A FAIRE KELTIC RENAISSANCE

DOUBLE KELTIC TRIAD 6

*LIZZIE STARR

To those who have traveled the tales of the Double Keltic Triad with me,
always wanting more...
For your encouragement and inspiration, your love of the Faerie
Otherworld, your acceptance of my tales... this book is yours, now and
always.
You have blessed me.
A storyteller wishes no more than that.

CHAPTER
ONE

The castle was nearly complete. Only a crenellated tower remained, needing just a couple more cardboard tubes. Jayse stepped back and surveyed the work with narrowed, critical eyes. Then a smile burst over his face and he chuckled. It seemed like he'd been working on his castle his entire life. And in a way, he had.

That dream he'd had when he was little more than four, a dream where an ornate castle imprinted on his brain, now came to life in a storage garage. Under the smooth, plaster finish, an array of plastic wrap tubes, bread boxes, and other assorted kitchen items...

Slowly circling the castle, Jayse shook his head at the evidence of his construction skills at ten. The model had grown, but he wouldn't change the rough walls and crooked balustrades of his early work.

College had put an end to his youthful obsession until a few years ago when he began to dream again of the castle, perched at the edge of a cliff above a wild sea. Compulsion urged him to pull the partially constructed building from a storage area in his aunt's Otherworld palace. He sighed, remembering the care with which she'd had her servants place the rickety construction into safe keeping. Though he believed he'd passed childhood by then, she'd still indulged his childish whim.

Perhaps, it wasn't so childish, now that the castle occupied nearly the entire floor of a rented garage, as well as his plans for the future. Coated in plaster, the castle stood stark and white against the unadorned stud walls and stained concrete floor.

He hadn't quite decided how to finish the outer walls. A collection of small, smooth river stones from the Otherworld was piled to the side. He chose a couple stones and manipulated them through his fingers—a contemplative movement he'd learned from Bryce. The stones might work for at least part of the castle. Maybe he'd etch square blocks in a gray plaster above the stone foundation. The finish details were still vague in his mind's eye, yet he had no doubt when he hit upon the correct look, he'd know.

Just as he knew his dreams would come true. And soon.

The tiny phone in his pocket chimed and as he tossed the stones back to the pile he glanced sat the screen. "Hey, Sis."

"Hey, bro."

"Lara, what's up?"

"Your voice's echoing funny. You in that garage again?"

Jayse grinned at his sister's mock dismay. Happily, in his family, odd eccentricities were more than tolerated; they were cherished and encouraged. Although, he had suffered more than his share of teasing over the castle from the moment he placed the first two cardboard tubes together. Feeling a bit rebellious at the continued bantering, he frowned. He'd show them.

"Jayse? Is anything wrong?"

"Nothing. Yeah, I'm here. In the garage. Just trying to decide how to finish this project."

"I'm sorry."

"For what?" He arched his eyebrows. That sounded like a serious apology. What could Lara have done that would need forgiveness? Then he rolled his gaze. Sisters.

"Uh, Dad asked me to give you a call."

"And..."

"And let you know that he needs to talk to you."

Jayse gave a soft snort. "He couldn't call himself?"

"He was summoned to the Otherworld. I don't know why, so don't ask. He'll be back at the office early afternoon."

"Hey, what are you doing here in the human world?"

Lara chuckled. "Brought the twins to see their gramma. Both sets. Mom's been reading one of her favorite old books to Belle and Antin."

Jayse joined her laughter as he turned from his castle and flipped off the overhead light. "Not *The Bobbsey Twins* again. Don't you have enough just living that life with your double doubles?" He locked the door and turned toward his car. "I've got work at the office, so I'll be there whenever Dad gets back."

"Hey, Jayse?"

"Yeah?"

"Come to supper some night. Soon?"

"Sure. Love to. I've got some ideas I want to toss around with Iain anyway. Talk to ya later, then?"

"Bye, bro."

Jayse took a deep breath. Deep in his gut he knew why his father wanted to talk. But he wasn't ready for that discussion. Not yet. Not until the castle was complete.

"I'd like you to take over the business as soon as possible."

Startled from his contemplation of the file before him, Jaysson Zeroun jerked his gaze to his father who leaned back in his chair, arms folded casually. Jaye's somber expression faded to worry as Jayse remained silent.

Finally, Jayse cleared his throat. "Uh, Dad? Can we talk about this another time?" He'd known this moment was coming. Zeroun's had been in business for over thirty years—an amazingly successful thirty years. All due to his father's—and his business partner, Tommy's—vision and hard work. It was natural his dad would want him to take over.

"Later?" The tiny lines over the bridge of Jaye's nose deepened. "Why later?"

"I'm, uh, in the middle of a project and..." Jayse shrugged and slipped the folder he'd been studying under a messy stack of invoices.

A low chuckle resonated from across the small office. "Another project? Son, don't you think it's time you got your head out of the clouds? I'm... tired. This mess with Feidhlim's taking more time than I can give. Even though his magic has been destroyed, and he's held in the world between worlds, I've still got this anxious knot in my stomach. I don't have time for business."

Then why not retire and close Zeroun's on a high note? Jayse winced at the thought. He didn't dislike catering, especially the specialty-themed events Zeroun's was famous for, but he wanted to do something else. Needed to live the dream he'd held close in his heart since he was a boy.

Jaye filled the strained silence with an exasperated breath. "Okay, son. We'll talk later. But, not much later."

"Thanks, Dad. Promise, it won't be long and I'll be able to give you an answer." As his dad turned back to paperwork, Jayse breathed out a soft sigh of relief. He wouldn't be able to postpone this discussion forever. He touched the edge of the hidden file folder with his index finger. One call, all he needed was to receive one call.

Not much later the soft sounds of the office door opening and closing drew Jayse's attention from the stack of invoices before him.

"He's gone."

"Who's gone?"

Jayse glanced at the woman who faced his father's wide, oak desk. Over the past months, the young Native American shaman had become a welcomed part of the extended Zeroun clan. Now, as Catori stared at his father, Jayse frowned at the worry creating a double line over her straight nose. Like his father, he leaned forward to hear her answer.

"The evil one. Feidhlim."

Jaye shook his head. "No, the Watchers wouldn't let him go."

Catori gave a soft snort filled with derision. "I don't think they let him go. Even without his magic, he still has followers who risk their lives for him."

After wearily rubbing his eyes with his fingertips, Jaye shook his head again. "No, I don't see how that could be possible."

Perching on a corner of the desk, Catori glanced at Jayse and gave him a grimace as if to make some comment about the older generation. He bit back a chuckle—his father was far from settled into being an elder. His aunt, the Queen of their Faerie clan, had recently crowned his dad as ruler in her stead. The sense of responsibility and leadership drew Jayse to his feet. Immediately after accepting the Faerie rule, his father had named him as *his* heir.

"Don't you think we'd better check this out, Dad?"

Jaye leaned his chair back as far as it would go without tipping and stared at the ceiling. "Aren't we ever going to be rid of Feidhlim and his evil?"

Catori snorted again. "Not until he's dead, Jaye. Not until his spirit no longer walks this world—or any other. His magical powers have already been taken from him and destroyed. His fey blood now runs red as human blood. He has nothing left—but revenge. Don't underestimate that power."

A tiny chime sounded, signaling the request to open a Faerie portal. Jayse nodded to himself—that had been a good idea. With him and his dad trying to run a human business and deal with the occasional problems of the Faerie Otherworld, there had been too many times when fey and human paths had nearly crossed. It could have very well ruined their business credibility.

"Enter." At Jaye's command a portal formed and a lean, dark skinned Faerie stepped into the office. He paused when he caught sight of Catori, then bowed slightly toward her and faced Jaye.

"Feidhlim is no longer in the world between worlds."

Catori gave Jaye a smug grin. "See."

He acknowledged her expression with a lift of one eyebrow then gestured toward a chair. "Have a seat, Gowthaman."

Instead, Gowthaman faced Catori. "You know this as well?"

"Yep. I've been keeping watch over him during some of my drum journeys. Today, my circle grew cold—icy. When I sought the world between worlds, all I found was emptiness. Even the Watchers withdrew from my presence." She rolled her eyes. "I don't think they wanted us to know that he's gone. And, I don't think they did anything to keep him from escaping."

Gowthaman turned to face Jaye. "He has returned to the human world. You must be wary."

Jayse rose and paced around his workstation to join Gowthaman and Catori before his father's desk. He extended his hand and after a brief pause, Gowthaman clasped his forearm. "You must take action to protect your family, Jayse."

"How did you learn of his escape?"

The warm chocolate brown of Gowthaman's skin paled. He cast his gaze around uncomfortably then met Jayse's curiosity with a steady gaze. "Since my time in the world between worlds there has been a... connection. I do not understand. Nor do I wish to know more than I am now forced to know of that... place. It is as if when Feidhlim's seeker... touched my mind, she opened my consciousness to that place of nothingness. When he was no longer there... I simply knew. I do not doubt that knowledge, as you should not."

"We don't, Gowthaman. This just came as a surprise."

Gowthaman closed his eyes and inclined his head, a quiet acceptance of Jayse's statement.

His father spoke softly. "I suppose we shouldn't ever be surprised by what Feidhlim is capable of." His eyes unfocused for a moment and he frowned. "Searlait?"

The portal opened again and a tall, blonde woman bounded through, her agitated breathing loud in the room. She paced back and forth before the others. "The Watchers have spoken to me. They havena done so since they released me from the world between worlds. I dinna ken at first, fer I dinna believe I waud ever hear such again." One of her hands slid to her side as if in search of a weapon. "I should have finished him then. Finished this all when given the chance. Jaye, my king, I beg yer forgiveness fer my failure."

"No failure, Searlait. We have been complacent, believing him to be defeated and held in a place where he could never touch this family again."

"He will try. An' soon. Carrie's child is due to be born."

Jayse took her place pacing the room. "Dad, we've got to do something."

"Do you have any ideas, son?" Jaye shook his head. "How many times have we thought we were rid of Feidhlim only to have him appear as if out of nowhere? At least this time we have some warning."

The young faerie lifted her hands in supplication. "But, Carrie—"

"Searlait, we will do what we can to keep her safe. I know he'll try and find her, no matter where she might go. Though we hesitate to admit it, he did father her child. I'm sure his followers have been watching her, watching the whole family. We'll just have to find him first."

Catori brushed her hands together. "Good. If there's anything I can do, just let me know. I'm here early, but I'll wait to go back to Arizona until after the baby's born."

"You came all the way here just to tell us about Feidhlim?" Jayse touched her shoulder as she turned toward the door.

She spoke without looking at him. "Of course. Would you have believed me over the telephone? Besides, how could I do any less? It's my duty as a shaman." She glanced sideways at him. "And as a friend. Maybe, since he's human now, you need to use the talents in the human world to find him. Take care."

She slipped through the door before Jayse could respond. He looked helplessly at his father. Jaye shrugged. "I don't know, son. I just don't know."

· · ·

Lucidea backed from the small room, her gaze lingering on the desk she'd occupied for the last eight years. Though she wasn't leaving for good, tears still burned the back of her eyes, blurring her sight. Since the bulk of the new forensic equipment remained in the room, she'd be back. She tried to smile. The equipment was hers, after all, and she was only loaning it to the department.

Thankfully, her boss wasn't at his desk when she passed the open door to his office. She wouldn't be able to face the crusty captain's censure and keep her composure. He'd thrown a royal fit when she told him her unspecified leave of absence had been approved and had been only slightly mollified when she agreed to leave most of the equipment she'd earned during her assignment in Scotland under his care at the lab.

Scotland. She needed to return, but she wasn't ready to face the memories and responsibilities she'd willingly left there. A single tear left a hot trail down her cheek. To find her uncle, then lose him the same day she finished the forensic sculpture proving that her father was dead... A second tear followed the first. She had to get out of the lab before somebody saw her moment of weakness.

Taking a deep breath, she tucked her laptop case closer to her side. She'd spend some time at home completing the sculpture of her uncle she'd begun when she'd returned from Scotland. Then, maybe she'd find a way to come to terms with her heritage and the responsibilities of leadership that fell into her lap at Morghan's disappearance.

Maybe.

A shiver of dread ran across her shoulders, a signal that somewhere, something was happening that would directly affect her.

Before she opened her car door, Lucidea glanced at dark gray clouds dancing across the sky. Gray... there was something particularly ominous about the gray. She shook her head and the dread slowly faded. Maybe the odd feeling was just the electricity of an oncoming storm.

Unwilling to face the quiet loneliness of her townhouse, Lucidea drove out of the city to one of the small nearby recreational lakes. Halfway around the water lay a small cove shaded by ancient cottonwoods and elms. The quiet seclusion of the space reminded her of the loch on her uncle's property in Scotland. Her property now, until Morghan returned.

After parking, she sat in her car for a long time letting indecision gnaw at her insides. Until with a huff of breath, she let her frustration escape and climbed from the car. Stretching, she stared toward the distant horizon and the streaks of sunset colors crossing the sky. The bright orange ball of the sun settled lower as she shaded her eyes from the sparkle off the mud-tinged water. She stood in silent contemplation until the sun disappeared from the sky.

Too bad those contemplations didn't steer her any closer to what she should do. If she'd been asked, at that moment, what she'd been thinking about, she would be hard pressed to form an answer any more coherent than her thoughts. Lucidea gave a short chuckle and leaned back against the car fender to watch the stars twinkle to life in the twilight sky.

Soft splashing drew her attention to the dark lake. Expecting to see fish feeding on late evening mosquitoes, she gasped when a pixie-like face grinned at her from the shallows. Warily, she moved closer to the lake as her friend, Coralie, rose from the water and walked toward her.

Coralie shook her head, sending a spray of tiny droplets over Lucidea.

Lucidea laughed and brushed at the moisture on her face. "Coralie, how'd you get here?"

The young woman frowned and squeezed the water from her long, curly hair. "The watery passages of course."

"To here? I know there's waterways between the lochs—but to reach the other side of the planet?"

"Aye," Coralie nodded. "No' so many ken how to use them. Still, those who do are able to find the way."

"Uh, Coralie."

"Milady?"

Lucidea sighed. She'd tried, over and over, to get Coralie to not call her 'milady', but the honorific seemed ingrained and any attempts to change Coralie's way of thinking met with quiet stubbornness. Lucidea turned and reached into the back of her car for a light blanket. "Wrap this around yourself. There might be someone else here. This lake's not as secluded as Nas Duirche Ness."

Coralie chuckled and made a toga of the soft cotton. "I ken. I had to speak with ye."

Leaning back against the car, Lucidea wrapped her arms around herself and peered through the darkness, trying to read Coralie's enigmatic expression. "You could have called, or sent an email."

At the shake of Coralie's head, Lucidea sighed. This wasn't going to be good news.

"I couldna trust mechanical means to contact ye. Pagas watches me closely and had me followed." Her white teeth glistened as she smiled. "But they couldna find their way to the passageways of this land. No' without the knowledge given me by the creatures met along the way." She shrugged, then adjusted the slipping blanket and glanced around her. "Still, I dinna wish to speak of these things so close to water."

"Would you like to come to my house?"

Even as night stole the last bit of light from the sky, delight sparkled in Coralie's eyes. She executed a deep curtsey. "Milady."

Huffing out a breath of air that stirred the loose hair around her face, Lucidea shook her head. "You can't call me that while you're here. Lucidea. Say it, at least once, Coralie. Lucidea."

"Lucidea. I shall no' promise to remember at all times, yet, I shall try."

"That's all I can ask. Come on, then. Get in the car. I, umm, think I might even have some clothes at home that will fit you."

"Aye," Coralie chuckled and moved to the passenger side of the car. "I hadna thought about that. 'Tis much easier to swim in only m'skin."

Once Lucidea had driven a few miles from the lake in silence, she glanced sideways at Coralie who, eyes wide, stared out the window into the darkness. "So..."

Coralie jerked against her shoulder belt, then turned a guilt-ridden expression to Lucidea. "I beg forgiveness. I am... astounded by yer country. I have ne're been here."

"So, Coralie, why are you here?"

"There's no telling what Feidhlim might look like now," Jayse said as he slumped back into his chair, matching his father's contemplative pose. "How can we fight against that?"

Jaye shook his head. "Like we've always fought him, I suppose. With lots of luck. Although, the destruction of his magic changes the odds, wouldn't you say? If his followers—"

"If? I don't doubt there's still a number of misguided Faerie who cling to his supposed ideals."

"True, son. His followers may be able to use magic against us, but he'll never harness that power for himself. From what I understand, he should no longer have the ability. We'll be able to protect the family against any Nechtan-Cattee trickery."

The two men sat in silence for a time, each absorbed in their own contemplations. Jayse guiltily let his thoughts drift to the final stages of a project he'd kept secret from the family and he ducked his head to hide a grin. Keeping secrets in his family was a challenge, though an enjoyable exercise in secrecy. If... no, he corrected himself... when his offer on the land was accepted, he'd make a formal announcement to everyone. And ask their help in completing his extensive plans.

A thick cardboard tube rested on one end on the corner of his desk. He'd been collecting the tubes from commercial plastic wrap since he was six. A year ago he'd transferred the sprawling cardboard construction to the empty storage garage near his apartment and completed the structure with an adult's artistic eye. Almost. One last tube, one last tower, attached and plastered would complete the castle he'd dreamed about his entire life.

He picked up the tube and turned it over and over in his hands. His cardboard castle would be completed at the same time he launched into a massive, full sized building project. There was something ultimately—satisfying about the way one project flowed into the other...

"...some way to imagine him in different guises."

"Uh, sorry, Dad. What did you say?" Guiltily, he lowered the tube from his eye and tossed the cardboard to the desk where it landed with a hollow thunk and rolled until stopped by his in/out basket.

"Daydreaming again?" Jaye laughed and shook his head. "Maybe someday you'll get your head out of the clouds."

"I hope not."

"Jayse, stay with me here for just a bit."

"Sorry, Dad."

His father stood and paced before his desk. "Do you remember the police artist who talked to Carrie?"

"Sorry again, Dad. I wasn't there."

"Hmm, that's right." Jaye leaned on his son's desk. "She used a computer program to create the face Carrie remembered. Then, erased a moustache and Feidhlim as I knew him was easily recognizable. I was thinking, maybe she'd be willing to help us out here. If she still has the picture, maybe she could alter it to give us ideas of how he might choose to look." Straightening, he shrugged. "It's worth a try."

After years of sharing the office, his father's thought processes were evident and Jayse took a deep breath. "And you'd like me to talk to her." At his father's nod, he continued. "No problem. I'll stop by the police station on the way home and see if she's there."

"A phone call and an appointment might be easier."

Reaching over the cardboard tube for the phone book, Jayse chuckled. "This must be why you're the Dad."

. . .

Feidhlim lay on his back, staring at the water-stained ceiling. Anger distended his nostrils as his breath came hard and heavy. Hands fisted, he beat a fierce rhythm on the mattress, raising puffs of dust to hang in the stagnant, musty air.

With a sudden movement, he rolled and sat on the edge of the bed, arms dangling between his legs, his chin touching his chest. He surged to his feet, paced around the end of the bed and flopped back to the same position on the other side to stare into a large, dirty mirror.

Why? Tightening his muscles, Feidhlim concentrated, straining to feel... feel anything. He cupped his hands, waiting for a zing of power, a tingle of magical electricity, a tremor of ability. He waited for... nothing.

Passing one hand over the other, he imagined forming a ball —a bright orange ball under his control. In his mind, the ball grew from a tiny pinpoint to a firm weapon and the hint of a smile eased the tension from his face. If he could just...

Shaking his head, he slapped his palms together. There was no concentration of power, no orange ball that would do his bidding.

Without even a chance to fight back, every bit of magic had been taken from him—stolen by the so-called Watchers in the world between worlds. Stolen and destroyed.

Emptiness, vast and cold, filled his belly. Overflowed into his heart. Inched a frigid path to his brain. Where his magic should be was nothing but... nothing.

He growled low in his throat. Anger warmed his cold skin, heated his blood until his heart beat hopeful in his chest. They would pay. There would be a way to take the magic from Zeroun and absorb the power into himself. There had to be a way.

Feidhlim scrubbed his hands over his face and rose to lean straight armed over a low chest before the mirror. A haggard, hollow-eyed visage stared back at him. The Watchers had kept him alive, though what pleasure the gray beings found in his torment eluded him. Basic needs had been provided, but he never saw another being, heard another voice, felt the presence of anything. The nothing had nearly stolen his will, broken him as the watchers had broken his magic.

As he would break Zeroun.

He leaned closer to the mirror and tried to imagine a new face, a disguise for his attack upon the usurper. But all he could see were dull, lifeless eyes in a drawn, thin face. It would do. He would attack Zeroun with the face the usurper made him wear. Let his enemy see the truth that would haunt him in his defeat.

Wild laugher burst from his lips.

Laughter that died in a sob. Feidhlim stared in amazement as tears spilled down his gaunt cheeks. Tentatively, he touched the damp trail with the tip of one finger. He cried? Dashing the tears away with fierce, jerking swipes, he bit the inside of his cheek to stop the welling of pain. He would not show weakness.

But the cry of his despair burst through his clenched teeth.

Nothing remained to him but revenge. He tore his hands through his hair, yanking at the length as though the pain would focus his thoughts, and spun in a tight circle. He couldn't stop the tears. Fisting his hands against the mirror, he panted, the combination of anger and pain tearing harsh breaths from his chest. With a low growl, he drew back his hands, paused, then slammed his fists against the mirror.

Spider web cracks radiated from the impact. A second attack shattered the mirror and sent shards of sharp reflections about the room.

Feidhlim stared into the bits of mirror still within the frame. Fractured. He was as fractured as his reflection.

The anger disappeared. The pain faded. Inside, he was as empty as the world between worlds.

The door behind him burst open. "My lord?"

Slowly, Feidhlim lowered his fists to his side and turned to stare at the concern etched across his follower's face. His follower. Despite his... disability, many still looked to him as their lord. He gave a derisive snort.

"My lord," the faerie whispered. With a wave of one hand, the broken mirror repaired itself.

Anger rushed to fill Feidhlim's emptiness. Though he paused to relish the feeling, any feeling, he lowered his brows and glared at his underling. "Never," he said slowly. "Never use magic in my presence." He turned his back. "Until such time as I am restored, I will not allow the exhibit of power before me."

One side of his mouth twitched to a smile as he heard the fool prostrate himself.

"Your pardon, my lord. I forgot my place."

Feidhlim grunted a response.

"How may I atone for my transgression?"

Bring me forgetfulness. A memory fought its way through the haze of anger. He could forget. There was a way. Why shouldn't he travel that path? Was there a reason to ignore the craving... one thing he could feel? He faced the prostrate faerie. "You wish to regain my favor?"

"As always, my lord, my wish is to serve you."

Feidhlim sighed. Would he be able to turn back once he spoke the words? Scrubbing his face with his palms, he pressed his fingertips against his eyes. "Bring me drink."

The faerie lifted his head. Eyes wide, he stared at Feidhlim. "My lord? But—"

"I shall allow no dissention." Feidhlim took a step forward and lifted a clenched fist. "You will do as I say, or you will be gone from my presence. Do you understand? I do not tolerate the questioning of my actions."

"Oh, no, my lord. Of course, my lord. Immediately, my lord. I shall bring the finest of Faerie ale."

The mention brought a flood of remembered flavor to Feidhlim's mouth and he closed his eyes to savor the smooth bite and flowing forgetfulness. No. NO!

"No! Again you forget yourself. I am no better than human now. Bring me human ales."

The underling crawled backwards from the room. "Yes, my lord. As you wish."

Feidhlim gave the man his back. "Do not allow my glass to become empty until I give permission for it to be so."

The door closed silently behind his follower. Feidhlim turned his gaze to the ceiling. "Bring me human forgetfulness," he whispered.

Then, letting his anguish find voice in a drawn out cry, he shook his fists in the air. Damn Zeroun. Damn the usurper and his entire clan. Crying out again, he collapsed to the bed. Damn him to every imaginable hell.

D rumming his fingers on the steering wheel, Jayse sat for a few moments before exiting his car. He'd called the police station and discovered that the artist, Lucidea Galvagin, had taken a leave of absence. Starting that day. Just his luck. But, maybe it was luck since the Captain had taken his name and his request and Lucidea contacted him only an hour later. Maybe the fact that Feidhlim was wanted by human law enforcement was a factor in her decision to see him.

He stared at the row of townhouses before him. The modern structure had tried for a Victorian appeal and he supposed the builders had succeeded—to a point. Neither as charming nor as homey as his folk's neighborhood and the house he grew up in, the complex was, nonetheless, clean and well kept.

Taking a deep breath, he ambled to the numbered door and knocked. He looked around as he waited, absently wondering about the woman with the soft contralto voice. The voice that, even in his memory, thrummed through him with sensual promise.

A soft giggle sounded through the fiberglass door and he took a half-step back, waiting expectantly. The door opened.

His eyebrows lifted. He took another step back. A petite woman stood before him. Dressed in nothing but a large towel.

TWO

Lucidea didn't leave the tiny space designated as a workroom when she heard the knock on her door. Coralie's immediate, "I shall greet the visitor, my... Lucidea," allowed her to continue searching for the disk containing the rendering of a perp's face for the man she assumed was at her door.

But, when she heard the deep, surprised tones, she paused at the drawn out, "Oh. Umm."

She drew her brows together in consternation, then opened her eyes wide. Coralie. Now what?

Rushing to the entry, she discovered a tall, dark-haired man staring at anything but Coralie. Lucidea followed his gaze to the ceiling, then closed her eyes. At least he'd come in and shut the door behind him.

She glared at the grinning Alfar-Sindhu, who bobbed a tiny curtsy then turned and scurried down the hall to a bedroom.

Lucidea took a deep breath and turned slowly. "Uh, I'm sorry about that. My... friend is just returned from the pool." Unable to look at his face, she hoped he'd accept her lame apology.

"No problem. She just surprised me."

Wondering if he was interested in Coralie, Lucidea chanced a glance at the man. He'd angled to face her, his lean body filling the small living room. A half-grin stretched his lips, and a twinkle filled his dark eyes. With the swipe of hand, he brushed a shock of wavy hair from his forehead. "Lucidea?"

The way he said her name sent a vibration to settle low in her belly. Although he had a typical Midwestern accent, his manner of speech in just that one word lent an exotic air to his formidable presence. She tugged her lower lip in between her teeth and bit down. Distraction. She needed to distract herself from the distraction of the man before her. The tremble of understanding, of deep, sensual knowledge fluttered just below her heart. She loosed her lip and frowned. The feeling had never been this strong before.

"Lucidea?" His brows lowered and concern chased the sparkle from his eyes. "Is something wrong?"

Blinking did nothing to clear her mind, but she was able to focus on his face. Short, amazingly thick lashes surrounded his eyes. His nose, long and straight—oh, but his eyes. They weren't black as she'd first thought when he stood in the shadowed entryway, but more of a golden, dark honey brown. Reluctantly, she let her gaze slip from his eyes to freeze at his lips.

His lips moved. Intrigued by the combination of firm lines and soft fullness, she didn't comprehend his words.

"If this is a bad time..." Jayse leaned subtly forward. A flush of male pride swirled through him at her obvious appraisal. He liked the almost physical feel of her gaze, the caress of her eyes, the interest sparking in the dark brown depths. An interest he realized he shared.

She blinked and took a short step back. "I'm sorry, what did you say?"

"If this is a bad time, I can stop by another day."

"Oh, no," One of her hands lifted slightly as if to restrain him. She canted her head toward the hallway. "Sometimes, Coralie doesn't think before she acts."

Jayse grinned. She'd spoken quite loud, obviously intending for her friend to hear. The laughter ringing from behind a closed door was a testament to the success of her words.

Keeping his gaze fixed on her face, Jayse waited for her to speak again. Already he craved the sound of her voice, the low, naturally sensual pitch so many women tried to cultivate—with utter failure. The twitch in his groin when she nibbled at her lower lip made him slightly adjust his stance. Yes, he needed to know this woman better.

She released her lip and cast him a tentative smile. "No need for you to make another trip. Come on back to my workroom. I haven't found the disk I stored that rendering on, but it shouldn't take too long. Then we'll boot up the computer and make any changes you want."

She turned and moved down the hall, still speaking. "So, you think that this perp will return? What's he got against your family that would bring him back here when he's a wanted man?"

Unable to keep a grin from his face, Jayse followed her easy stride to a small, cramped room. He skimmed his gaze over the bank of computers and electronics but stopped and stared at a pair sculpted faces. The clay of one sculpture looked long dry, the features aquiline and strong. Glass eyes looked out over the room and Jayse restrained a shiver at the life that seemed to emanate from the clay. He turned his attention to the second face. Similar in appearance, this was a work in progress, the clay dark, damp, and partially covered with a cloth.. If Lucidea had sculpted these, she was far more than just a forensic artist. She was... "Fantastic."

"I beg your pardon?" Lucidea turned from an overflowing CD file. Her finely shaped brows drawn together, she glanced from him to the sculptures and back again.

Oops, he'd said the thought out loud. "These sculptures are fantastic. Are these—"

"The one that's finished is my... father. The other is my uncle Morghan."

"I can see the family resemblance." Jayse moved around the

small workbench, studying the heads. He frowned at strange flaps molded into the skin behind her father's ears then shrugged the thought away. Perhaps an accident had caused the strange, parallel lines. "It must be interesting to pose and watch your face grow out of a lump of clay."

"I... wouldn't know. My father disappeared when I was a kid."

"Oh, I'm sorry." He mentally slapped his forehead for a thoughtless, insensitive statement. "You have a good memory then."

"No, not really. That face is an actual... actual forensic reconstruction. From a skull found near Morghan's loch."

Boy, he was really wracking up the stupidity points here. Her eyes shimmered as tears gathered on her lashes. Jayse turned from the sculptures and held out one hand. "You don't need—"

"No, it's okay." She gave a delicate sniff and squared her shoulders. "It was just such a shock to discover my father and an uncle I didn't know all in one day."

"Finding your uncle has been a comfort then?"

Lucidea bit her lower lip and shook her head. Jayse wondered if she had any duct tape. He could certainly use a long strip to keep his teeth from scraping the skin from his foot.

Then she lifted a sad gaze to him and attempted a smile. "He's disappeared, too. Part of the reason I took this leave from work is to find him. Bring him home. To do that, I've got to spend some time in Scotland."

Scotland? Jayse's heart tumbled from his chest to his feet. She couldn't leave, not when he'd just met her. Lucidea had turned away and, thankfully, hadn't seen the loss he knew must have crossed his face. This instant attraction was amazing and he held himself still a moment to savor the feeling.

Cringing a little inside, Lucidea fumbled through the CD file. Now why did she tell him that? She hadn't even decided how soon she would have to leave. So much depended upon the news Coralie hadn't yet told her. If strife riddled Morghan's kingdom, then she'd have to return to the loch sooner rather than later. But if any problems could be handled from here...

There might be time to really get to know Jaysson Zeroun.

Her body's reaction and the lingering sensual connection centered physically in her chest gave her notice. This man would undoubtedly become more than just someone looking for a perp's face. How much more, she had no way of knowing. Ah, but it had been a long time since a man had so completely captured her interest. She ached to feel more, to experience that joy of discovery.

A tiny voice, a hope she seldom allowed to escape to merge with the concerns of the real world, spoke softly to her mind. So soft, if spoken by an actual voice, she would have to strain to hear the imaginary words.

Maybe... him.

Maybe.

She gave a soft snort. Dreams and fantasies. Just as such thoughts of lasting relationships had always been. She looked up at a soft rap on the doorframe. Coralie had dressed in a loose fitting, sleeveless dress that flowed nearly to the floor. Lucidea gave her a thankful smile. At least she put on some appropriate clothes.

"I was wonderin' if ye wished fer some tea while yer workin'."

"Oh, uh, sure." Lucidea turned toward Jayse.

"No, thanks. Never been much of a tea drinker."

"Coffee then?" Coralie asked. "My... Lucidea prefers coffee herself."

"Now, that I could go for." Jayse grinned as Coralie bobbed a curtsey and disappeared from the doorway.

Focusing on the drawer of disks that had to be purposefully hiding the one she wanted, Lucidea jumped when warm, square-tipped fingers slid into view and covered her hand.

"Can I help look?"

By turning her head just a fraction she looked into the concern filling those honey eyes and stopped breathing. The intake of air didn't matter—she could survive on nothing, but being lost in his eyes.

"I'm sorry."

"Wh—what?" She closed her eyes at the inane syllables she hadn't been able to force smoothly from her mouth. When she lifted her eyelids, the concern still hovered in his eyes, mixed with another emotion. Dark. Smoky. Smoldering.

"I'm sorry. Bringing up the memories of your father and uncle. I should have—"

"No," she barked at him, then softened her voice and continued. "No, that's okay. It's only been a few months since I discovered... what happened to my father. But, I'm dealing with it. And with Morghan's disappearance."

"Still, I must have said some pretty insensitive things... from the way you're acting."

She was saved from having to analyze her actions by Coralie's return to the room. Lucidea snatched her hand from under his and rushed to take the heavy tray from the small woman. When Coralie resisted, Lucidea glared silently at her, opened her eyes wide in what she hoped was a meaningful manner, and gave a minute shake of her head.

Coralie chuckled as she released the tray and backed away. "Call if ye be needin' anythin'."

The aroma of fine coffee drifted from a steaming carafe. Jayse's nostrils distended in pleasure, he'd half expected instant coffee. Watching avidly as Lucidea busied herself filling two large ceramic mugs, Jayse imagined every morning beginning this way, sharing coffee and moments of quiet with Lucidea.

She glanced back over her shoulder. "Want anything in your coffee?"

"Nope, as is." Jayse offered her a grin when she handed him the mug. He lifted the coffee in salute.

After returning his grin and the acknowledgement, Lucidea turned back to the CD file, flipping through the disks with practiced ease as she drank. Jayse sipped the coffee then, eyebrows lifted, stared into the mug. "This is great. I usually drink Sumatra—"

"Me, too. But the Mill was out. This is a new blend from The

Blue Moon Coffee Shoppe. The beans are only roasted for a couple of months every year. If I wasn't such a good customer..." She looked up from her search. "I'd never be able to afford more than the beans for one pot."

Before he took another sip of the bitter, smooth liquid she sloshed the coffee over the edge of her cup as she set it on the table and held up a disk in triumph. "Here it is. Now, let's see what we've got."

Leaning slightly, she pushed the button on her computer tower and the low hum of booting electronics surrounded them. Jayse nodded in surprised approval at the speed with which the computer started, accepted the CD and displayed a face on the extra large screen.

Churning anger, mixing with stark cold terror, filled his belly. "This—this—" He couldn't think of a word bad enough, evil enough to describe Feidhlim. "He'll be back," he growled.

"Huh?' Lucidea turned a frown to him.

"Awhile ago, you asked what would bring him back here when he's a wanted man. He tried to kill my father. He kidnapped my aunts when they were babies, and almost destroyed them. All my life I've known the threat he is to my family. And now, when we thought he was defeated..." Jayse scrubbed his free hand over his face and shrugged one shoulder. "Sorry, it's just that... I don't think the... man has anything left but revenge. Retribution because my father was born."

"I don't understand. He doesn't look old enough to have been a threat to your father."

Uncomfortable with an odd spark in her eyes, Jayse lowered his gaze to his mug and shook his head. "Nevertheless," he mumbled. "We've got to be prepared and find a way to stop him. He's like a cat, only he's had more than nine lives. Nine dangerous lives."

Lucidea turned back to the monitor and tilted her head to one side to study the composite she'd created not that many months ago. Jayse was hiding something, something about this perp, or about his family. She wasn't sure which. Then she let a long breath escape through pursed lips. She had no right to poke into someone else's family secrets, not when she was still afraid of what she might discover in her own heritage.

Her own, unbelievable genetic make-up.

THREE

L ucidea took a deep breath and leaned back in her chair, only to jerk forward when her shoulder brushed against a hard thigh. She glanced down at Jayse's feet. He wore strange boots, the uppers made of dark suede that disappeared under his pant leg. She couldn't see the soles, but he moved so quietly she was sure they weren't hard leather.

The full breath caught in her throat as he leaned over her shoulder and peered at the monitor. "He's a master of disguise, so there's no telling how he might appear when he returns. That's what Dad's worried about, and why I'm here." He reached toward the screen, but pulled his hand back into a fist before touching the picture. "Can you... say, do a number of different looks for him?"

This kind of a request she could deal with easily. "No problem. All it'll take is a few clicks on the mouse. If I remember, he had a moustache just before he escaped."

"Yeah." The word was flat and emotionless, as though the man at her side fought to control his emotions. Maybe if she kept him talking, he'd relax a bit. And, she'd be able to listen to his voice. Now, if only she didn't have to watch the screen so she could stare into his eyes... "So, what's this guy's name?"

"Feidhlim."

"Odd name." She shrugged, not that Lucidea was common. "Has he used any aliases?"

"He called himself Aubrian when my sister met him. Then, when he orchestrated Tommy's kidnapping, he was called Titus Avery. Now... who knows."

"You told me some of what he's done, but not why. Jayse, why is this man so intent on harming your family?"

Dead silence met her question and when she glanced at Jayse, he had half turned from her, concentrating on a spot near the doorway. Okay, so this wasn't a question he was willing to answer. Knowing reasons wasn't important for the work she had to do now. She didn't have to understand the whys to make a face look different.

But, she wanted to know. Desperately wanted to understand. And that desperation gave her a moment's pause. Another why added itself to her questioning mind. Why was it so important to her that she know the details? Did it have something to do with the sudden, magnetic attraction she'd felt when she'd seen him standing in her living room?

The silence dragged on and she tried to fill the uncomfortable emptiness with keystrokes and clicks of her mouse. When the quiet settled painfully in the tense muscles across her shoulders, she twisted in her chair. "I'm sorry. I have a hard time reigning in my curiosity."

The frown he bestowed upon her faded slowly until his lips were a straight line and the furrow disappeared from his fore-head. "That's okay. Curiosity I understand. I guess that as much as we've talked about him in the family, it's difficult to go be—"

The gentle, chirping melody of a cell phone halted his words.

Giving her an apologetic shrug, Jayse reached into a pocket, tugged out the phone and slid his thumb over the surface before lifting it to his ear. "Zeroun."

Well, wasn't that good timing? Lucidea shook her head. The moment was choreographed almost as if some movie director called the action, both slowing the action and increasing her tension. Movie director? She turned her attention back to Jayse.

He paced the narrow, clear area in the room. "Now? But..."

Lucidea bit back a chuckle as he shook his head and crossed his eyes as if mimicking the caller. "Yeah, I understand. But..." He closed his eyes. "Okay. Fifteen minutes." With a flick of his wrist, he pocketed the small rectangle. "I've got to run. I'm, uh, in the process of trying to buy this amazing piece of property and the seller's finally ready to talk. Crusty old farmer. If I'm not there in fifteen minutes, he won't talk to me. Probably ever. Can you—"

She rose and touched his arm. "I'll print out some different faces for you. Call when you've got some time, and I'll get them to you. I know you don't want to wait on this... any more than you want to keep that farmer waiting." Giving a gentle push, she guided him toward the door.

Silent, they walked to the living room and paused in the entry. Lucidea ached to touch him again, to feel the heat radiating from his lean muscles. Instead, she gripped the edge of the open door, tightening her fingers on the wood so she wouldn't give into temptation. Her palm still tingled from the earlier contact.

"Good luck, Jayse. I'll have the faces done later this evening, if that's okay."

"Fine. I, uh..."

He planted his hand on the door, just above hers and tilted his body toward her. Those dark honey eyes glistened and she matched his lean and tipped up her face. If she stood on her toes, right now, she could kiss him.

"You'd better go," she whispered.

"Aye, I should."

Blinking at the tiniest bit of accent in his words, she eased back and let her hand drop.

W hy hadn't he kissed her? Jayse slammed his hand on the turn signal then strangled the steering wheel. He'd wanted to. By God, he still wanted to. She'd tilted her head in unconscious invitation, drawing something from deep inside him. Okay, he knew what that something was. Lust. Pure, but not so simple.

Lingering behind the lust, lay a nodule of feeling he hesitated to examine. So he pushed the feeling away and concentrated on the streets leading him to a broad, gravel road. He slowed to safely maneuver the recently graded surface, stretching his fingers from their death grip on the steering wheel. He needed to clear his mind for the meeting with the property owner. As he mentally ticked off bargaining points, his shoulders relaxed and the tight knot at the base of his neck loosened.

Thoughts of Lucidea Galvigin wouldn't be ignored for long, though. He knew that with a certainty that pleased him.

A shallow, tentative knock sounded on the battered wood door.

"Enter."

After the rattling of the doorknob, the door swung inward and a dark haired woman entered, balancing a large silver tray. She glanced curiously at him and set the tray on the dresser. Then, she turned and slowly peeled the clothing from her body. "I was asked to bring you this," she said as she indicated the tray with a leisurely wave of her hand. "And anything else you wish." Her painted lips quirked on one side as she appraised him. "Anything."

Feidhlim remained silent, returning her inspection. For a human—the imperfections of her body vividly showed her heritage—she might have one time drawn his interest. Except for the hard, knowing glint in her eyes, made violet no doubt, by the use of contacts. His followers knew his tastes. A willing faerie maid he would gladly use, but humans were only pleasing when taken with the anger simmering inside him.

Dispassionate, he watched her slink toward him, hips undulating in an unnatural way, hands roaming over her own body. Disgust burned at the base of his throat.

Longing drew his gaze from the whore to the silver tray and

the three tall bottles reflected in the mirror behind them. Those would be a start, but hardly enough to even dampen the memories, let alone bring him the forgetfulness he sought.

Strong scents, the mixture of cheap, flowery perfume, sweat, and a woman's musk swirled around him. The woman leaned over him, hands planted on the arms of his chair. Her breasts swung before his face then she inched closer until her skin touched his cheek. Inviting. Tempting. Disgusting. "I have ropes," she breathed against his ear.

He jerked back, lifted his hands to her shoulders and shoved her from him. "Get out," he growled. "No doubt you have been well paid. Leave me."

She planted her fisted hands against her hips and stared down at him. A flash of disappointment darkened her eyes then she huffed and turned away. "Your loss, mister."

Moments later her naked backside disappeared through the door.

He had hardly expelled a breath to release the woman's smell from his senses before the door inched open and an underling peeked into the room. Feidhlim waited in silence until the faerie knelt before his chair. "Your... initiative is admirable. However, I have no need for companionship. I have no need except more..." He waved his hand toward the bottles on the dresser. "Triple that, and it shall be enough for a time. Watch, and do not let the tray empty. Send me nothing more than that I demand of you. Do you understand?"

"Yes, my lord. I shall do as you require of me."

"Yes, I know you will. Go."

The faerie rose and backed from the room.

Weary beyond reason, Feidhlim stumbled across the room and leaned again on the dresser to stare into the mirror. This time he avoided his reflection, staring instead at the duplicated bottles. Which should he choose? He closed his eyes and pounded a fist against the wood, making the bottles rattle. Did it matter?

Without another glance at the bottles, he closed his fist around one tall neck and twisted the cap. Now he watched himself in the mirror, tried to discover a reason for not completing the action that shook his hands and made his stomach clench in powerful anticipation. There was no reason. There was only the need for bleak forgetfulness.

In one swift motion, he lifted the bottle, tipped his head back, and drank deeply.

'''T is something different about that man."

Coralie's words barely registered as Lucidea stared at her computer monitor. "Huh?"

"I said 'tis somethin' different about that man."

The pleasantly sensual vision of the masculine angles of Jayse Zeroun's face, his smile and oh, those eyes wavered then burst into sparkling fragments. She jerked and angled to face Coralie. "What? Who? Him? She pointed at the composite of the perpe- trator on the screen.

"Mayhaps, but 'tis no' about who I was speakin'." Coralie chuckled, crossed the room with a filled coffee carafe in her hand, and topped off Lucidea's cup.

"Uh, thanks. Who do you mean?"

"The one yer thinkin' about."

"I'm working on some different looks for this guy." Lucidea took a sip from her mug and glanced over the rim at her friend. Maybe she could bluff her way out of this one.

"Aye, mayhaps. But 'tis no' the man ye be thinkin' of now."

Giving a nonchalant wave of one hand, Lucidea turned back to face the computer. She set the coffee aside and rested her fingers on the keyboard, feeling the tiny ridges on keys along the home row. "I don't know what you're talking about."

"Ye do. Deny if ye wish, but I ken. But, since ye dinna care to admit it, I'll be tellin' ye. Jaysson Zeroun. 'Tis somethin' different about him. Somethin' fey."

"Oh, you must just be imagining things." She tapped a series of keys and the hairstyle on the slender face changed. With another stroke, she made the color darker. A word broke through her attempt at appearing to concentrate. Her fingers stilled. "What do you mean... fey?"

Coralie leaned against a file cabinet and crossed her arms. "I mean, Lucidea, that I feel some difference in him. If ye concentrated, I'm sure ye would sense somethin' as well."

"That's not my—"

"Nonetheless, 'tis yer heritage. Try, then I shall tell ye what I felt."

"You're determined to get me to accept a heritage I never even knew existed until only a few months ago, aren't you?" Lucidea frowned at the other woman who calmly returned a steady gaze. "What is it you want from me, Coralie? I can't believe that by default I'm the ruler of an entire world, a world that isn't even the one where I grew up. If I asked anybody on the street, they would say that world is imaginary, it's not possible—that I'm crazy. There can't be such a thing as parallel worlds, places where magic is the norm. A place..."

Lucidea stared helplessly at Coralie. She wanted to deny the facts, wanted to sink back into her old routine, the things she knew and understood. But she couldn't deny the pull in the center of her chest; a deep inner knowledge that what she didn't want to explore or believe was true. How could it not be, with Coralie standing before her? How could it not be, when she had seen her uncle Morghan sucked into another of those parallel worlds? How could it not be...?

She sighed. "I'm still having trouble believing in you, Coralie. How can I find a belief in even more?"

Coralie leaned and touched her hand. The warmth of the woman's touch made Lucidea realize how chilled she was, a chill that reminded her of Nas Duirche Ness. Her loch. Loch Dark Ness. The place where, finally, she'd felt at home.

"Okay, I'll try and suspend my disbelief." She cast Coralie a strained smile. "Sometimes, it's not difficult to believe that my father is... was from a parallel world, a world where the beings have gills and breathe underwater. Sometimes, when I look at his face," she glanced at her sculptures, "I think that's easier to believe in than the fact that I'm now the ruler of those people. Coralie, how am I to reconcile all this? How am I supposed to understand the whys, the hows... anything?"

"Time, milady. Time no' available to yer questioning. I shall tell ye of Pagas after we decide about Jayse. Try, Lucidea. Concentrate on him an' tell me what ye see."

"How many times do I have to tell you? I have no magic, no abilities beyond what I already know."

Coralie merely lifted her eyebrows and cocked her head to one side. Lucidea chuckled. "Okay, I'll try. But I promise you that there won't be anything."

Closing her eyes, Lucidea tried to concentrate on Jayse, but knowing Coralie watched her made her shift uncomfortably in the chair. When she wasn't concentrating she had easily brought his face into her inner vision, now she couldn't even seem to be able to even describe him verbally to herself. She took three deep breaths and tried again. There had to be an honest effort made, before her failure, in order for her to finally convince Coralie she was a lost cause.

A slight pressure on her shoulder and the clasp of Coralie's hand focused her back to what she was supposed to be trying, not how to avoid it. She took three more breaths, relaxed her shoulders and... there he was.

Not just his face, but his full, lean figure. A brief, wicked thought as she wondered how he would look without clothes made the figure waver and grow dim.

"Concentrate," came Coralie's whisper.

That's right, she was supposed to concentrate on why Jayse seemed different to Coralie, why she thought he had a fey background. When Coralie's hand left her shoulder, she mentally squinted to try and bring him back into focus.

Ah, there. She smiled to herself. If nothing else, he was a joy to look at. Relaxing further, she studied the figure. What was different?

A faint haze of color surrounded him. Okay, she understood a little about auras from long ago discussions with a college friend.

But, these colors shifted, swirled, never remaining static. Colors merged and coalesced over his chest and forehead, smaller patches covered his hands. Sparks of silver shot through the colorful mix then concentrated at those four points.

The gasp escaping her lips jerked Lucidea from her vision and she turned, wide-eyed to Coralie. "What was that?"

"Magic."

"No... that can't be."

"'Tis. An' no amount of denyin' will change that. Look at me, Lucidea. What do ye see?"

"I see—"

"No, look with yer inner eye. What ye saw with yer vision, ye can see with yer eyes, if ye ken how to look."

"How?" If only Coralie would stop being so... mystical and just tell her what she needed to do. And how. This 'you can do it because you know how' mumbo jumbo was getting on her nerves. Shrugging, she settled into her chair and squinted at Coralie.

When her friend grinned and nodded, she stared harder, straining until she thought her eyes would pop from their sockets.

"Nay, yer forgetin' to relax."

"Oh, sure." But she tried and a strange lassitude overtook her for a brief moment. A clear, turquoise aura shone from Coralie. The Alfar-Sindhu smiled gently and spread her hands. Sparkles of a darker blue-green danced around her hands, at her forehead and over her heart.

"Oh... my... God. I can see it. You're turquoise and sparkles."

"Aye, 'tis the magic within me. Ye have the sparkles as well, my lady."

"Me? No way. But..." Lucidea stared down at her hands. After only a heartbeat, she was able to discern a distinct violet, laced with faint, pulsing spots in a paler color. "Oh. Is this real?"

"As real as ye or I, Lucidea."

Lucidea glanced sideways at Coralie. "He's Alfar-Sindhu?" That might explain... something.

"Nay, I dinna think so." Coralie sat cross-legged on the floor next to Lucidea's chair. "Different. Nor is he of the Alfar-Andras nor of Alfar-Domovii. 'Tis verra different, yet not so."

"You're not making much sense."

"I dinna suppose so. However, my... Lucidea. If the three clans of the children of Dea Anu each touch upon the human world in a way we are able to pass from one world to another, might there no' be other worlds as well? Worlds such as where milord Morghan is held."

"You think Jayse comes from there?" Pain shot through her chest and pierced her heart. She'd only known her uncle a few days before he had been ripped from this world into a gray oval that felt of nothingness. How could a vital man such as Jayse come from a lifeless place? Another tremor of pain made her bow her head. How would her uncle survive?

Coralie said fiercely, "Nay. No' from there. But mayhaps from another place that also conjoins this human world."

The painful urgency of Morghan's plight fought to over-shadow their discussion. Still, Lucidea had to know. "Why don't you believe he's any of the three Alfar clans?"

"Ye saw the embodiment of my magic. Ye saw yer own. What similarities did ye see?"

Great, Coralie was in a teaching mode. Why couldn't she just say the words to give her an answer? Why all this didactic bullsh—

"Lucidea. What is similar?"

Lucidea tossed her hands in the air in a gesture of surrender. "Okay, okay. Let's see. Our auras were different colors, so that can't be it."

"Correct, milady. Each being's magic has a physical manifes-tation. However, that manifestation 'tis different fer each of us. What else?"

"Um. You had sparkles of a slightly different shade of color. I had pale spots."

"My magic is developed, yers isna." Coralie shrugged. "When ye accept and strive to learn more of yer magic, yer sparkles will form. Yer like an Alfar child in this."

"Great. I'm a kid again." Lucidea fell silent and her friend waited patiently, sipping at her pale, well-creamed coffee. With a suddenness that made Coralie jump, Lucidea slammed the flat of her palm against the desktop. "It does have to do with color, doesn't it?"

"Aye, but how?"

"Let me take a stab at this... The colors of Alfar sparkles, or the magic, are the same as the aura, only a little different in density or hue."

Nodding, Coralie set her coffee aside. "Correct."

"And Jayse—well, his aura wasn't even one color—"

"That puzzles me greatly, though I dinna feel anythin' disturbin'."

Lucidea continued as though Coralie hadn't interrupted. "But it was his sparkles. They were different. They were silver. Silver. That's strange. I don't ever remember hearing that silver was a typical aura color."

"And so, 'twould appear the man is no' so typical, either."

Consumed with thoughts of Jaysson Zeroun, Lucidea stared into a corner of the room. He wasn't typical. And neither was her reaction to him. Her normal, inner guidance, a strange force that had always steered her either toward or away from casual relationships, seemed to have gone haywire. Every nerve ending tingled with a subtle heat.

Heat she knew, deep in her heart, would grow, burn and consume her until she found relief in his arms. Only his arms.

Oh, God. This wasn't a good thing.

FOUR

J ayse crested the small hill and stood facing the light breeze. The crackle and colors of fall mixing with the dry, sweet scents filling the air made him smile. The faint rustle of paper when he touched his pocket brought a rush of satisfaction. This land was now his. Ever since he'd first ridden his bike along the trail following the old railroad right of way and seen this hill, he'd wanted it. Knew that having this piece of land would bring the fulfillment of his dreams that much closer. He'd never told anyone, not even his sister or Bryce or his closest friend, Macaire, of his dream. Who would have believed such a well-developed plan from a nine-year-old? Now, twenty years later, with a plan nurtured with an adult's eye and understanding, he was nearly there.

Taking in the three hundred and sixty-degree view from the hill, Jayse's imagination overlaid the land with plans formed over long years. There, that open space would be for the mundane such as parking and an entrance. He angled slightly to the right and shaded his eyes with his hand. There, wound through the trees covering the slightly rolling slopes, he pictured a maze of paths between tiny buildings and canvas awnings. He closed his eyes, listening to the calls of the merchants and the low rumble of bargaining. The sound of steel against steel and cries of huzzah turned him toward a large flat area, perfect for jousts and displays of fighting styles.

When he opened his eyes, the snapping flags and costumed crowd disappeared. But the drying pasture grasses and brightly hued October trees couldn't dampen his spirits. With a mild winter and the help of willing faerie artisans, he would be able to complete the centerpiece, the crown jewel of his development and hold a small renaissance faire in the spring.

Jayse leapt high, punching his fist into the air. "Yes!" he shouted, then laughed as the word echoed across the quiet land. A startled rabbit zigzagged toward the closest clump of trees and disappeared in the thick undergrowth.

This is mine. Jayse's shoulders sagged and he gave a rueful chuckle. *What have I gotten myself into?*

T he moan that jerked her awake hovered on Lucidea's lips, a building scream tightened her throat. The dream again, only worse.

The door burst open. Coralie ran into the room. "My la—"

Lucidea held up one hand and the Alfar-Sindu skidded to a stop on the polished wood floor. "I'm fine, Coralie. Just another nightmare."

"Ye still dream of Morghan?"

Weary to her bones, Lucidea fought her tangled covers and after plumping her pillows, sat leaning against the headboard. "I do. Almost nightly. But, they're not always nightmares. Sometimes I dream that I'm a little girl again and my father didn't disappear. He takes me to Scotland to meet Morghan." She released a long slow breath filled with longing. "Those are the dreams I wish were true. But the other dreams... I see Morghan just before he destroyed the fire elemental, just before he disappeared. I couldn't see his face when it happened, but in the dreams I see all the pain, the pure agony he felt at being ripped from this world. From me. From you. I wish I knew where he was."

Coralie sat on the edge of the bed and tentatively reached out to pat Lucidea's arm. "I believe he's being held in some kind of a prison. 'Tis a place between worlds, the place where Brandr Ur was held. 'Tis almost as if when the elemental was destroyed, his place in that prison had to be filled. With Morghan."

"But why?" Lucidea rubbed her gritty eyes. "At first when I returned from Scotland, the dream place where Morghan was held was a cold gray. Nothing but gray. He was lost in a mist of nothingness. Now, that's changed. There's no longer that feeling of emptiness. Now I feel a... a presence. And I feel Morghan's agony. Tortured. He's being tortured. Being driven crazy... Crazy..." she ended in a whisper. The agony tightened her muscles. In the dreams she felt everything Morghan felt. Was she going crazy?

"Aye, 'tis our fears come to life. I must show ye somethin'. Then 'tis finally time to tell ye of Pagas and his duplicity." She held one hand out, palm up and tapped the center of her hand with her fingertips. A tiny, rolled parchment appeared, laying across her palm.

"Whoa—how'd you do that?"

"'Tis only a minor magic, Lucidea. If ye show a talent fer this, I shall teach ye." Her slight smile faded and she closed her eyes as she tightened her hand around the document.

"What is that?" Lucidea cocked her head and stared at the brown-bag colored parchment. A wave of apprehension burst over her. "That's from... Morghan, isn't it?"

Coralie's eyes opened. The sea green shimmered as tears gathered along her lower lashes. She nodded. After a long pause, she opened her hand. "'Twas found not long ago, hidden in a place overlooked as we searched for meanings in Morghan's disappearance. We had thought to find answers within the palace, and had near given up hope. Only by chance 'twas it found stuck in an ancient book in the library. Though written to me, now I believe ye should know what yer uncle wished. And ye must know how dangerous Pagas has become. Mayhaps there is a meaning in yer dreams, a warning."

"I don't know if I want—"

"Ye must read this, Lucidea. Then I shall tell ye what else we have learned of Pagas."

Coralie held her extended hand steady. Lucidea stared at the roll of paper as if answers would come to her without actually touching the page her uncle had written on, without having to read what she suspected was his final communication before facing the fire elemental, Brandr Ur. Disappointment filled her. He'd written to Coralie instead of her. She shook her head. He loved Coralie. They'd only met a few days before that, and Morghan hadn't even known his brother had fathered a child with a human.

Human, she was only half human—the other half a race inhabiting the waters of a different world. She touched the skin behind her ear. If she really were half Alfar-Sindhu, why didn't she have the telltale gill slits?

"Ye ken we believe ye'll discover that bit of yer heritage when ye enter the waters."

"I've gone swimming, Coralie. I've never even had an itch there." She gave a dry chuckle. "So maybe I didn't inherit the ability to travel in your world."

"It matters little if ye have gills at present. Read this," Coralie pressed the parchment into her hand.

Hesitant, Lucidea stared at the far wall. She ached to know what the note said and the curiosity over what future it might hold for her overwhelmed her. As did the fear of that same future.

Taking a deep breath, she smoothed the parchment on her lap and glanced at Coralie who smiled encouragement. As she began to read the flowing script, she grinned at the archaic style of Morghan's handwriting and traced the initial larger letter with her finger. From the looks of the page, she half expected the document to be illuminated with scrollwork and drawings in colored ink. But the message was plain and even though the letters flowed smoothly, she sensed urgency behind the words.

Dearest love,

Pleased I am ye are no longer a sister to me.

She jerked her gaze from the missive to Coralie. "Sister?"

"Nay, not by blood, Lucidea. The then ruler of the Alfar-Sindhu, milord Morghan's father, took me into his household when my family disappeared. Much as he did with Pagas when he was but a boy and his father... died. Morghan and yer father, Lachlann, were well grown by the time I became part of their family. They had no sister, so named me such. Lachlann left to journey the human world shortly after." Coralie paused and shook her head sadly. "I dinna ken Lachlann well. I wish I had, fer I could tell ye more about him."

"That's okay. I do remember a lot, the important stuff."

"We shall talk of him another time. Please read."

Nodding, Lucidea began again.

'Tis not much time and I fear I shall not return from meeting the Fire Elemental. His power is great, built, I believe, upon ages of hatred and imprisonment. If it is true, and he is the Elemental who raped the Mother of the Three Clans, then I go to fight my own ancestor.

'Tis not an action I relish.

To discover Lachlann had a child, a beautiful daughter, now, is bittersweet pain. She is, of course, heir to my rule. She will not readily accept that rule, though she seems to accept that I and her father are of a race different than her human mother. Deep in her soul, she knows the truth of her heritage. Deep in her soul, she shall find the strength and the will to do what is right and true for our people. Help her, Coralie.

For my sake, and the sake of all Aljar-Sindhu.

I have not the time to tell all I must. Beware of Pagas. I have discovered evidence of his duplicity, but I dinna ken the extent of his sins against me and my people. I do ken it was he who called forth Brandr Ur.

When the second full moon of the month, the human blue moon, rises tonight, and similar moons also rise in many other worlds,

Lucidea furrowed her brow. Other worlds? How many parallel universes could there be? It was difficult enough to believe in two or three conjoined worlds—but more?

It is this accumulation of events that allows Brandr Ur to escape from his prison of ages. Pagas may have loosed additional magicks to defeat me. I am saddened by the loss of our time together.

Sweet Coralie. I believe Pagas make seek to harm ye, for the love he claims to bear for ye is yet no' love at all. He will focus his ill will toward my niece, my Lucidea as well.

"Pagas loves you?" Lucidea stared at Coralie who blushed deeply and shook her head.

"I dinna encourage him, ever. In fact, I barely tolerate his presence. He has always been cold, his touch clammy and..." She shuddered. "I canna abide him, but I fear such feelin's increase his determination to have me. I take Morghan's warnin' seriously. As should ye."

"What can Pagas do? When he's back at the loch in your world and you and I are here."

"Dinna underestimate the power of evil. 'Tis a mistake too often made. Please, read on."

Lucidea studied Coralie a moment longer, then turned her attention back to the parchment. There wasn't much more and the handwriting tilted at a sharper angle. Waves of anxiety and fear rose from the scrawled words.

I dinna ken what damages Pagas may have caused, or what other evils he seeks to inflict upon our worlds. Set watchers upon him. Protect Lucidea. Keep from her these worries as long as ye are able. Dinna allow Pagas to touch her.

This is my charge to ye, darlin' of my heart. 'Tis a dangerous burden, Coralie, one ye are well able to handle. Assist my heir. Her strength shall hold her in good stead. Accepting her heritage...

The pull to confront the Elemental can no longer be denied. Farewell, Coralie. Hold my love for ye in yer heart. Share that love

with Lucidea, for though I barely ken the lovely lass, she is Lachlann's
daughter and I love her well.

A seal, colored and embossed into the parchment, ended the missive. Lucidea ran her fingers over the raised design. She wished she could cry. Falling into that supposedly weak, female role would feel good right about now. She missed her father. She missed Morghan. She didn't want to rule a people she didn't know, a race she didn't understand. She wanted her old life back.

Creating faces—on paper, on a computer, or in clay—to find a criminal or bring closure to a grieving family... that's what she knew. That's what she was good at. That talent had gained her a certain notoriety in forensic reconstruction, which had garnered Morghan's attention and his initial request to her office, sending her to Scotland.

She glanced at Coralie. The look of concern increased the already large lump in her throat. She tried for a smile as she rolled the parchment. "So, I hadn't thought of it before, but, in a way, you're my aunt."

Coralie ducked her head, hiding the beginning of a grin. "If 'tis what ye wish. Though I would prefer to be yer friend."

"That works for me. Thank you for sharing this with me. It means a lot."

Nodding, Coralie took the parchment from her and closed her fist around the thin roll. It disappeared. Lucidea gasped and shook her head in amazement. Maybe knowing magic wouldn't be such a bad thing after all. "You really have got to teach me to do that."

"'Tis fer safekeeping. We dinna wish Pagas to realize how much we ken of his underhanded dealin's. Until we are certain of the extent."

"What kind of punishment do your... our people use?" It had better be severe. Maybe they even used that disappearing trick. If the man had even the slightest hand in her uncle's... "Do you think he may have had anything to do with my father's death, too?"

Coralie remained silent long enough Lucidea had her answer.

"I didn't trust him when he first offered his services after Morghan's disappearance. He gave me major willies. Now... please tell me there are punishments strong enough for his crimes."

"Aye, if ye deem them so. Fer, 'tis yer providence as our ruler, to mete out the rare punishment. As a rule, there are few transgressions, and rarely one that deserves severe action."

Lucidea narrowed her eyes and glared at her friend through the tiny slits. "This is one of those times."

"Aye, so 'tis. But first, we must be sure of our accusations. If we falsely accuse him of misdeeds..."

Smoothing the blanket over her legs, Lucidea fought for the calm detachment she'd cultivated for work. The first time she'd used an actual skull, amazing things had happened in her head. The bones came to life and she knew, not clearly, but she knew how the victim appeared when alive. That first time, she'd carefully set the skull into a protective clay ring, left the room—and burst into tears. She hadn't understood what she'd seen. Later, when she completed the reconstruction, she recognized the same face. She'd nearly given up the profession she quickly came to love.

When the vision came on her second assignment, she had ignored the pictures of her mind's eye and double-checked each measurement and ethnic determination with co-workers. And created an identifiable face that led to closure in the case of a missing child.

It took two years for her to accept her visions, and even now, two years after that, she still worried. What if she began to see not only the victim, but how that person died? Thankfully, fate had given her one concession and she only saw the person as they were in life.

The same queasiness that affected her each time she touched a skull and began a new project assaulted her now, filling her with an odd vertigo and way too many 'what ifs'. Where was the calm? "Tell me what you know of Pagas' activities."

There, she'd said that with the proper amount of detachment needed for an investigation. Now if she could only maintain the ruse.

"May we speak in the livin' room? The sun rises and this tellin' shall be the better for all the light we are able to surround ourselves with."

"Light?" Lucidea glanced toward her heavily curtained window.

"Aye, milady Lucidea. Light. To counteract the darkness of evil."

S hivering in the damp early morning, Jayse sat at the crest of his hill, watching the sun rise over the horizon. The moon hovered low at his back and he felt the blessing of both celestial bodies as he faced this new journey, this adventure of his heart.

It would be difficult telling his dad that he couldn't take over Zeroun's. His dad had a dream, and at the same age Jayse was now, had started his own business. It was an accomplishment Jayse longed to emulate. But in his own way, with his own determination and dreams.

The morning calls of geese from the small pond nestled between two hills drew his attention, and his smile. The mist rising from the warmer water into the cool air hid the large birds until, with a noisy flutter and a darker swirl in the ethereal white, they burst into the sky and arrowed toward a recently harvested field. As the geese settled in the distance, satisfaction settled in Jayse.

He could do this. With the business experience he'd gained at Zeroun's, he could imagine few problems he couldn't at least fake his way through. Years of attending renaissance faires and participating in the local society for creative anachronism honed his medieval skills. Time and further education in the Faerie Otherworld gave him an edge on which he planned to capitalize on shamelessly. His permanent faire site would offer more—with a subtle difference—to his patrons. Human and fey alike.

Cold seeped through his jeans, chilling his skin. Sitting in frost-covered grass wasn't the driest idea he'd had lately. He pressed his hands against the crisp grass, then laughed as he rose. A cold butt couldn't dampen his spirits now. He couldn't wait to share his dream.

With Lucidea.

As he turned back to his car, Jayse drew the image of the woman into his mind. Would she understand his passion for this project?

Once before—and only once—he'd mentioned this dream to a date. She'd offered polite interest, but he'd later overheard her laughing with a girlfriend. The pain of that moment lingered years later. Why was his dream so different than any other entrepreneur? Because it was historically based and not on the cutting edge of technology? Because fantasy played a prominent role in the dream? Any person, any woman who would laugh at this—he turned back and nodded at the expanse of land—could never accept him. His family. His life.

Scrubbing his hand through his hair, Jayse grimaced. Lucidea's life was wrapped tightly in reality. How could it not be? She worked for the police. Drew criminals. Sculpted victims' faces. No fantasy there.

Yet, when he'd visited her with the reality of his family's need, he'd sensed... No, all he'd felt was a physical attraction. All right, a strong physical attraction. An attraction threatening to tighten his jeans then and there.

Maybe he could just bring her out and show her the land. He didn't have to explain how he planned to develop the rolling hills. Not yet.

Would she even be interested? There had been a spark in her eyes, then a glimmer of what he thought was sadness when he'd left yesterday. The spark might be there for him again today. After meeting the lawyers and slashing the final signature across the deed, he'd stop by and see her. He had to check on her progress with the computer sketches of Feidhlim. It was a good excuse.

Climbing into his vehicle, he admitted a difficult fact to himself. Excuses aside, he just wanted to see the long legged, auburn haired beauty again.

CHAPTER
FIVE

"Demons? You mean like ugly monsters with horns and slobbery fangs that prey on innocent people?" Lucidea caught her lower lip between her teeth to keep from laughing. The slight, downward turn of Coralie's mouth showed her seriousness, but Lucidea had a hard time believing in demons.

At least, she used to believe they were a function of wild imaginations.

"Aye, demons. But no' such as ye describe. Though I have no doubt they exist as well. There is much unknown in all the worlds."

"Nobody knows that better than I do. It wasn't that long ago I didn't even know about another world, a parallel world." She closed her eyes and leaned back in her chair, cradling her coffee mug against her stomach. Drinking the dark, aromatic liquid had done nothing to warm the disturbing chill deep within her. Maybe she could warm herself from the outside in, so she tugged a throw around her shoulders. "So, Pagas has somehow been in contact with a world populated by demons?"

"Aye, as near as those set to watch him are able to discern. He is able to hide himself from us, so what we ken is mostly assumption. That, an' scraps of parchment found in his rooms, an' scrolls, verra ancient texts, that have disappeared from the library. 'Tis as though he hides his activities yet flaunts them at the same time."

"Then why do you suspect demons? Maybe he's trying to free another elemental."

Coralie shook her head. "There are creatures humans now call elementals, but they have no' the powers of the ancient beings such as Brandr Ur."

"What did Morghan mean when he said he was going to fight his ancestor?" At the deepening of Coralie's frown, Lucidea hurried to explain. "I'm not trying to change the subject. I'm struggling to understand how all this fits together." Although she seldom participated in extensive forensic investigations beyond what her job description allowed, the curiosity now rose strong in her, and the need to know chased her concern over Pagas' activities.

"Ye havena' had a chance to learn more of the history of the Alfar-Sindhu, of yer family, have ye?"

"No, you know I haven't. At first, after Morghan's disappearance, you kept me busy trying to come to terms with just knowing about the Alfar-Sindhu. Then, when I came home, it was easy to pretend everything that happened in Scotland was only a dream. Now..." She leaned forward. "I need to know more. Tell me short history again. The one Morghan told that...that morning. That will be enough for now. I'm sure everything's all interconnected anyway."

Coralie took a deep breath. "I suppose 'tis best the more ye ken." She rose and drew the curtains wider, letting in more light from the rising sun.

Wincing at the brightness, Lucidea angled in her wide, over-stuffed chair and, clutching the throw tighter, looped her legs over one arm. Maybe with a retelling of the information she'd be able to piece together more of the whys and think of a way to free her uncle from his Otherworld prison. Then she wouldn't have to worry about learning how to lead an entire race.

After refilling her tea and Lucidea's coffee, Coralie sat cross-legged on the couch, took a quick breath and began.

"Ages upon ages upon ages ago, there were few people in the world of the Alfar." She paused and touched her fingertips to her lips as if a strange thought filled her mind. "Or perhaps it was yet another world. I am no' so sure now. How ere it may have been, all the people lived upon a single island. Three gods there were, one worshiped above the others, much to the anger of the goddess of the seas. She destroyed the island and all the people."

"Atlantis?" A rush of excitement flushed through Lucidea. She'd always been drawn to tales of the city, and the mysterious island of Mu, said to have once been in the Pacific Ocean and destroyed the same way.

"There is no recorded name of this place, and those who lived there were called simply 'The People'."

"But, if everyone was destroyed—"

Coralie lifted one hand. "The god, one called the Great Master, and his consort, protected and saved two of the people from the violence of the sea."

"Like Noah and his ark?"

A smile softened Coralie's tense expression. "There are similarities in this history to tales of many religions in this world. However, in this case, I believe Zale and Haven would be more like to yer Adam and Eve."

"Oh." Lucidea sipped at her coffee. There were legends of creation and of a flood in almost all of the religions she'd ever heard about or studied. Interesting. This was something to explore further. But later. When she had time. "What did this have to do with the fire elemental?"

Coralie nodded as she spoke. "Brandr Ur was of a race even older than the gods of The People. The sea goddess, in her quest for supreme power and worship from The People, loosed him from captivity."

"He was imprisoned then, too? What did he do?"

A shrug tensed Coralie's shoulders. "I fear his indiscretion is lost to legend. I would suspect the fire elemental also desired ultimate power and worship from The People. He destroyed the sea goddess.

"However, this goddess had a son, born and grown by the same magic that held Brandr Ur captive. Released, the elemental fought the young god and nearly destroyed the world itself."

Lucidea thought she understood. "For killing his mother."

"Nay." Coralie shook her head fiercely. "For Wodhan had already turned from his dam's search for power. Nay, he fought the elemental for the love of the babe newly born to Haven and Zale. They fought and Wodhan defeated the elemental. They fought for the love of Dea Anu."

She heard echoes of that name in her own. A sprite of fear tripped along her spine and tingled across her shoulders.

Staring unseeing out the window, Coralie continued, "Aye. She is the mother of all Alfar."

"How? If Brandr Ur was defeated..."

"He gave false promise to the new triad of gods—Wodhan of the seas, A`mhathair, the mother goddess and her horned consort, Rawdan."

"Horned god?"

"Aye." Coralie grinned. "Again similarities to human legend. May I finish yer history?"

Lucidea laughed. "Aye." It felt good to laugh. She had a feeling laughter might soon be difficult to come by as she dug deeper into the treacheries of Pagas' activities.

A comfortable silence that settled over the women, calming the churning of Lucidea's belly. Nerves, nothing but nerves.

"So, Coralie, about this Dea Anu... you said Wodhan beat the elemental."

"Aye. Brandr Ur said he loved Dea Anu, while Wodhan held fast to his claim she was the mate destined fer him from the beginning of time."

"Why didn't Dea Anu make her own decision and stop the fighting?"

"How could she? She was but a babe, born only moments before the battle began."

"But, how can that be?"

Balancing her cup in one hand, Coralie spread her arms. "Many say the love of yer soul is determined long before birth. I dinna ken the truth of that belief, but Wodhan so believed. As did Dea Anu. As she grew older, Brandr Ur continually pressed his suit, but she had eyes, and heart, only fer Wodhan."

While Coralie paused to sip her tea, Lucidea stared into the bright orange sun hanging over the buildings across the town-home community's green space. Somewhere, deep in her heart, or in that soul Coralie spoke about so blithely, lived a wish for just that kind of love. Not one known from birth, of course, that was silly. But a love of now—for now—and for the future. She grimaced into the dregs of coffee in her mug. That was a dream. Wasn't it? She'd never met anyone who remotely...

"Brandr Ur kidnapped Dea Anu from the home she shared with Wodhan. Kidnapped and raped her. Thrice he came to her, thrice he planted his seed within her."

"What?" She'd been only half listening to Coralie's tale but the word 'raped' pulled her immediate attention. Lucidea struggled to believe what she'd heard. "He claimed to love her and he forced...? That's not love."

"Nay, 'tisn't. But, Brandr Ur could ken nothin' else. Dea Anu escaped and the punishment upon her attacker was swift and, so the gods believed, permanent. Until Pagas discovered the way to call him from that captivity."

"The blue moons."

"Aye."

"Wait. You said he raped her three times."

Coralie nodded.

Lucidea squinted at her. "And three times he 'planted his seed'?"

"Aye. Dea Anu gave birth to three, the only children she was ever able to conceive."

"Whoa, that's not fair. How did Wodhan handle that?"

"'Tis no' fair, but Wodhan was a true father to each child, cherished and loved them, fer they came from his beloved Dea

Anu. From those children come the Alfar. Each child had, umm, talents, and so each clan has dominance over differing parts of the world. The Alfar-Sindhu, such as we are, rule the waters. Alfar-Andras, the air. And the Alfar-Domovoii, the earth itself. 'Tis been long since the clans have come together. I fear many try to forget our shared heritage."

"So, to back up just a bit here... that means that Brandr Ur would be Morghan's great, great, whatever grandfather?"

"And yers."

"Eww." Lucidea scrubbed her hand over her face as if to wash away the concept. "I hadn't thought of that. Eww," she moaned. "I don't think I like having him in my family tree. Are you sure?"

"Yer birthmark."

She had one, but she hated to admit it. The brown mark reminded her of some wild animal, and had been the focus of teasing when she'd worn a two piece bathing suit as a teenager. Even now the thought of a bikini sent shivers of dread down her spine.

"Remember Morghan told ye Dea Anu's father was the chosen of Rawdan, the horned one. It was Rawdan who protected Zale, and Haven, from the sea goddess' wrath. As chosen, Zale bore a mark, the symbol of a stag upon his shoulder. It has been said that descendants of this man, of his daughter Dea Anu—those who are of the ruling family—bear a similar mark. This is true in each of the three clans." Coralie lowered her head and looked up at Lucidea through her thick lashes. "Ye saw where Morghan carried such a mark upon his calf. Lachlann, his brother, yer father, bore his mark much as Zale did, upon his shoulder."

Lucidea shook her head. But even as she did, she lifted her tee shirt to peer at the brown birthmark just to the left of her navel. No doubt about it, the mark looked like a deer.

How would she explain this to Jaysson?

Lucidea blinked and tucked her shirt over her stomach. Where had that thought come from? Why Jaysson? He was a guy she'd met only—was it really only yesterday? And this thing on her stomach. It was just a birthmark—lots of people had them. So hers just happened to have the widespread, multi-pointed antlers of a proud stag. No big deal. The birthmark she could explain, then ignore. But her birthright?

"Coralie? What am I going to do?"

CHAPTER
SIX

The expressions greeting Jayse when he opened the office door plummeted his heart to the pit of his already tortured stomach. He had the completed paperwork for the land purchase in a thick folder clutched in his fist, and believed himself ready to face his father. But not the number of calm, unreadable expressions facing him.

While his dad sat in his usual chair, Tommy perched on a corner of the desk. At least with both business partners there, he'd only have to explain once. He hoped.

"Uh, hi, everybody."

His mother rose from the chair at the second desk, crossed the room, and brushed a soft kiss across his cheek. "Have a seat, Jaysson."

His heart pounded once, then fell the rest of the way to his feet. Mom almost never used his full name. This wasn't going to be good. Maybe he should have called and said he wasn't coming in for awhile and gone back to absorb more peace from his land. He tossed the folder to the desk as he passed. His land. His decision. His life. That was how to explain it.

Settled in the chair, he waited until Allyn sat, then he leaned forward, drew the folder toward him for courage and took a deep breath. He felt like he was seven again, and he and Bryce had just broken a window with a well-aimed chunk of rock. "Dad, I—"

"We need to talk, son." The firm line of Jaye's mouth softened as if he held back a grin, then straightened. Jayse wondered if he imagined the fleeting humor.

"Yeah, we do. Dad, I—"

"I'll speak first, if you don't mind."

Jayse's reply sputtered to a halt before he even formed the words. Dad used the same tone of voice when facing the Faerie council. His stomach joined his heart at the soles of his feet. This wasn't good. It could only mean...

"Feidhlim?"

Jaye's eyebrows lifted and he shook his head. "No, nothing new there. We still have no clue to his whereabouts."

"I was planning on stopping by Lucidea's—the forensic artist —later to pick up the renderings she worked on for us."

"Great. I'm sure that will help. No, son. We need to talk about the business. About Zeroun's."

If Dad and Tommy were both there, it meant only one thing. They were going to pressure him into taking over. Jayse stiffened his spine. He had to remain steadfast in his decision to follow his own dream. "Dad, I—"

"I'm not done talking, Jaysson." Again the authoritative voice.

The rod in Jayse's spine disintegrated and he slumped back in his chair.

Allyn leaned forward. "Jaye, don't torment your son." She gave Jayse a gentle smile and a quick wink.

Now what? He was getting thoroughly mixed messages. "Somebody please tell me what's going on."

Tommy crossed one ankle over the other. "You've done a great job with the business. You've a natural talent, just like your dad. Zeroun's has always been well in the black. Thanks to hard work from the entire family."

Great. Now they were laying on the guilt. Jayse remained attentively silent, but seethed inwardly. Why couldn't they just let him live his own life? Because, he was an idiot and never told them what he want.

Jaye took up the conversation. "As we discussed yesterday—briefly—I've taken more responsibility within the clan and the Otherworld. I don't have the time or energy, or even the desire any more, to devote to the business. Tommy feels he needs to spend more time with David. The boy has adjusted well to life in this crazy family, and there's still hope that someday he may regain his sight. Tommy and Derrik want, and need, to be there for him."

"Of course." Jayse understood perfectly. The entire family longed for the abused child's return to a normal, love-filled life.

"And they need to be close to help Carrie," Allyn added. "As leader of the Alastriona, and the child's granda, Derrik will see to extra security to prevent Feidhlim from ever coming in contact with the baby—or Carrie." She shivered and Jayse silently cursed the Faerie who caused her, and the entire family, such pain.

Staring at the folder centered on the desk, Jayse drew a long, shaky breath. "And you want me to take over as soon as possible."

He'd said it and now, how could he refuse? What were his wishes, his dreams, when tempered against the health and safety of his family? Nothing. He realized he'd do anything, including sacrifice himself, body and soul, to keep each and every one of them from harm.

A part of him, of his soul, died at that moment.

Allyn rose and hurried to his side. Wrapping her arms about him, she rested her cheek on the top of his head. "Jaye?" she prompted.

"No, son. We don't want you."

Still in his mother's embrace, Jayse jerked upright. They didn't want him? "I don't—"

"Understand? We've discussed this at length, Jayse. It's time to retire the Zeroun's name. Time to close the business." Jaye's chair squeaked as he pushed back from the desk and stood. A broad grin stretched his mouth.

Jayse stole a glance at Tommy. A similar smile relaxed his

expression. Jayse leaned back and turned to Allyn as she straightened. "Mom?"

"It's true, darlin'. Your dad's retiring. Tommy doesn't want to run the business by himself. And you..."

"You, my son," Jaye continued, "have too much of your grandmother in you. Yes, you're good at business, but your heart lies elsewhere. Much as you think you have kept this hidden, I see it in your daydreaming, in your interests, in the time you've spent in Faerie. You'd take over the business—"

"Of course I would, Dad."

"—be the consummate businessman—and be perfectly miserable. I'm glad for the years you've given us, Jayse. Thankful for the chance to work with you and know you as the man you've grown to be. Not all fathers are able to say that."

Jaye crossed the room and tugged his son to his feet and into a bear hug. "I'm proud of you, son. I'll be proud of you, no matter where your dreams may lead you. Your happiness is more important to me than—"

Jayse shrugged from his father's embrace, then leaned to kiss the older man's cheek. "Getting kinda schmaltzy there, Dad. I know. I love you, too." He glanced at the tears in his mother's eyes, then at Tommy's proud grin. "All of you. So, you're really going to close Zeroun's?"

Jaye returned to his desk chair. "Yep. As soon as we come up with a hell of a final event. We're not going to fade away. Zeroun's is going out with a bang that people are going to remember for a long time. I'm counting on you for this, kiddo. I hope you can come up with—"

Jayse burst into laughter. His parents' stunned expressions made him laugh all the harder. "If... you can... wait..." He paused to catch his breath and reached for the folder he'd brought with him. "If your retirement can wait until spring, I've got the perfect... the absolute perfect event."

· · ·

A shaft of bright, painful light slanted across Feidhlim's face, piercing his half-open, dry, burning eyes. He managed a groan and rolled to his side. The torn, loosely hanging drapes and rising sun were now at his back, but the light reflected from the mirror directly into his eyes. He groaned again and tugged a thin, smelly pillow over his face. The musty, choking odor gagged him and he shoved the pillow away as he struggled to sit.

Wild, whirling, tilted. The room sped in circles around him. He pressed his palms against his temples in a futile attempt to stop the motion. His stomach roiled. but the bile remained in place, creating fresh agony in his belly. He couldn't even manage another groan from his parched throat.

The door eased open and a face, a faerie he didn't recognize, peered around the edge. Feidhlim squinted at him through one eye and the faerie smiled.

"Good morn, my lord."

The cheerful tone pained Feidhlim nearly more than the burning sunlight. "Go 'way."

The faerie stepped fully into the room. "My lord, Feidhlim. Your spies have returned but bear little information."

"So?" The idiot's tenor voice made his teeth ache.

"What plans now, my lord?"

Plans? They wanted plans? He had no plans. Feidhlim leaned forward to cradle his head in his hands. Only to make the pain go away. The only way he knew how. Sinking deep in a bottle was no longer a pleasure, but it was preferable to the misery of climbing from that liquid forgetfulness. He lifted his head and tried to focus. He needed something. What?

"Your followers await."

Feidhlim slashed one hand in a silencing motion then grasped at his head. "Let them wait. They wait for nothing. I am nothing."

"But..."

"Shut. Up."

The astonished faerie backed toward the door, knocking an

array of empty bottles from a small table. The continued clinking as he tried to gather the scattered bottles drove Feidhlim to his feet. Wavering side to side, he cupped his hand, drew it back and tossed—nothing at his follower.

"Ahh," he wailed. That was what was missing. What he needed. His magic, his power, his... anger.

Before the wide-eyed faerie could back from the room, Feidhlim lurched forward and wrapped his empty fist in the man's shirt. Using his other hand, he pointed to the bottles. "Take those from my sight."

He leaned closer and the trembling faerie shrank from his advance. His throat made a rasping sound as he tried to speak, tried to choke out the words. "And bring me more."

J ayse glanced at his watch and rolled his eyes. It was well past noon and he had planned on stopping by Lucidea's no later than midmorning. He'd shown his folks the sale documents for the land, and Tommy had read through the legalese carefully. Finally, they believed he was a land owner and settled back while he outlined his plans for the hilly pasture, tree-lined stream, and large pond. Pride emanated from them in almost touchable waves as he explained how his castle would grow from cardboard and plaster to the real life centerpiece of his land. Never mind that he was almost thirty, parental approval meant much to him.

As did the catering agreement he made, and signed with his dad and Tommy. The opening of the permanent faire site would be Zeroun's farewell event.

Tomorrow he would take the family not that far from the city and let them walk over his land. He doubted they would feel the same sense of peace and belonging he did, but he wanted them to experience the hills and valleys, and sit by the pond before he began construction. He didn't doubt that he'd receive more ideas than he could use, more suggestions than he would be able to keep track of, and more offers of help that he'd gladly accept.

Today, he would succumb to the odd need for Lucidea's approval.

Perhaps she would go with him that afternoon. Maybe the offer of supper would convince her.

Jayse pulled into the visitor parking lot across from her townhouse. Before he could change his mind, he was out of the car and standing at her entrance. The door opened before he knocked and Coralie grinned at him. He avoided looking lower than her eyes—just in case. Now, if Lucidea answered the door au naturel, he would be a lucky, lucky man. And more than willing to look down. More than willing to do a lot.

"Oh. Master Jayse."

Master Jayse? Where was this woman from anyway? Much of her speech sounded similar to Derrik's, but there were enough subtle differences to confuse him.

She angled to one side. "Will ye come in, please? I'm off to the pool fer a swim."

Pool? In October? Jayse blinked and shook his head.

"There is a pool inside the clubhouse. Lucidea says I may swim there while I visit."

"Oh, of course. Sorry, my mind's elsewhere."

"I dinna doubt."

What was it about the knowing timbre of her voice that shot longing coursing through his veins? He glanced at the young woman and breathed a soft sigh of relief. She wore a bathing suit under a long, lacy cover-up.

Coralie passed through the doorway and paused two steps down the walk when he called out to her. "Wait. Shouldn't you wear a jacket or something? It's chilly out here."

She glanced at him over her shoulder. "I thank ye fer yer concern, but I'm accustomed to the chill. Lucidea is in the office... workin' on yer faces." She twirled in a pirouette and waved. "'Tis a beautiful day."

A smile spread across Jayse's face. "It sure is."

· · ·

S ending Coralie off to the pool gave Lucidea a chance to think over all the things they'd discussed in the early morning light. The revelations of the previous day, the mere thought she might actually have some magical power intruded into those fearful thoughts.

She couldn't wait to see Jayse again, and try looking at him in the way Coralie taught her. She wanted to see his aura. For some reason, testing her budding skills on him—with him—was unusually important to her.

She had a stack of renderings of the perpetrator's face with a multitude of looks ready for him. Should she call him? Maybe, invite him for supper?

As she reached for the phone, a movement in the doorway caught her eye. Fear rose in her as she slowly stood, Coralie's warnings against Pagas ringing loud in her mind.

SEVEN

Lucidea closed her eyes, took a few short, choppy breaths, and whirled, one leg kicking high. She heard a satisfying grunt when her foot connected. Her eyes popped open. A hand closed around her bare foot and a soft voice said, "Lucidea, it's me. Jayse."

He held her foot securely against his stomach, then supported her calf with his other hand. Trying to clear the fear from her brain, she shook her head. "What are you doing here?"

"Coralie said it was okay that I come in. I met her as she was leaving to go swimming." His fingers moved against her foot and she held back a sigh at the gentle caress.

"Uh, you can let go." Not that she wanted him to; she was enjoying the subtle pressure of his hands way too much. But she couldn't stand on one foot forever. "I'll keep both feet on the ground."

"I'm sorry to frighten you. Even though Coralie let me in, I should have knocked. My fault."

"No, I'm just a little jumpy. I... nightmares kept me awake last night."

He still hadn't let go of her foot and she shifted to grab the back of her chair to keep her balance. "Nice defense, by the way."

Jayse chuckled and the sound vibrated from his body, through her foot and along her leg. A sudden weakness nearly collapsed her and he immediately dropped her foot and reached for her arm to steady her.

"Careful."

"Well, if you wouldn't have snuck up on me." She pouted her lower lip.

He hadn't released her arm and moved a step closer. Her heart pounded—from the scare, nothing else. Then he blinked and stepped back, letting his fingers drag a soft trail along her arm. A delightful, mischievous light sparked in his eyes.

"So, want to... teach me that move?"

"Move? Oh, you mean the kick?" She leaned back and eyed him, appraising him and his motives as he shifted under her scrutiny. "Only if you show me how you blocked it so easily."

"Deal." Jayse held out his hand and she pressed her palm against his. Instead of shaking to close the deal, he turned her hand, lifted it and brushed his lips against the back. He wasn't playing fair.

She needed to sit before she collapsed. "How about some coffee?"

A knowing grin stretched his lips and she shifted uncomfortably. "Okay."

The office was too small to contain the essence of Jaysson Zeroun—and her desire for him. There. She admitted that much to herself. "I... I just finished up a bunch of faces for you. Let me bring them into the kitchen and I'll let you take a look." She turned from the heat of his gaze and a chill cascaded over her. Turning her head, she caught his smile and the warmth returned. Flustered, she couldn't even seem to gather the neat stack of papers from the printer tray.

Jayse eased past her and picked up the few sheets that had fallen to the floor. "I have an even better idea—unless you need to stick around until Coralie comes back."

"No, she has my spare key. Otherwise she couldn't get into the

pool. There's a lock, but every townhouse key opens it." Blathering. She was a blathering idiot.

"Good precaution. She won't worry if you leave?"

"Leave? No, I could write a note... or we could stop by the pool
on our way. Yeah, that'd probably be better." Although Lucidea
had a sneaking suspicion Coralie knew, and wouldn't mind
spending the rest of the day alone. "You want to go somewhere?"

Oh, now that was intelligent. Of course he wanted to go
somewhere, otherwise he wouldn't have suggested it. That was
what he was suggesting, wasn't it? She bent to the task of evening
the edges of the pages in her hand to concentrate on something
other than the amber of his honey eyes.

"I'd like to show you something. Actually, it's the reason I
rushed away yesterday. I'd like your opinion."

"Mine?" she squeaked. Why would he want her opinion? The
why really didn't matter, as long as she could spend time with
him and get to know him better. Much better. He turned toward
the door and she let her gaze roam from his shoulders down to his
firm butt and the thighs that stretched the legs of his jeans. Next
to eyes, she was a sucker for man-thighs.

"Yes, yours."

"Huh?" She clutched the papers to her chest.

"Yes, I'd like your opinion." He turned back. "Will you take a
drive with me? About ten miles outside of town? I'll bribe you
with supper at the restaurant of your choice."

She grinned at that. "My choice, huh? I haven't been out much
lately, what if I picked the most expensive place in town?"

He shrugged and her mouth dried at the way his cotton shirt
shifted over his chest. This was bad—no, good—so good it was
bad. What in the world was she thinking?

"Doesn't matter. I'm celebrating. And I'd like it if you helped
me celebrate."

"What are we celebrating?"

"We?"

"Of course you can bribe me with a meal. Especially with a
gooey chocolate dessert. Food can also be the way to a woman's

heart, you know." She gasped and stared at him. She'd just said that?

"I'll remember, Lucidea." Infinite promise resounded in the simple statement and he held out his hand. "Let's go. It's getting dark earlier and we'll need the light."

Pushing further questions aside, she carefully took his hand then, after he angled to the side so she could leave the room before him, led him through the townhouse as she gathered her purse and a jacket.

In the parking area, she pulled him to a halt and pointed to the squat building across the green space. "Let me just run over to the pool and tell Coralie I'm leaving. That'll be quicker than driving through the complex. The front gate's on the other side of the building. How about if you meet me there?"

He nodded understanding and she imagined the heat of his gaze as she trotted toward the clubhouse. She was at the door before she heard the smooth rumble of a car engine. She turned and waved before entering the building.

Coralie was alone, lying on the bottom of the pool with her eyes closed. After a moment of panic Lucidea slapped repeatedly at the water to gain her attention. After berating the Alfar-Sindhu about lying like that where anyone could see her and think she had drowned, Lucidea rushed back outside, Coralie's laughter and promises to be careful echoed behind her.

Jayse waited at the community entrance, tapping his finger on the steering wheel in time to the soft music from the radio. Fighting to keep his nerves at bay, he fiddled with the seatbelt and frowned at the dust on the dash as if his expression would make the light gray coating disappear. Then he picked up the papers Lucidea thrust into his hands before she'd run off to the clubhouse but didn't glance at the computerized drawings.

A smile replaced the frown. Running, she was joy in motion. Standing still, she was beauty. Flustered, she was all he wanted. The frown returned. Was this love at first sight? No, it couldn't be. Could it? He hadn't been looking to fall in love. No, it was just that marvelous physical attraction. He squirmed in his seat. And boy, she sure attracted him.

She knocked once on the window before opening the door and slipping onto the cloth seat beside him. He dumped the papers unceremoniously over his shoulder and chuckled as they rustled to cover the back seat.

Lucidea shook her head at him, but smiled. "So, tell me. Where did you learn that defensive move?"

He swallowed heavily. Where indeed? Long hours of practice with Derrik and Macaire had sharpened his fighting skills, and his adaptability. However, this wasn't the time to bring up the fact that he was a quarter Faerie, or that the practice had taken place in the Otherworld. "I do some medieval style fighting, though mostly with swords. The kind of stuff you might see at a renaissance faire."

"A ren faire? I love those things. I was really upset to have missed the big one down in Kansas City this year. I usually go once or twice a season. I don't remember seeing you there, though."

The tone of her voice made it sound like she would have noticed him. And, she loved faires? Maybe... the spark of hope blossomed in his chest. Maybe she wouldn't laugh at his dream.

"I've never fought there. They're pretty strict about sticking with the people hired for the various parts each year. It's a huge competition to be selected to be a part of the faire."

"Oh, I'm sure. I've always thought it would be a kick to be one of the actors."

"And what part would you play, milady?"

Lucidea angled in her seat and tilted her chin. "The queen, of course."

The Queen of Hearts... of my heart. "Oh, I beg pardon, milady. Who else could you be?"

"Who else indeed." She laughed then returned to the conversation. "So, do you fight with the Society for Creative Anachronism?"

"Not usually, although I have done some teaching. They use

padded weapons and I fight with the real thing—with a sword. Makes it more difficult to find a challenger."

"I'm sure it does. But, if you use a sword to fight, how did you block my kick so easily?"

"Many people think that once a warrior has a sword in his hand, there's some code of ethics—that chivalry thing—that binds our actions. In reality, if you were fighting for your life, you would do anything to win. Down and dirty, that's the reality of fighting. You use whatever means you can to stay alive, to win."

"Sounds pretty intense."

"It can be." He shrugged one shoulder.

"So, have you ever blocked a sword the same way you blocked my kick?"

"Yes."

"And..."

"I wouldn't recommend it. Sliced the heck out of my hands."

"Oh, no." She reached for his hand and he let her draw it from the steering wheel. Concentrating hard on driving safely, he tried to ignore the way she drew her fingertips over his palm and along the length of his index finger. And the way his body responded.

"I don't see any scars."

"I..." He swallowed heavily. "... had a good doctor." When Macaire had seen the blood streaming from his hands, the faerie had bypassed the healers and taken him directly to his father. Dad's talents healed the wounds and restored the strength that had flowed from him along with his blood. Thankfully, his dad had never questioned him about the incident, though Macaire, and later Derrik, had both chastised him at length for the foolish action.

"Bet you never did that again."

Laughter filled his chest and escaped to be joined by Lucidea's low, sultry laugh. "Nope, not until today."

"Good thing I didn't have on stiletto heels, huh?"

"Very good thing. We're here."

Jayse pulled off the gravel road onto a rutted path little more than parallel stripes of dirt across a field. Watching how Lucidea clutched the armrest, he drove carefully until he neared the crest of an impressive hill. He parked and silence surrounded them when he turned off the engine. "We'll walk the rest of the way, if that's okay."

She smiled. "Sure is. I left my stilettos at home, remember?"

Lucidea took his offered hand and they climbed to the top of the hill. The sounds of the city were far away and the peace of the countryside seeped into her soul. She wasn't able to forget the threat Pagas held over the Alfar-Sindhu, nor could she ever escape the pain of her uncle's imprisonment, but she needed this brief respite more than she realized. The fact she shared this time with a man she was unaccountably attracted to only deepened the power of the moment.

Holding a chuckle inside, she mentally berated herself. She'd made this time more important than it was. Sure, she was pretty sure Jayse was as attracted to her as she was to him. He'd never be able to hide his true feelings from her with those intense amber eyes.

Turning her head to look at him, she found those eyes, his expressive gaze hard upon her. The interest she expected to see was tempered by a dulling of doubt, of worry. If he brought her here to show her a place of quiet reflection, he needn't worry. He drew a deep breath and her breathing matched his.

"You said you enjoy renaissance faires?"

She tilted her head to one side and stared at him. Not expecting his question, she stumbled for an answer. "Yeah, I do. I haven't been to many, and afterwards I always think I'm going to create a persona, or at least a costume before the next one. But I never do."

"If you don't mind sitting in the grass, there's a great spot just a little further overlooking the pond."

"Let's go." Wanting to erase the doubt from his eyes, she waited until he nodded then threaded her fingers through his. He smiled, a gentle, sweet smile, a smile so innocently sensuous she probably needed to jump into that cold pond, not sit next to it.

"This is the reason I had to leave yesterday. I bought this land."

Jayse stopped and took both of her hands in his then spread his arms. "I first saw the area when I was nine, riding my bike along the old railroad tracks. I knew, even then, someday this would be mine. I even told the farmer who owned it that I would buy this whole section. He didn't even laugh at me."

"Why would he laugh?"

Jayse shuffled his feet through the ankle-high, dried grass. "I was twelve at the time."

"Oh. Not many kids have a dream like that—one they carry with them into adulthood. I admire such dedication."

"That's not all of the dream, Lucidea. Before today, I've only told one other person about my plans."

The fear returned to haunt his eyes, the doubt strong enough to dull the excited sparkle. What was he afraid to tell her? Why? "What's troubling you, Jayse?"

He shook his head and angled to face the pond.

"Don't turn away from me, Jaysson whatever your middle name is Zeroun. Tell me what's wrong."

"Allen."

"Huh?"

"My middle name's Allen. Sit with me?"

After she nodded, he held her hand as she folded her legs into a cross-legged position, then lowered himself so he sat facing her. Knowing he'd speak when ready, she waited in silence. Content with watching him, Lucidea let her gaze lose partial focus until it was as if she looked at him both with her physical eyes and with her mind's eye.

A faint, rainbow-colored haze surrounded him, the colors swirling and pulsing like the beat of a heart. But, she wanted to see the sparkles, even though she was sure that she had only imagined the tiny silver lights. Sparkles meant magic, after all, and unlike her, Jayse was human. She gnawed at her bottom lip to hold back the sudden onslaught of a silly grin. She'd done it. She saw his aura without really trying.

Focusing her gaze on his face, she guiltily released her lower lip.

Jayse watched her intently, but the moment her eyes locked with his, he glanced away and stared over her shoulder. "The first date," he began slowly, "my parents had was to a small renaissance faire at the Arthur Hills winery. Until a few years ago when the faire outgrew the space they had available, the winery held a faire every spring. My family attended religiously. It's almost a compulsion with us—much like seeing every production of *A Midsummer Night's Dream*."

"Shakespeare?"

Nodding, Jayse gave her a crooked grin. "You'd be amazed at how my family connects to that play."

A great deal remained hidden behind that statement, and Lucidea vowed to eventually find out those secrets. The possibilities, vague and fleeting, intrigued her, but the distraction wasn't enough to pull her from learning more now. "Okay, so your family loves Shakespeare and ren faires."

"It wasn't just owning this land that's been my dream for— oh, all my life. It's the development of the land. Look around you with your artistic eyes, Lucidea. Over there, winding through the copse of trees, lanes filled with small shops and pavilions. On the flat area at the top of that hill, in an area surrounded by colorful flags armored knights upon battle ready steeds await a tournament. And here, were we sit, a castle, built in traditional fashion of timber, stone and mortar, home to spectacular fêtes and feasts. In the pond, fountains shower the still water with sound."

Jayse closed his eyes and she held her breath waiting for him to continue. Waiting for him to look at her again. He spoke without opening his eyes.

"That's my dream, Lucidea. To own a permanent faire site. A place with facilities for parties and receptions, a place for lovers of fantasy and history to come together." A faint, ruddiness colored his cheeks. "I've even been building a model of the castle—since I was ten."

Finally, his lids lifted, exposing dark, cloudy apprehension.

Lucidea blinked, even the swirl of colors in his aura had slowed, becoming murky and dull. Realization dawned in her. He was afraid of what she would say to his admission to a life long love of—fantasy. The beat of her heart surged with hope. Maybe there was a chance for them.

"What happened the last time you told someone about this?"

"You mean other than when I told my folks today?" His gaze skittered to the side. "She laughed. Not to my face, but later."

Foolish woman. With a response like that, the... she didn't deserve a man like Jayse. "Idiot."

"What?" He jerked as he faced her, the honey-brown of his eyes turning to chocolate.

She was an idiot, too. He thought she'd meant the word about him. "No, Jayse. I mean she was an idiot for not admiring you. Your dedication to a dream. Too many people either don't have a dream, or lose sight of it somewhere along the way." The warmth of his hand when she touched him made her smile softly.

The tentative return of a smile brought light back to his eyes and a shower of silver sparkles to the aura she forgot she could see.

"Oh."

"Lucidea? What's—"

"Nothing. Just a stray thought. I think your plans sound wonderful. I can't imagine how great it will be to have something like this so close to home."

"Thank you. That means a lot."

"So, how soon do I have to have my outfit done?"

Instead of answering, Jayse leaned forward, planting his hands on the ground at either side of her hips. The breath caught in her throat and she nervously licked her lips. He was going to kiss her.

"What's you're middle name?" he whispered.

"Huh?" That wasn't the usual prelude to a kiss.

"I told you my middle name. Now, I'm asking yours."

"Anne."

His mouth hovered only a breath away from hers. "Nicknames?"

She wanted to shout 'just kiss me', knew that if she tilted her face a little to the right, she could initiate the kiss. But she wanted him to be the one... yes, she wanted him to be the one. "No, not that I like anyway." Her voice softened to the barest of whispers. "Except when Daddy called me Dea Annie."

"Dea Annie, I'm going to kiss you."

"I know. Please..."

He lifted his hand to cup her cheek and she covered his hand with hers. Gentle pressure of his fingers created the final angle and she closed her eyes. Warm, firm lips touched hers and she swallowed her verbal response of longing. Ah, even better than she imagined. He slowly moved his mouth and touched the tip of his tongue to the seam of her lips. There was no question in her mind as she parted her lips and invited him with the quick touch of her own tongue.

Leaning her back as he crawled forward, Jayse slid his hand from her cheek to the back of her head, cushioning her against the hard ground. He sprawled beside her, pulling her close against him, trailing quick kisses along her jaw before returning to possess her mouth.

Lucidea threaded her fingers through his hair and held him close. The man could kiss... could kiss her senseless... and she wouldn't care. He pulled away and stared down at her, his eyes bright with desire. He touched her cheek and she felt as though sparkles shot through her, igniting the blood in her veins. The analytical part of her mind attempted to decipher the odd experience, but feeling overtook logic. "Please."

Jayse grinned and stroked a strand of hair from her forehead. "Please, what, Dea Annie."

"Kiss me again."

The grin widened and she knew he was happy to oblige. When he pressed her close, she wrapped one leg over his and arched against him. He groaned into her mouth and danced his tongue along her inner lip.

An odd chime penetrated the sensual haze he created around her. Jayse lifted his face from hers and said, "Don't answer that. Let voice mail pick up."

The chiming stopped but as he turned back and she searched for his lips, the phone rang again. "Jayse, that's your phone."

"I know." He groaned and stared into her face. "Ignore it. This is better."

"Important?" she managed before he lowered his mouth to hers.

The annoying sound ended and she gave herself to his kisses. Until the third time the phone rang. Then she shoved at his chest, but tempered her actions with a smile and a caress. "Three times, must be important."

Jayse rolled to his back and dug in his jeans pocket. Lucidea dragged her swollen lower lip between her teeth as he pulled his phone from the tight, straining denim. He closed his eyes, tipped his head back to the ground, and cleared his throat before he answered. "This better be good."

CHAPTER
EIGHT

"What? Now?" Jayse struggled to his feet. "I'm there." With an easy motion he tucked the phone back in his pocket, and held out his empty hand to Lucidea. She stared at his fingers and his heart collapsed into a tight pain as the desire faded from her eyes. After a moment she took his hand and he pulled her to her feet and into a loose embrace.

"I'm sorry, Dea Annie. We've got to go."

She leaned her forehead against his chest. "So I assumed."

Afraid she thought he used the phone call as an excuse to end the sensual moment, he pressed his lips to her hair. "I wish we could continue—"

"That's okay, you don't need to say anything. I understand." The soft, sad tone of her words said she didn't. Not by a long shot.

"No, you don't. But I don't have time right now to show how much I didn't want to stop." He tightened his arms and felt her sigh. "You remember Carrie?"

Her shoulder stiffened then relaxed, and she wiggled to lean back far enough to look into his face. "Yes. She's the reason I did those facial changes for you."

"Yep." Unable to help himself, he kissed the tip of her nose then smiled. "She's in labor. I've got to get to the hospital. Her husband, Bryce, is like my brother... closer probably."

Lucidea's forehead furrowed and he longed to kiss the cute wrinkles. Her expression showed a touch of concern. "This is the baby that's a result of the attack?"

"Yes. And I don't have any doubt that if Feidhlim doesn't already know that she's in labor, he will soon. I need to be there to help protect them."

Caution joined the concern in her expression. "What do you mean? You don't honestly think that just because he raped Carrie he'd try and do something to the child? I'm sure he's long gone from this area."

Jayse kept his arm around her shoulder and turned them toward the car. He couldn't explain to someone outside the family how important this child might be to Feidhlim or how the disgraced faerie could use the innocent life to further his own purposes.

Lucidea eased them into a quicker pace. "But then again, you never know what kind of sick ideas some perpetrators come up with. We'd better hurry. There won't be time for you to take me all the way across town, so unless there's a problem, I can go to the hospital with you. I'll get a taxi or something from there."

He admired her matter-of-fact manner and the way it eased the painful concern in his chest. A little. He, and the rest of the family, had imagined a multitude of scenarios involving Feidhlim and Carrie's baby. Although Feidhlim had no magic, that didn't mean his followers still wouldn't do anything for him. Even situations dictated in purely non-magical terms were too horrible to consider. No, if he and the Alastriona had to stand guard on Bryce's family twenty-four seven, they would. Until Feidhlim was dealt with—permanently.

At the car, Lucidea turned to face him and he engulfed her in a tight embrace. "Thank you," he whispered against her hair.

She nodded then pressed a kiss to his cheek. "We'd better hurry. Babies won't wait if they're ready to greet the world."

On the drive back into town, Jayse convinced Lucidea to come to the maternity ward with him. Her agreement came with a slight grin that told him she wanted to stay close to him as much as he wanted her by his side. The fact that she could show the different looks she'd created for Feidhlim to the family weighted her decision in his favor.

"After all," she said as she hurried to gather the renditions scattered over the back seat of his car. "Even though to the parents babies may not seem to wait, the wait will seem interminable to everyone else. This isn't the happiest of things to discuss, but under the circumstances..."

"I'm glad you understand."

She glanced up at him and shut the car door with a shove of one hip. "No, not really. But, that's okay. I'm... happy to be here... with you."

There was time for only one quick kiss before they hurried into the hospital, and after getting lost in the maze of hallways and oval, pod-like nurses' stations, finally found the maternity waiting area.

Oddly, there were no other impending births in the ward, so the extended Zeroun clan took up the entire space. After Jayse rushed to speak to a man who could only be his father, Lucidea stood in the doorway clutching the stack of papers to her chest. There were so many of them. Jayse hadn't been kidding.

A tall, blond man with fine, aristocratic features advanced, took her arm and gently guided her into the room. "So, ye came with Jayse? D'ye remember me? I'm Derrik." He stood a bit straighter. "Soon to be a granda again."

Lucidea grinned at his evident pride. "Of course I remember. You're the partner of the man who was kidnapped."

The tall man's shoulders slumped and Lucidea wished she hadn't unthinkingly brought up the painful memory. "Aye. But, my Tommy's here now, an' we're waitin' fer our new grandson to enter this world. Come, join the family."

Lucidea glanced around at the small clusters of people perched on the uncomfortable waiting room furniture. She recognized only a few from the times she had visited with

Carrie to draw the face she now held as a pile of wrinkled copies.

"Come with me." Derrik chuckled and she smiled in response. "If Jaysson dinna wish to introduce ye around, then I shall. With yer permission, of course."

"Of course." She liked this man. Before, he had been haunted and drawn, then absorbed in the return of his lover. Now, it appeared life was good to him. In fact, he seemed barely old enough to have a young child of his own, let alone a grandchild.

He took her directly to Jayse's side and she cast him a grateful look. He grinned. "This is Jaye Zeroun, Jayse's da. Allyn, his mother. An' my Tommy."

Jayse took her hand and the strong grip helped her relax. "I was showing Lucidea my land when the call came."

His father's eyebrows rose and he appeared ready to make a comment when Allyn pinched his arm. At his sideways glance, she gave him a meaningful look and he shrugged. Then Allyn turned her attention on her son. "We called three times," she admonished dryly. "Glad you could make it."

Shortly after Jayse handed the pictures of Feidhlim's face to his father, a commotion at the door silenced the low hum of conversation. Derrik snatched the papers from Jaye and held them behind his back as a frantic man burst into the room and rushed toward them. "Da, Pop, it won't be long now. We're headed for the delivery room." He did a double take then clasped Jayse heavily on the shoulder. "I'm glad you're here. Hi, artist person—I'll remember your name later. Carrie's doing great—she's stronger than... Gotta go."

The whirlwind of soon-to-be father rushed back into the hallway.

Lucidea leaned close to Jayse's ear. "What was that all about? He looked really worried despite what he said." She basked under the glow of his smile and obvious pride.

"You're very observant. But, I guess that's part of your job isn't it?"

Shrugging away the statement, she responded. "I've always

been pretty good and reading people and gauging their emotions." She paused in thought. Could that be part of her abilities, of the magic Coralie said she would continue to discover within her? What about the visions she often had when she touched a skull—could that be another special ability? A gift of her non-human bloodline?

"But, he said everything was fine. Other than the concerns about... that man..." She didn't want to speak the name of the man who raped Carrie, not while they were waiting for her to give birth.

"No. There's more than that." Jayse tugged her to a tiny space near the center of the room not already occupied by a family member. He nodded his head toward a group of children playing quietly in one corner. "Breanna, the little girl in the pink overalls, is Bryce's daughter. Her mother... wasn't strong... and died when Bree was born. Despite everyone's assurances, that's got to weigh heavily on his mind."

"Oh, that's understandable." She watched the children play. "Poor baby, not to know her mother." She had been lucky to know her father, at least for a little while. A wave of loneliness for the man she barely remembered washed over her.

Jayse gave a soft snort. "There's plenty of mother figures in this family. She hasn't lacked for anything. You know, Bryce gives her one hundred percent of the credit for finding Carrie and insisting she would be her mommy."

"How cute." Lucidea leaned against Jayse's side and they silently watched the children play. Breanna jerked her face toward the door and froze, her hands clasped before her chest. A bright smile infused her face. Lucidea consciously struggled to keep her mouth from dropping open in astonishment as glowing sparks of bright pink danced around the child, whirling faster as her smile grew.

The girl clapped her hands and ran toward the door. "Gowtham," she cried and when the man who entered knelt beside her, she wrapped her arms tightly about his neck. Sadness lingered in his dark eyes as deep red sparkles danced with the pink for a brief moment then disappeared. The man touched a kiss to his finger then pressed it to the girl's nose before gently untangling her arms from his neck.

Lucidea glanced around the room. A rainbow of colors, flashes, and sparkles that soared and danced then settled lightly around each person assaulted her senses. In one corner, a man sat on the back of an overstuffed chair, a woman holding a tiny child perched on the seat before him. Involuntarily, Lucidea shrank back against Jayse. The man's aura coalesced at his back in the form of—wings. Butterfly wings of silver and blue. Oh, God. This was more than her battered emotions could handle. She'd only just discovered this ability—now, she wanted to turn it off.

"Something wrong?" Jayse's arm tightened about her shoulder.

She shook her head. These were his family and friends. It was just... if what Coralie had told her about the physical manifestation of magic were true? Then these people were... She shook her head again.

No, that couldn't be.

"There is something wrong, Lucidea. How about getting out of here? My family can be overwhelming at times. Even for me."

Overwhelming? That was an understatement. Not just the presence of so many people in a small room, but now besides the strong, vibrant colors, she could almost feel something in the air. An uncomfortable sensation tingled along her shoulders and came to rest at the base of her neck. She wanted to rub at the area, but knew the action would do no good. The dam holding back her unrealized magic had been opened and she was on definite overload. What other explanation could there be? Suddenly she didn't want to discover more talents within herself—and wasn't so sure she wanted what she already had.

"Come on." He leaned close to her ear and his warm breath tickled her neck. "Dea Annie, let's get out of here for a bit. How about some wonderful hospital cafeteria coffee?"

Laughter burst from her lips, drawing a few smiles from those nearby. She poked Jayse playfully in the chest. "I've had more than my fair share of hospital coffee. It's far from wonderful, unless you like thick coffee muck. But, yeah, I could use a little time. This is quite a group."

"It would have been better for you to meet them a little at a time, and I'll introduce you to everyone—later. Ah ha, I see my sister and Iain have just slipped out as well. Unless you'd rather find a place to be alone..."

"No, I'd like to meet your sister." She took a deep breath and a chance. "Alone can be later." The heated promise of his smile melted her against him as he pressed one palm flat at the small of her back to hold her closer. Intent on the brush of his lips against hers, she forgot the raging colors and the crowded room.

His mouth traced a smoky line to her ear. "Sorry. I couldn't wait until later. We'd better go, everybody's watching."

Lucidea stiffened, but he still held her close. "Relax, Dea Annie. My family's very loving—and demonstrative. I hope... you'll get used to it."

"I'd like that."

When he released her, she kept her head lowered, but glanced around surreptitiously. Except for a few fond grins, no one seemed to have paid much attention. Relieved, she gave Jayse a smile. "Coffee now?"

He nodded and turned them toward the door just as a young Native American woman entered. She seemed familiar. Lucidea didn't believe she'd ever met the woman, however, that kernel of knowing her blossomed strong. When the woman canted her head to one side and lifted her eyebrows to acknowledge her, Lucidea realized that more than by appearance, she was strongly reminded of Coralie.

But, how could that be? Coralie wasn't American, native or otherwise. Still the shape of their faces, the set of their eyes, the slight tilt of her head... Hmm, more mysteries.

Before they left the waiting area, the blonde child skipped across the room to her and took her hand. "I'm Breanna. My mommy's having my brother."

Lucidea bent closer to the charming imp. "A brother? Are you sure it's not a sister?"

"Oh no." She shook her head fiercely, tossing the wild, white blonde curls. "It's my brother."

"Are you happy to have a brother?"

"Oh yes. He's important." The girl touched Lucidea's cheek. Her brilliant blue-green eyes grew wide and round. Her mouth formed a perfect 'O'. "You're important, too."

Jayse ruffled the girl's hair. "Yes, she is Bree. She's my friend. This is Lucidea."

"No, Unca Jayse." Bree shook her head slowly. "I mean, yes." She executed a tiny curtsey. "Pleased to meet you, Lucidea."

Then she turned her attention back to Jayse. "Unca Jayse, I mean she's a mermaid."

Jayse stared at Breanna and shook his head. Her eyes widened further and she covered her mouth. "Sorry," she mumbled through her fingers. "I was surprised and I forgotted."

"Forgot," came a calm, melodious voice from one side.

Gowthaman came closer and rested his hand on Bree's head. "Forgot what, little missy?"

Bree looked up at him and pointed to Lucidea. "My new friend doesn't know."

"Know what?" Lucidea asked.

Trying to think of some plausible explanation for whatever Bree thought Lucidea didn't know, Jayse bit the inside of his cheek. What would he do if Bree spilled the family's secrets? Any one of the many?

Gowthaman gave Lucidea a shallow smile. "Breanna has a very active imagination. I cannot imagine what she may believe you do not know. I am sure it is nothing but the whims of a small child."

"Oh, I understand. Does she have an imaginary playmate?"

"Not no more," Bree piped up. "She's here now."

"Not any more," Jayse corrected automatically. He tugged on Lucidea's arm before Bree dug the family into a deeper hole, one he wasn't sure he'd be able to easily cover. "We'd better go."

"Yes. I shall watch the little missy," Gowthaman stated with an incline of his head.

"Thanks, friend." Jayse hoped Gowthaman understood how thankful he was for the intervention. He wasn't sure he could have diffused the possible uncomfortable situation.

With a slight bow, Gowthaman acknowledged the thank you. "The pleasure is mine, Jaysson. Come, little missy, we must talk about your... imagination."

He'd understood. Letting his breath out slowly, Jayse guided Lucidea out the door without further delay. They walked the hospital hall in silence for a few minutes but when they waited for the huge, stainless steel elevator Lucidea gave him an odd look. Tense and wondering what must be going through her mind, he tried to read the expression in her eyes.

"Your family has an interesting cast of characters. A great place to study faces. I tend to look at people with respect to their racial and ethnic origin—the characteristics I use when I do reconstructions. Like the broad shouldered man who leaned against the back wall. I'd like to say his ancestors come from the American southwest, but there's something, hmmm, just a little different from the indigenous people of that area. Oh well, with the continual mixing of races, such oddities are bound to occur, aren't they?"

"I suppose. And, I'm impressed." If she focused on appearance, maybe some of the other eccentricities would go unnoticed. The elevator doors opened after a double chime indicating the downward direction of travel. They entered and Jayse pushed the well-marked button for the cafeteria level.

Lucidea tapped her index finger against her lips. He watched her think, wondering what pathways her thoughts sought. Would there be difficult questions to answer? Questions about people and situations he couldn't talk about without revealing his fey heritage?

"That man who took care of Breanna, is he East Indian?"

Letting relief wash through him, Jayse chuckled. "Gowthaman is a friend of the family. I don't know exactly where he's from. I've only known him since he worked with my aunt on a research project in the Sahara desert."

"The Sahara? Wow. That's someplace I'd love to visit. I've not been much of anywhere except my recent trip to Scotland."

The touch of sadness in her eyes intrigued him. He ached to wrap his arms around her, to protect her and keep sadness far from her. "That was when your uncle disappeared?"

"Yeah." She gave him a crooked smile. "And I do need to go back there soon. To... take care of some family business."

The knowledge he wouldn't see her during that time settled like a lead lump low in his belly. Even the prospect of beginning the development of his land couldn't chase away the sudden bout of loneliness.

Lucidea touched his hand as the elevator doors opened. "I'm not leaving right now. How about that wonderful coffee you promised me?"

They found Lara and Iain at a small round table. After Jayse introduced Lucidea the small talk turned to Lara's tales of raising two sets of twins. Jayse watched Lucidea's reactions and let his mind wander to the day when he might have kids. Then he would have silly stories to share with friends and family, too.

"I just hope Bryce and Carrie have decided on a name for the baby."

Jayse focused his attention on his sister and her off-handed statement. "I'm sure they have," he muttered, afraid of what Lara was planning to say next.

Her eyebrows rose and she chuckled. "Although Bryson isn't such a bad name, it'd be nice to have something different. You know how confusing it gets sometimes with you and Dad." Lara chuckled again and turned a canted, mischievous grin toward Lucidea. "Did you know that when Jayse was born, our folks couldn't decide on a name. Everyone kept calling him Jaye's son. Ta da. There ya go. Jaysson."

"Gee, sis, thanks for telling her I don't even have a name of my own." Jayse thrust out his lower lip, crossed his arms and slumped in the hard, plastic chair.

Muffled snorts erupted from Iain in his attempts to stifle his laughter. "Sweet, ye shouldna tease Jayse. 'Tis no fault of his... he must forever be... known as the son."

Lucidea adopted a serious expression and touched his arm. "I like your name, Jaysson Allen Zeroun."

Enough to take it as her own? Jayse straightened, relaxed his pout and closed his eyes for a brief moment. It was way too early in their relationship to be thinking those kinds of thoughts.

When he opened his eyes a faint shimmer drew his gaze to a far corner of the cafeteria, partially hidden behind a grouping of tall artificial plants. His spine stiffened and his muscles tensed in defensive preparation.

Time and breath halted as a Faerie portal opened.

CHAPTER
NINE

Vibrations from Jayse's tensed muscles bounced against Lucidea's hyper-sensitive senses. She stared in wonder as his aura colors deepened and the silver glinted across his forehead. He exuded power, pure power that went beyond masculinity. The force of his emotions reminded her of how Morghan had gathered power before he fought Brandr Ur. Was it possible that this man beside her had magical abilities?

Iain clasped Jayse's shoulder. "Easy, man. 'Tis only Macaire."

Jayse shook his head as if trying to clear his thoughts and the silver sparkles danced away to resume a smooth flow through his aura. A faint light shone around Iain's hand as his fingers tightened, then released Jayse's shoulder

Jayse remained tense and alert until Iain leaned back casually and spoke again. "Mayhaps Macaire brings news of the birthin'. We should return to the rest of the family." He angled his smile to Lara. "Sweet?"

Lucidea glanced quickly at Jayse s sister who gave her a bland smile, then at the tall man approaching their table with long, easy strides. Gads, were all the men associated with this family good looking? She admired the man, but suddenly realized she didn't care about the other men, just Jayse.

He rose and met the advancing man a few steps from the table. Leaning forward on the balls of his feet, he whispered, his hands moving in jerky, urgent swipes through the air. Lucidea tried to listen without listening. Maybe she could catch a clue as to why he'd suddenly become so tense.

"...more careful... public place... portal..."

"So, Lucidea," Lara said just a bit too loudly, "what do you think of the family?"

"Trying to distract me?" At Lara's blush Lucidea softened the accusation with a grin and continued. "Overwhelming doesn't begin to describe it." Not only the sheer numbers—though as an only child she'd had little experience with large families—the explosion of colorful auras and strange visual images crowded her mind. She'd need a time alone for quiet reflection to even begin to put the sensory overload into perspective. That, and another long talk with Coralie.

Jayse returned and leaned on the back of his chair. "Macaire says it's almost time—so we'd better get back upstairs." As the group left the cafeteria, Jayse introduced Macaire as his friend as well as Derrik's assistant. She ached to ask what Derrik did for a living, but suspecting it was some form of law enforcement—possibly covert—she remained silent. Everyone was entitled to a few secrets. She was accumulating more of her own to tuck away from the real world.

Excitement throbbed through the waiting room, increasing the intensity of the colorful auras. Unsure she could deal with the images until she found a way to turn off the ability, she left Jayse talking to his aunts and inched her way to an amazingly unoccupied corner and slid down to sit on the floor. Tired beyond what little she'd done that day, she scrubbed at her eyes with her fingertips and leaned her head back against the wall. Maybe she could try and imagine... no, she was sure that childish technique wouldn't work. Maybe she'd just keep her eyes closed as much as she could to limit her contact with the colors.

"Mind if I join you?" The woman's voice soothed her jangled

emotions and for a brief moment she thought Coralie had somehow joined her. She glanced up through narrowed eyes to avoid taking in the full force of an aura. "Of course not. It's tough to find a space with all these people."

"It's quite the family. Good thing there aren't any other people who need to use the waiting room this evening." The woman eased next to her. "I'm Catori. But, please, just call me Tori. I haven't been a part of this group for very long either."

"Who are you with?" Lucidea hazarded a full glance at the woman and breathed a soft sigh. While Catori had a strong aura, it was somehow muted, as though hidden behind a thin film of gauze. Thankful for the visual respite, Lucidea offered a smile. "I'm Lucidea."

Catori nodded. "I know, Jayse's friend. The forensic artist. I'm not with anybody, I'm just a family friend. I got to know everybody while helping with a... situation." She turned her face to the side and her jaw worked as though she chewed on the inside of her cheek.

Suspecting that this situation had something to do with the perpetrator who had fathered the child about to be born, Lucidea closed her eyes again. "I think I understand. They're really concerned he's gonna show up, aren't they?"

She felt the intensity of the young woman's gaze. "Carrie is well guarded and protected. By every means the family has at their disposal."

Lucidea looked into Catori's dark eyes. "I'm sure of that. Just look around. There are more than just the usual pre-birth, waiting in a little room nerves here. You can feel the watchfulness." Now that she'd voiced the words, the feeling intensified and she rolled her shoulders.

"You look a little stressed."

The comment gave Lucidea a fit of giggles. Astounded, she covered her mouth. "I'm sorry," she mumbled through her fingers, "I guess I am."

"No problem. There's this breathing technique I learned

recently that really seems to help when stress gets to me." Catori hesitated. "I could teach you. It's amazingly simple."

Again the odd similarity between this woman and Coralie struck her and without question, she trusted Catori. "That would be great. How about a couple of days ago?"

Their shared laughter released the tension from Lucidea's neck and when she looked around the room, the auras seemed to have faded. After only a few minutes of quiet instruction, she discovered a gentle rhythm of breathing and pausing that further eased the intensity of the surrounding auras. Ah, much better. Better still was the man weaving through the crowded room, his focus and his smile shining on her.

Jayse sat at her other side and casually slipped his arm about her shoulder. "Okay?"

Snuggling against his side, she wasn't sure if he asked if it was okay to hold her, or if she felt okay. In either case... "Okay," she answered with a smile.

Catori leaned forward to peer at him. "So, what's the word?"

Relaxed, and with her tension headache fading, Lucidea didn't want to do anything but savor the feeling of warm man next to her. But her new friend's question triggered the active, investigative part of her mind. This went beyond a simple question—like so much of what she'd experienced and heard today with Jayse. There were layers upon layers of meaning. She angled a tiny bit so she could watch his face as he answered.

"They thought the arrival of the newest MacAlister was imminent, however, it seems baby has other plans. Carrie's totally stressed because Nightshade's not here. Nobody's heard from him in days."

"Nightshade?" The odd name was familiar, but Lucidea couldn't put a face to the name.

"Hmm. Nightshade's been a family friend for years. Then, we come to find out he was also Carrie's manager when she was a... dancer. He was Carrie's best friend—until Bryce came along, that is."

"And nobody knows where he is? Does he always just up and disappear? Isn't that suspicious?"

"Ah, the mind of my forensic investigator." Jayse touched his fingertip to her temple. "Always thinking."

Lucidea felt her face heat from his comment. He'd said *my* investigator. "Oh, no. I'm not really an investigator. Just the artist who puts together facial clues to discover how someone looked."

He stroked his finger from her temple to the fullness of her cheek. "Still, I'd say some of those investigative techniques rubbed off on you. You get this look in your eyes when you're trying to figure something out."

"Uh, you guys," Catori interrupted, then laughed. "There are other people in the room."

The gentle heat remaining from Jayse's praise burst into flames across her cheek.

"Oh, no. Don't be embarrassed." Catori hesitated, then touched Lucidea's arm. "I didn't mean to make you uncomfortable."

"You didn't." At Catori's disbelieving expression, Lucidea continued. "Not much anyway. Just more of the overwhelming aspects of this family."

Catori sighed. "I know what you mean." The sense of camaraderie brought a smile to both faces.

The matching expressions eased a measure of worry from Jayse's heart. He hadn't realized how nervous he was about Lucidea meeting his extended family and was glad she had found a friend.

A commotion at the door silenced the room. Jayse surged to his feet. The same rush of adrenaline that brought him to defensive tension in the cafeteria now prepared him for this new intrusion. He'd seen the shadowy forms of faerie warriors and received acknowledgement from the Alastriona silently patrolling the hospital corridors, so no danger should reach the family. Still, he set his jaw and waited, restraining the urge to leap forward.

A figure burst into the room, arms flowing in grand gestures. "Where is my Carouselle?"

"Nightshade." Jayse breathed the name in relief, but narrowed his eyes at the confident, dark woman who followed Nightshade closely.

Lucidea rose and cocked her head to one side. "That's Nightshade?"

Accustomed to the flamboyant man, Jayse tried to see him from Lucidea's perspective. Dressed in his usual tight blue jeans and flowing, billowy sleeved silk poet's shirt, the man moved with a lithe grace beyond the skills of his stage presence. Of all the characters in the family circle, Nightshade was easily the most... interesting.

Lucidea tugged lightly on his sleeve and he glanced at her. What was she thinking in that analytical mind he admired—and feared?

Forgetting Nightshade's grand entrance, would she somehow discover the secret of the Otherworld, of his fey bloodline, of his family? Then what would she do? Would she believe her conclusions or laugh them—and him—away as foolishness?

Her mouth twitched with suppressed emotion. "I think I saw one of his shows a couple years back."

"And?" Nightshade. She'd been thinking about... but what had she thought then? Would she accept...?

"He's very talented. My date didn't believe she was really a he. When I finally convinced him, he never called again. No big loss there. I guess he thought a drag show had something to do with race cars." She shrugged and chuckled. Jayse closed his eyes to capture the low, throaty sound deep within him.

"So...?" He had to know what she thought.

"If you're asking, no, it doesn't bother me in the least. In fact, I'd love a chance to talk to him. Maybe he could even give me a few makeup tips. I remember wishing I could look so good."

Laughter rumbled from him. Dea Annie grew more and more special to him with each moment. He hugged her to his side. "I think that could be arranged, But you don't need any tips from anyone. You're beautiful." She ducked her head and he pressed a kiss to the hair that had fallen over her temple. "Very beautiful."

Nightshade caught his eye and gave a brief nod. A serious glint shone in his eyes. Nightshade had changed since Bryce met Carrie, since Tommy had been kidnapped. But the chameleon-like man hid his secrets well, and Jayse respected the unspoken boundaries.

As Derrik led Nightshade from the waiting room, he tossed a loose wave over one shoulder, then whirled back and gave the woman he'd arrived with a gentle shove. "My... associate, Forsythia Jones. Her kindness got me back in time for this grand event. Make her welcome."

The woman scowled at Nightshade, rolled her eyes, then smiled at the gathered family. "Call me Thia, please."

"I'm off to see my dear Carrie and offer encouragement. From the looks of you, this has gone on long enough. She always listens to Nightshade. Ta, all." With another broad gesture of farewell, Nightshade disappeared into the hall.

Lucidea gasped and Jayse held her tighter as he stared at the retreating figure. The hem of Nightshade's loose shirt swirled up when he turned, revealing the unmistakable hard, black grip of a handgun.

No one else seemed to notice, so Lucidea tucked her astonishment away under a calm expression Maybe he always carried a gun. But when she glanced at Jayse, his eyes mirrored her surprise. So, the weapon wasn't a usual accessory. There must be more concern over this Feidhlim guy than she realized. What hold, besides fear, did he have over these people?

Slowly, Jayse turned and gave her a puzzled look before leaning close to her ear. "I can't believe Nightshade's got a gun. I can't imagine he knows how to use it. I've got to talk to—"

She stilled his lips with her fingertips. "No, you don't. If he wanted you to know... Jayse, sometimes you've got to give up trying to figure out so many whys. Just hope that if he's got a gun, he also has a license for it and does know how to shoot properly."

Jayse frowned at her. "But..."

She wrapped her hands around his forearm, holding him in place. "Everyone in the room is concerned, worried about what..."

She lowered her voice further. "... Feidhlim might do. If Night-shade is as good a friend to Carrie as you say he is, wouldn't he do anything... including wield a gun... to help protect her and the baby?"

"You are a wise one, aren't you?" A smile replaced his frown.

"No, not really. I'll take practical—at least in this case." If she were wise, she'd have already determined a way to free her uncle. Or why an entire family had sparkles in their auras. Or at least faced the responsibilities of her newfound heritage.

"I'm still concerned about the gun." Jayse fidgeted, glancing around the room.

"Then ask him about it when you get the chance."

Jayse slapped his forehead. "Dumb. Of course. I'll ask. Guess I've got so much going on, I lose track of my thinking processes."

Lucidea thought she understood. Whenever she was near him, or simply thinking about him, it was as if her brain cells simply gave up until focused on him again. It was a wondrous feeling— yet frightening. Between wanting to explore her feelings and create a strong relationship with Jayse, and Coralie teaching her about the Alfar-Sindhu and magic, there was too much to keep in focus. And she realized now she'd added to that list of concerns.

The Zeroun family's fears were rapidly becoming hers as their concerns wormed a path into her conscious thought. She closed her eyes briefly and silently vowed to do whatever she could to keep the family safe. The powerful inner promise surprised her, but there was no way she'd refute that vow.

Silence intruded on her thoughts; all conversation in the room had ceased. She opened her eyes, glanced around then focused on the lean form waiting in the doorway. Nightshade gestured broadly with both arms and bowed. "It is my pleasure to announce the arrival of Chance Evan MacAlister. About five minutes ago he came squalling into the world. Mother and son are doing fine. Bryce, on the other hand..."

Soft chuckles filled the room. After a decidedly theatrical pause, he continued. "You will all be able to see the newest member of the family in a little while. He's rather... upset at being thrust from his warm nest." Nightshade gave a delicate shiver. "But Mom and Dad are requesting the immediate presence of Tommy, Derrik, and Breanna."

After a round of congratulations, kisses, and back slapping, the trio left the room. Nightshade executed another perfect bow then winked. "I told you Carrie always listens to Nightshade."

B
right stars shone in the inky sky and Lucidea squinted against the lights of the parking lot, searching the southeastern sky for Orion. She had no idea why that particular constellation called to her, but on clear winter nights she always sought the triple star belt.

Emotionally drained, she leaned against the side of Jayse's car, waiting for him to finish speaking with his father. The two men stood just beyond the hospital doors, silhouetted by the blazing interior lights. She suspected they were talking about Feidhlim. The man's ever-present non-presence had been an uncomfortable undercurrent the entire evening. In many ways, she was glad to be leaving the large group of people, but in another part of her heart, she was already lonely.

Long strides brought Jayse to her side and that strange loneliness receded with the glint of his smile in the artificial light. "I'm starved. Haven't eaten all day. How about that meal I promised you hours ago?"

He wanted to be with her, extend their time together. Happiness washed away the fear she hadn't recognized until that moment. A fear that for some reason, she hadn't met some unspoken standard or expectations. "Oh, that sounds wonderful." She glanced at her watch. "The place I would have chosen is closed now, though."

Jayse lifted her arm and peered closely at her watch. "It's only a little after eight." Before he released her, he turned her hand and kissed the palm.

Shivers of delight danced across her skin. With feelings like this, she never wanted to go home.

"I know, but they close early. It's just a little place, close to the railroad tracks on the other side of town. It used to be a railroader's café in a miniscule building."

"The OK? Hmm, I haven't been there in ages. Do they still have the best roast beef in town?"

Surprised he knew about the small, family oriented, out of the way café, she took a moment to answer. With Zeroun's reputation, she expected him to frequent only the classier places in the area. "Yeah," she finally said. "I'll admit to nothing less than a passion for their hot beef sandwich."

A glimmer in his eyes brightened when she said 'passion', and even though she no longer saw his aura, it seemed silver sparkled through his dark hair. A trick of the streetlights. That's all.

"We'll go there another time then." The husky rasp of his voice promised not only a trip to a well-liked restaurant, but a trip to passion as well. She pushed away from the car, placed her hands on his waist and looked deeply into his eyes.

"I'd like that."

Jayse rested his hands on her shoulders and caressed the exposed skin of her neck with gentle strokes of his thumbs. Silent, they stood in the hospital parking lot, their gazes locked, as if each searched for meaning in the other's soul.

Perhaps she did. Perhaps he did hold such a meaning, a truth within him, that somehow, by knowing him... somehow she would find whatever it was she thought she was looking for.

Love. No, it couldn't be. She'd accept that she wanted this man, wanted him stronger, faster than any other man. But love? She didn't have time for love. She had to save Morghan. She had to learn about her heritage and find a way to protect her people from an evil disguised as Pagas, the High Chancellor. She didn't have...

The soft touch of Jayse's mouth upon hers shattered her thoughts into uncountable shards, sparkling silver and violet when her eyelids lowered. His lips lingered against hers, moving gently, never pressing for more. A kiss to caress every cell in her body. Every nerve ending sang a soft refrain. The nearby street sounds faded until all she heard was the beating of her heart.

And his.

TEN

The scent of fear touched his alcohol deadened senses long before his follower tentatively opened the door. Feidhlim let a modicum of satisfaction temper his pain. Mayhap not all was lost to him. Unable to shake the drunken haze from his mind or the heavy lethargy from his body, he remained sprawled in the chair. A tingle of inner knowing told him hours had passed since the dark forgetfulness first took his mind. The awareness threatened to send him rushing back to bottled oblivion. But first, he would suffer the fool before him and hear what he had to say.

"Speak."

"My lord, I have news."

Feidhlim opened one eye and tried to straighten. The effort became too great, so he remained at an uncomfortable angle. The faerie danced from foot to foot, vibrating excitement. Watching the movement wrenched Feidhlim's stomach painfully.

"Hold still and speak. And softly, fool."

The faerie froze, then leaned forward and spoke in a low, soothing tone. "My lord. The time has arrived. Your son is born."

The underling waited expectantly. Let him wait. Let them all wait. "So?"

"But, my lord, this is marvelous news. When the tidings spread that your son has come to you—when you hold him in your arms before us... Think on it, my lord."

Think? Pain arched through his brain.

"My lord, Feidhlim." A second faerie entered and stood without the usual bowing and scraping. Intrigued by the lack of obsequence, Feidhlim squinted up at him. "The child is a healthy boy, for what other child could come from your loins?"

"What indeed?" Feidhlim grunted, struggling to remain unaffected. But the seeds of ancient ambition, lying fallow since his magic had been stolen, germinated and grew swiftly. The apathy returned and quickly faded. As his magic was stolen, so would he steal the child from beneath the usurper's watchfulness. "Tell me more."

As the faerie launched into a tale of how Feidhlim's followers observed the birth without the Alastriona's knowledge, he straightened and shoved away the nearly empty bottle tucked between the chair cushions. When his follower regaled him with the physical perfection of the child—his child—he slid to perch on the very edge of the stained cushion.

After a slight pause, the faerie bowed low and said, "One final, glorious thing, my lord."

Feidhlim lurched to his feet, conquered the swirling room, and stiffened his spine. He lifted his head, regal despite the agonizing throb in his temples, and rested his hands on his hips. "What, then, is this glorious thing?"

The faerie's lips stretched to a wide, satisfied smile while relief and pride mixed in his expression. Feidhlim fought the urge to make a sarcastic, disparaging remark and angled his chin higher.

"My lord. There had been concerns about the child."

Feidhlim cocked one eyebrow and tilted his head slightly. The movement pulled at muscles in his neck, tight and painful from his awkward position in the chair. He withheld a grimace. "Concerns?"

"Yes, my lord. Unfortunately, since the woman who bore the

blessed babe is... human..." A look of distaste twisted the faerie's features before he composed his expression with a visible shudder. "Many were concerned the child would be as the mother and have no magical ability."

Would that be so bad? Startled by the morose direction of his thoughts, Feidhlim stared into the air above the other's head. "And what of those concerns now that the child—my son—is born?"

"The concerns no longer exist. From the moment your son drew his first breath, the observers felt the power of magic... beyond that experienced when a true Faerie child is born."

Feidhlim lowered his narrowed gaze. "And my son is not a true Faerie?"

"No, my lord, he is not." Even when Feidhlim took a menacing step forward, his follower stood firm and unflinching as he spoke. "Your son carries mixed blood, the taint of humankind flows through him. Once, at your wishes, we sought to destroy such children, destroy those who would mix human with fey. Once, we were nearly successful in eliminating the usurper and all he loved. Once... but once is gone, my lord. We have only the now."

The first faerie who had entered his room made a soft sound of dismay, drawing their attention. Having forgotten there was another in the room, Feidhlim turned and stared. "You. Out." When the faerie remained in place, Feidhlim jerked one finger toward the door. "Now."

The fool scurried from the room and with a look of profound sympathy at his fellow, carefully closed the door behind him.

Feidhlim rolled his shoulders and focused on the faerie calmly returning the intensity of his gaze. "Continue."

The other indicated a table, miraculously free of the clutter of bottles and moved to again face Feidhlim. "With your permission, shall we sit, my lord, so that my words shall be more comfortable to you?"

"Considerate of you," Feidhlim snapped. Did this one consider him weak? Anger heated his face and the room receded then advanced, the pulsing motion bringing sour bile to the back of his throat. Perhaps sitting was a good idea. Feidhlim stepped carefully through the now spinning room, sat opposite his underling, then waved his hand. "Sit then as well, if it is your wish."

"My wish is only to serve you, your ideas, your son." He sat, but his expression showed no attitude of service.

Giving a soft snort, Feidhlim squinted across the table. "Your name."

"Osric, my lord." A calculating gleam appeared in his eyes. A strong sense of déjà vu surrounded Feidhlim. The actions and expressions of the faerie reminded him of someone. But the fuzzy edges of his brain couldn't seem to wrap themselves around who.

In one smooth move, Osric reached to one side then slipped a full bottle on the table. He held the opaque blue cylinder between his palms, rolling it back and forth.

Avidly, Feidhlim watched the hypnotic motion. He swirled his tongue across the roof of his mouth, feeling as though he'd been licking the filthy orange shag carpet. A drink would moisten his mouth. Make it easier to speak, easier to listen... to think.

Osric held the bottle by the slim neck and angled the forgetfulness toward him. Knowing how easy it would be to reach out his hand and snatch at the bottle kept Feidhlim's palms flat against the table.

The hint of Osric's smile made Feidhlim frown. What was he up to? Why did he tempt when no temptation was needed? Why did he seem so familiar?

"My lord?" Osric held the bottle toward him.

"What games?"

"No game. I only offer—a choice."

A choice? Bottled forgetfulness or what? A blast of insight blurred his vision. A choice. A slow smile tugged the memory of past satisfaction from Feidhlim. Retribution. Payment for the wrongs done to him. Revenge. Sweet revenge.

Feidhlim slapped the bottle from Osric's hand, sending it flying across the small room.

"Yes. Very good, my lord." Osric took a deep breath. "It will be difficult. And painful."

Feidhlim kept silent, watching Osric, trying to place him, analyze his motives. He remembered the pain. How could he not? He remembered the agonies when his body had cried out for human drink, how he had shivered with heat and scratched at non-existent insects crawling on his skin and through his veins. Was this torture to his body and mind worth the pain?

He had a son. Yet only a babe, but a vehicle of power he could use against Zeroun. There may no longer be a place for him in the Otherworld, but revenge would know no boundaries of worlds.

Revenge was more potent than the forgetfulness. Zeroun would pay... dearly.

"Tell me of my son."

"Very good."

Leaning his head into his hands and staring at the tabletop, Feidhlim ignored the tone and lack of proper address and rubbed his temples. Satisfying as the prospect of revenge may be, his head throbbed until he could barely think. "My son?" he ground out between clenched teeth.

Harsh laughter sounded and Feidhlim lifted his head as Osric reclined in the hard chair. "You know me not, do you, my lord. Yet, I am familiar to you. Am I not?"

Feidhlim took a shallow breath and lunged across the table, wrapping his hands about Osric's neck. "Who are you? What have you done with my son?" As he spoke the words, fear gripped his chest tightly. If anything happened to the child before he found a way to use him... He shook Osric and tightened his grip. "Who?"

The laughter ended with a grunt and Osric brought his hands up to encircle Feidhlim's wrists. Power burned along Feidhlim's veins, a human power of physical control. Nearly as pleasant and satisfying as a magical attack, he gave a final press above the quivering lump of Osric's Adam's apple then shoved the faerie away. "You will tell me."

A grimace crossed Osric's features as he rubbed his throat. "Forgive me, my lord. I go too far."

Staring hard at him, searching for subterfuge, Feidhlim nodded. "Speak. Mark me well. If I do not care for what I hear—"

"I understand, my lord." Osric dipped his head and spoke to the tabletop. "I challenge you only—"

"You dare challenge me?" Hands planted on the scarred wood, Feidhlim focused on the cowering faerie.

"No. No, I..." Osric lifted his hands in a negative gesture.

Feidhlim smiled. His headache began to fade. Relishing the control over another, he waited.

Finally, Osric met his gaze. "You knew my father well, my lord. Entrusted him with much for the glory of the Nechtan-Cattee. My father... was murdered by the cousin of the leader of the Alastriona. His life's blood drained by a knife drawn across his neck."

"Searlait." The name brought an even fouler taste in his mouth.

"Yes, my lord."

"Torquil was your father? I didn't know he had a child." Amazing possibilities cleared pathways through the haze in his mind.

"Few did." A flush crept across the faerie's pale features. "He barely acknowledged me. But, I... I have followed you since his death, securing the methods to prevent you from being banished a second time to an unknown place. I found the ways to thwart the cursed Alastriona in their attempts against you. Then, when you were held in the world between worlds, I—and others..."

Feidhlim's lips twitched. Osric's reluctant acknowledgement of others said much. He was ambitious—and daring. As long as the ambition could be controlled, the daring would be useful. "For those actions I offer my thanks."

Osric brightened, the pleasure increasing his resemblance to his father and highlighting the subtle differences. Torquil, while doing Feidhlim's will with little question, had always seemed to follow a secret ambition of his own. There was no duplicity in Osric's expression. Placing a tentative, uneasy trust in the young faerie, Feidhlim leaned back.

"Yes, I see you have done much for me. To do secret battle with the Alastriona takes either courage or foolhardiness."

"Perhaps a bit of both, my lord. Now, shall I tell you of your son, and plans that await your approval to be set in motion?"

Feidhlim lifted one eyebrow and waited.

Launching into a quick telling of the birth time, the faerie spoke in a low tone, emphasizing his words by poking the table surface with his finger. Feidhlim relaxed as Osric spoke, yet wondered if he made a grave error in trusting Torquil's son. Wondering if his concerns were real or shadows caused by alcohol.

He closed his eyes briefly. How difficult would the road be this time? Already his stomach cramped with need and he could think of little but easing the agonies. He burned inside, yet cool sweat formed on his brow. Very difficult, he acknowledged, but not beyond his power. If control of his addiction was the only power allowed him, then he would use that control to his greatest advantage. He opened his eyes and made a subtle gesture with one hand. Immediately, Osric fell silent.

"I must leave this place. What has occurred here is past—an unspoken past."

"Yes, my lord. A place more... suitable... has been made ready for you. Well hidden from Alastriona spies, yet close enough to continue our observations."

"Good. I will allow no other to attend me until... until the..." He could say no more.

Osric dipped his head. "I understand, my lord. I shall be your voice to the Nechtan-Cattee until you stand before us whole and strong once more."

Whole? He doubted that, but he would let Osric have his ideals.

"Now, Osric. What thoughts have you on how I can use the child's birth to my best advantage?"

Osric slipped a folded page from a pocket and slid it across the table. "I propose, my lord Feidhlim, to first send this message to Zeroun."

· · ·

For once, waking early didn't bother Lucidea. Rather than facing a dull, drearily normal day, her first thoughts were of Jayse. She smiled. Her last conscious thought when she finally crawled into bed had been of him as well. Hooking her fingers around the scroll design on her cast iron headboard and pointing her toes toward the end of the mattress, she stretched.

They had settled on fast food and driven back to Jayse's land for a cold, in the car picnic. Then, they'd held hands and talked as they watched Orion move across the sky. And made out like a couple of teenagers until the windows fogged over. Laughing together, they'd wiped away the gray evidence of their behavior with leftover paper napkins.

Coralie had been reading when she floated through the door and had only given her a knowing smile before turning back to her book.

Lucidea relaxed her stretch and curled on her side. Her dreams had been non-existent. After months of reliving Morghan's disappearance each night, a night where she remembered no dreams was significant.

She shrugged and vowed to enjoy the peaceful night, even if it was—she glanced at the alarm clock—only three and a half hours long.

Knowing she'd never be able to go back to sleep, she scooted to the edge of the bed, but didn't yet climb out from under the covers. Was Jayse awake yet? She covered her mouth and bit back a giggle. What was it about him that made her act like a schoolgirl in the throes of her first crush?

Heeding a siren's call, she tossed back the comforter with a fluid movement and stood. Coffee. She needed dark, blessed caffeine to start her day. They had made no plans, but she was sure Jayse would call her. Maybe after he took his family out to look at his property.

She needed to get some work done first so she wouldn't feel guilty spending time with him.

The guilt stopped her with one arm halfway into her robe

sleeve. Every moment she spent on herself or with Jayse was time Morghan remained a prisoner. She fought with herself to hold on to the guilt, but the pleasure of just being with Jaysson Zeroun tumbled her concerns to the far recesses of her mind.

Shaking her head, she tied the thick chenille belt and tiptoed down the short hall to the kitchen. She had to come to terms with her feelings and put both Jayse and her uncle into perspective so she could deal with each appropriately.

She hummed while she prepared her coffee, then leaned her hip against the counter and watched the dark liquid drain into the carafe. How could she find time to build a lasting relationship when she needed that same time to find a way to free Morghan? But, how would she be able to concentrate on her uncle when her mind kept returning to Jayse? It wouldn't be long, and she would have to return to Scotland. Then how could she maintain a budding love? Except in the case of Morghan's captivity, she felt a strong belief in 'out of sight, out of mind'. Hadn't that been the reason her previous relationships had sputtered and died?

After filling a huge mug with half the coffee in the pot, she sat at the tiny kitchen table holding the heavy cup in both hands. She lifted the mug to her lips, but didn't drink, staring over the rim and seeing nothing but her worries and concerns.

The sound of water running in the sink alerted her to Coralie's presence as her friend filled the teakettle, then set it on the burner to heat. Lucidea allowed herself a small grin. Much as she never learned to drink tea, Coralie normally refused coffee. Once the kettle sputtered in preparation for a shrill whistle and Coralie prepared her tea, she crossed the room with her own, much smaller cup, and sat at the other side of the table.

Deep lines at the corners of the Alfar-Sindhu's eyes suggested worry. Coralie had voiced her concerns about Pagas, his repeated attempts at a coup, and how his ambition directed him to seek leadership of the people—at any price. Including being instrumental in Morghan's disappearance. As well her father's death so long ago.

The sorrow in Coralie's eyes told her much. When she looked

more closely, she noticed her friend's aura was dull and streaked with gray. That reminded her, she needed to ask about better ways to tame her newfound ability. She steeled herself for more bad news.

"I have received communications, milady."

"So formal this morning, Coralie?" Lucidea took a long swallow of coffee. She was going to need the fortification.

"Lucidea, word came this morn. Pagas has disappeared. He bypassed those set to watch him an' canna be found."

"I would think that if he was gone, it would be a good thing. I mean, one less problem to worry about, right?" She knew it wasn't, but voicing the possibility was worth a try.

Coralie shook her head. "I ken ye wish it so. But, I fear he shall be more dangerous to ye, and milord Morghan, if he is where we canna watch him. The castle is in an uproar. I ken ye dinna wish to, but now ye must."

"Must what?" She did know what she had to do but didn't want to hear her knowledge confirmed. Lucidea held her breath.

"Ye must return to Nas Duirche Ness. Now."

A t Carrie's insistence, Bryce left off hovering over her and joined Jayse in a short trip through a portal to his new property. After emerging in a thick copse of cotton-woods, Jayse led his family to the crest of the highest hill and proudly described his vision.

His plans were applauded and acclaimed a success and the last bits of his trepidation faded. His family was behind him one hundred percent. As he watched the others wander the property in small, talkative groups, he realized that perhaps this vision gave them welcome relief from the constant threat Feidhlim posed. They would be able to focus energy on a pleasant task for a time.

Korin climbed the hill to stand beside him, his tiny daughter snug in his arms. "I remember well our first faire experience."

Heat rose in Jayse's face and he ducked his head. "I was a total ass."

Korin smiled and shifted his daughter. "That you were. But, you were only protecting your aunt... and you redeemed yourself when you enabled us to pass through the crowds, with my full wings visible. For that—"

Jayse lifted one hand. "Enough already. It's long past. Now, I have a favor to ask of you."

"And that is?"

"I'm going to ask family members to play different roles for the opening of this site. Later, there'll be actors and others who will want to be a part of the faire who will take over. Did you know many of the larger faires have waiting lists of participants?"

"I didn't. Amazing humans would want to play at what is right beside them if they would only see. But, do you wish of me?

"I want you to be my fairy king."

Korin cocked his head to one side at Jayse's pronouncement. One eyebrow arched high.

Jayse blinked as a vision formed—of Korin crowned with a circlet of entwined silver, gold, and emerald. The symbol he wore when he ruled as his ancestor Oberon had ruled—as the true fairy king. How had the fairy artisans created a thread of solid emerald, then woven it in an intricate pattern with the precious metals? He blinked again and the vision was gone.

Korin's eyebrow lowered. "Really?' he drawled.

"How did you do that?" Jayse gave Korin a crooked grin.

"Nothing but fairy glamour, nephew."

"Speaking of..." Jayse glanced pointedly at Korin and Nanceen's daughter. She gazed up at him with wise, sleepy eyes. "How well does she adapt when you keep her wings hidden?"

"The magic doesn't seem to cause her any distress. However, we may have to keep her grounded, so to speak, when she gets older. Already, the experiences with her wings are quite... interesting. She will be a handful."

"Better you than me." But as Jayse said the words he knew he didn't mean them. As long as it was his and Lucidea's child that was the handful. He couldn't imagine a more joyous time.

"I'd be proud."

Korin's words startled him. "Huh?"

A teasing glint sparkled in Korin's eyes. "I know what you're thinking about," he said in a singsong tone, then chuckled. "Or, should I say who? About time, don't you think? And don't deny it, everyone noticed last night."

Just the kind of teasing reaction he should have expected from a descendent of Robin Goodfellow. There was a great deal of Shakespeare's Puck in Korin. "No denial."

"Good. And I'll still be proud—to play your fairy king." He threw his shoulders back and regally lifted his chin. "Would you prefer Oberon?" Then he danced a quick jig, making his daughter trill soft giggles. "Or Puck?" Finally he hunched over and bared his teeth ferociously. "Or perhaps the Fir Dhaerrig?"

"I would prefer Korin Goodfellow, the current king."

Straightening, he clasped Jayse on the shoulder. "Ah, I shall have little trouble maintaining that ruse, my friend. You have a marvelous plan. I'll do whatever I can to help."

"Yeah, this is gonna be great." Bryce joined them and Jayse turned to him. His friend was drawn and looked exhausted, but he supposed most new dads had the same look. Except this father had a host of additional concerns to shoulder.

"Thanks. Carrie okay?"

A deep breath preceded Bryce's nod. "Yeah. I think so. Like me, she's worried about Chance's safety."

"And you're ready to go back to the hospital to check on them."

Jayse understood. He was ready to go as well. "I have an errand to run for Derrik, so we can leave and check on them together."

"Thanks. What's Da got you doing on this beautiful day?"

"He hasn't been able to contact Searlait since last night."

Bryce gave a casual shrug that didn't fool Jayse for a moment. "Ever since she was returned to the family from the world between worlds, Da's been protective. Almost to the point of obsession. I think it drives her crazy sometimes."

"I'm sure. Derrik can be intimidating." His dry tone had the desired effect and Bryce chuckled, easing the worry surrounding his eyes.

"Come on." Jayse wrapped an arm around Bryce's shoulder. "Let's get back to the hospital, then I'll find Searlait. I have a sneaking suspicion she's with Macaire anyway." Like he wanted to be with Lucidea. He'd make his visit to the Otherworld as quick as possible, then... Ah, Dea Annie.

"Probably. Good thing. And if she's there, it'll get you back to Lucidea..." Bryce's grin widened. "See, I did remember her name. Let's go then." He glanced around Jayse to Korin. "Got it bad, doesn't he?"

Jayse affected a wounded expression to hide the fact that Bryce had hit his emotional nail squarely on the head. He did have it bad for Lucidea Galvagin.

After mentally checking the safety of their destination, he opened the portal. Five strides later, he and Bryce stepped into Carrie's room.

The bassinet sat empty at the end of the bed. Carrie cradled her child and Nightshade was perched on the bed next to her, holding her tightly. When Bryce shook off Jayse's restraining arm and rushed to her she lifted a tear-stained, fear-filled face.

Derrik relaxed from his defensive posture at one side of the open portal and held a sheet of dark, ink stained parchment toward Jayse in his shaking hand. "'Twas found in the crib. 'Tis from Feidhlim."

ELEVEN

J ayse hesitated before the door to Macaire's chambers. The words of Feidhlim's missive burned behind his closed eyelids.

The birth of MY child heralds the end of Zeroun. The clan obliterated. The Alastriona destroyed. The Otherworld brought to its knees. Before me. Before my son. Await and fear.

How had the message been placed in the bassinet? Other than the portals he and the family had used, Derrik could sense no use of magic anywhere in the hospital or the surrounding neighborhood. The portable crib had never been out of Carrie's room, and she had never been left alone. Could one of the nurses have placed the note there when they checked on the new mother? Could a member of the hospital staff be in league with Feidhlim? The possibilities were... endless.

He knocked and waited impatiently. After a grunted summons, he entered and found Macaire sitting on the edge of his bed, blocking the other occupant from view. A seemingly casual fold of the sheet covered his lap. Despite his worry, Jayse couldn't help but grin for a brief second.

"Sorry to disturb you."

"You should be." Macaire gave him a mock scowl. "What is it?"

"There's been... communication from Feidhlim. Somehow, he managed to leave a message in Chance's crib at the hospital."

Macaire surged to his feet, searching for his scattered clothing. Behind him, Searlait rose to her knees, holding a silken sheet over her body.

"Nay," she wailed and struggled to push her tangled mass of hair over her shoulder. "I shouldna have left. I canna protect them if I..." A sob strangled her words.

Macaire dropped his tunic on the bed and crawled across the surface to gather her in his arms. He stroked the hair from her eyes and kissed her forehead. "We didn't have any idea a thing such as this could happen. Derrik and others of the Alastriona remained close." He glanced over his shoulder at Jayse. "How did this happen?"

"We don't know. There must be someone in the hospital. Someone either in league with Feidhlim or coerced by him to leave the parchment. But I don't understand how. Carrie and the baby were never alone."

Searlait twisted from Macaire's embrace. "I must go to her. I dinna mean to shirk m' duty. Nay, Macaire, let me go."

"Be calm, love. You can't help if your emotions are in an uproar."

Her shoulders slumped, and she looked at him, pleading. "Nay. Yer right. But, I must go."

"Aye, we'll both go."

Jayse turned his back when she rose to dress. Moments later, Macaire's hand landed lightly on his shoulder. "Is there anything else you know?"

"Everyone except Derrik and Nightshade were with me. I came back early with Bryce. Derrik had just found the message. I don't have any idea how long it had been there. Dad's bullied the hospital staff into opening one of their conference rooms for the family. The hospital administrator's probably afraid of a lawsuit." He shook his head. "We've got a lot to discuss."

Searlait joined them and Macaire wrapped his arm about her. "Ready, my love?"

She nodded and gave a wry chuckle. "'Twould appear m' readiness 'twas needed sooner." She touched her fingertips to his frown. "Dinna fasch yersel'. I've nay regrets about what happens between us. Only the timin'."

Jayse led the way, his own thoughts on the vagaries of timing. He shrugged away his business plans; his faire site could be worked on and completed at any time. But, how would he find time to work on his relationship with Lucidea if all his energies were concentrated on the evil surrounding Feidhlim? Worst of all —Jayse paused after opening a portal and let the others cross to the human world before him—what could he tell her that she might believe and accept? He needed her to wait until this was over so they could start again.

He didn't have any clues, but was sure any answer there might be for him in the universe wouldn't present itself now.

Even before he passed through the portal into the conference room, the sound of heated discussions assaulted him. Hoping the raised voices didn't carry as clearly into the hallway, he slipped into an empty seat near the door. An Alastriona stood just inside the door and Jayse assumed a second warrior or two loitered inconspicuously in the outer hall. He glanced around, set his personal concerns aside, and listened intently to his father.

His dad stood at the head of the oval conference table, hands planted firmly on the shiny mahogany surface. "We must find a place to secret away Carrie and... no, we must hide Bryce's entire family. I believe Feidhlim will concentrate his efforts on taking Chance, pretty much ignoring the rest of us—for the time being."

Jayse agreed with his father's assessment. Feidhlim would make threats to the rest of the family, initiate actions to make them sweat, but wouldn't harm anyone until he had Chance under his control.

Jayse nodded to his sister as she led her older daughter and Breanna from the room. 'Potty break' she mouthed at him, then spoke softly to the Alastriona at the door. Jayse nodded to himself. Each and every one of their precious children would be doubly watched and protected until Feidhlim and the Nechtan-Cattee were no more.

L ucidea dropped Coralie off at the lake so the Alfar-Sindhu could make her watery trek back to Nas Duirche Ness. She'd tried to convince Coralie to fly, but the young woman avowed, with a shiver of dread, that she was no Alfar-Andras and would not survive flight. It was just as well, for it seemed everyone and their brother were traveling and the best Lucidea had been able to arrange was getting her name on every stand-by list she could.

Now, with her bags ready to go at a moment's notice and stowed in her trunk, she was at the hospital. Unable to reach Jayse by phone, she assumed he'd probably be visiting the new baby. Needing to talk with him as soon as possible, she hurried inside.

She had mentioned returning to Scotland, but definitely not the reason why. What kind of a story could she concoct now to explain a sudden departure? She wanted a relationship with Jayse, but not one based on lies and half-truths. Unfortunately, there was nothing else she could give him now. The truth was unbelievable, even to her. No matter how involved with fantasy his dreams might be, how could she explain to him that she was the unprepared, reluctant ruler of a fey race that inhabited a parallel, underwater world? That she, herself, was half Alfar-Sindhu.

Feeling the need to compose her frazzled nerves and smooth the flyaway tangles of her hair, she slipped into a restroom and leaned against the sink to study her reflection. There was nothing about her to indicate that other race. She looked the same as she always had. She ran her fingers over the smooth skin behind her ears. Coralie said she would develop the gill slits once she ventured into the deep water.

She wasn't sure she wanted that particular confirmation of

her heritage. She'd never find a way to explain that to Jayse. Even if the young girl—Breanna—had called her a mermaid.

A ruckus outside the door startled her into reaching for her purse and a comb in an attempt to appear normal. Her hand froze as the little girl she'd just been thinking about pushed through the door, followed by another child, not much older, but with dark hair. And Lara.

Lucidea breathed a sigh of surprised relief as Lara herded the girls into the stalls then propped herself against the wall and nodded. "Nice to see you, Lucidea."

"You, too."

A half smile lightened the worry on Lara's face. "You looking for my brother?"

"Well... yeah, I am. I couldn't reach him by phone this morning." She stuffed the comb back in her purse unused. "I need to talk to him."

"Stand in line," Lara muttered.

"Is something wrong?" Moving from the sink as the girls emerged to wash their hands, Lucidea leaned close to Lara. "Has something happened?"

Lara gave her a long look and she had a difficult time remaining still under the probing examination. Then Lara closed her eyes and nodded as if to herself. "Let's get the girls back to the conference room and I'll give you a quick rundown."

Bree slipped her hand into Lucidea's. "Hi, Lucidea. This okay?"

"Of course it is, sweetie." The damp warmth of the small hand and the trust in the little girl's expression filled her with calm. It was almost as if the child knew how worried she was about everything, and healed that worry. She gnawed on her lower lip. All this fantasy stuff was getting to her.

It was a short walk to the conference room and the muffled voices paused as the door opened. Lara shooed the girls inside then turned to Lucidea. "You know quite a bit about what's happened in this family lately."

Lucidea nodded. "Enough."

"Our fears are rapidly coming true. Somehow, Feidhlim

placed a threatening message in Chance's crib. Here in the hospital. We're trying to decide what to do now. If he can get into the hospital unseen, who knows what else he might be able to do? We've got to find a safe place to hide Bryce's entire family. That's what they were talking about when I left with the girls and I imagine they're still at it. Jayse is sitting just inside the door and unless someone else has shown up—and I can't think of anyone —the seat right next to him just happens to be empty." Taking Lucidea's hand, she gave an encouraging squeeze. "It's not always like this... all the drama. Although, we seem to have had more than our share lately. Come on, Jayse could use your support right now."

Before she could speak, Lara had dragged her through the door and given her a gentle push in Jayse's direction. He glanced at her when she sat, then returned his attention to the conversation surrounding them. His cool palm covered her hand and his whisper floated to her ear. "I'm glad you're here, Dea Annie."

The young woman who reminded her so much of Coralie spoke. "I thought my home in Arizona would be a safe hideaway, but Grandmother called this morning and said the visitors to the reservation have been—different. Watching, not doing anything, but making the elders uncomfortable. We can't go there."

"And the Other—" Jaye glanced sideways at Lucidea and shook his head slightly. "—places we've talked about are sure to be watched as well."

The East Indian man rose and spoke softly. "At one time, my library and the oasis would have been a haven. However, it has come to my attention that certain information, previously known only to myself and this family, has been studied. The volumes have been disturbed and rearranged upon the shelf. I do not know the extent of the stolen knowledge, but fear we must expect the worst."

"Aye," Derrik said as Gowthaman returned to his seat. "The evil 'tis far reachin'. I fear any location where this family has previous connections will no' be safe. He kens too much."

Silence fell over the large group. Lucidea shifted in her chair.

She'd only known this family a very short while. Maybe this perpetrator hadn't connected her with them. Maybe she could offer a solution.

"Uh, could I say something?" Her face heated uncomfortably when every pair of eyes turned to her. She glanced at Jayse and he encouraged her with a nod. "Uh, I know you haven't known me for very long, but you've trusted me with some knowledge of what's been going on. I may have a suggestion."

"Go ahead," Jaye said. "At this point, we'll listen to any option."

"I came here to tell Jayse I was leaving." Soft gasps sounded around the room and Jayse jerked his hand from hers. "Oh, no," she said and looked directly at him. "Not that way. I mean, I own some property in Scotland and an emergency has come up. I need to get there as soon as I can. I'm waiting for a flight."

She turned back to the rest of the gathering. "Anyway, the manor house is huge and there would be plenty of room for Carrie and her family. Since you don't really know me, then this guy, Feidhlim, probably doesn't know too much about me either. He wouldn't think to look near a secluded loch in northern Scotland. Except," she slouched in the chair. "I don't even have a flight for myself, let alone think there's seats available for a whole family. And a baby. My God, can you even fly with a newborn?"

At a curt nod from Jaye, the man at the door exited. "We'll find out. Are you sure you want to do this, Lucidea? To be honest, it could be dangerous for you. While we'll try and keep our homes and lives here appearing as normal as possible, there's no way of knowing if and when Feidhlim will find where you are. We can't provide a great deal of obvious protection."

"I'll go with them, Dad." Jayse regained possession of her hand and gave her a half-smile. "I've had enough... training to be effective if need be. And, I know Lucidea can take care of herself."

She ducked her head. She'd had plenty of self-defense courses, but would it be enough to help protect a woman and children? What in the world prompted her spontaneous offer? When she looked up, expressions of gratitude circled the table. That was why. Because a group of strangers—a large group of strangers—took her in when she didn't even know she needed a family. Maybe doing what she could to help now, would protect someone else. She hadn't been able to save Morghan. A deep breath calmed her nerves.

"But, Jayse," she said finally. "What about your project?"

"There's nothing as important to me as this family. The faire can wait—indefinitely if need be. I've held it in my mind for so long, what's a little more time to plan and dream?"

He'd spoken so everyone could hear, but Lucidea imagined there was extra meaning just for her, that somehow she was now included in those plans and dreams. "I'd appreciate it if you could come."

Jaye sat and leaned his chair back on two legs. "That was solved remarkably easily."

"Nobody's asked me what I want to do." The focus of the room turned from Lucidea to Carrie. Sitting in a wheelchair, one hand clutching the portable hospital crib, she scowled at the family. Bryce touched her shoulder and Lucidea caught a quick wink pass between them.

"What do you want, Carrie?" Jaye asked softly.

"Protecting Chance is our major concern, right?"

Heads nodded in affirmation.

"Then I think Lucidea's plan is great. Chance and I are ready to go immediately. I just wanted to be consulted." She chuckled, a desperate attempt at normalcy. "Besides, I've always wanted to go to Scotland."

Lucidea grinned and softly applauded the brave new mother. With that attitude, they'd get along just fine.

"So there's just the remaining problem of how to get everyone to Lucidea's property. We don't want to be hanging around the airport waiting for a flight. If Feidhlim's infiltrated the hospital, I'm sure he's watching any routes we may take to hide Chance." Jaye leaned his elbows on the table and closed his eyes wearily.

Silent until then, Nightshade rose from a seat in the far corner.

Lucidea studied him through narrowed eyes. Gone was the flamboyant entertainer. The man who stood before them now was filled with the deadly calm she'd witnessed in officers facing dangerous assignments. Did he still have the gun? With his expression, she had no doubt he knew how to use it—and would, with little provocation.

"I have the solution you need." He waved behind him. "Forsythia has generously offered the use of her jet. We have to get back to our assign—our business quickly and since that takes us to the other side of the world, it will be no problem to drop the travelers off in Scotland."

"What kind of business?" Carrie asked.

Nightshade shrugged. "Not important, honey. However, Thia and I need to be in the UAE as soon as possible."

"UAE?"

"Hmm. United Arab Emirates."

"Why there?" Carrie asked the question, but by the interested expressions Lucidea witnessed around the room, everyone wanted to know the answer. Including her. If she had more time, she'd relish a chance to try and figure out Nightshade.

With an affected glare, Nightshade planted his hands at his hips. "No more questions, honey. Do you want a ride, or what?"

The whirlwind of planning surrounded Lucidea with strange contentment. At last she had something concrete to do. In pursuing the actions of helping Jayse's family, she'd soon be in Scotland. After settling her guests and seeing to their safety, she'd be able to slip away and face the problems caused by Pagas' disappearance. Through it all, Jayse would be there and they would have the time to get to know each other. Much better, she hoped.

After the explosion of action at the hospital, Thia spoke little on the way to the private airstrip and merely smiled at Lucidea's amazed exclamations at the sight of the sleek Cessna Citation. When asked what she could do to help, Thia gave succinct directions for preparing for take off.

Jayse jogged across the tarmac, a bulging bag bouncing at

each hip. The smile he had for her as he climbed the narrow stairs didn't brighten the worry in his eyes. He'd barely stowed his bags in a tiny compartment when a plain sedan stopped next to the jet. Tinted windows, the only concession to secrecy, hid the occupants until Bryce opened the door. Breanna bounded up the stairs and into Jayse's arms.

"We're going flying."

"I know, darlin'. You let Lucidea help you buckle into a seat, okay? I'll go help your mom and dad."

"And my brother, too."

Finally Jayse's eyes twinkled and Lucidea caught her breath. Those warm honey-brown eyes would be her undoing. "And Chance, too. Here, you take this seat for right now." He glanced up as Thia passed them and she leaned close to the little girl.

"How about later, you have Nightshade bring you up front and we'll show you how we fly the plane."

Breanna clapped and bounced in her seat. Jayse turned to help Bryce secure what seemed to be an overly large amount of baby equipment. As Lucidea snugged the seatbelt around the small girl she half listened to Bree's excited chatter and added a new bit of information about Nightshade to her mental file. Thia had said 'how *we* fly the plane'. That meant Nightshade could pilot a jet.

"You sure it's okay to fly with a newborn?" Jayse asked Carrie as they tightened a seatbelt through the supports of an elaborate car seat. Carrie nodded then brushed a kiss across Chance's fine, blond hair. "As long as he's sucking..." She turned bright red. "Uh, when we take off and land, that'll equalize the pressure in his ears. The hospital gave me some saline nose stuff to counteract the dry air. We should be okay. Right, my precious boy? Are you hungry, or is it binky time?"

Lucidea turned her face away to hide her smile. Knowing how too often women were unable to love a child that was a result of rape, she treasured the strong bond exhibited in Carrie's actions. This was a family worth preserving.

Thia cleared her throat. "That's it, folks. As soon as Nightshade's on board..."

"And Nightshade is here, my dears." He waved a small yellow teddy bear over Chance until Carrie grabbed the stuffed animal and hugged the man. Then he knelt next to Bree and placed a similar pink bear in her hands, making a show of receiving her kiss of thanks.

Lucidea caught a quick, silent communication between him and Thia before he waved broadly toward the front of the plane. "Thia? Shall we?"

Shortly after they disappeared at the front of the craft, the jets roared to life. Lucidea sat next to a small, round window and peered through the haze of encroaching evening to the tower and maintenance building. Jayse took her hand as they inched forward over the rough airstrip.

Before she turned her attention to the man at her side, a figure ran from the building, arms waving high in the air. Lucidea pointed out the window. "Jayse. Who's that? They're trying to get our attention."

Jayse unfastened his seatbelt and leaned over her. She stared into his profile. The hard set of his jaw relaxed in surprise. He turned his head and shouted. "Nightshade, stop the plane. It's Tori."

CHAPTER

TWELVE

T he Citation slowed to a crawl and Nightshade appeared
from the cockpit to open a narrow side door. Wondering
at Catori's sudden appearance, Jayse joined his friend at
the door as the jet did a slow pivot until the opening faced the
running woman.

Jayse tried to read Catori's expression in the dusty twilight.
Normally a bastion of calm in a stress-filled situation, there was
now stark fear twisting her features. What now? Why was Catori
chasing their plane?

As Catori neared the small jet, she lifted her arms. Jayse gave
Nightshade a quick look, received a single, sharp nod in return,
then joined him in leaning out the door. Following Nightshade's
lead, he wrapped his hand around Catori's wrist and they pulled
her up and into the cabin.

"Got her, Thia. Go." At Nightshade's command, the Cessna's
engines rose to a high whine and the jet picked up speed. While
Jayse guided her to a seat, Nightshade strained to close and secure
the door. Before turning back to the controls, Nightshade paused
at Jayse's side. "Well done," he whispered. "Find out what
happened."

He straightened and rested his hand on Catori's shoulder.

"Well folks. Looks like we have another passenger. Ever been to Scotland, honey?"

Panting heavily, she shook her head. Nightshade gave her shoulder a gentle squeeze. "Relax, girlfriend. You're safe now. Nightshade's not gonna let anything happen to any of you." In a breath he was gone.

Jayse buckled Catori's seatbelt for her then returned to his own seat. "Whenever you can..."

She nodded and rested her head against the high-backed leather captain's chair. The soft sounds of Bryce and Carrie's conversation rose behind Jayse. A pleasant pressure covered his hand where he gripped the armrest and Lucidea stroked her thumb over the back of his hand.

"She'll be okay, just give her a moment," Lucidea said.

"Thank you." Jayse let out a long breath. "You're a calming influence, Dea Annie."

The throaty chuckle he loved eased through him. "Calm? In this mess? I don't know about that. But, I have interviewed more victims than I care to count. I know the signs—she'll be fine."

Jayse's stomach lurched as the jet lifted smoothly from the runway. He swallowed around a heavy lump in his throat and tightened his death grip on the armrest.

"Don't like to fly?"

Closing his eyes, he shook his head. "Flying's okay. If only we didn't have to take off or land."

The deep, rich sound of Lucidea's laughter shot down his tension and he turned his head to look at her. "You'll be fine, too. I see the signs," she whispered.

Before he answered, Catori leaned as far forward as her seatbelt would allow. She smoothed her hands over her hair and stared at a spot just to one side of the small window. Twice she started to speak and twice her words died on her lips. At Lucidea's gesture, Jayse waited, reigning in his impatience to learn what happened.

Nightshade returned, pausing at the first quartet of chairs to whisper a few words with Bryce. Then he kissed Carrie's cheek and moved fluidly to crouch next to Catori. Like Jayse, he waited silently.

"I was... I was searching for answers with a dream journey. They were waiting for me." Catori turned a wide, brown-eyed expression to Jayse. "I'd hoped to find some clue to... his whereabouts, or his plans. But they... his followers were waiting for me. They tried..." She shuddered and wrapped her arms about herself. The trail of a single tear dampened her cheek.

Nightshade rested his hand against her thigh. "You're safe here, honey. We won't let anything happen to you."

"I know. It's just that I've never been so frightened. They tried to contain my soul in the spirit realm. But, when I fought them, they just let me go. If they wanted to hold me there, I don't understand why they let my spirit return."

"Maybe it was their way of sending another message to the family," Lucidea ventured.

Concern faded for a moment as Jayse treasured the way Lucidea said 'the family', as though she claimed his family as her own. He glanced at her. Her brow wrinkled in concentration and she had pulled one corner of her lower lip between her teeth, worrying at the fullness.

The lump returned to his throat and he fought to swallow. When he had the chance, he'd kiss away the worry, sooth the growing redness with his tongue. Dragging his thoughts from the delightful possibilities, he focused his gaze on Catori. "If it was a message, the meaning's clear," he stated in a flat tone.

"No matter where we are, Feidhlim can find us."

Catori ignored him and her gaze grew distant. "They didn't speak, except for one phrase. Over and over. Like a chant."

"Tori." Jayse unbuckled his seatbelt and slid forward to take her hands in his. "Catori, stay with us here. What did they say?"

She remained still and silent until he was tempted to shake her gently to gain her attention. Finally, her gaze moved to lock on his. "*An fhoil a'cho gaidh.*"

A chill skittered down his spine. His father and the Alastriona had expected no less, but the confirmation brought their struggle against Feidhlim's evil into sharper focus. If the evil one claimed—

"I can still hear the chant in my head, throbbing like a drumbeat. What could it mean?" Catori shook herself and the haunted expression faded, though a glimmer of fear remained in her eyes. "Well, that's a new mystery for us, isn't it? Why send a message through me?"

Nightshade rose from his crouch to check Bryce's family then perched on the arm of Catori's chair. "They're okay. Listening, but okay." He glanced down at her. "As to why, honey, probably because you were involved in Feidhlim's imprisonment."

"He was in prison?" Lucidea jerked her hand from Jayse. Dismal cold settled over him at the loss of her touch. "I thought he was still at large."

"He was held, though not in a hu—a normal jail. He escaped before... the authorities could do anything." Jayse stumbled over his explanation, hoping she wouldn't question his words too closely.

Lucidea gave him an odd look. "Uh-huh." He knew the subject was far from closed as she turned her attention to Catori.

The young shaman faced her calmly. "We're talking about imprisonment in a spiritual sense here, Lucidea. Feidhlim has..." She paused and rolled her gaze to the rounded ceiling. "... issues that go far beyond his transgressions against Carrie and this family. Sometimes when one is forced to face these thoughts, to deal with one's actions and the consequences of what's been done, it's like a prison. Through a drum journey, I... umm... assisted in helping Feidhlim see the errors in his thinking."

Lucidea stared at the dark haired woman for a long, silent minute. Jayse held his breath waiting for her response. Finally she gave her head a disbelieving shake. "Uh-huh. I'll settle for that explanation for now. So, does anyone know what those words mean?"

Nightshade shrugged and stared pointedly at Jayse. Uncomfortable with the intense scrutiny, he shifted in his seat. He did know the meaning of the words, but remained silent.

A sharp poke in his arm focused his attention on Lucidea. "You know, don't you?" The accusation twisted like a knife plunged between his ribs. If Dea Annie thought he kept this knowledge from her, how would she react when she learned the truth flowing through his veins? He had to tell her. Soon. The realization she might not accept him then, twisted the knife deeper.

"You do, Jayse. What does it mean? How can we fight without knowledge?"

"We? You mean to stand beside me, beside my family in this?"

She leaned back and crossed her arms. "Well, duh. No. I'm here on a private jet, taking people I hardly know to my manor in Scotland—running from some crazy, perverted perpetrator—for the sheer fun of it. Now... what do those words mean?"

Nightshade snorted with laughter. "Good job, sweet cheeks. You put our boy right in his place."

"She's got you, Jayse." Bryce's laughter joined Nightshade's and, for a moment, Jayse forgot the evil words and relaxed in the joy of the company of friends and family. She did get him. She had him... now and forever.

"Jayse?" Warning echoed in Lucidea's tone.

"*An fhoil a'cho gaidh*. Literally, it means blood war. For Feidhlim and his supporters, it is vendetta."

"Ah, I understand." Lucidea's brows drew together. "Does he have many people working for him?"

"We don't know. He can be extremely charismatic, and others have been known to follow him blindly."

"That's been true of many considered evil throughout history. Vendetta? Like in crime families?"

"I'm sure it's similar." And like those organized crime operations, Jayse was sure Feidhlim held sway over a far reaching network of misguided faeries and despite his lack of magic, held tight reign over the Nechtan-Cattee.

"Yikes."

"That's putting it mildly, honey." Nightshade stood and stretched.

Breanna peeked over the back of her seat and waved at the

serious foursome. "My brother's sleeping now." A fetching smile brightened her young face. "Unca Nightshade? Can I fly the plane now?"

"Again, my lord. You must make another attempt."

"Leave me alone." Feidhlim cringed as the sound of his own voice ripped through his head. Osric clasped his upper arm in a rough grasp, but he had no strength to twist away.

"You chose this path, my lord. Now you must abide by that decision. You willed my assistance. You shall not turn me away. Until you have returned to your true self, I shall guide you."

Feidhlim bared his teeth. "And what gain do you expect?"

Releasing him, Osric stepped away then fell to his knees. "You shall determine my reward, lord Feidhlim, when my task is completed." He bowed his head.

Feidhlim's fingers twitched. How easy it would be to throttle his tormentor and take the painless oblivion from the bottles placed prominently about the room. 'To conquer the temptation', Osric had said when they arrived at the large, secluded farm-house. Fool.

"*An fhoil a'cho gaidh*, my lord. Revenge is nothing. Now is the time of vendetta."

"Vendetta? Of what purpose is this blood war if we are unable to locate the child? Get off your knees, Osric."

A satisfied smile stretched Osric's thin lips. The fool had a way about him—the conniver—so that Feidhlim found himself in actions he longed to ignore and ignoring actions he longed to take.

Only a day's time had changed Osric from a concerned follower to one with layers of his own desires, hidden yet evident. Did Osric hold some control over him? How did another's magic affect him now that he had no magic of his own?

"I beseech you, my lord. Communicate with the child. The bond between Faerie parent and child should overcome your disability. The child showed evidence of great magic, of power enough to strengthen that bond between you."

"I said off your knees." The advance of raw paranoia created a quaver in his voice and Feidhlim motioned toward the door. Even with the tentative trust he once placed in the underling, Osric would not witness his agony as he fought the effects of his desire for drink, the physical and mental tortures of his body. "Leave me for a time."

"My lord?"

Feidhlim tightened his muscles against an onslaught of need. "Leave me. I'll call for you when I am... rested. I shall attempt this bonding you so desire then."

"Of course." The knowing glint in Osric's eyes added explosive fuel to Feidhlim's paranoia making him barely able to control an outburst of useless anger. Osric turned without bowing and left the room, latching the door behind him.

Alone, Feidhlim succumbed to the tremors coursing through his body. Unable to fully control his muscles, he stumbled to the bed and curled onto the mattress. Wailing silently, he clutched first his belly then pressed against the pain at his temples with his palms.

After endless moments the agony subsided and he lay dazed and panting. Why was he so cursed? No other Faerie suffered so. Even the humans—curse them—he'd seen fighting drunkenness had not suffered so greatly. Why?

Another attack of need would soon consume him, but in the brief respite, he lay on his back, tucked his hands beneath his head and stared at the smooth plaster ceiling. Osric demanded much of him, and in moments of clarity such as this, he understood and appreciated.

Some would condemn Osric's methods, but Feidhlim knew them to be successful. Painful though his need was, each time he suffered less and for shorter duration. Osric deserved rewarding —Feidhlim grinned—but perhaps not the reward the fool anticipated.

Still, much as Feidhlim disdained admitting, Osric made valid points and had proven dependable despite his flares of attitude. Feidhlim's bark of laughter startled him and he sat. Rather than acting in ways similar to his father, Osric's actions were those he himself would take. Yes, Osric would bear close observation.

Folding his legs into a meditative position, Feidhlim took a series of slow breaths. Establishing a bond with his child would increase his knowledge of the Zeroun clan and vendetta would be the more satisfying. Destroying Zeroun from within the clan... and with a babe...

Feidhlim focused his concentration but had no clue what to search for, what it might feel like to receive an indication or acknowledgement from a newborn babe. Was there a bond such as the one he sought between a human parent and child? How might such a thing manifest?

Human. The word burned behind his closed eyelids. Without his magic, he was little better than the lowest human. He fought the despair and imagined a fiery sword slashing through the letters, shattering the word into dull, lifeless shards.

Fighting his impatience and refocusing on his child, he waited.

Just as the dull throb of need began again, he saw a tiny light. Faint, yet pulsing with power, the light danced before him. He reached out, but the spark flitted away. Each time he tried to touch the indigo light, it escaped him.

The presence was his child. His son. He tried a soft, mental call and the flickering paused as if listening.

"Come, my child," he whispered. "Show yourself to me."

Lucidea curled in her seat, the tiny bundle of baby boy snug in her arms. After watching Carrie yawn repeatedly while feeding Chance, she'd offered to care for him while Carrie slept. She hadn't expected the baby to be placed in her arms. Leery because she hadn't held many babies, she tried to encourage Carrie to place him in his carrier.

But once the warm body was nestled along her forearm and tucked against her body, her concerns faded.

Soft voices drifted from the cockpit where Thia, Catori, and Nightshade kept Breanna occupied. Carrie and Bryce both napped. She glanced sideways at Jayse. His eyes were closed but she didn't think he was asleep. However, he needed private time for his thoughts, so she tilted her head and watched Chance.

He looked up at her and his mouth puckered. How much did he recognize at such a young age? She'd read babies didn't see clearly at first. Or, was it the other way around? She couldn't remember and it didn't matter. What was important was that he appeared to be looking at her, his bright blue eyes clear and strangely intense. She ran the back of her finger along the soft curve of his tiny cheek. His eyes squeezed shut and he squirmed. Adorable. There was no other word for him.

She'd have children someday. Lucidea moved her caress to the cap of fine, down-like blond hair covering his head. What would her children's hair be like? Dark brown and wavy. That's what she'd like, along with brown eyes, warm as amber. Jayse's eyes. Jayse's children.

Chance grew restless, waving his tight fists, kicking against the light blanket swaddling him. He made soft sounds, cries she imagined were sounds of angry denial. Odd that she would think something like that.

The wiggling increased and Chance's eyes opened wide to stare at her. Unbidden by her thought processes, the child's aura flared around him, the inner vision overlaying her outer sight. Swirling and agitated, the indigo aura pulsed against a bright orange surrounding and containing the vibrant color like a shell. Fingers of orange struggled through the baby's aura until they nearly touched his squirming body.

"What's wrong, Dea Annie?" Jayse leaned toward her and touched her arm. "Is something the matter with Chance?"

"He just started fussing and moving around like this a moment ago. I don't know what's wrong." How could she tell

Jayse that it looked like something was trying to force through the baby's aura, to make contact, to touch him?

"My brother," Breanna shouted from the front of the plane. She ran to Lucidea's side, the commotion of her passage between the crowded seats rousing her parents. Without hesitation she pressed one hand to Chance's forehead and waved her other hand through the advancing orange. "Go 'way. Leave my brother alone."

Lucidea gasped when the orange shell popped out of existence and the baby's indigo aura immediately calmed. Bree kissed Chance's cheek and looked up at her father who stood close behind her. Carefully, she patted the baby's forehead. "The bad man was here."

THIRTEEN

Astonishment at the small girl's actions and startling statement lasted long after Chance had been lifted from Lucidea's arms and cuddled protectively by his mother. Bryce, Nightshade, and Jayse had moved their low, heated conversation to the rear of the cabin. She longed to join them, but despite her part in providing an out of the way location to hide the beleaguered family, it wasn't her place to intrude. She wasn't family.

She closed her eyes at the sadness threatening to overwhelm her. How did she get into this emotional mess? On her own for a long time, the need to be part of a family rose so sharply in her now. Did it have anything to do with finding out she had an uncle then losing him? Did knowing her father had been killed—sacrificed—make her need to protect another family and lead her to take unusual actions? She took a deep breath and let it out slowly.

She sensed Jayse next to her before he stroked an errant strand of hair from her forehead in a soft caress. She looked up at him and he leaned close to brush his lips against her cheek. "Are you okay, baby?"

She nodded but wondered if she really was.

"You sure?"

Damned perceptive man. Why couldn't he be like any other guy she'd dated and take an answer he didn't really care about anyway at face value? Still, she should have given him an honest answer in the first place. "Just a little shook up."

He took his seat and angled the swiveling chair to face her. "A lot's happened in a short time. I hate to keep pounding away at this..."

"No, that's okay. I understand. We need all the facts we can uncover to keep your family safe." The nagging regret that she hadn't taken advantage of more seminars relating to forensic discovery taunted her. Maybe then she'd be able to help more and not feel so helpless.

"Did you...?" Jayse glanced at where Breanna lay in a puddle of blankets on the floor beside her mother's chair. Lucidea followed his gaze and grinned at the protective way the girl touched her brother as they napped. She had no doubt that if Bree had anything to do with it, nothing would ever harm her beloved sibling.

Jayse cleared his throat. "This might sound silly, but... did you notice anything odd? Anything about Chance or how he was behaving?"

This was it. Should she admit to what she'd seen and reveal how the image remained in her mind? Unpleasantly. Making her shiver with unknown dread. How much could she confess without him thinking she was nuts or some throw back, new age kook?

Watching him, she studied his profile until he turned to face her. Any information, however uncomfortable it was for her to admit, might be important in the long run. Besides, if she continued to see auras, eventually she'd let the fact slip, whether she wanted to or not. The question was how much to tell him right now. He waited patiently, a bland, 'I'm ready whenever you are' expression on his face. She didn't know that much about her ability to see auras, so there wasn't much she could tell him either.

"Chance and I were just watching each other. He's a good baby."

Jayse nodded encouragement. But before she continued, Lucidea noticed Catori's unrestrained interest and gestured for the young woman to join them. Catori had recognized her discomfort when Jayse's family's auras assaulted her senses at the hospital, and hoped her presence would help now. Maybe the young woman would be able to help her sort through the images still burning in her brain.

"Chance started getting restless, wiggling around and kicking. I thought he might be hungry again, or needing a change, but I didn't want to wake Carrie. Then, I noticed..." She stared down at her tightly clasped hands and made a conscious effort to relax her white knuckled fingers.

"First, let me tell you this. Now, whether you believe in such things or not, just recently I've begun seeing... auras. You know, colors surrounding a person."

One of Jayse's eyebrows lifted and he gave a sharp nod. She released the breath she'd been holding. At least he hadn't laughed outright.

Catori crossed her arms and leaned back. "Recently? How recently?"

Lucidea glanced to the side at the dark sky outside her small window. "Only a few days."

"Ah, so that was what was bothering you at the hospital. You couldn't control what you were seeing."

"That's right. How did you know?"

Catori chuckled. "I've noticed sometimes when a person develops a new ability, or discovers a... gift within themselves, that ability goes haywire at first and is difficult to control." She leaned forward, hesitated, then touched Lucidea's arm. "Are you still experiencing that onslaught on your senses?"

Lucidea shook her head. "No. I think the breathing exercise you explained to me helps. I don't think I have much of any control over what I see, but at least it's not all the time now. I'm really looking forward to introducing you to my friend Coralie.

She's the one who taught me how to open my senses to the auras in the first place."

"Uh, I hate to interrupt, but... Chance?"

Both women turned guilty gazes to Jayse, who just shrugged and gave a weary grin. "You'll have time to explore all this later. Now, we need to know what you saw, Dea Annie. Something in Chance's aura?"

He didn't discount her ability. In fact, it appeared he would take what she said as credible information. His reaction made it so much easier to express what she'd seen and what she'd felt. And maybe... later... he might understand when she told him who and what she really was.

"It wasn't until Chance started getting fussy that I noticed his aura. It's indigo by the way." She closed her eyes to visualize what had happened. "His aura grew agitated, like storm clouds of the same color swirled around him. Then I noticed how the edge of his aura wasn't hazy and indistinct any more. Instead there was... umm, it was almost like there was a shell closing in around him. It was bright orange."

She opened her eyes at Jayse's sharp intake of breath. "Something significant about that?'

He glanced sideways at Catori before he answered. "Maybe. Go on."

There was something important, but she couldn't tell which part of her explanation caused his reaction. "Then, it was as if this shell wasn't solid after all. Little bits of it pressed in through Chance's aura. Like... tendrils or fingers or something. That was when the baby really got upset. When Bree touched him and said 'go away,' the orange shell popped and disappeared. And the baby settled down."

In one fluid movement, Jayse rose. "I need to talk to Bryce and Nightshade."

"But..."

He leaned down and kissed her, but she could tell his mind was already on his conversation with the others. She had questions, too. It was becoming imperative for her to know more about what they faced. Warm breath touched her cheek. "Try and get some rest, baby."

Curious as she was, a little part of her consciousness slid to the side and held on to how he'd called her baby. That was twice now, and each time heat pooled low in her body. It was almost enough to dim the force of her curiosity. Almost, but not quite.

"I need to know what's going on."

Bronze flushed over his face. "I know. Later, okay?"

"No, it's not okay. It was tough for me to admit to you that I can see auras. I've hardly had time to come to terms with that ability myself, let alone have to admit it to someone else. If what I saw means something—and I think it does—I have a right to know. Bree knew something was happening with Chance. How is that possible? What did she do to make the orange invasion disappear? Why did she say the bad man was here? Did she mean here in the plane, or here as in the aura around the baby? See, there's so much going on, and I don't know even the half of it. That's not okay, Jayse. You can't smooth this over. Later's not okay. Now, Jayse. I need to know something now."

Keeping silent, Jayse agreed. She did have the right to know, especially now when she was so deeply involved. But, that would mean explaining more about Feidhlim and telling her about the Faerie Otherworld. He wasn't ready to make that admission. His own feelings aside, Bryce's family needed her and the safe haven she'd offered. He couldn't risk their being turned away now.

"Can you give me just a little more time, baby?" He needed that time to come up with an explanation he thought she'd accept and understand.

Lucidea crossed her arms and glared at him. "Jayse, I don't like this. I don't like being in the dark. You've trusted me enough to allow me to bring the newest member of your family halfway around the globe to a place you've never been." Her eyes softened briefly. "You trusted me with your dreams."

"Lucidea, I..."

The spark burned in her eyes. "Oh, I know. Later. You have to figure things out first. Fine. Go plot with Nightshade. Keep your blasted secrets. When you're ready, I might not be." She glanced around then stood and snatched a blanket from a pile near the sleeping children. "Go on. Go have a discussion with everyone else. I'll just join the little ones in a nap. Wake me when we get to Scotland."

She plopped back into her seat, angled it toward the window, and shook out the blanket. By pulling the soft, cream colored covering up to her shoulders and turning her back on him, she built an effective wall.

Jayse reached one hand toward her even though she couldn't see the action. "Lucid—"

"I'm napping. Don't disturb me."

Frozen in place, he barely recognized the presence of Catori at his side. She patted his shoulder as she squeezed past him in the narrow space. "Good going. Very... male of you."

Lucidea made a soft sound, but he couldn't tell if it were a sob or muffled laughter. Either way, he had been called to task... and rightfully so. He took a step but she tugged the blanket under her chin.

She was being stubborn, didn't she realize...? No, she didn't. How could she when he kept his secrets, his family's secrets, tucked deep inside?

Jayse turned away. They were fighting. This was their first argument. A sad, half-grin pulled at his lips. Great. Well, maybe the argument itself wasn't so hot, but none of the few women he'd dated recently had the gumption to stand up to him. Always it was 'yes, Jayse, whatever you want'. Good for his ego, perhaps, but not very conducive to relationship building.

Dea Annie cared enough to stand up to him, and a revelation exploded within him. He liked being challenged. Especially when the prospects of making up were so delightful. But satisfying any need of his wasn't going to happen until he could satisfy her need to know.

Distracted by his thoughts, he returned to the discussion with Bryce and Nightshade. Catori joined them, remaining silent as he explained the phenomenon Lucidea had witnessed.

Nightshade kept his voice low. "I thought Feidhlim's magic had been destroyed."

"His followers are still faerie, still have their abilities," Jayse said.

"And, for the most part, they've somehow been able to mask their presence from the Defenders. How they placed the message in the crib is a prime example."

"So, he could be tapping into another's magic?"

"I might think that, except for the fact that the only color Lucidea saw attacking Chance's aura was orange—the color of Feidhlim's destroyed power. We each have a unique color associated with our abilities and there was no evidence of additional magic." Jayse fell silent. Everyone with even a tiny measure of fey blood had a magical color. One color. Except him. He'd been told his aura swirled with many colors, but no one had been able to explain why. Having a colorful aura had been a point of contention and teasing when he'd been young. Over the years he'd grown used to being an anomaly.

Catori blew out a breath and gave him a disgusted look. "You realize, of course, that even non-magical creatures like us poor, simple humans also have auras."

"Yeah, I know that." At Catori's shaking head, he amended his sharp statement. "Okay, I forget sometimes. There's so much..." He cast a quick glance at Lucidea. The steady rise and fall of her breathing indicated she had fallen asleep. "...so much magic surrounding me, that it's the norm. Besides, you're far from a poor, simple human, Tori."

She canted her head in wry acknowledgement. "My point, magic boy, is that your enemy may be magicless, but since Chance was conceived while Feidhlim still owned those abilities, maybe the baby has magic of his own."

Nightshade rubbed the side of his nose with a finger. "Excellent point, honey. But how might that relate to the... attack on Chance?"

"Maybe it doesn't. Chance didn't seem frightened." Catori spoke Jayse's thoughts.

"Honey." Nightshade chuckled. "How can you tell with a newborn?"

Shrugging, Jayse tried to order his thoughts but the jumble in his mind eluded his attempts. Attack. Had the occurrence been an attack?

Despite Breanna's reaction, he hadn't picked up on an overriding sense of violence. Wouldn't a sense of menace have made the baby cry out? Except for a few soft sounds, Chance had been quiet.

Catori continued. "I'm thinking that Feidhlim might be trying some human meditation techniques—like I use with a drum journey. He might be trying to find Chance, or he may just be trying to contact his child. There is a connection between parent and child that grows and becomes more evident if nurtured, or fades and dies if ignored."

"So, honey, you think this could have been nothing more than an attempt at communication? A parent-child bond?" Nightshade gave her a skeptical roll of his eyes and waggled one hand in a loose wave. "Dearheart, knowing what you do about this creature, how can you even suspect anything so benign? There's got to be an ulterior motive."

"Maybe." She tapped one foot. "After my recent encounter with his followers, I'm sensing more about them—and him. This incident just doesn't feel evil. At least, not completely."

"My thoughts exactly," Jayse said. "However, we definitely need to remain vigilant. Any suggestions?" Both Nightshade and Catori had thoughtful expressions, but neither spoke.

He had no ideas either, except to keep a tight watch on the tiny boy. If Feidhlim was able to contact him this high above the surface of the earth, how easy would it be for him to find their hiding place in Scotland? At the first sign of trouble they'd have to leave again, probably through a faerie portal despite the danger of the enemy learning their destination. He glanced at Lucidea. How would he explain that to her?

· · ·

rawing on the sleep feigning skill she'd honed during her days with an obnoxious college roommate, Lucidea easily kept her breathing slow and even despite the rapid, unorganized clatter of thoughts racing through her mind. Jayse had no right to withhold information from her. Okay, it was his right because this all revolved around his family. But she was smack in the middle of the possible danger. And by her choice. That should count for something.

The heaviness in the pit of her stomach had nothing to do with their flight from a perpetrator. She curled a bit more tightly around the pain. Standing up for herself was one thing, but this sure felt like an argument and she disliked confrontation, as much as she disliked dishonesty.

Jayse hadn't been dishonest with her. By not explaining what was going on, he was guilty only of omission. She, on the other hand, had so many secrets tethered tightly inside her, how could she look on the fact she couldn't tell him the entire truth as anything but lying. Was being with him worth the risk of continued arguments? When she accused him of withholding information, she was guilty of the same thing.

If only she could figure out the meaning behind some of veiled statements he and his family had made, know what thoughts and words were halted part way through then changed, hear the whispers from the rear of the cabin. If one thing, just one bit of information, became clear, she was sure it wouldn't take her long to understand the rest. Guilt by forensic association. The phrase relaxed her frown and she shifted positions, releasing the tight set of her shoulders.

She wished she could fall asleep. She'd been out late with Jayse... her lips tingled at the memory of his delightful kisses, but she restrained the urge to touch them with her fingertips. Then, she had gotten up early because she couldn't sleep. Concerns, first of Pagas' disappearance and her need to be at the loch, followed by fearful concern for Jayse's family had finally drained any energy adrenaline might have given her.

As she reviewed the situation involving the baby's aura over and over, her mind seemed to create a new energy. She straightened with a jerk and a soft gasp. Looking around quickly, she snuggled back under her blanket. The others were either asleep or involved in conversation. No one had noticed.

What was she going to do now? As she'd replayed the encounter, details became clearer and the sharper focus showed her something more she didn't understand. When the fingers of orange pressed close to the baby, glitter-like sparkles had risen from his hands and forehead to rebuff the advance. Did this mean the child had magic?

She'd discounted evidence of magic in other members of Jayse's family. In Jayse himself. Coralie had told her the magical indications appeared when one of the Alfar-Sindhu grew old enough to utilize their inborn talent—a puberty kind of thing. But this... this evidence of magic at only a couple of days old? In a human child? It couldn't be.

She ran through the scene again, this time letting her memory continue until Bree had somehow chased away the orange shell.

Lucidea clutched her chair arms and shrugged off the blanket. "Oh, my God," she whispered.

Jayse stumbled against a seat in his rush to her side. He clasped her hands. "You're freezing. What's wrong?"

She stared at their hands, trying to collect her thoughts. She couldn't imagine the expression on her face and didn't want to look at him until she could compose herself. How could she explain what she'd seen, what she now remembered with vivid clarity?

Jayse rubbed the back of her hand. "Lucidea?" He leaned close to her ear. "I'm sorry I can't tell you anything right now. Be patient with me, baby. Please... forgive me?"

She shook her head. Not tell her everything? If she told him what she'd just remembered... there'd be no need for forgiveness. The men in white coats would be waiting when Thia landed the jet.

Jayse dropped her hand and stepped back. Knowing he'd

misunderstood, she managed a terse smile and held out her hand to him. "I'll be patient."

"Then, what's wrong?" He returned her hand to his firm grasp and lightly chafed her fingers.

Nightshade appeared at his shoulder. "Sorry to interrupt, my dears, but it won't be long until we land. Time to get everything stowed and buckled in. Thia's arranged for a rental van to be waiting at the airstrip, so you can leave as soon as possible."

Jayse acknowledged him and took the seat next to Lucidea without releasing her hand. "We'll talk soon, okay?"

"Yes."

Lifting her hand to his lips, he pressed a lingering kiss to her palm. Then, after a longing gaze into her eyes, rose again to help Bryce and Carrie situate the children.

Thankful for even the brief reprieve, yet dreading the length of time she had to wait before she told him what she'd seen, Lucidea folded her blanket and placed it in the seat across from her. Her quick smile at Catori received a quizzical look in return. When Jayse returned to the seat and took her hand she turned her attention to him.

No matter what he might think of her and her crazy notions, she had to tell him.

She had to tell him how, when the orange came close to Chance, the baby fought it not with tiny sparkles the color of his aura, but with silver sparkles. That when Breanna's hand had entered the plane of her brother's aura, bright pink surrounded her fingers, sparkles rising to merge with the baby's. When the orange had touched the bright blending, the shell had disappeared. How could she tell him she'd seen... magic?

FOURTEEN

F eidhlim didn't know whether to dance for joy, scream out his frustration, or wallow in indulgent self-pity.

He had made contact with his son.

Joy bubbled along his veins like the first sip of long awaited ale. Even without magic, he'd made contact and felt the power within his son's tiny body. The power he would be able to use to reestablish himself in the Otherworld. Power to destroy Zeroun.

The euphoric bubbles burst. His son had denied him and used the power to fight against him. Feidhlim had been able to come close to his son, but could not touch him. He rose and paced the sparsely furnished room. How did a child so small, so insignificant, have the power to deny him? He'd almost beaten back the infantile evasion when another power had joined his son's.

Whose? He hadn't recognized the magical signature as belonging to any of the Alastriona. Nor had it felt like any belonging to the cursed Zeroun clan. Had they found another protector for the child?

The force that had touched his non-magical advance was powerful, well beyond the average faerie. Who was this power, this magic he could not recognize? And why did they align with his enemy? It was enough to draw him to forgetfulness.

He glanced at the bottles arranged about the room. He had conquered the demon of need within him and no longer needed the reminder of the pitiful failure he'd recently overcome.

When he jerked open the door, Osric stumbled through the opening.

"Watching o'er me—or simply watching me, Osric?"

"My lord, I... No, my lord, I do not." Osric stepped back. "How may I serve you?"

"Remove the bottles. There is no longer a need." There was. It grew in his belly and in his mind even as he spoke the denial, but he would never again succumb. He snatched up an empty carafe. "Bring to me the freshest of juices. The clearest of waters from the Otherworld, that I may cleanse my spirit in the bounties of my true home."

Feidhlim waited as Osric summoned servants and remained silent as his underling relayed his orders to the simpering creatures who still claimed to follow him. A cleansing of his followers was needed, where he would strip away any pretenses they might hold, any thoughts of rising to glory with him. He would be the one to hold the glory—none other. None, except for a short while, his son.

His son. He felt an unaccustomed smile pull at his lips. "Osric."

Osric flinched at his name and when he imagined the fear caused by the guilt from planning against his lord twining through Osric's mind, Feidhlim's grin drew wider.

Osric composed his expression, squared his shoulders. "Yes, my lord?"

"I have achieved contact with the child, my son."

Osric brightened. "Success, my lord? That is marvelous. Where have they hidden the babe?"

Feidhlim held back a rush of failure. "That I do not know as of yet. There is time. We have much to accomplish before we take the child."

His stomach lurched, sending pain searing to his brain. The

need blossomed. "Go now. When I again call for you, have ready the refreshment I have ordered. Then we shall plan."

Osric attempted to hide his satisfaction while Feidhlim gloated in the renewal of control over another. A feeling more powerful than drink, Stronger than the need. A new magic. His magic.

L ucidea stood beside the partially loaded van. They'd landed on a small, private airstrip, and while the family settled in the van, Nightshade drew her aside.

"You can find your way from here?" His gaze skittered over the landscape as he waited for her answer.

"I got really lost when I first came to the loch. And I passed this airstrip a number of times before I found my way. I remember and I won't get lost again. It should only take about fifteen minutes to get to the manor."

"Good. I'll return as soon as possible. Baring any... unforeseen disasters, our business should be concluded fairly quickly."

She watched him as he pressed a kiss to his fingers and bent at the waist to wave at Breanna perched on the van's rear seat. The man was a study in contrasts. His loose grin faded when he turned back to her and handed her a slip of paper.

"If you need anything, leave a message at this number. Is there a number where I can reach you?"

"There's no phone at the manor, but I have my cell and I'm sure Jayse has his."

Nightshade nodded and scanned the horizon. "Give me the number and directions to the manor from here."

"It's kind of complicated. Lots of short, curving roads. Let me write it down for you." She reached into her bag for a small notebook.

Nightshade stilled her hand. "Just tell me, I'll remember."

He closed his eyes as she recited directions and finally her phone number. His lips moved soundlessly for a moment, then he opened his eyes and grinned. "Got it, sweet cheeks. Now, you get these folks home safely and Nightshade will see you soon." He hoisted himself into the jet, gave a flamboyant wave, and slammed the door. With a roar of engines, the jet taxied to the far end of the airstrip.

Once the jet was airborne, Jayse moved to her side. "Everyone's ready. Want me to drive?"

"Can you handle driving on the other side of the road? I had a tough time when I was here before."

"As long as you give me directions, I should be okay."

She took his hand. "Thanks. We'd better go. Looks like it'll be light soon. I think we should be home by then."

Home. She'd never considered the manor home, but somehow, with the presence of this family, it just might feel that way. At least for a short while. Until she told Jayse her secrets.

With only a couple of turns, which landed them on the wrong side of the road, the short trip to loch Nas Duirche Ness was uneventful. Even after the long plane trip and short van ride, Bree still bounded from the van when Jayse opened the door and rushed around, exploring the front of the manor.

Lucidea stood back remembering the first time she'd seen the imposing stone building. Wild winds emanating from a greenish vortex above the loch had shaken her small rental car. Met by the man she later discovered to be her Uncle Morghan, she'd begun her time in a world of secrets. Secrets she still didn't completely understand.

Morghan. Her heart cried out for the man she barely knew, imprisoned in some other world after destroying the fire elemental Brandr Ur. There must be a way to free him. She hadn't really wanted to return to Scotland, but now that she was here, perhaps she could finally find a way to help.

The front door eased open and her heart stopped for a moment. Had Morghan found a way to free himself? Was he here? But instead of the tall, dark, glowering figure she wished for, Coralie stepped onto the stone stoop.

"Welcome." Her bright smile and open arms released the tension in Lucidea's shoulders. There had been no way to contact

Coralie earlier, but from her welcome, she'd obviously expected them. Maybe the concentrated thoughts Lucidea had tried sending to her had worked. Or, more likely, Coralie just knew.

Breanna skipped to Coralie and took her hand. "I like it here. You'll help keep my brother safe, won't you?"

Coralie glanced across the parking area at Lucidea and grinned. "Aye, that we shall. Ye've had a long trip. Come inside. 'Tis a bit of breakfast and a rest ye'll be needin'.'"

Jayse unlocked the back of the van, but paused, staring at Coralie.

"How'd she get here so fast?" he muttered.

Lucidea reached in for an overstuffed bag. "She was able to get a flight out right away."

"Hmm. Good thing. Maybe you should go introduce everyone."

"What? Oh, of course, how thoughtless of me. I'll take these bags." She had brought strangers together and they at least needed to know each other's names. Standing at the doorway, she made the introductions as each person passed through the narrow door and crowded into the entryway. Jayse was the last to enter.

"I'll bring in the rest of the stuff once we know where to put it." He looked from Lucidea to Coralie. "Rooms?"

Coralie chuckled. "'Tis a suite of rooms suitable fer the family. The room across the hall fer Catori. Jayse, I shall allow Lucidea to show ye yer room, fer yer in another wing."

There were only bedrooms in two wings that, along with the dining hall and kitchen, made a triangle around an overgrown courtyard. That meant Coralie probably intended Jayse to use the room next to hers. The room with the connecting door. At that moment she regretted allowing Coralie to move her from the guestroom she had originally occupied into Morghan's suite. Perhaps it wasn't regret; maybe she simply didn't trust herself to keep the door closed.

While the others followed Coralie she turned to Jayse. He stared after the slowly moving cluster of family. "There's something... really similar about Tori and Coralie. Almost like... oh, I don't know... like they were related somehow."

"You noticed that, too?" Surprised, Lucidea looked at him and belatedly closed her mouth when he grinned.

"Yeah. I can't put my finger on it. It'll be interesting to see how they get along. I didn't sleep much last night or get much of a rest on the flight. I'd just as soon skip breakfast and sleep for a while."

He gave a low whistle when she opened the door to the darkly paneled room. A stone fireplace dominated one wall and a bank of windows set into the thick masonry looked out over the loch. He moved to the windows. "This is spectacular. How could you leave such a view?"

She didn't want to answer and couldn't explain her reasons, so she gave him a brief tour, indicating the wardrobe and the narrow hall to the tiny bathroom. Nodding his pleasure, he dumped one bag on the high bed then turned toward the main hallway. "Guess I won't get my nap until the van's unloaded." He paused by a door nearly hidden in the paneling. "Where's this door go?"

Ducking her head, Lucidea tried to avoid looking at him, but he cupped her chin in his palm and lifted her gaze to his. The question in his eyes sparkled as though he knew the answer.

"It's to your room, isn't it?"

Heat flamed over her face, burning, but not as hot or fierce as her need to kiss him. Afraid of what she might say if she spoke, she nodded. Jayse smiled and leaned closer until his lips brushed her cheek then traveled to the shell of her ear. "As much as I want to, Dea Annie, I won't open that door. But, if you do, I won't ignore the invitation."

Gently, he tilted her chin then molded his mouth over hers. The intensity of his soft movements, the darting touch of his tongue along the seam of her lips, weakened her knees until she grasped his shoulders to steady herself. He speared the fingers of one hand through her hair and angled her head back to trail his kisses down the column of her neck to the hollow at its base. He teased the skin there with flicks of his tongue.

Splaying his other hand at her waist, he took a step forward until her back pressed against the wall and arched his hips into hers. He wasn't fully aroused, but with his sinuous movements, it wouldn't be long. The pressure of him against the juncture of her thighs brought a low moan to the back of her throat.

She dragged his mouth back to hers. The duel of their tongues, the silky glide of heat against heat, stole the breath from her lungs. She should stop this now. She should stop this... she should stop... she should...

"Hey, Jayse." Bryce's call came from the intersection of the hallways. "I could use some help here."

"Damn," he said against her lips.

Her sentiments exactly. Unfortunately, Bryce's interruption fell into the realm of good timing. She had guests to settle, and she really needed to talk to Coralie. "We... we'd better get the rest of the baby's stuff. Before they come looking for us."

Jayse pulled his fingers from her hair, but kept her captured against the wall with his hips. He smoothed the errant strands and kissed the tip of her nose before laying his forehead against hers. "God, baby. Will you open that door?"

Would she? Right now, the answer was a resounding yes. But in a few hours... would common sense prevail, or her hormones? She shook her head. "I..."

"Don't say anything until you can say yes, Dea Annie. Please don't." He took a deep breath and stepped away. "Let's get everyone else taken care of. I'll take my nap. You see what you can do about that emergency you've got here. Then we'll talk... then..." He popped his head out the door. "Be right there."

When he faced her, she cast a quick glance at his lower body. He followed her gaze, shrugged, tugged his shirt from his jeans, and tried to smooth the wrinkled fabric. She giggled nervously. "Like that's gonna not make anyone ask questions."

"Best I can do."

· · ·

True to his word, Jayse disappeared after unloading the van.

Coralie herded the rest into the dining hall and mothered them with hot oatmeal, thick with raisins and cream, and deep mugs of coffee. Breanna chatted happily throughout their breakfast while the adults discussed how long it would take to adjust to the time change. Once Lucidea had given them the tour of the manor, and settled the active young girl to watch a movie in the modern television theatre, she escaped to Morghan's workroom.

The wide deck cantilevered over the loch, and despite the cool, damp breeze she leaned on the rail and watched tiny waves disappear beneath her feet. Out there, in the middle of the loch, was a watery gateway leading to the world where she was the unwilling ruler. She gave a soft snort at the irony of her life. For so long, she'd been alone.

Then, within a few days time, she found family. And lost them again.

Now, when all she wanted to do was explore a relationship, her two worlds careened on a collision course. Some sixth sense had always directed her in choosing relationships, and ending them. Once she learned to listen to that inner voice, she'd never been steered wrong. Was this actually a magical ability that she might be able to translate to other areas of her life?

She closed her eyes and thought of Jayse. A strong sense of right, of belonging tightened her chest. If her feelings were true this time, then this relationship was meant to be. Taking a deep breath, she opened her eyes. But how could that be? How would she be able to balance a home and a family with Jayse while still keeping her fey life secret?

And if not secret, how could she expect him to understand and believe her wild tales of parallel worlds and non-human magical bloodlines?

Fighting the hopelessness, she turned from the dark water. Coralie stood just inside the doorway, an expression of sad understanding shadowing her face. Lucidea took a deep breath and pushed away from the railing. "So, tell me about Pagas."

Stepping onto the deck, Coralie handed her a woolen shawl. "Evening comes an' the air is cool."

"Evening? But, we just finished breakfast not that long ago."

"Nay, ye have been out here for many hours. Thinkin'. Yer guests are resting again afore the evenin' meal. We have time to talk."

Lucidea dropped onto a cushioned chaise and Coralie nodded. "I see ye ken nothin' new fer yer love of Jayse."

"Love?" She avoided admitting the emotion to herself, but she did love him. Desperately. "Oh, Coralie, what am I going to do?"

Coralie sat in a nearby chair. "Ye shall tell him, of course."

"Tell him what?"

"That ye love him. Dinna make my mistake and keep yer love to yerself. To do so only wastes precious time. I understand how ye feel, 'tis no' that much different between Morghan and I." Coralie's somber expression turned to a gentle smile. "Then, ye must find a way to speak of yer life beyond the human world. Dinna believe ye can hide that from him. Dinna believe he shall turn from ye. I dinna ken that within him. Aye, milady, I do ken how he loves ye as well."

"There is this physical attraction."

"Aye, the blind can see that." Coralie chuckled and winked.

Trying to hold any thought in her mind to counteract the heat rising in her face, Lucidea faced the cool breeze. "I don't... yes, I do. Coralie, I've never had such intense feelings for a man. I almost believe... believe we could be together. But, I've got this little problem. I'm not one-hundred percent human."

"Ye believe 'twill make a difference?"

Lucidea spread her hands. "Why wouldn't it? If what you say is true, I need to jump in that loch and discover if I truly will be able to breathe in the water. Then, how do I explain to him, or anyone else, about having gills? I need to find a way to lead a race of people I don't know. How do I justify time away from my job to do that ruling? What if I can't...? What if I'm a failure? At swimming. At ruling. At loving Jayse."

"Ye'll no' fail in these endeavors, milady. An' I believe yer love will stand beside ye. He is a guid man, Lucidea. He shall understand, accept, and be a partner fer ye."

"Are you a prophet now, Coralie?" Even though she disagreed with Coralie's assessment because she knew any man would find her secrets difficult to deal with, she appreciated her friend's attempt. It was a relief to have spoken of her fears to another. Maybe the practice would make talking to Jayse easier.

She doubted it.

"Nay, fer if I was, I'd be tellin' ye where Pagas has taken himself off to. I'd be tellin' ye what actions ye must take to rule this world of ours. I'd be convincin' ye that the one ye love returns those feelin's."

Lucidea blew out a slow breath. "First order of business— Pagas. What's so bad about his disappearance?"

While Coralie explained how the historians had discovered additional information concerning the conjunction of blue moons in many different worlds, Lucidea fought to focus on the problems. What she really wanted was to think about Jayse. Then Coralie spoke about a partially destroyed volume filled with Pagas' handwriting outlining spells and incantations. Lucidea carefully touched her lips at the memories of Jayse's kisses and the deep, longing promise in his honey amber eyes. While Coralie outlined the guards' and palace staff's opinions on the high chancellor's actions and disappearance, she imagined a home filled with love—and Jayse.

A knock on the workroom door brought Coralie to her feet.

Rubbing her arms beneath the wool shawl, Lucidea followed more slowly. She'd just stepped into the workroom when the light from the open doorway surrounded the man who'd filled her thoughts.

Rumpled from his nap, he looked delicious. When he grinned at her, her insides melted like butter.

"Sorry to disturb you, ladies. But the rest of us are kind of mixed up on the time. Everyone else was hungry, so I took the liberty of making some sandwiches with that marvelous bread you must have made today, Coralie."

She dipped her head, then smiled. "Aye. Workin' the dough helps me think."

Lucidea wrapped the shawl more tightly about her shoulders. "You had time to make bread?"

"Aye. Dinna I tell ye more time has passed than ye realized?"

Jayse stepped into the room and draped an arm about each woman's shoulders. "Well then, I'm sure you must be hungry, too. We've set up supper in the TV room. Bree says she found a movie she just has to watch tonight."

"Oh, aye? I dinna think there were many children's movies in the library."

Jayse guided them from the workroom. "We'll just have to see what caught her eye. She doesn't normally choose something inappropriate."

Coralie slipped from under his arm and hurried away. "I shall meet ye there," she called back over her shoulder.

Stopping them in the middle of the hall, Jayse turned Lucidea so they faced each other. The eyes she'd thought about all afternoon sparkled with surprise when she stood on tiptoe and kissed him.

"Have a nice nap?"

"Sure did. I was more exhausted than I thought." But not tired enough to chase the thoughts of her from his mind or the lingering effects on his body from holding her close. Despite his yawns and gritty eyes, he'd lain awake for nearly an hour, imagining her beside him, beneath him. Then he'd dreamed, active, potent dreams that left him aching for the reality of her touch.

Now, she was in his arms. And he wanted her more than he thought humanly possible. She affected him, got under his skin, thrilled him... completed him more than any other woman. Now he finally understood that stupid movie. This was the woman he'd waited for, planned for, dreamed about forever. They were connected, but right now he didn't want to search for the reason why. He only wanted to kiss her.

Holding himself slightly away from her, he stroked his hands down her arms and entwined his fingers with hers. He meant to kiss her gently, as chastely as he could but she inched closer and slipped their hands to the back of her waist. Working her fingers free, she flattened her palms against his chest, one hand over the fierce beating of his heart. She initiated a deeper kiss and the mating of their tongues.

Loving her so quickly and wanting her with such a fierce desire might not be right. He didn't care. He crushed her against him, molding the soft curves of her body to his. He bent his knees slightly then lifted her to her toes as he slipped one leg between hers and lowered her to rest against his thigh. After capturing her gasp in his mouth, he trailed kisses over her cheek and drew his tongue around the shell of her ear.

Her breath halted and she pressed her breasts to his chest. The firm nubs of her nipples matched the rise in his groin. The moment was unbearable, a torture he never wished to end. Taking possession of her mouth, he mimicked the thrust and retreat...

CHAPTER

FIFTEEN

L oud, off-tune whistling penetrated the haze filling Jayse's mind. Lucidea gasped, struggled, and stepped to the side a split second before Bryce rounded a corner.

"Oops, sorry guys." Jayse glared at him and Bryce's smirk said that he wasn't a bit sorry. Still, maybe the interruption was a good thing. Making love to Lucidea in the middle of a hallway wasn't his style.

Bryce shrugged. "I'm just off to the kitchen for some drinks to go with those sandwiches. Bree's getting impatient to start her movie, so you'd better hurry. Can I bring you something?"

"Coffee," Lucidea said with a slight tremor in her voice.

"Me, too," Jayse added.

"Coming right up. I'll just bring the whole pot."

He disappeared in the direction of the kitchen and Jayse expelled a ragged breath. Ready to apologize, he glanced at Lucidea. The pink flush of her cheeks accented the passion sparkling in her eyes. Full and reddened, her lips begged for more kisses. Her breasts rose and fell in sharp, short breaths. She blinked and the passion in her eyes receded, hidden by some determination he didn't understand. Didn't she want him the way he wanted her?

She lifted her hand to his shoulder, then stroked her palm down to cover his heart. "You go on. There's something I've got to do. Be there in just a couple minutes."

"Yeah. Okay. I'll see if Bryce... Lucidea?"

"Shh, Jayse. Let's go watch the movie. I am kind of hungry."

So was he. For her. He had the sinking feeling—or maybe it was elation that burned through his chest—that he would hunger for Lucidea Galvagin now and forever.

"And I could really use that coffee."

"Huh?"

"Coffee, Jayse. I need strong, black coffee. Go on now, I'll be right there." Without another word, she moved away. He watched the sway of her jean clad bottom and tried to bring moisture to his mouth.

She turned one way and he found the strength to stride down the hall in the opposite direction, following the smell of brewing coffee.

Out of breath from her rush, Lucidea beat the men to the TV room. Carrie sat in a rocker brought from another room with a light receiving blanket draped over her shoulder. She nodded at Lucidea, then switched the baby to her other breast. Bree stood bouncing from one foot to the other before the large television screen, a movie disc hidden behind her back. Catori pulled a heavy drape over the window she'd been looking out of and sat in a leather, theatre style chair.

Lucidea's eyebrows rose at the woman's outfit. Hadn't she seen Coralie wear something similar? Catori glanced down at herself, then gave a shrug of one shoulder. "Since I came with no luggage, Coralie loaned me some of her clothes. Good thing we're the same size, huh?"

"I thought the outfit looked familiar." Hoping Jayse would join her and they could cuddle discretely during the movie, Lucidea chose a leather loveseat. She'd hated ending the moment

in the hall, but hallways weren't high on her list of places to...
well, at least not when there were other people in the house.

The enticing aroma of Sumatra blend coffee preceded the men
into the room. Bryce set the pot on a sideboard next to a plate of
sandwiches. Jayse added mugs to the display. He turned to her
and lifted his eyebrows in question.

"Please."

Jayse filled two mugs and placed them on a low coffee table in
front of the loveseat.

Catori rose. "Thanks for offering. I'll get my own." She
laughed at Jayse's stricken expression. "Don't worry about it."

Soon Coralie joined them and Carrie had placedd Chance in
his carrier at her feet where she'd curled up on a second love seat.
Bryce pulled her close and grinned at his daughter. "Okay, darlin'.
What movie are we watching?"

Breanna blew out a breath that lifted her pale blonde bangs.
"Finally. I've been waiting forever, Daddy." She waved the movie.
"My favorite. Will you put it on, please?"

"Let me." Jayse returned his mug to the coffee table. "You look
too comfortable."

"Yep. Thanks." Bryce kissed his wife soundly.

Jayse took the movie from Bree, read the cover, and groaned.
"You're not going to believe this." He put the disc in the player
and brought the remote back to his seat. "Remember I said my
family has a fascination for a certain movie as well as the original
play—"

"Oh, Bree, you didn't." Carrie patted the seat next to her. Bree
curled against Carrie's side. "Yes, Mommy. It's my favorite."

Mendelssohn's overture sounded from speakers hidden about
the room. Lucidea took a sip of coffee. She recognized the music.
Even with the dark screen, she grinned—she knew the movie.
"Hey, this is one of my favorites, too."

"You're kidding." Jayse lifted his arm and she snuggled against
his warmth.

"Well... except some of that high pitched singing's a bit much."

But there's no better Puck to my mind than Mickey Rooney. And I just love Cagney as Bottom. It's a marvelous tale."

A strange, unreadable expression flitted across Jayse's face. Yet she sensed a mingling of hope and apprehension. The look faded. "I agree, and because of my family's obsession, I've seen every movie, every local production. All of them. I still like this version the best, too."

"Shh," Bree admonished with a finger to her lips. "I can't hear my movie."

Half way through *A Midsummer Night's Dream*, Bryce and Carrie said goodnight and took their sleeping children to bed. Catori and Coralie left soon afterwards, saying they wanted to visit. Cuddled under the wool shawl, Jayse had slipped his hand under her blouse and softly stroked her side. Lucidea returned the favor, unbuttoning one button of his shirt and tucking her hand against the warmth of his body.

Lovers, to bed; 'tis almost fairy time.

Jayse's abdominal muscles tensed until his skin trembled beneath her palm. Something about that line affected him. His hand twitched against her side. Affected him a lot. Maybe it was the statement sending lovers to bed.

Puck spoke his final lines and Jayse turned off the movie. They remained unmoving in the silent darkness. A spell surrounded her, a fairy spell of contentment and longing. A combination as potent as the man beside her.

Jayse tossed the remote to the coffee table. *Lovers, to bed.* The very thing that had been on his mind through the entire movie. Part of him was glad Lucidea's hand had strayed no lower than his waistband. Part of him, hard and uncomfortable against his zipper, wished otherwise.

'Tis almost fairy time. How could he make love to her—even contemplate the feel of her, welcoming and surrounding him—when he hadn't told her about his family's true nature? Long ago he'd vowed never... unless his partner knew.

"Jayse?"

"Yeah, baby?' The roughness of his voice sounded as if the

tones carried every bit of desire and longing within him. Did she notice?

"Let's go to bed."

Was this the invitation he ached for, or simply an expression of her weariness? Whichever it was, he wouldn't... couldn't push her if she wasn't ready. The signals her body gave—oh, God. He closed his eyes. And his body received, translated into a desire he prayed matched his.

With a light touch he wrapped his fingers around her wrist and moved her hand from his skin. He kept her fingers in his and helped her to rise. Hand in hand they walked toward their bedrooms.

He paused before her door and she leaned close to kiss him. He waited, but she didn't deepen or prolong the contact. "Good night, Jayse."

So. This was how it would be. He swallowed his disappointment and stroked her cheek with the backs of his fingers. "Night, Dea Annie."

He felt her gaze on him as he took several reluctant steps toward his door and turned to look at her before he entered his lonely room. He froze at the promise in her smile. She blew him a kiss and disappeared into her room.

The wooden door was cold against his forehead. He had to take several breaths before calming his heart, his body, and his soul enough to face the long, empty night. Finally, he entered the room.

Instead of the expected darkness, a pale light shone from one side.

From an open doorway. The doorway.

Had she? Was this his invitation? His body leapt in anticipation as he crossed the magical threshold. Lucidea stood in the center of the room, her back to him.

"The... the door was open," he stammered.

"Yes."

"This means..."

She turned and slipped her blouse from her shoulders. "Yes."

Close the door and come to bed." Lucidea waited, her arms spread slightly, her breasts rising and falling with her heavy breaths.

A subtle force slowed his movements, and he felt as though he was walking through deep water. Odd. The sense of magic surrounded him. Unlike the magic of the Faerie Otherworld, yet similar enough to make him doubt the tingling of his nerve endings.

Or perhaps it was only the woman waiting with a soft smile of welcome meant only for him. Yes, there was the magic, a cauldron filled with simmering emotions, spilling over with desire. And love.

Did she love him? They hadn't spoken of love. They had never spoken of desire either. Only acted upon their mutual wants and needs. Was this moment only that—only a fulfilling of needs?

He wondered why he thought so much. Lucidea had opened the door and he was a fool if he ignored the glistening look in her eyes or the soft pout of her lips. But, more the fool if he ignored his personal vow. He stopped before her. "Dea Annie, ah, baby, we've... I've got to say..."

"Hush." She ran her finger down the front of his shirt and slipped two more buttons from their moorings. With a sigh that heated his exposed skin, she tucked her hands under the material and rested her cheek against his chest. "No discussion now, no worries about later."

She lifted her head and gazed at him, her lower lip pulled between her teeth. He groaned.

A smile burst across her face. "That's it. That's the only kind of sounds I want to hear. No talking, unless it's to tell me what pleases you."

"You." He captured her face between his palms and lowered his mouth to hers. Fierce, intense, the meeting of their lips pulled the magic along his veins, shooting heat to the throb at his groin. Afraid his ardor was too strong, he tried to pull away. She followed his movements, sliding her lips against his.

"Yes, you," Lucidea whispered. Tearing at his shirt, she bared more of his chest and moved her kisses to the ridge of his collarbone. When she nipped lightly at the base of his throat, his response rumbled through her sensitive lips. His hands rested on her shoulders, but only for a moment before he crushed her against his body. His hard, hot body.

One hand splayed over her bottom and she willingly arched closer. Oh, the better to feel the hard ridge that had tempted her all evening. His other hand moved to the clasp of her bra then held her steady as he bent her backwards to remove the confining cotton lace. She watched his face in the dim light from the single small lamp she'd left burning. The apprehension had disappeared, replaced by pure passion.

His aura flared, the multitude of colors bright and alluring. Silver exploded around his head, then the colors were gone, leaving only the man.

His amber eyes darkened and he glanced toward the bed. "Lovers, to bed?"

Hands tangling together, they shed their clothing while they crossed the room. Rough in his action, Jayse yanked the heavy comforter to the end of the bed while Lucidea slid the top sheet aside. But before she climbed into the bed, Jayse lifted and tossed her, squealing, to the center of the mattress. He crawled next to her and they melded together as he pressed kisses along her jaw and the length of her arched neck.

Frustrated, wanting more, Lucidea wove her fingers through his hair and pushed his head lower. He chuckled, then traced patterns along the side of her breast with his hot, wet tongue. Nibbles and kisses followed her ribcage. Never having realizing the underside of her breast could be so sensitive, she gasped in delight.

He covered the damp skin of her breast with his palm, massaging the fullness as he tongued and kissed her other breast. "Jayse, please," she whimpered.

"Please?" He teased the upper swells with light strokes of his fingers, giving her a wicked grin as he moved his hands with her writhing movements, ignoring the touch she wanted next. "This?" He brushed his thumb over her pebbled nipple.

"Yes," she sighed.

"Or this?" He bent and firmly pulled the nipple into his mouth, laving the peak with his tongue.

"Oh." The sharp sound of pleasure echoed in the night-quiet room.

"I'll take that as a yes," he mumbled, barely lifting his mouth from his ministrations.

Lucidea sank into the pull of his mouth, the brush of his fingers over her skin, the press of his erection against her leg. She touched him, desperately needing to know the feel of his skin. Damp heat covered her, covered him and their bodies slid together as they moved, igniting her past the point where she knew she should burst into flames.

Rising on one arm, Jayse looked down at her. Heavy lidded, her eyes sparkled with an odd violet light. Her lips moved and he couldn't resist tasting her growing passion. When he slipped his tongue between her parted lips and stroked the soft inner surfaces, she responded with soft sounds, a lover's song. She clung to his shoulders, then moved her hands to his buttocks. The pressure she applied inched his hips closer, and she angled her body, inviting him to cradle himself between her thighs.

He captured one of her legs beneath his and rubbed against her, arching his back and biting his lip against the powerful sensation. Not yet. He couldn't... not yet.

Cupping the soft cushion of curls at the apex of her thighs, he pressed lightly with his palm, rotating, caressing, stroking. He timed the thrust of his tongue against hers with parting her folds and drawing slick moisture up to the small firm nub. She jerked, cried out, collapsed against the soft pillows, cried out again. Pressing up against his hand, she wordlessly directed his touch, teaching him to please her.

He found joy in pleasing, knowing he took her to higher planes of desire as he changed the speed and angle of his touch. Her body convulsed around him when he entered her with his finger and she sobbed with loss when he withdrew. The instrument of her body played a symphony he'd never forget, made him feel the master musician.

Feet planted against the mattress, Lucidea arched with a sharp cry and the crescendo brought a gasp of pleasure to his lips. He held her tightly until her body calmed and she lay back, limp, her skin glowing in the soft light. Beauty in fulfillment. How had he been so lucky?

Her satisfied smile changed subtly and she reached out to stroke her fingers down his chest, slowly over his belly, and... and cradle him in her palm. In time with his heavy, rapid breaths, she stroked the underside, curving her little finger up over the ultra-sensitive head.

Lucidea dragged her tongue over her lips. He was so hard, steel covered in velvet and silk. She needed him in her, but sensed his hesitation. He hadn't taken her earlier hint, although the outcome of that had been... amazing. Now, she wasn't about to take no for an answer.

She kept her strokes light, touching only the ridged underside and moisture-laden tip. His hips arched toward her with each glide of her hand. With one final long stroke, she cupped her palm over the head, then encircled his length and stroked back to the base.

"Baby!"

"Jayse, I want..." The suggestive motion of her hand should leave no question to what she wanted. Instead of covering her body with his, Jayse rose to a crouch and sat back on his calves. He leaned forward and lifted her shoulders, repositioning her until she straddled one of his thighs. Wondering at his actions, she watched his expression and returned her hand to his erection. He wrapped his fingers over hers, indicating changes in pressure as he directed her strokes. He captured her mouth and dueled with her tongue as their hands moved between their bodies.

Jerking his face from hers, Jayse gasped, tensed, and as he moaned her name his heat burst over her belly. She slowed her strokes and kissed the hard line of his clenched jaw. Moments later, he smiled and laid her back against the pillows. Taking a handful of tissues from the bedside stand, he wiped her skin clean and tossed the tissues to the floor.

"You have a birthmark." He touched the brown mark with his tongue, then lifted his head to peer closely at it.

Lucidea shivered when he traced the design with a fingertip, then tensed. What would he say about the stag shaped mark?

"Relax, baby." He canted his head as if to take a better look. "Interesting, like some sort of horned animal. Anybody ever—"

She slipped her hand over the birthmark. "When I was younger, kids teased me about it. It's embarrassing."

Lifting her fingers, he covered the birthmark with his palm. "Shouldn't be. Just interestingly shaped. But..." He sighed. "I know how kids can be."

The tone of his words led her to believe he'd been the brunt of childhood teasing. She couldn't imagine why. "I recently found out it's a family birthmark. My father and uncle both had—have similar birthmarks."

He gave her a gentle smile, then he bent and kissed the spot just below her navel. "Then it's all the more special."

The tenderness in his voice and actions was her undoing and tears filled her eyes. She tugged carefully on his ear until he lifted his head. "I love you," she whispered.

"Dea Annie, you're more than I had ever dreamed." He turned his head and looked out the window toward the loch. "There's something I have to tell you."

So, he didn't love her. She sighed and squared her shoulders. It wasn't the first time an affair hadn't worked out the way she'd wanted. But, nothing inside, no indication from her special sense had warned her that her love would follow a downward path this time.

He captured her chin with his fingers and held her gaze. "I do love you, baby. I do." After a lingering kiss, he reached down and drew the sheet up to cover them and tucked her against his side.

"A long time ago, when I first discovered... women, I made a vow to myself. While I wouldn't deny myself the pleasure of female companionship..." He paused and the endearing bronze flush flared across his cheeks. "Well, I am... human. But, I vowed never to have intercourse until my partner knew about my family."

"What about your family? They're wonderful, caring, loving to the extreme."

He kissed her. "So are you. However, there is something about my family, about my bloodline. There have been a couple occasions I almost told a woman about this part of me. Something always stopped me. Lucidea, baby, until I met you, I never truly wanted a woman to know this... secret. I've never told."

Pushing gently against his chest, she looked hard into his eyes. She really didn't care about family secrets. His... or hers. "That means, despite what we just did... if you never... technically..."

"I'm a virgin." He lifted one shoulder in a shrug. "In that one technical area, anyway."

"And you want to give me that part of you?" Was this rush of feeling, of loving tenderness, what a man felt when a woman saved herself for him? The power of emotions spilled more tears from her eyes.

Jayse kissed the tears away. "Don't cry, baby."

"I'm... honored. Jayse, and I do love you. What is this awful secret?"

With a tentative grin, he sat and faced her. "I never said it was awful. First, I'd like to ask you a question."

Confused, she nodded and he continued. "Have you ever thought about the possibility of parallel worlds connecting to this one?"

SIXTEEN

After a long, drawn out moment of silence and a muffled snort, Lucidea burst into a fit of wild laughter. She sat up, reached for him, pulled back and wrapped her arms about her belly. Fat tears trailed down her cheeks as the sound of her deep laughter took on a hysterical edge.

Not the reaction Jayse expected. All this for just a question? How would she react when he explained the reason?

She rested her hand on his knee. "I'm sorry." Laughter overtook her and the low sounds rumbled through him, pooling hard heat in his groin. He tugged the sheet over his lap as she visibly struggled for composure. "It's just... I've been thinking about that exact question recently."

"You've considered parallel worlds? Why?"

Turning her face almost hid a flash of guilt from him. Interesting. Why would she feel guilty about the concept of parallel worlds?

Unless she knew more about him than he expected. Since she accepted him, loved him, maybe all his worry was unfounded.

"Oh, I don't know." The guilt in her eyes burned brighter but she met his gaze fearlessly. "Why do you ask?"

Jayse took a deep breath and released it slowly. "Baby, I have something to tell you that might be difficult for you to believe. But, trust me, while this might sound nuts, I'm not crazy." He took another long breath.

"Jayse, sweetheart, it's okay. Tell me." She crossed her legs and scooted so she faced him squarely.

A flush rose from the engorged tips of her breasts to her face and he wondered if she was recalling moments ago when they'd faced each other on this bed. He was. His body remembered. The ache to repeat, no, to do more held him silent for a moment. "Are you cold?"

She shook her head, but tugged on the sheet and tucked it under her arms. "This might make it a little easier... to talk." Though her expression was serious, she chuckled and took his hand. "Tell me."

"Okay, it's like this. There is a world, a parallel world, connected to this one by magical portals. This other world, the Faerie Otherworld, is populated by people who look like us, but who have magical talents. And long, long lifetimes."

"The stuff of fairy tales." Lucidea nodded.

"The stuff of Shakespeare. As if the play, *A Midsummer Night's Dream* was history, not imagination. In the Faerie Otherworld, the rulers are descendents of Oberon and Titania. The winged fairies, the tiny boggarts, other creatures of fantasy reside there as well."

"I can believe that. I've always thought that tales of such beings are too common, too widespread to be mere stories. There had to be some truth behind them."

Her matter-of-fact manner gave him courage, as did the way her hand tightened around his. But when he stared into her eyes, that touch of guilt remained, tempered by a violet light. Violet? There was no violet in her deep brown eyes. He tipped his head to one side.

"There's more, isn't there? What is it you have to tell me before we... change your virginal status?" A smile twitched her full lips.

He sent a silent plea that she would still want him. "Yeah, baby, there's more. My granda discovered a way into the Otherworld and met my grandmother. Because he loved her so much, he remained. My father was raised in the human world to protect him... from evil. My mother is human. That makes me... a quarter faerie. And as we recently found out..." He hardly dared say this and closed his eyes. "... a direct descendant of Oberon."

The room was so quiet, he imagined he could hear the disbelief whirling through Lucidea's mind. He ached to look at her but couldn't face the denial he'd see. Loving Dea Annie was a dream, beautiful while it lasted but fading in the realities of the light of day.

Lucidea studied his face. He'd closed his eyes, but a myriad of expressions still flowed over his features. Mostly fear that she'd not believe him. How would he guess she'd recently discovered her heritage was so very similar to his? Now her fears seemed unfounded and there was no doubt he'd accept her as half Alfar-Sindhu. The Alfar didn't sound that much different than his faerie race.

How much time had they wasted worrying and being afraid of things over which they had no control?

She moved her hand from his and he shrank in upon himself. Moisture dampened his lower lashes. Amazing how much she'd come to love this man in such a short time. Leaning forward, she planted her hands on the bed at his hips and kissed one closed eye. He tensed and she kissed the other eye then held her lips against his forehead. Tingling danced through her lips, a physical representation of the magic she'd seen in his aura. Now, she understood.

Barely lifting her mouth from his skin, she whispered, "Do you have magic?"

The touch of his hands at her waist was tentative. "Yes."

"It's silver."

"Dea? Baby?" He tugged at her waist until she leaned back. The hope in his honeyed eyes made her heart pound against her ribcage.

"What you've told me is unbelievable, but..." She caught his face between her palms to keep him from looking away. "I do believe you, Jayse."

"You do?"

She chuckled and kissed his mouth. "Yes, I do."

Relief soared through him, hope and love danced along his veins. Every nerve ending sparked. He caught his breath at the power surging through him. "I love you, Lucidea Anne Galvagin. I love you."

She sat back and gave him a thoughtful look. "Mmm, and I love you, too, Jaysson Allen Zeroun. There's something I should tell you, but right now..." Running her hand under the sheet, she stroked along his thigh. "It's time to change your status."

She slid her hand over his quivering belly, across the tight rise and fall of his chest to his shoulder, and pushed until he lay back. His expectant, glowing expression chipped away at the hiding place she'd created in her mind for her guilt at not telling him her parallel world connection. But, this moment was about him... for him... her news could wait.

But she couldn't. She straddled his thighs, rubbed her aching breasts against his chest, and rested her hands along his collarbone.

She was ready for him, and from the hard ridge captured between them, he was ready—and willing. Angling up to kiss him, she closed her eyes and the memory of her loss of virginity reared an ugly head.

She'd thought she loved the guy, but like many opportunistic college students, he'd moved on almost immediately. The next night.

Jayse twisted his mouth from hers. "What's wrong?"

Damned perceptive man. Smiling, she shook her head and returned to the pleasure of his mouth, sucking on his lower lip until his groan vibrated through every inch of her body. This was his time and her memories had no business here. Maybe, in the special time of this sharing, she'd be able to purge the pain, both physical and mental, of her first time. And make his moment a memory for them both to cherish.

Rising to her hands and knees, she carefully slipped to his side.

"Tell me what you want."

"You."

When she glanced at his groin the joy of her laughter filled the room. "Obviously."

Jayse rolled to his side to face her and cradled his hand in the indentation of her waist, his thumb moving against her skin. "I'm not naïve, nor totally inexperienced, you know."

"Mmm, I remember." She wanted to purr under the gently sensuous movement of his thumb and stretched languorously.

"Shall we just... see what happens?" He slid his hand to her ribcage and teased the underside of her breast with his soft, stroking thumb. Her nipples peaked.

"See what happens?" She gasped when he moved his thumb in a firm stroke across her nipple, then grew serious. "I can't believe you chose me, that you've never... You must have driven women crazy."

Like he was driving her to the edge of consummate desire.

He shrugged but continued teasing her body. "Maybe, but once they realized what I wouldn't do, I was pretty much left alone. I wasn't always happy at the time, but now—baby, I don't have words."

"Then don't talk. I'm tired of talk. Kiss instead."

"As my lady commands."

My lady. Her world. Her problems intruded for a flash then faded. Disappeared. Forgotten. Only Jayse.

Soft murmurs and sighs filled the night, mingling with the rustling of bedding as they moved together finding pleasure in the exploration of their bodies. They kissed, touched, stroked, and nibbled until the sensitivity of every inch of her body screamed for completion. Jayse's heavy breaths burst across her skin as they lay tangled.

"It's time, Jayse. I'm gonna die if we don't." She raked her fingers through his sweat-damp hair and traced the shape of his ears with her thumbs.

"The little death?"

She tried to catch her breath. "Oh, it's gonna be a big one. Jayse, please. Don't make me beg."

He moved over her and poised between her thighs. "I should be... the one... begging you, baby."

Arching up, she took possession of a fierce kiss and wrapped her fingers around the length destined for her. "Now," she said to his lips and encouraged him closer.

He froze when the tip touched her heat and swallowed a strangled cry. Lucidea feathered her fingers over his face. "I want to hear you."

Wiggling, she guided him, positioned him, and planted her feet flat on the mattress. The sound of his astonished joy when her hips surged up to encase him wrapped around her own cries of sudden release. Joined, they lay still for a long moment, breathing harsh, staring into each other's eyes.

Then Jayse moved, withdrawing slowly and returning, letting the tremors of her inner muscles pull him deeper. He'd never be able to describe this moment but knew he'd experience these same feelings with her all of their lives. As he thrust, he learned her joyous responses. With an adjustment of angle this way, she cried out wordlessly. More speed and she clung to him, her eyes shining. Slower, she lay back, gnawing on her lip, her hands roaming over his body. A spiral pulled through every muscle, every nerve, and tightened to an aching of pleasure-pain centered on the joining of their bodies.

"Jayse, oh!"

Her cry, her orgasm, her... Forcing their hips deep into the mattress, he threw back his head and with a groan that shook the bed, spilled his heat into her. His eyelids closed to darken the whirls of colors blurring his vision. He'd imagined, but never imagined.

Resting his forehead against hers, he sighed.

"Jayse?"

"Am I too heavy?" He didn't want to move. Held in her arms,

surrounded by her slick heat, he was more at home than he'd ever been.

"No. But, look at this."

The only thing he wanted to look at was her, to watch her nostrils flare softly as she strained to calm her breathing, to see the sweet, sweet sheen of satisfied passion covering her body, to experience the love in her eyes. She poked his shoulder. "Look."

Slowly he opened his eyes and turned his head. She held one hand, palm flat, near his face. Dancing over her palm, a tiny vortex of silver streaked with violet sparkled with vibrant intensity. Amazement brought a smile to his face. When he could tear his gaze from the whirling, glittering configuration he looked straight into her confused eyes. "God, baby, I don't believe it."

"What?" A tinge of fear melded with her confusion.

Jayse stared again at the colored sparkles then kissed her, keeping his gaze on her hand.

"Jaysson, what does it mean?"

His chuckle ended in a moan as her body clenched around him. "It's part of my heritage, Dea Annie. Something that appears when souls are meant to be together. Like..." He searched for an explanation that she would understand. "It's called soulfire. Like a special aura surrounding soul mates. It means, sweet darlin', that we're meant to be together."

"Soulfire? How long will it last?"

"Forever, Dea Annie."

"No, I mean now. Will it... I mean, will we have to explain..."

He held his palm under hers. The soulfire flared then the vortex spun and danced until it faded from sight.

"Soulfire only appears during moments of intense feeling. Those who have magic, or like you can see auras, are usually the only ones to see it."

"Oh, it's so beautiful," she sighed. "But I don't need auras or colored lights to tell me we're right where we're supposed to be."

He wanted her to know how unusual the expression of a soulfire was. "Soulfire doesn't appear for everyone."

One side of her mouth tilted in a grin. "Oh, so we're special, huh?"

The kiss he offered her and her enthusiastic response shot fresh, intense desire to his groin. He turned so she lay on top of him and rolled his hips.

"Jayse!" Eyes wide, she lifted her upper body, shook her head and smiled at him.

He reached to cover her breasts with his palms. "I've got some time to make up for."

Sunlight spilled across the bed, coming to rest directly in Lucidea's eyes. She winced, stretched and covered her eyes with her forearm. With her other hand, she carefully patted the bed next to her until she found a warm body. The dream-like night had been no dream. Happily she curled closer and snuggled against Jayse's chest when he wrapped his arms around her.

"It's morning." Surprise laced his tone.

"No kidding. I should have closed the drapes last night."

"I enjoyed the moonlight. The sheen of your skin." He stroked the birthmark on her belly. "The sparkle of our soulfire." His hand moved higher.

She stopped his advance by covering his hand with hers. "I suppose we should get up."

"Mmm, up." Jayse nuzzled her neck. "'S what I had in mind."

Slapping at him playfully, she scooted to the edge of the bed. "I love you, but not now. I need a shower."

Jayse rolled after her and grabbed her around the waist. "I'll join you. The shower in my bathroom's pretty small. Is the one in here any bigger?"

"Oh, I think so." Taking his hand, she walked backwards toward the bathroom. She wanted to see his face when he first spied Morghan's hedonistic shower. The space still amazed her.

She reached behind her for the latch and pressed her back

against the wood to open the door. Standing to one side, she watched Jayse.

At first he didn't look at anything but her, then, obviously realizing she waited for him, he turned his head. His mouth dropped open. He shook off her hand and stepped to the center of the expansive room. "Wow."

"I feel that way every time I come in here." Lucidea shuffled her bare toes through the thick, shaggy rug. "And the first time I used the shower, I must have been in there an hour. Just... looking."

Jayse turned in a slow circle then moved toward the smooth, stone shower. "Your uncle... uh... wow."

Yes, her uncle had built a masterpiece, a shower made to enjoy, to experience, to share. She wondered briefly at that fact, then dismissed her thoughts. He had been—he was an extremely handsome man. No doubt he'd had no lack of willing partners during his long life—before he admitted his love for Coralie.

The far wall of the shower, a panel of thick glass from floor to ceiling, faced the loch. The rocky shore disappeared under the overhang. Jayse turned back to her. "It'll be like taking a shower outside."

"Wait." Biting back her grin, Lucidea reached for a small set of handles. Warm water fell like rain around the perimeter of the enclosure. Jayse grinned and held his hand under the gentle flow.

"Wait," she said again and flipped a switch beneath a sliding panel. With a faint mechanical whir, stone slid away and shower-heads moved into place. After a moment's thought, she set the controls and water pulsed, the jets alternating a variety spray patterns.

Throwing his head back, Jayse spread his arms and laughed. He turned, following the pulsing spray. She admired the droplets cascaded over his body to create a sexy, steamy sheen. When they entered the shower, he'd been aroused. Now when he faced her, he was proudly erect. Lucidea's mouth dried and without pause, she stepped under the pulsing water and into his embrace.

The force of his kiss pressed her toward the stone wall. His hands, slick on her skin, stroked her quickly to a fevered pitch. Standing under the soft waterfall, he tugged her earlobe into his mouth and sucked until she sobbed out his name.

"This room, this shower was made for sex," he whispered.

"Probably," she responded, barely able to catch her breath.

"No probably about it, baby." Grasping her waist, he lifted her to a shallow ledge. She held onto his shoulders as he positioned himself between her legs and sheathed himself in her body. "See," he gasped. "Just the right height."

L ater, after they'd left the sensual comfort of the still warm water and managed to dress, they followed the sounds of lively conversation to the dining hall. Lucidea sat at the table while Jayse moved to the sideboard. When he placed a mug of coffee before her, she smiled up at him. "You certainly are magic."

Bryce jumped up. "Magic? Did you say magic?"

Jayse sat next to Lucidea and shook his head. "Uh, Bryce..."

Bryce ignored him and rounded the table. He paused as if in thought then leaned forward and touched a finger to Lucidea's ear, pulling away a shiny coin. Bowing, he handed it to her, lifted a finger to keep her from speaking and produced a coin from her other ear.

Lucidea clapped and chuckled.

"Uh, Bryce," Jayse tried again.

"Hush." Bryce took the two coins and manipulated them over and under his fingers until, with a flourish, the two became four.

Jayse cleared his throat. "Bryce..."

Bryce shot him a dirty look. "Quiet. She said magic and since I'm the resident magical person—"

"You're a magician?" Lucidea cocked her head to the side and winked at Jayse. "I love magic."

"Me, too," Carrie called from the other end of the long table.

"Thank you, darlin', my ever faithful wife."

Carrie stuck her tongue out at him.

Bryce bowed deeply once again and flashed the coins through his fingers. "A magician, yes. Landscape architect by trade, magician by design."

"Uh, Bryce..."

An impatient grimace contorted his expression and he whirled to face Jayse. "What?"

Jayse took a long sip of coffee. "She knows."

SEVENTEEN

Blatant speculation filled Bryce's expression. Even without further comments, heat feathered up Lucidea's neck. Wishing she'd left her hair loose rather than pulling it back into a ponytail, she thought seriously about crawling under the table.

"She knows what?" Eyebrows lifted high on his forehead, Bryce leaned over the back of a chair.

Jayse took another sip of coffee. At that moment, she wanted to punch him for dragging out her misery. Why was she so embarrassed anyway? So she knew a little about the Faerie Otherworld and Jayse's family.

"The Otherworld. The family. Me," Jayse said.

The knowing smile gracing Bryce's face brought a renewed burn to her skin. "So..." he drawled. "You finally did--it."

Oh, no. He hadn't said... meant... Lucidea covered her cheeks and stared at Jayse. Although that gorgeous bronzed flush tinted his cheeks, he'd angled one arm over the back of his chair and slouched back, totally at ease. "Yep."

A wordless sound of astonished dismay burst from her mouth. He hadn't... he didn't. The dim recesses under the table looked better and better. How could he?

But before she could slip under the table, Bryce pulled her to her feet and into a bear hug that nearly cracked her ribs. He twirled them in a dizzying circle and kissed her cheek before letting her stumble away. "Welcome to the family, Lucidea."

Carrie was right behind her husband. "I'm so glad. Welcome."

Lucidea accepted her hug, then turned to Jayse. Planting her hands at her hips, she tried her best to glare at him. He stared back at her as if he had no clue as to what he'd done. "Does everyone know?"

"Yes." He nodded while fighting a mischievous grin. "Everyone in the family knows about the Otherworld."

"Ooh," she growled. "That's not what I meant and you know it." She gave him her back.

"Lucidea. Dea Annie. Only a couple of people in the family know about my personal vow." He moved behind her, wrapped his arms about her waist, and leaned his chin on her shoulder. "Bryce has always been my brother by choice. If Derrik and Tommy hadn't been able to adopt him, my folks would have. Then he would have been my brother in fact. Of course I would share such an important promise with him."

She remained silent and stiffened her spine. She crossed her arms. Carrie tugged on Bryce's shirtsleeve and they moved away.

"I'm sorry I embarrassed you. What we did last night is one of the most important moments of my life, the most joyous, most beautiful, the most—"

"Stop." Lucidea stared at the high corner across the room and tucked her hands under his arms enough to loosen his grip so she could turn to face him. "Yes, I'm embarrassed, Jayse. And I share your feelings about last night... and this morning." She kissed his chin. "As long as we don't have to replay this with every member of your family."

"Nope, only Bryce and my sister."

"Lara?" Well, that might not be quite so embarrassing.

"The three of us shared just about everything, all our hopes and dreams. When we were kids, we became blood brothers.

We'd watched this old musical where they talked about how one drop of another race's blood made a character part of that race. Since, as far as we know, Bryce is totally human, Lara and I gave him part of our blood so he could be faerie, too."

"That's beautiful." She dabbed at the corner of her eye with her fingertips.

"Yeah, but we got in a boatload of trouble for stealing one of Derrik's daggers to do the deed." He lifted his wrist. "If you look close, you can still see the scar."

This man, so perceptive and caring had harmed himself to make another feel better. She didn't deserve even knowing him, let alone loving him. Holding the inside of his wrist against her cheek, she smiled. "I adore you."

"Hey?" Bryce asked loudly from the far side of the room. "We okay, Lucidea?"

While Jayse captured her lips with a kiss that seared her all the way to her toes, she gave Bryce a thumbs up signal.

"Thanks. Carrie says this calls for a celebration."

Turning his face, Jayse barely lifted his mouth from hers. "I am celebrating."

"Tell me, Osric." Feidhlim leaned his back against the thick trunk of a towering Cottonwood and rubbed at an itch on his shoulder blade.

Osric glanced up from the parchment he studied. "Yes, my lord?"

"Was it difficult to learn how the librarian disguises his travel through portals?" Though he knew the answer, he wanted to experience the discomfort of his fool.

"The concept was easy to master. The skill? Only three have managed to completely conceal their paths."

"And you are one of these three?"

Osric lowered his gaze. "Yes, my lord."

The false humility created a sour taste in Feidhlim's mouth.

"And what, in your esteemed estimation, is the reason others have not been able to achieve the same success?"

"To hide one's passage is more than a learned ability. There must be a natural talent to build upon."

"I see." Feidhlim angled to rub another part of his back against the rough bark. "We have missed no nuance in the information provided by the seeker?" Petula, once vibrant, talented, and well suited to his varied needs, had discovered much within Gowthaman's mind. But when brought before him that morning, she had been reduced to little more than a babbling idiot, destroyed by the Zeroun clan. Another heavy weight piled high upon the scale against them.

Osric lifted the parchment. "This is as it was recorded at the time. I find nothing else of importance to be learned from the one known as Gowthaman. Have you attempted another contact with the child?"

Grinning despite his displeasure, Feidhlim stared at the faerie. "Changing the focus from your failure to mine?" At Osric's wide-eyed denial, he waved one hand in dismissal. "I have not made the attempt. I would... understand the reason I was rebuked so my next contact will have greater success. What information have you on the abilities of each of the usurper's family? I'm convinced one of them has prevented me from knowing my son, but I didn't recognize the power source."

"My lord, I shall request that information immediately. Perhaps when we return to the farmhouse..."

Osric's hopeful expression turned Feidhlim's stomach. "Yes, later." Did no one understand the urgency? Each passing moment the tentative connection with the child grew weak and slipped further from his grasp. From his control. The feeling was—unacceptable.

He set aside his concerns over the child and swept his hand toward the evening horizon. "This is the land? You're sure?"

"I studied the documents myself, my lord. Only a few days ago this vast tract passed into the possession of the usurper's son. I

know not what he plans for these hills, but the ownership is
sure."

"Good. Fortuitous the land you obtained for my use is adjoining.
The possibilities..." He rubbed his palms together, then stared into
the empty space between them. He closed his eyes to hide the
nothing that screamed his lack of power. Not that long ago his magic,
bright and fiery orange, would have gathered between his palms,
awaiting his command. But no more. He slapped his hands together.

"Osric. We go. I am in need of a longer run. We shall circle the
extent of this land before returning."

A faint darkening of dismay filled Osric's eyes before he bent
to the task of folding the parchment and tucking it into a pocket.
"Yes, my lord," he sighed dramatically.

Feidhlim checked the laces of his running shoes then started a
slow jog, grinning to himself as he chose a rough, steep path to
the top of a hill. The lengths of time he'd been forced to exist in
the human world had toned his body to a point beyond what
most faerie achieved, except perhaps the Alastriona. But even so,
they depended heavily upon magic. With no magic, he would use
the advantage of a powerful body and his superior mind to defeat
his enemies. Each Defender, each warrior, and every member of
the cursed Zeroun clan. Adult and child. Faerie and human.

He chuckled at Osric's labored breathing and heavy footfalls
and easily increased his pace.

"I'd like to do something to begin repaying you for your
hospitality." Bryce paced back and forth in front of the
windows facing the enclosed courtyard.

Charged with setting the table while Carrie and Jayse
prepared pancakes and strips of thick bacon, Lucidea paused with
her hand full of forks. "That's not necessary. Besides, what's
family for?"

She loved how that sounded. Family. Being able to help a
family, a family she'd claim as hers even if she and Jayse ended

their budding relationship. A painful possibility she had to seriously consider since she still hadn't been able to tell him about the Alfar-Sindhu.

Bryce picked up the pile of knives and began placing them precisely next to the plates, blades all facing the same way. Lucidea couldn't help but chuckle when he smoothly repositioned the forks so all the flatware handles were even with the bottom of the plates.

"You've worked with catering, haven't you?"

Glancing down at his handiwork, he grimaced. "More hours than I care to think about. Don't get me wrong, working for my dad helped pay the bills and get me through school. And I don't mind helping, but I like working with plants. Which brings me back to my offer."

"Okay, what do you have in mind?"

He moved back to the windows and placed one palm flat against the glass. "It looks like your courtyard hasn't had any real attention for a long time."

Sadness pounded at the happiness in her soul. No, probably not since Morghan was sucked into the vortex. Landscaping had been the furthest thing from her mind.

"Anyway, I'd like to clean up the area, see what plants might be salvageable, then create a new design for you. This isn't the best time for a lot of planting, and I'll need to study up some on local plants and those acclimated to this area. And, with your permission, I'd like to create a play area for children."

"Aren't you jumping ahead a bit there?" Lucidea joined him at the window. Children would be great, wonderful in fact, but... Her stricken reflection stared back at her. How many times—with no protection?

Wrapping an arm around her shoulders, Bryce gave a friendly squeeze. "We need to somehow return the rental van today. Maybe a stop at a drug store for... a few items could be arranged."

Another perceptive male. Damn, she had to stop blushing.

Ignoring her discomfort, Bryce continued. "Besides, if you extend the invitation, you'll be overrun with family. And plenty of kids. This would be a great play space—enclosed so it'd be easy to keep track of the little ones."

"Why would you want to do that kind of work right now?"

"Honestly? It's gonna drive me crazy sitting around waiting for something to happen. Plants are what I'm good at. I lose my worries while working in the dirt."

A commotion at the entryway produced Carrie and Jayse hefting laden platters. "Coralie went to find Bree and Tori. Let's get started while everything's hot. And look." Carrie pulled a bottle from the pocket of a voluminous apron she'd donned. "We found some real maple syrup."

Breanna bounded into the room as they were taking their places. "Can I play outside after breakfast?"

"May I?" Bryce corrected. He gave Lucidea an 'I told you so' look.

"I know, Daddy. Sorry. But, can I?"

Lucidea choked back a giggle and focused on the pancakes Jayse plopped onto her plate.

"I don't know, darlin'. I'm not sure it's safe yet."

"Daddy, I wanna."

"Breanna. Behave."

The little girl climbed onto a chair, thrust out her lower lip, crossed her arms, and kicked at the chair rungs. Bryce rested his hand on her lap. "Stop."

"Beggin' yer pardon. I dinna mean to interfere, but the court-yard should be safe enough fer playin' outside." Coralie set a flask of juice on the table and sat next to Lucidea. "I spoke to yer palace guards an' they have placed additional spells surroundin' the manor. No' evil shall be permitted to enter, an' they should be able to track any attempt back to the source. Alfar-Sindhu magic shall protect ye and yers."

Lucidea's fork dropped to her plate. "Coralie," she was finally able to choke out past the panicked lump in her throat.

Coralie frowned. "Wasna correct, Lucidea? To use our magic to protect the magic of yer new family and of their faerie world?"

"Coralie." Frantic, Lucidea shook her head. "I haven't... I didn't...Wait, how do you know about them?"

"Ye dinna?" Coralie shoved back her chair and it tumbled sideways with a wooden clatter. She fell to her knees, clasped her hands before her and bowed her head. "Milady. Yer pardon. I dinna ken. The conversation in the kitchen was open an' honest. I thought ye told him, told him of yer world, as easily as he spoke to ye of his."

"Coralie, get up." Lucidea glanced at the others around the table. Even Bree was still and silent. Lucidea tapped upward on the underside of Coralie's arm. "Get up."

"Nay, milady. 'Tis failed ye I have."

"Stop calling me that. And get up. You haven't failed me." The failure was entirely hers. How could she face Jayse now? Her lies of omission ran strong, tight bands around her heart. The pain drew tighter, yet she silently begged the pain to completely destroy her heart before losing Jayse ripped the organ from her chest.

Her heartbeat stalled when his hand came down lightly on her shoulder. This was it. The end. Before they'd barely had a beginning.

"Lucidea?"

Not Dea Annie. Not baby. She shook her head and gnawed on her lower lip as Coralie rose and backed away, head still lowered. How much worse could this moment get?

Replacing the repentant Alfar-Sindhu, Jayse knelt before her but she couldn't look at him. Couldn't look at anything but the floor at her feet, wishing the flagstone would swallow her the same way the vortex had taken her uncle.

"Please look at me." Jayse kept his voice low and she couldn't identify his mood.

"Dea Annie, please, look at me." If she was part of another world, Jayse understood her reluctance. But, why hadn't she said anything last night when he'd bared his soul and heritage to her? He glanced at the floor and smiled. They hadn't given each other much time to talk.

Now, they'd have to make that time. And soon.

She remained staring at the floor, looking like she waited for a hangman's noose. He wasn't angry, and what temper churned in his belly was more at himself for not noticing any magic within her that went beyond the magic of his love for her.

Coralie moved to his side. "Milord Jaysson." At his startled expression, she gave him a tentative, sad smile. "Milady Lucidea has no' long been aware of her blood heritage, or of the Alfar-Sindhu, her people. Only when Morghan was taken to yet another parallel world bare months ago, was she forced learn of us to become our leader."

"Leader?" Jayse sat with a thump.

"Aye. Reluctant though she be. When I heard ye talkin' with Carrie about yer Faerie Otherworld, my heart leapt fer joy. Fer, if Lucidea had learned of yer world, then assuredly, she must have spoken of her own. I, an' many others, have long held belief in these many conjoined worlds. Yer proof of that. 'Tis forgiveness I beg of ye. Forgiveness fer my presumptions. I shouldna have spoken so freely until Lucidea gave me permission so to do."

"No, Coralie. It's okay, I understand." Both turned to Lucidea.

She'd lifted her face and while dampness glimmered along her lower lashes, no tears dampened her face. "I understand. I should have said something sooner. I should have. But, I was so afraid he would..."

Lucidea reached one hand toward Jayse, but pulled back before she touched him. "So afraid you'd be disgusted and walk away from me. I was... I am... so afraid I'll lose you."

Jayse rose to his knees and gathered her in his arms. "Baby, how could you believe that of me?"

The wet trails of her tears burned his cheek. He'd seen enough relationships beyond his family that hadn't lasted past the effects of outside influences. His family, perhaps because of their faerie blood and the soulfire, pledged themselves for life. And beyond if that were possible. But, how was she to know all that. They'd only known each other for a lifetime. A glorious lifetime that had actually been only a few days.

"Why would you want me around when I lied to you?"

Jayse leaned back and brushed the tears from her cheeks with his fingers. "Did you?"

She sniffed softly. "By not telling you the truth right away."

"Then, by your own definition, I lied to you as well. I didn't explain the Faerie Otherworld to you the first day I met you, did I? I didn't tell you that my dad's the leader of our clan, did I? I didn't tell you I have magical abilities I seldom use, did I? So how are we going to measure my guilt against yours?"

The redness of her lower lip, abused by her teeth, called to him and his kiss was gentle. Then he tilted his head waiting for her answer.

"We... we can't?'

"I don't think so, baby. If we were to put it into strictly human terms, it might not be a whole lot different than admitting to a horse rustler in my past."

She chuckled, then looked around guiltily. "Oh, I think our situation's a bit different than that. Will we be okay? Can we work this out?"

"You have a lot to learn about my family." Jayse sat at her feet facing her and held her hands tightly. "Briefly, let me tell you this much. My aunt Nanceen married Korin, who is a true fairy. He's given up his wings and his tiny size to be with her. My other aunt, Kaelea, recently married a man who suddenly appeared in the Sahara desert from a parallel world. My sister had to go back in time to the ninth century to find Iain. If they can work through those differences, can't we deal with ours?"

Lucidea glanced at Bryce and Carrie who sat watching, the breakfast before them cold and ignored. "What about them?"

Jayse waved one hand. "Them? They're both human. No worries."

"Hey," Bryce complained.

Lucidea smiled at his reaction, then turned her smile on Jayse. Like the sun bursting from beneath the grayest of clouds to bring rainbows, he knew hope again. The despair he'd fought over the past moments shattered when she took his face between her hands and kissed him deeply.

"Lookit, Mommy. Sparkles."

"Yes, darlin', that's the soulfire. That's how much they love each other." Carrie's soft voice carried a note of wistfulness.

"Like yours, Mommy. You and Daddy."

"Oh, no, Bree. I don't think so. Your Daddy and I—"

"Have sparkles, too. Pretty ones. You just can't see 'em. I can. That's how I knowed you was supposed to be my mommy."

"How I knew..." came Bryce's automatic correction.

"That's right, Daddy, I knew."

Jayse ended the kiss. "And I know Lucidea and I have a lot to talk about today. And not just sparkles." As he hoped, pink infused her face. They'd be fine, once they had time to sort through the problems plaguing all of their worlds. Convinced now that her emergency reason for coming to Scotland had to do with this Alfar-Sindhu world, he hoped they'd be able to work together, solving each of their difficulties and bring the conjoined worlds closer together. Such action could only benefit all of them.

"I suppose I've ruined breakfast for everyone." Lucidea spread her hands. "I'm sorry."

Bryce picked up a strip of bacon. "Actually, I like cold bacon. But, soggy pancakes? I don't know about that."

Coralie rushed to clear the pancakes from the table. "'Tis my fault yer meal was interrupted. I shall make more." She paused. "Oh, and mi—Lucidea, I have sent one of yer guards to return the van. No' record of ye nor yers will appear fer the evil to find."

Bryce tilted his chair back on two legs. "Well, that settles today then. I'll start work on the courtyard, with the help of my lovely wife and daughter. Especially if we can talk Coralie into watching Chance for us."

Coralie beamed. "Of course. 'Twill be my pleasure."

"Great. Then you two are free to see how much of your lives you can get sorted out."

Jayse nodded his thanks. "Appreciate it. Lucidea, where?"

"I really need some energy first, some of those fresh pancakes. And more coffee. Then, how about the workroom deck?" She glanced around the dining hall. "Wonder why Tori hasn't joined us."

As if summoned by her words, Catori stumbled into the dining hall and sank wearily onto a chair. Dark, puffy circles deadened her eyes. The muscles in her jaw were tight, and she rested fisted hands on the table. "I must take a drum journey."

EIGHTEEN

"Y ou can't, not after what happened last time."
After Catori's blunt announcement, she'd been
encouraged to eat, though she only nibbled at toast and
toyed with a glass of fruit juice.

Now, Bree entertained her brother with small stuffed bears
while the adults talked. Jayse gave the tabletop a soft slap. "It's
too dangerous. There's no telling who, or what, might be waiting
for you there."

"You don't understand." Catori rubbed her temples. "I was
younger than Bree when the spirits called me as a shaman. I can't
ignore this. I can't not attempt the journey."

"Why now?" Lucidea asked. "Could this be a trick? Something
of Feidhlim's doing? Oh, I'm so dumb." She cast her gaze to the
ceiling. "Took me long enough. This evil guy, he's not just some
weirdo out to ruin your family. He's faerie, too, isn't he?"

Jayse nodded. "Sort of. I mean, he was, but his magic was
stripped from him when he was banished a couple years ago.
Somehow, his followers found a way to bypass the wards set by
the Alastriona, our peacekeepers, and his magic was returning to
him. That's when he... attacked Carrie." Concerned over her
emotions, he sent her an apologetic look. "I'm sorry."

Wrapped tightly in Bryce's embrace, Carrie shrugged one shoulder. "It's history. Horrible as it was... now we've got Chance. We'll get Feidhlim before he can do anyone else harm."

"My brave wife." Bryce kissed her. Once again Jayse admired her calm strength. Not many women would react so positively in a similar situation. He hoped no one else had to find out how they would react.

They had to get Feidhlim and put him out of their misery.

"A little more quick history for you, Lucidea. There's a place we call the world between worlds. It's a place of nothingness, of vast gray mists."

She gave a little gasp and leaned forward eagerly. "That sounds a lot like the place where Morghan is being held." She took a deep breath. "You're all confused, so here's my quick history. My uncle Morghan fought a fire elemental trapped in a place like you've described. When he destroyed the elemental, the vortex took him instead. I thought it was the vortex that was the prison, but now, I wonder. Whenever I dream of Morghan, it's all gray. Maybe... oh, maybe what you know can help free him."

"I hope so, Dea Annie. Sounds like we could be talking about the same place. And if your uncle is there, we'll find him. Maybe Searlait could help. She was in the world between worlds there as punishment until the time when she, Bard, Gowthaman, and Tori joined forces against Feidhlim there.

"There are watchers in the world between worlds. These powerful beings not only stopped the return of Feidhlim's magic, but utterly destroyed his power. There's nothing left, and no way for him to ever regain his own, or any other magical powers." Deep satisfaction brought a grim smile to his face.

Lucidea rested her fingers against his arm. "Are you sure? From what you've told me about him, it sounds like anything's possible."

"The watchers assured Searlait before they released her. As for trusting their word, she seems to believe them. It's all the hope we have, now that he's escaped from the world between worlds. His followers still possess magic though, and we don't know the extent of his influence since he is basically human. The very thing he fought to keep from being part of the Otherworld." The thought of hating someone for the race of their birth was a foreign concept for Jayse.

Hate itself was a complex emotion he didn't understand. But, if he ever chose to hate, Feidhlim would top his list.

Catori moaned, shoved her plate to one side, and rested her head upon her crossed arms. "I've got to go. But I don't have my drum."

The hopelessness in her voice churned through Lucidea. A similar compulsion often consumed her when she first held a skull she was assigned for reconstruction. There was no way she'd ever been able to avoid the faces that rose in her mind, nor their emotional pleas for identification. If Catori felt the same internal distress, there must be some way she could help the young woman.

"I'll be right back." If she remembered correctly, she should find it in the library. She rushed from the table down the hall to the small library and quickly found what she sought in a deep drawer. Holding the aged item against her chest, she returned to the others and placed the flat drum before Catori. "Will this work?"

Jayse stood and leaned over Catori to thump his knuckle against the highly decorated skin head. A sharp thrum sounded through the room. "A beautiful bodhran. Very old, isn't it?"

"I suppose. I just remembered seeing it while I was searching for information about my uncle's disappearance. Why do you think it's old?"

Catori rested her fingers lightly on the drum. "You'll have to see his collection sometime."

"Collection?"

"I... uh, have a small—"

Bryce laughed loudly. "Small? It takes up a whole wall in his apartment."

Jayse gave him a disgusted look and continued. "A collection of ancient musical instruments. Drums being my main focus."

"Plays 'em, too." After receiving another frown Bryce spread his hands. "How's she ever gonna learn anything about you if you don't tell her?"

Lucidea blew Bryce a kiss. "Thanks. Now, Tori, do you think this drum will work?"

With slow, deliberate movements, the shaman drew the drum closer. She caressed the head, then lifted the bodhran and cradled it in the crook of her arm. After a few test taps at various places on the drum, a smile finally lightened the darkness of her expression. "This drum feels... yes, it will work. Thank you. Under the circumstances, I think it will be important for someone to watch over my body while my spirit journeys. She glanced at Jayse. "Will you?"

"I'm going with you." Jayse rested his hand on her shoulder. "The others will watch here, I'll be with you to protect your spirit."

"You can't." She shook her head. "It would be too dangerous."

Lucidea held her breath. Jayse wouldn't do something stupidly dangerous, would he? She looked into his eyes and recognized determination and another powerul emotion she couldn't identify. Nothing she or anyone else in the room might say would sway him from this decision. Still, she had to try and clutched his arm. "Are you sure? What if... I don't know much about drum journeys, but I'm sure there's so much that could go wrong."

Catori nodded. "She's right. I don't even know why I'm called so strongly. You'd be putting your spirit in danger unnecessarily."

"Tori, with everything happening in both my worlds right now, what else can I do? Lucidea, I don't even know about your world's troubles yet, but they're mine now, too. Doesn't it seem we have to do whatever we can, all that we can, and without hesitation? There's no time to call for an Alastriona if Tori needs to undertake this journey so desperately. There must be a reason. I'll be fine. Watch with the others and keep us safe here. We'll return."

Fear clawed at Lucidea's throat and she struggled to speak. "I won't lose you."

"No, you won't." After a long look, so full of promise Lucidea would never dare doubt him, he turned to Catori. "I trust you, Tori. But, I won't let you attempt this alone."

"You're as bossy as your father." Her smile softened her words. "We must do this now."

Bree dropped the stuffed bears and came to stand beside Jayse. "Unca Jayse?"

He knelt and brushed her pale curls back from her face. Tears stung Lucidea's eyes. This gentle man... if he didn't come back, she vowed she'd find him and give him a major piece of her mind. And, no matter what, she'd bring both her uncle and him home.

Jayse grinned at the little girl. "Yes, darlin'."

Serious, she stared at him, then touched his forehead. After a moment, a pink glow surrounded the small hand. Just like when Bree had touched her brother. Jayse closed his eyes and took a deep breath.

Then Bree kissed the same spot on the center of his forehead. "There, Unca Jayse. Now you'll come home. And Tori, too."

He glanced up at Catori as he gave the child a hug. "Breanna, thank you. I'm sure that will help. Will you do me a favor?"

"'Course."

"Will you stay with your folks and Lucidea until we come back?"

Her bright smile brought grins to the worried adults. "Sure, Unca Jayse. We can talk about mermaids."

C atori gave explicit instructions to those who would be waiting for the travelers' spirits to return from the drum journey. Lucidea listened carefully, although all they could really do was wait and not panic when the bodies sitting in the courtyard became unresponsive. She focused on what to do in case either Catori or Jayse seemed in distress.

Carrie remained inside with the baby, but after Breanna's refusal to remain with her mother, Bryce held his daughter's hand tightly.

Since this was to be a journey of spirits, Coralie didn't believe the Alfar-Sindhu magic would inhibit the travelers, but had contacted the palace guards to be wary and prepared to drop their shielding at a moment's notice.

Finally, when Lucidea thought she would scream with frustration, Catori positioned herself cross-legged on the ground and had Jayse sit behind her and place his hands upon her shoulders. She glanced back at him. "Remember... no guarantees."

"No guarantees," he responded then turned his face to Lucidea and mouthed *I love you*.

Pressing her fist against her mouth, Lucidea nodded, then closed her eyes. *Please. He has to come back.* She didn't know to whom her mind whispered the prayer, didn't even know if the Alfar-Sindhu had anything like deities anymore. It didn't matter who heard, as long as they listened. *Please*.

The touch of a small warm hand in hers made her look down to Breanna's confident smile. "Don't worry, Auntie Dea. They'll be okay."

The soft, rhythmic beat of the bodhran startled her. The sound rose around them until her heart and breathing matched the beat. In the middle of a beat, Catori's head slumped forward and the drum slipped from her hand. Two seconds later, Jayse's head tipped until his forehead rested against the back of Catori's neck. Lucidea stared, willing Jayse to take a breath. She'd counted to twenty-five before his shoulders rose and fell with a shallow breath. Another count of nearly thirty—another breath.

So far, so good.

She hoped.

Once Catori began the steady beat on the drum, Jayse concentrated on the sound. Bursts of light flickered behind his closed eyelids with each beat. The analytical part of his mind attempted to find a reason, so he forced his concentration to his senses. Surrounded by the sound, he bit back surprise when Catori's shoulders drooped under his hands. No more sound. Nothing—like he imagined the world between worlds to be. A spark of panic centered in his darkened vision. A blast of pink chased it away.

"Jayse..." Catori's voice called from an unimaginable distance. "Jayse..."

Conscious of nothing but the echo of his name, he followed the call through a smothering nothingness to a place not much different than the American Southwest. Catori's home. Only... this was different. Clearer somehow, yet hidden under a faint haze. Colorful, but dull. A breeze cooled his face then swirled around him hot as the sun. Filled with a peace that burned him in anger, he froze in unbearable agony.

"Jayse, do not linger here."

As if she took his hand, he followed the pull, leaving the world of contrasts. The tugging ended and he stopped, looked around, and waited. If the spirit world looked the same, would his spirit appear like his body? Hesitant, he lifted his hands and looked through them.

The shape was right, he felt the same, but he was transparent. Before he thought much about the oddity Catori appeared beside him, smiling.

"I didn't know if this would work. Welcome to the seventh world. Not a parallel world such as you know, but the spirit world of a shaman. Confusion could not hold you, so you are welcome here. I know. It takes awhile to get used to seeing through yourself. But, you can talk to me normally."

"I... whoa, I'm not sure what I expected. I'm not sure... so— this is how our spirits look?"

She glanced around searching the area. "Sometimes. In this place. I've been to other spirit worlds. I'm not so pretty there." She gave a wry chuckle. "Now, we wait and hope the reason for the strong calling appears soon. I'm not sure how long I can hold both of us here."

"Any clues what we're waiting for?"

She continued to scan the horizon. "Hmm, nope. I've met animals, people, plants, and creatures I can't even begin to describe. But when it appears, I'll know."

A second presence approached his side and he tapped Catori's shoulder. The amazement that her transparent form felt solid kept him silent a moment. Shaking off the feeling, he said, "I've got a pretty good idea whom we're waiting for. Bard, what are you doing here?"

Bard's dark eyebrows shot high into his forehead. "Jayse? I wasn't expecting anyone but Catori. How did you come to be here? No, never mind, there is much to discuss."

"I managed to tag along with Tori. Why are you contacting us this way? What's going on?"

"No one has been able to use a portal to your location." Bard gave Jayse a reproving look. "Since no one knows where you are."

"Yeah, we wanted to keep that from Feidhlim. What about my cell phone?"

"No connection. And, we weren't able to send a magical call. For some reason any magic directed to you bounced back."

"Uh, looks like I've got a lot of explaining to do, a lot to tell the family."

Catori slumped against him. "Hurry, your presence here is draining me. Not long."

Bard gave her a concerned look. "We must arrange a meeting, then. If only there was a way to show me where you are so I can create the portal."

Catori gasped and pointed. "Look, Bard. Quickly."

Jayse followed her indication. A perfect representation of Lucidea's courtyard floated before them surrounded by a faint pink glow. Bard nodded sharply. "Got it."

"I'll get the Alfar-Sindhu to drop their protective shield."

"Shield? What is Alfar? Jayse, explain."

"No time." She wrapped her arms about Jayse and he cradled her spirit as a whirlwind spun them with blinding, dizzying speed. His spirit jerked into his body and he straightened, blinked, and caught Catori as she collapsed back into his arms. Taking a moment to realize he was in the courtyard and truly back in his body, he breathed deeply. Warmth attacked him from one side and Lucidea rained kisses over his face.

"Where's Coralie?"

Lucidea pulled back, gave him an odd look, then stroked his hair. "She's here."

"She needs to lower the magic shield right away. My family's been trying to contact us."

"'Tis done," Coralie confirmed.

"Good." Jayse gave Lucidea a quick kiss. "Told you I'd be back, baby. But, the ordeal exhausted Tori."

"No, I'm all right." The woman in his arms struggled to sit up straight. After swaying drunkenly for a moment, she grinned. "It worked. This is amazing."

"Now, can we talk?" Bard's question rang through the courtyard.

U nable to sleep, Lucidea strolled through the manor's dark halls, finally taking refuge in a small parlor near the front door. It wasn't late, but the day had been exhausting for everyone. She, Jayse, and Bard had spoken long concerning options for Chance's safety. Adding Alfar-Sindhu magic into the mix lightened a measure of concern, but even her limited knowledge took quite awhile to explain. Calling on Coralie helped, however now her lack of knowledge and ability weighed heavily on her heart. There was so much to learn.

She plopped into a chair and turned on the table lamp. Jayse's dad was the leader of a faerie clan, much like she was now leader of the Alfar-Sindhu. Maybe she'd eventually be able to go to him for answers, to pick his brain in effort to understand how to be that kind of a leader. He seemed wise and thoughtful. His suggestion to continue with family obligations, keeping only Bryce's children secreted away, seemed a viable plan. Maybe they'd be able to draw Feidhlim out into the open sooner.

So, in the morning Jayse would use a portal and start implementing the plans for his faire site. Bryce, on a generous parental leave from his firm, would stay with his family. Catori chose to remain in Scotland as well.

She slouched further in the chair and stretched her legs out before her. She'd use the time while Jayse was away to work on her problems surrounding Pagas. Hopefully Coralie would be in one of her teaching moods. It would be great fun, and a release of tension, to be able to show off some magical ability when Jayse came home. A moment of commiseration for Bryce's lack of magic in a magical family brought a tear to her eye. She knew how he felt.

Dashing the moisture away, she stretched. She must be overly tired to be so emotional. It couldn't be all the happenings and disclosures of the past few days, could it? She should return to bed.

With so much to do, Jayse wanted to leave early.

She rose and reached for the lamp switch when an odd noise from outside made her pause. The wind—had to be the wind. Coralie had assured them the shield was in place so they would know if magic were being used against them. She was only being jumpy. Imagine that.

A soft double knock sounded on the front door. Whirling toward the parlor entrance, she stared at the wall at the other side of the foyer as if she could peer through the thick stone. If she ran to get Jayse, whoever was there might be gone before they got back. Not knowing who had knocked would be more frightening than answering the door alone. If she didn't check now, that person might try and enter another way.

The urge to protect those within the manor blazed through her. A heavy sphere from a bookcase would make an effective weapon and the cool stone was a comforting weight in her hand. If she had to, she could smash the stone against an attacker's skull. That should stop anybody whether they had magic or not. Glancing down, she frowned at the violet sparks circling her hands.

With her mouth set in a grim line, she advanced into the narrow entryway. Knowing she had magic on her side, even if she didn't understand how to use it, made her brave. Or simply foolish.

The knock sounded again. Why hadn't Morghan installed a peephole? Modern gadgets and technology filled his home, but not a single, simple security measure to protect everything. Yeah, but he knows how to use magic.

One hand on the latch, she weighed the stone ball in her other and lifted her weapon shoulder high. One jerk and the door flew open. The visitor jumped back, out of range of her possible attack. The stone ball fell to the flagstone step and cracked. She stared, mouth open. "Nightshade?"

N ightshade glanced down at the stone that barely missed his Birkenstock clad feet. "Sweet cheeks, you need to hang on to your weapon for it to do any good."

Lucidea forced her words past the knot in her throat. "What are you doing here?"

He met her gaze and chuckled. "Happy to see you, too."

Lucidea looked past him to the empty parking area. "How did you get here?"

"Thia... dropped me off. It's been a long day, mind if I come in?"

"Oh, sorry. Everybody else is in bed. You were lucky I couldn't sleep."

"So, wore our boy out early tonight, huh?"

Damn the blush heating her face. She never blushed this much. Nightshade ignored her discomfort. "I saw the light and hoped someone was awake. If the house would have been dark, I'd've waited until morning."

She stared at him. "What? Sleep outside. It's October."

"Wouldn't be the first time. Now, honey, I really do need to get off my feet."

"Go ahead and leave your stuff in the hall. We can talk in here."

She motioned toward the parlor. Nightshade kept a small bag tucked under his arm but tossed the large pack to the corner. Dark, lightweight material fluttered from under a flap and the soft clinking of metal against metal sounded as the lumpy bag settled. Curious, she crossed the hall and fingered the slick, thin material.

"What's this?"

"Silk for a new outfit." Daring her to contradict, Nightshade lifted one eyebrow.

Ignoring the look and the evasive answer, Lucidea asked again. "How did you get here?"

Nightshade matched her crossed arm pose. "I said Thia dropped me off."

She swung one hand toward the pack. "That's a parachute."

He shrugged elegantly. "I said I'd be back once our... business was concluded. My part is. Thia's cleaning... taking care of the last details. There wasn't time to land, so she... dropped me off. Can we sit down, please?"

"But, how did you get here?"

"You gave excellent directions." He moved into the parlor, dropped the smaller bag at his feet, and eased back to sprawl in a chair.

"What kind of business?" Determined to learn something about the strange man, she tugged a second chair close to him, preparing to bombard him with questions.

For a moment his expression firmed, mimicking her determination. "I think you know I can't tell you."

"Who *are* you?"

His lips twitched and he gave a loose-wristed wave. "I ain't nothin' but your average, run of the mill drag queen, honey."

"Uh-huh. Okay, so don't tell me."

"No worries there, sweet cheeks."

Silent, she studied him and he calmly returned her examination. Suddenly, he winced and leaned forward. "Let it be enough for you that I do know what I'm doing and by whatever means available, I will protect this family." Carefully angling back in the chair, he crossed one leg over the other. "So, you and our boy find the... magic yet?"

"Wha... what do you mean?"

"Lucidea, don't play coy games with me. You two are more than meant for each other. Any fool with one eye and half a brain can see that. Besides..." He gave her a sly look. "...I'd say your magics are extremely complimentary."

"Ma... magic?"

"By now Jayse has told you about his Faerie Otherworld, yes?"

"Yes." Fearful of Nightshade's next words, she drew out the word. "Have you told him about your magic? I haven't figured out where it comes from yet, but you are a carrier, honey."

"How?" How could he suspect something like magic? She'd been careful, hadn't she?

"I'm obsessively observant. It's kept me alive for this long, no reason to change now. So, am I right or—am I right?"

Nodding, Lucidea experienced a rush of relief. "My father was Alfar-Sindhu, a race much like the Faerie as far as I can tell. The entrance to their world—my world, I guess, is here in the loch."

One of Nightshade's eyebrows arched as though she'd surprised him. Less than a second later, his calm, neutral expression returned. "Interesting. We must explore this later, sweet cheeks, after I've had some rest. Maybe the little lady who's hiding around the corner can point me in the direction of a bed."

Coralie peeked around the edge of the entryway and bestowed an impish grin on Nightshade. "I'm Coralie. If ye follow me, Lucidea may return to her own bed."

Nightshade snatched up his pack and he surged to his feet. He leaned close to Lucidea's ear. "And Jayse," he whispered. Then his soft laughter disappeared down the hall.

· · ·

O nly vaguely aware Lucidea had left the bed because her skin was cool when she returned and snuggled against him, Jayse held her tight against his body. "Where... been?"

"Nightshade's here."

"'Kay. Good." Even the concern that their friend returned much sooner than he'd expected couldn't keep sleep from taking him. He floated, the air around him cold and smooth as a winter wind. No, it wasn't air. Water. Dark, inky black.

He looked around, searching for light but there was none. Struggling against the cold, he sank and shivered. How could he survive?

Warmth touched his palm then twined through his fingers. The touch comforted, stroked, held him steady. He no longer fell into the darkness. Darker than the dark, a shape loomed before him. Ancient, prehistoric, the animal undulated past him, returned and touched surprisingly warm, dry skin to his. The face, reptilian yet filled with intelligence that humbled him, hovered close. The rounded nostrils blew air across his face. Startled, he followed the trail of the breath, bubbling through the darkness until it swirled into a vortex, creating a watery tornado of silver and violet.

A shaft of silver rose through the vortex. Carved. Jeweled. Glinting sharp. A sword. The sword. The blade was a weapon. No, it was an answer. What was the question?

He reached for the blade, but it danced away. He tried calling, but no sound emerged from his open mouth. The sword was his, he knew the truth as he knew... what did he know? During his confusion the blade sank back into the vortex.

The creature slid beneath him, lifting, carrying him from the darkness until he floated half in dark, half in light. A voice, so beautiful it brought a lump to his throat and tears to his eyes, spoke into his ear. In one hand he held a small sheet of parchment, in the other, a quill. As the voice spoke words he knew but that his mind refused to comprehend, he copied the prophecy onto the parchment.

He cried in earnest when the voice ended, his tears pooling golden in the water lapping his chest. Golden threads streamed from him, formed an ever-tightening spiral dancing above the water.

Caught in the spiral, the blade returned, spinning until the blur shot out and sliced the parchment in two, severing the prophecy, tearing the page from his hand.

He fought to regain the halves but watched helplessly as part sank below the black water's surface. The other floated through the air to slip through a shimmer to another world. When he looked for the blade, the sword, too, had disappeared.

Cold, he was so cold. The tears froze upon his face and while his fingers cramped, aching to feel the reality of a sword haft clutched in his grasp, the darkness covered him. Jayse lay still, trying to decipher the strange dream images.

Staring into the dark, he wiped cool moisture from his face and shivered with remembered cold. Except, his other hand was warm. He carefully lifted the slender fingers entwined with his. Lucidea pressed their palms tightly together. Turning to his side, he watched her sleep, grinning at the tiny smile on her full, sensuous lips when he stroked his thumb over the back of her hand. Comforted by her presence, the dream faded and he slept.

T rying to ignore whoever shook his shoulder, Jayse groaned and buried his face in his pillow. "Time to get up, sleepyhead. It's late. You wanted to be gone by now." "I don't care." The aching in his body intensified when he moved. Loving Lucidea shouldn't have... no, it was the dream.

He rolled and captured Lucidea beneath him and nuzzled her neck. "I'm not on a real time schedule, baby."

She threaded her fingers through his hair and tugged at the short, sleep tangled strands. "We've got company anyway. Do you remember me telling you Nightshade was here?"

"Barely. I had this really odd dream. Probably why I slept so long."

Lucidea chuckled and the vibrations arched straight to his groin. "That's not what Nightshade thinks."

"Mmm." Moving against her like this... He increased the roll of his hips, angling his body, urging her silently to grant him entrance.

"Mmm is right." She bent her knees and he pressed against her heat.

"What about Nightshade?" His tongue followed his question into the shell of her ear.

"Who?"

"That's part of what I wanted to hear." He slid one hand down her side and cupped her bottom, lifting as he entered her with a long, slow stoke.

"Oh, Jayse."

"That'll do, baby."

Arms about each other's waist, Jayse and Lucidea strolled toward the kitchen. "We're going to have to set the alarm clock earlier if you expect to get up in time." She patted his side.

"Didn't I get up in time this morning?" His innocent expression was tempered by the glow of satisfaction in his eyes. "Can I help it if I'm randy as a teenager with you?"

"Randy? I thought your name was Jaysson."

As she'd hoped, he captured her laugh with a lingering kiss. When she was breathless, he stepped back. "Maybe I should change my name. Or my actions."

She rested her hand over his heart. The rapid beats matched her own. "Don't you dare—on either count. Come on. I'm starved."

With the material crushed in her fist, she tugged him forward by his shirtfront. Laughing they entered the kitchen.

To freeze at the sight of Nightshade's bare back. "Oh, my God," Lucidea whispered.

Coralie set a bowl of water and a soft cloth next to where Nightshade leaned on the table. He looked back over his shoulder. "Sorry, didn't want anyone to see this."

Wooden legs scraped against the floor as Jayse jerked the chair next to Nightshade from under the table and sat. "Who did this to you?"

Nightshade sighed. "Just a part of the business, honey."

Lucidea found her voice, but had to support the sudden weakness of her body by leaning against Jayse. "How did you hide this from me last night? There was no... how did you keep the pain from me?"

"Like I said, a part of the business. Hurts like hell this morning though, sweet cheeks. Coralie said she'd give me a hand."

"You need more than a hand, Nightshade. You need a doctor."

"No."

Lucidea gnawed on her lower lip and stared at the thin wounds criss-crossing Nightshade's back. "You do, some of them are bleeding. What did this? A whip of some kind?"

"Cane. A very narrow, flexible cane." Coralie touched the damp cloth to one stripe and his intake of breath hissed through his clenched teeth. He bared his teeth in a vicious grin. "Poor baby broke it, though. Before we broke him."

He jerked his hard gaze to Jayse. "Like I told Lucidea last night... I ain't nothin' more than a drag queen. Anything more than that..."

"I know, you can't tell me. But, you've got to have your back looked at."

Coralie cleared her throat. "I could summon yer healers, Lucidea."

Before she answered, the soft sounds of a child singing entered the kitchen. Followed by Breanna. Luckily, she entered through another door as Lucidea moved behind Nightshade to try and cover the wounds on his back. Bree moved directly to him and he angled to face her.

"Hi, Unca Nightshade."

"Breanna, my darling. How's my girl?"

She gave him an adult look of reproach. "Better'n you. Your color is all dirty."

Nightshade glanced back at Lucidea. "My color?"

"You know. The color all around you. You're blue, like the stones in Tori's necklace."

He shrugged and winced. "Do you mean turquoise, honey?"

She nodded happily. "Yea! You knowed what I was talking about. But, it's all dirty. I can fix it, if you want. I'm always supposed to wait for you to ask, but you don't know how. Can I make it better?"

Jayse expelled a sharp breath. "She has shown a talent for healing. Maybe she can at least help with the pain."

"I can," Bree announced. "Helping hurts is easy. I need to touch you, touch the owie to make it go away."

Nightshade shook his head. "No, honey, that's okay. I don't want you to see my... owies."

Bree closed her eyes and shook her head with such a look of disgust; Lucidea had to turn her smile from the adult expression. "You don't want me to see because you think it'll be too icky for me." Her eyelids lifted and she touched his face. "I already seed the stripes on your back. I've seen icky stuff before. Once I fix you, it won't be icky anymore. Won't that be good?"

"That'd be very good, but maybe we should ask your daddy first." Nightshade covered her hand with his and tugged it from his face.

"You need to listen to me, Nightshade." Bree shook her free hand at him. "Daddy'll be right here and we can ask. He's gonna say yes. He doesn't like for you to hurt either."

"Damn right I don't. Oops, sorry Bree." Bryce stepped into the kitchen and rested his hand on his daughter's head. "Guess I owe a quarter to the jar, don't I?"

"The jar's getting full, Daddy. You're gonna have to watch your mouth."

"Hard to do when it's below my eyes, darlin'. Now, did Nightshade ask you to help?

Bree shook her head. "He doesn't know how. But I asked him if I could help. He thinks it's too icky."

Bryce eased around the table to look at Nightshade's back. He closed his eyes and turned his face away. Lucidea touched his shoulder. Seeing wounds like this, even after studying photos of similar injuries in seminars, was a shock. There was no way they could allow Breanna to see the effects of a vicious caning.

"When my Gowthaman was hurt here..." Breanna touched her forehead. "It was icky, but I fixed him quick. Please Unca Nightshade. May I fix your hurt?"

Bryce grimaced. "Bree, it really does look icky. Are you sure?"

"He's my family, Daddy. I can't let his owies hurt if I can help, can I?"

Coralie leaned her hip against the table. "Can ye heal the hurt even if ye canna see it?"

"Don't know. I guess. But, I gotta touch him." Bree shrugged, then tugged on the hem of her tee shirt.

"Mayhaps, I could be allowed to guide yer hands to Nightshade's hurts, an' ye can keep yer eyes closed."

The sudden brightness of the little girl's smile eased the thick tension. "I'll try. Daddy, is that okay?"

He flashed a relieved half-smile to Coralie. "I think it's worth a try."

Nightshade hissed in another pained breath. "Honey, if we're going to do this..."

Coralie moved beside Breanna. "Close yer eyes, child." When Bree complied, she took the small hands and inched them both toward where Nightshade turned his back to them. Then she gently lay Bree's palms against the worst of the bleeding stripes and held her hands just over the child's.

A grimace of pain distorted his features, and Nightshade arched his back but remained silent. A soft pink glow spread from under Breanna's hands and crept along the wound. The bleeding stopped. The bright, raw redness faded. The skin knit together leaving no indication of a wound. Bree nodded once and Coralie repositioned the girl's hands. The process was repeated until every stripe of pain on Nightshade's back was healed.

Holding tightly to Jayse's hand, Lucidea stared at the miracle before her. The child's magic was... she couldn't begin to describe her amazement. Maybe it really had been Bree who had chased away that orange shell from Chance. If that was so, what else was within the child's power? She glanced at the others. They appeared as amazed as she felt. Hadn't they any idea how strong the little girl's magic showed in her aura?

Finally Bree patted Nightshade's back. "All fixed."

Nightshade rested his head in his arms and took a deep breath. "Thank you, honey. You did a wonderful job."

F eidhlim took the roll of parchment from Osric and gave a dramatic sigh. "Now what is it you wish me to look at?"

Osric schooled his expression. The emotions that flitted across his underling's face had been confusing. Unable to discern whether Osric was anxious to show him the scrolls or fearful of his reaction, Feidhlim set the parchment aside.

"My lord. This information has recently been obtained from the library at Alexandria."

Feidhlim smiled. "More information from my friend, Gowthaman?"

Osric shared the smile. "Indirectly. His is the hand that has transferred the information to this form, however I believe it was compiled by the usurper's sister. You may find this information... enlightening."

"Perhaps." He would concede nothing to this fool. Still, Osric had brought him something that engaged his curiosity. He opened the scroll and scanned the chart scribed there. "So, it's a family history. Of the usurper's family." Why would he want to read the names of progenitors of one he hated?

"You may find the name of the first ancestors interesting. Another page, my lord."

Rolling his eyes, Feidhlim turned the page and followed the ornate lines to the names Oberon and Titania. He jerked his gaze to Osric's satisfied gloat. "What does this mean, fool?"

"That fiction is truth, my lord."

"And Zeroun knows this?"

"Yes, my lord." Osric pointed again to the parchments. "Here also are the genealogies of liaisons Oberon had with females of many fey races. The next history shows the bloodline of one Robin Goodfellow, son of Oberon and ancestor to Korin, member now of the Zeroun clan."

"Interesting. But, what use is this to me if they also hold this information?"

"One final history, my lord. That of Oberon's lady, Titania. She had not her lord's wandering eye and only once dallied with another."

Feidhlim laughed. "You don't mean to tell me that part of Shakespeare's tale is truth as well?" At Osric's grin, he laughed again. "With an ass-headed human? And what child now bears the stigma of that union?"

An odd light brightened Osric's eyes. Feidhlim paused, cocked his head to one side, and studied the dark-haired faerie. What was in this scroll that delighted the fool? Trepidation churned in his belly, mimicking the need he fought daily. Slowly, he returned his gaze to the parchments and turned to the final page.

The name Titania, ornate with swirls of colored ink, headed the page. Directly below, the name of the human—Bottom the Weaver.

Feidhlim quickly scanned the remaining names, knowing what he might find, dreading the confirmation. He took a deep breath. There. The final faerie generation. Feidhlim.

He waited for anger. There was none. He waited for despair. He felt only a numb emptiness. The absurdity struck him like lightning and he broke into wild laughter. All his life he'd fought against the taint of human blood within the Faerie Otherworld, a taint he believed destroyed the sanctity of the Faerie race. His goals, to rid his world of that taint, had precipitated the formation of the Nechtan-Cattee, followers who believed as he did and who worshiped him and his ideals. Now, what was his hatred of the usurper, whose human taint only carried back one generation, compared to his, a taint as old as time? He laughed at the fact that all his life he'd carried hidden human blood and now he was no more than human.

Osric remained silent, a smile frozen on his face. Obviously, Feidhlim's reaction was not what the fool expected. That thought made Feidhlim laugh all the harder. He slapped the parchments and gasped for air.

"My... my lord?" Osric took a step backwards.

"Fear not, fool. Despite this... enlightenment you brought me, my goals do not change. I shall destroy the usurper. Perhaps we shall rethink my charge to the Nechtan-Cattee, eh?"

"My lord? You are... well?"

"Well enough, fool." Good, the surprise faded from Osric and anger at being the fool returned. Feidhlim needed the faerie's anger, no matter what focus he gave to the emotion. "Well, enough, my friend."

Osric took another startled step back, his face registering confusion. Feidhlim leaned back in his chair, satisfied. No, not satisfied. Satisfaction would come later. "Osric, I wish to celebrate this new information. Bring me... companionship."

He bowed. "Yes, my lord. There are many faerie maids awaiting—"

"No." Feidhlim slammed his fist on the desk. "Bring me a human woman. One to fulfill my... desires."

TWENTY

With hearty, yet good-natured complaints, Nightshade allowed Breanna take his hand and tuck him back into his bed. Coralie prepared strong coffee and dishes of her thick, rough-cut oatmeal while the others remained silent in their own thoughts. Halfway through his cereal, Jayse laid his spoon aside and caught Bryce's attention. "Did you know she could do that?"

"We've suspected her healing talent was really strong, but other than small cuts and scrapes, I've never seen her do anything like this."

"What about Gowthaman? She's always maintained she 'fixed' him."

Bryce swallowed his mouthful and washed it down with coffee. "I don't know. Neither one of them will say anything much about what happened. Good God, Jayse. His back was bloody raw. Now, there's absolutely no indication there were ever any wounds there. And what did she mean that she'd seen the stripes? I was right behind her. You and Nightshade did a great job hiding his back when she came into the kitchen. There was no way she could have seen that gruesome sight." He scrubbed his face with his fingers. "How am I going to deal with this?"

Lucidea stirred another spoon of brown sugar into her cereal. "With your strongly knit family. Like you all have dealt with so many, many painful issues lately. There must be someone, some doctor or healer person in your Otherworld who can help."

A sour bile settled at the base of Jayse's throat and he shook his head. "The healers are... sorry, Bryce, but there's no other way to explain it. They're afraid of her. A few magical talents manifest while a child is young, but usually, a faerie's true magic reveals itself at puberty. Sometimes even later." He shrugged one shoulder. "Our family seems to have an abundance of overachievers in the magic department."

"Aye," Coralie said, "'tis much the same fer the Alfar races. Mayhaps magic is no' so different in our different worlds. If ye wish, I shall speak wi' the Alfar-Sindhu healers."

Bryce nodded. "I'd appreciate any help. I don't want to deny her any ability. But, she's so young. I don't want her to feel out of control, or become a pawn in some power struggle. I want her to be a child and know the joys of being young, with few responsibilities. How did it happen? How did a child with so much obvious power come into a family with two human parents?"

"Bree's birth mother was Faerie."

"Yes, yes, Jayse. I know that's where the magic stems from. And everything comes down to dealing with her and her talents. I'd feel a lot more competent if I had more of a grasp on the hows and whys."

He forced a smile. "I know the family will always be here for us. Carrie and I will do the best we can. I'd better go check on my little healer."

Jayse watched him rise and exit slowly through the wide kitchen arch. Even growing up surrounded by magic and seldom calling upon his own magic, he thought he understood. He'd heard how difficult it could be to have a child who was extraordinarily intelligent, or gifted in music, making in nearly impossible for some to stay a step ahead of their child's needs. But magic? How would they handle Breanna's talents?

He glanced sideways at Lucidea who sipped thoughtfully at her coffee. How would magic manifest in their children? And there might be children... they'd never used any protection. The thought brought a silly grin to his face and he hid the expression by focusing on the dregs of oatmeal in his bowl. Before he worried about magic in their children, he needed to learn more about her and her fey race. They needed time together, time he didn't have just then.

"I really should get going." Late the previous night he'd called and set up a meeting with Bryce's partner, Garr Logan, who he'd asked to do some of the architectural renderings. Today he'd see if Garr would oversee the needed permits and begin routing utilities to the land. He needed someone to be his eyes and ears at the faire site since he planned to spend as much time as possible with Lucidea.

"I know." The soft, secret smile of lovers pouted her lower lip. He'd need to call upon Lara to create a time portal for him anyway, maybe, just a little longer. Her eyes widened slightly. "Oh, no you don't. You get going. Coralie and I have a lot to do today. I'll... be here when you get back."

Promises passed silently between them and he rose before kissing her deeply. She tasted of fine coffee and homey oats and love. "I do love you, Dea Annie," he whispered to her lips.

"With every beat of my heart, Jayse."

"Will you come to the courtyard and see me off? I hate using a portal since we don't know if anyone's watching, but there's no other way. I'll make a few transfers to make it more difficult to trace my route."

"Is it that dangerous?"

"Nah. I'll take you to the Otherworld soon. Promise. Come with me to the courtyard?" The more seconds he could spend with her, the better. In fact, he could return only moments after leaving if Lara would time it for him. No, that would make his portal use even more risky.

Lucidea took his hand as they passed through the dining hall and out the wide, glass doors. "How does this portal thing work?" she asked. A tremor of fear shook her voice.

Was she afraid of the simple means of getting from one place to another? Jayse hurried to explain. "It's a magic that seems innate in every member of the Otherworld, no matter how diluted the fey blood is. All you have to do is have a clear picture in your mind of where you want to go. Some must speak a few words, others of us can create a portal by sketching a magical sign in the air. Others, like the Alastriona, create portals by thought alone. The key is that clear picture. If you don't know where you want to go, you won't go anywhere."

"I wonder if I could ever learn how." Growing excitement overcame the evidence of her fear.

"I don't see why not. Bard uses portals and he's not from either the human world or the Faerie Otherworld. Since you're my magical Dea Annie, you should have no difficulties. When we know using portals is safe from Feidhlim's observation, I can begin your training. If you'd like."

"I'd like."

"I'd like to kiss you again."

She cocked her head to one side. "You, my dear, are incorrigible."

"Damn right," he said, gathering her into his arms and slanting his lips against hers. He released her suddenly and took a step back. "I've... got to go."

But as he lifted his hand to create his portal, a shimmering oval formed to the side. Angling into a defensive posture, he moved between Lucidea and the glow.

Lucidea felt her lower jaw go slack at the amazing sight. Not much larger than a doorway, but oval and shimmering with intense magic around the edges, the portal showed an expanse of golden sand. A figure appeared in the opening and stepped into the courtyard. Brief surprise registered in the coffee-brown eyes, then a sad smile showed the edge of one slightly chipped tooth. The portal snicked closed as Jayse straightened and Gowthaman bowed.

Studying the two men as they spoke quietly, Lucidea gave a soft snort. Her courtyard was turning into Grand Central Station. Not bad for people who were supposed to be hiding. Swallowing her sarcasm, she moved closer to hear what the men were saying.

Gowthaman acknowledged her presence by closing his eyes and bowing his head briefly. Then he turned his gaze back to Jayse and lifted the flat, wooden chest in his hands. "It is uncommon for faerie magic to take the form of lengthy incanta- tions or a talisman. But, it is not unheard of. The practice was far more common in the long ago past. In this time of need, I have searched many ancient texts and devised a charm I believe may be of assistance."

Lucidea listened closely to the flow of Gowthaman's words. Like his appearance, his lyrical speech patterns were reminis- cent of an East Indian. Were there faerie folk similar to other human races? She added that to her growing list of questions for Jayse.

Gowthaman touched the latch three times then opened the chest to reveal a triple row of small, clear oval stones. Each was wrapped with silver in a precise, spiral pattern ending in a loop at the top.

"These charms, when attuned to the wearer, should disguise the use of portals from unwanted observers as well as provide a device allowing those monitoring this family to locate the bearer. In either the human or Faerie worlds. I need only to attune each stone and make one final test."

Jayse lifted his head from his study of the charms. "What test is that? Any way I can help?"

"I thank you. I need someone to use a portal so I may test the tracking ability of a stone."

"Great. I needed to head home anyway. I was set to open a portal when you arrived."

"I have but one request. I ask for you to chose to transfer to a place I do not readily know or would suspect as your destination."

The stones were so beautiful, Lucidea couldn't imagine how such tiny things could be used as Gowthaman suggested. But then, she really wasn't all that accustomed to magic yet. She held her hand over the box. "May I touch one?"

The sadness lifted from Gowthaman's smile and her breath caught at the exotic beauty of his eyes. "I have prepared one for you as well, Lucidea. It was hoped by many there would be a need."

She glanced quickly at Jayse. "Your family doesn't waste any time, do they?"

"Nope. They only want the best for me. And that's you, Dea Annie."

Blast the heat that filled her face then burned deeper at the odd, contemplative look Gowthaman gave her before he indicated the stones. "Chose a stone, but please, touch only one so as not to dull the connection with the charm's proper recipient."

Nodding her understanding, she scanned the stones. They were identical, each the same as the next. Yet, she sensed subtle differences. Holding her palm flat over the stones, she moved her hand slowly.

"Very good." Gowthaman's approval encouraged her to concentrate until, as her fingers passed over a certain stone, unmistakable vibrations zinged through her fingertips. "That one," she whispered in awe.

"Good. Now hold the stone flat upon your palm lifted before you."

When she did as he indicated, Gowthaman rested his hand over hers and spoke a single, sharp word. Tingling centered in her palm then with a flash of cold so intense it burned, the sensation ended.

Gowthaman nodded with satisfaction and lifted his hand.

Jayse and Lucidea gasped simultaneously. The once clear stone now held swirls of intense violet.

The speculation in Gowthaman's eyes deepened. "You have magic?"

Jayse cleared his throat. "It's a long story, my friend. We'll go into it all later, okay?"

Silently thanking Jayse for running interference, she cradled the stone against her chest.

"As you wish. Your choice, Jayse?"

After a moment's scrutiny, he gave Lucidea a lopsided grin and lifted a stone that had been next to her choice. The dark faerie repeated the procedure to reveal swirls of silver echoing the spiral wrapping on the stone. Then he produced fine silver chains from a pouch at his side and had them fasten the charms so the stones lay close to their hearts.

Gowthaman closed the box. "Lucidea, will you guard this while Jayse and I finish testing the stones?"

Honored to be trusted, she clasped the charm between her breasts and bowed. It seemed the proper thing to do. "Yes, of course I will."

He handed her the box as he spoke to Jayse. "A worthy choice. Now, if you will choose a destination I would not suspect, then wait to form your portal until I am inside." He glanced at Lucidea. "With your permission, of course."

"Certainly. I'm sure Bryce's family would like to see you—if there's time."

"I have a special stone for each of them, and will use the time to attune each to each. Jayse, I wish to allow all trace of the portal to dissipate before trying the charm. Please allow time for my discovery, and return here if I do not appear within a reasonable period."

"Understood. You said there would be someone always keeping track of these?" Jayse touched his finger to his chest.

"Yes. Only three are charged with this task in order to prevent an escape of information. Myself, Derrik, and Searlait."

"Okay. I know where I'm going. See you in a few."

. . .

With few in the family even knowing about his model, let alone where he kept the constantly evolving castle, Jayse figured the storage garage was a good location to test Gowthaman's charm. Besides, there were drawings there he needed to retrieve then drop off at Logan and Associates. As the portal shimmered to life, he let his imagination place his castle upon the cliff of his dreams rather than in a dark, dingy garage.

Without looking forward into his destination, Jayse moved through the portal. His first breath of clean air in the faerie Otherworld encouraged him to draw another. It had been too long since he'd tasted the fresh breeze, too long since he'd come here.

Frowning, he stared about him. Obviously, this wasn't his garage; it wasn't even the human world. How had this happened? Had his portal been somehow redirected? He turned a quarter turn and froze.

The taste of the salty sea caressed his senses as the wind tossed his hair back from his face. He took a single step forward, shook his head, and stepped back.

It was his castle.

Yet, it wasn't.

Rising from a flat plain to perch on the edge of a sea cliff, the immense structure glistened in the sunlight. The hill he stood upon was high enough he could see over the high outer walls into the bailey. There, that section was the first he'd built. And to the far side, the tower he'd only recently finished. The lack of movement about the walkways and courtyards indicated the castle was vacant.

Amazing. How long had he dreamed this place, and now, here it was before him, solid and real? He looked around but his gaze was drawn back to the castle. Where was here? All of his senses screamed he was in the Otherworld, but where?

Because he really wanted to run down the hill and explore the grand building, he hoped Gowthaman would be along soon.

Reluctantly, he sat, rested his elbows on his knees and stared at his castle.

He didn't know how long he waited but remained seated when the slight electric vibration of an opening portal hovered beside him. He smiled up at Gowthaman, unprepared for his friend's reaction. The instant he spied the castle, Gowthaman collapsed to his knees, hunched forward as if in pain, and covered his face with his hands.

Jayse crawled to his side, waited as Gowthaman took a series of shuddering breaths, then rested his hand in the middle of the faerie's back. Gowthaman stiffened, then relaxed and straightened. Haunted and filled with a whirl of terror and pain, Gowthaman's eyes begged him for answers. "Why did you come here?" he gasped.

"Here? I don't even know where here is. I've dreamed this castle since I was a kid. Through the years I've built a model of it and I was aiming for a storage garage in the human world where I keep the construction. I can tell we're in Faerie, but where?"

Visibly struggling for composure, Gowthaman closed his eyes and leaned his head back as though staring at the sky. His hands clenched and flexed over his belly. Tremors coursed along the corded muscles in his neck. Jayse hadn't seen such agony since... Gowthaman had returned from being held by Feidhlim.

Did Feidhlim use this place? Anger, deep, thrumming, and unreasonable surged through him. How dare evil use the place of his dreams? What had been done here to Gowthaman to cause such belated pain? A growl vibrated at the base of his throat.

"Jayse." Gowthaman's strained voice diffused part of the anger. "I am... in control." He struggled to his feet and Jayse followed. "I do not know where in Faerie this place is, but as you have surmised, it is where Feidhlim recently held court. The stench of his evil no longer lingers and perhaps his presence has been washed away."

"Will you tell me what happened here?"

Gowthaman gave him a long look. "Since you have dreamed of this place, it would seem appropriate for you to know of how evil came to be here. Perhaps, it is your destiny to finally cleanse this portion of Faerie. I do not know." He fell silent, staring at the tall, stone walls.

"If you can't say anything right now, I understand."

"No." Gowthaman managed a wry smile. "Mayhaps the telling will clear my soul as well. Feidhlim's minions brought me here. Here I met him, tasted his anger—and his power. Here, he made use of a seeker."

"I don't know what that is."

"Blessedly, few do. It is an extremely rare skill enabling the seeker to... travel the mind, the memories, the fears of another. Feidhlim's seeker... she entered my mind, destroying any defenses set against her and learned from me. Learned all that I know. Took all that I am. It is as though my mind was stolen from me and returned intact, and yet... There are moments I do not trust my own thoughts. Are these thoughts, these memories truly mine, or something left behind by the seeker?"

"Oh, my God."

"When the agony of my questioning becomes unbearable, the little missy is able to release the pain and ease my soul away from thoughts of... I do not know if I would still live, if not for Breanna."

"I had no idea."

Gowthaman laughed bitterly. "Few do. The Defender, Derrik. Your father as ruler of our clan. The little missy. And now you. Bard does not know the extent of what was taken from me. He understands, but does not speak of it. The seeker attempted to touch his mind and was destroyed." He paused and stared at the castle. "I never saw outside the cell of my incarceration, but this is the place. Mayhaps... there is a reason we both are here. Knowledge for you. For me, I do not know."

"I'll destroy the model. I was going to build a smaller version of this castle for a project in the human world, but I'll do something else. The reminders—"

"No." Gowthaman moved to stand directly before Jayse. "Do not change your plans for me. Even as we stand here, some of the initial pain fades. Mayhaps I must face the embodiment of my fear and torment in order to conquer myself and return to Gowthaman as he was."

Silent, the men turned to face the castle. Jayse had doubts, but in a confused way, what Gowthaman said made sense. Still, facing your fears was one thing, having a constant reminder of those fears was another. The pain his friend had suffered, still suffered was unimaginable. Maybe, with Gowthaman's permission, he and Lucidea could find a way to help him find peace.

Gowthaman took an eager step forward. "Do your dreams hold any strange symbols?"

The change in Gowthaman's mood made Jayse pause. "Uh, no. Just the castle and this location. Why?"

"Will you approach the structure with me?"

Jayse gave him a doubtful look. "You want to get closer? Are you sure?"

"Yes. There is something, a crest or symbol above the door that I must examine. It appears familiar, something I have seen while studying ancient texts."

"Okay, but at the first sign that anything's wrong, or if you feel... you know, we're out of here."

"Thank you, my friend."

During the short walk down the hill Jayse examined the castle and compared the structure to his dream memories. There was no doubt, this cliff side dwelling had haunted his dreams since he was four. How long had it stood here in the Faerie Otherworld, hidden from everyone—except Feidhlim? How had evil found it? Could the building be cleansed of that taint? There was no sense of evil, only of... waiting.

"There." Gowthaman stopped and pointed to an open arch rising high above a pair of huge wooden doors. "It is only in a certain light, at a precise angle, that I can see a crest hanging above the opening, suspended... from nothing. Unless, that is hidden as well."

Gowthaman mumbled and Jayse only half listened as he, too, studied the odd crest.

The meeting of two triangles, points overlapping to make a distorted hourglass, formed the white stone background. The blossom of a simple purple flower filled the upper portion of the crest. Below, the representation of water swirled with blue crystals with the haft of a heavily jeweled sword rising from concentric circles. The breeze shifted the crest and highlighted a golden disc behind the indent of the hourglass, sharp rays of clear, sparkling stone radiating from the edge.

In a few short seconds, the image burned into his memory and Jayse knew he would incorporate the symbol into the signage for his faire site. It was perfect. About to turn away, he stopped, then slowly turned to look again at the lower portion of the crest. The dream of the previous night—the dream he'd forgotten in his time with Lucidea—blasted into his mind with perfect recall. The jeweled sword of his recent dreams now hung before him, decorating the castle of his lifelong dreams.

He was no idiot. This meant something. And with the intensity of emotion churning his gut, it meant a lot. Maybe Gowthaman could tell him something. He discovered the librarian had moved a few steps away to stare up at a large open window. The same crest decorated the stones at either side of the opening.

"Do you have any ideas?" he asked Gowthaman.

"Oh, yes. I just do not believe the possibility."

"What?" This was no time for guessing games and riddles. It was suddenly imperative he know now. Jayse had no idea what it was he needed to know, but his need for knowledge couldn't wait.

Gowthaman tucked a strand of hair behind his ear and turned a true, relaxed smile to Jayse. He hadn't seen such a free expression from the haunted librarian since before Bard literally fell into the desert and joined their family. "What?"

"Jaysson, my friend. What you see, what we see, is astonishing. A confirmation of the history we have only recently begun to know. This is your heritage." Gowthaman waved his hand toward the castle. "I believe this castle was once the seat of fey power for both this and the human worlds."

"Okay?" The excitement lighting Gowthaman's face made Jayse wonder if seeing the castle had taken his friend's tentative hold on reality. With the little Gowthaman had exposed of his past with this place, it would be understandable.

"Jayse, do not worry. I have complete control of my mind. And of this fact I am sure. As truly as you are descendent and heir to the power of Oberon and Titania, so is this castle the place from where they ruled. I recognize the crest from drawings in the journal of Oberon, that same book that gave us your lineage and that of Feidhlim. This symbol is the crest of Oberon."

TWENTY-ONE

L ucidea didn't think she was ready for and really didn't want to face her new responsibilities, but after Gowthaman followed Jayse, she searched out Coralie. Time for some Alfar-Sindhu damage control.

She found her friend in the workroom studying an array of papers spread on the table before her. Idly Coralie moved the tiny slips of parchment as if she were placing pieces of a puzzle. An apt analogy, Lucidea supposed, for Pagas had left behind a confusion of possible clues.

Coralie glanced up and sighed. "Lucidea, I dinna ken what Pagas has done."

Pulling a chair next to her, Lucidea sat, angled slightly to face Coralie and folded her hands. "Tell me what you do know."

"He has gone."

Lucidea cleared her throat. "Well, that's obvious. You said he slipped his guards and disappeared?"

"Aye." The forlorn expression showed that Coralie held herself responsible for the disappearance.

"You had nothing to do with his escape. I know that. And you know that. This guy's obviously slippery as an eel."

"Nay, dinna be maligning a fair creature."

The women laughed together and Lucidea laid her hand over a pile of parchments. "There, now that your unfounded guilt is under control, we can get to work. So, we need to find Pagas because there's no telling what he might do next, right?" She paused. "Just like Feidhlim. Damn, we don't need to be worrying about two crazy men who want to take over the world. Even if it isn't the same world. Oh, my God, Coralie. Does Pagas want to destroy my family like the other one wants to destroy Jayse's?"

The hesitation gave her the unpleasant answer to her leap of logic. "He does, doesn't he? I remember... he was involved in both my father's death and Morghan's disappearance. But, I don't think he's ever tried anything against me."

"We began watchin' him as soon as 'twas known ye were Lachlann's daughter. Wasna chance fer him to take such actions. Until now."

"Oh, great. And if he disappeared from under the guards' noses, he could probably bypass the shield you've placed around the manor."

Now what was she going to do? Bryce and his family were protected by Alfar magic—maybe faerie magic could shield her from Pagas. She'd check with Jayse when he returned.

"'Tis a concern. However, I spoke with Gowthaman afore he left an' he promised to ask the Alas—Alastriona, the faerie defenders, to form a protection fer ye similar to our shield about the manor. Dinna seem to believe 'twould be a problem."

Lucidea tugged on the chain and pulled the tiny stone from under her shirt. "And I've got this. That should count for something."

"Aye. All in this house are similarly protected."

"You, too?" It didn't surprise her that in protecting Jayse's family any who were pulled into the family circle would be cared for as well.

Coralie blushed a faint pink when she nodded. "I dinna believe 'twas needed, but 'twas insisted upon. I see the wisdom in the action. Milady?"

"Yeah," Ignoring the use of the honorific, Lucidea answered

absently as she stared into the tiny stone. She'd thought the swirls of violet were encased in the crystal, but as she watched, the soft clouds of color moved through the stone. Hypnotizing... she chuckled to herself—kind of like a retro lava lamp.

"Further evidence has been discovered."

Evidence. The word drew her back to the problems at hand. Evidence she understood, much better than the abstract concept of magic. Evidence she could focus on, deal with, use to solve the problem. She slipped the crystal charm back under her shirt. "Tell me."

"From what yer guards were able to find in Pagas' rooms, an' in the area of the library he'd used fer his spell castin' to call upon the fire elemental, 'tis certain he is no longer within the Alfar world. Nor are there signs he may be hidin' in this world. He dinna ken the Faerie world... at least so we believe. Gowthaman has informed the defenders and asked them to watch fer Pagas."

"Then where could he be? Another parallel world? How many of these things are there?"

Coralie laughed. "Only a few days ago we dinna ken more than the Alfar an' human worlds, an' the place holdin' Morghan. An' now I have heard tales of at least two more—"

"Two?"

"Oh, aye. The Faerie Otherworld an' the world where the traveler Bard is from."

"That's right. Jayse told me a little about Bard. I'd forgotten."

"Milady, imagine the possibilities. There may be worlds upon worlds, mayhaps as many as the stars in our skies. Mayhaps each star is a world. Mayhaps as many as grains of sand boundin' the seas. Mayhaps..."

"I get the picture." Her brain was rapidly being forced into overdrive again, so Lucidea fell silent. Only a few months ago she was happily—okay, maybe not all that happily—ensconced in her world of forensic art and police work. That was her world. Not an underwater kingdom she still didn't have the courage to visit. Still, she'd accepted the world of the Alfar-Sindhu. And, only days ago, she'd accepted that the man she loved was part of the ruling family of yet another interconnected world. But, to even consider the concept of hundreds, thousands, maybe even millions of those similar yet different worlds. Where were Carl Sagan, or even Rod Serling, when you needed them?

"So, then the upstart of this is that Pagas has taken himself off to some world, and we have no idea which one, probably to work on some way to kill me off so he can come back and take over the Alfar-Sindhu."

"Aye, that sums up the situation."

"Great. That makes my life sooo easy." Lucidea propped her elbow on the table, supported her cheek in her hand and stared at Coralie. "Just great. Now what?"

"All ye can do is wait. 'Tis no' action we ken to find where he went. He dinna provide us with a locating device." Coralie touched a spot between her breasts.

Lucidea sighed. "Okay, we wait and watch. And, I see by the hesitation in your face, there's more we need to discuss. I could use some coffee first."

"The carafe on the warmer in the corner is full." Coralie grinned as she rose and moved toward the small counter. "Yer very predictable in this, Lucidea."

"I lived on coffee in college, sometimes I don't believe I can think without the jolt of caffeine. Oh, I know that's not true. There's just not much I love more than that bitter-smooth bite as it flows over my tongue."

"No' even... Jayse?"

Lucidea accepted the mug and cupped her hands around the warming ceramic. "No, for him I'd give up coffee in a second. I don't have a clue how our relationship is going to work out. We're literally from different worlds." She snorted with a short laugh. "That sure puts a slant on romantic songs and stories, huh? That lovers really can be from far reaching worlds? Yikes, I'm not ready to explore that line of thought. What else do we have to talk about?"

Coralie shifted a few papers nervously then lifted a narrow

slip of what appeared to be a very old parchment. She studied it for a moment then handed the page to Lucidea.

"What's this?"

"'Twas found among Pagas' notes. None of our scholars has been able to translate the words, fer 'tis in no language of the Alfar world."

Lucidea set her mug aside and cleared a spot on the littered table. Leaning close to the slip of parchment, she studied the flowing, ornate handwriting. From the length of the lines, she assumed it might be a poem and Coralie agreed. Something about the writing called to her soul, and her heart ached to know the meanings of the words. Tracing the writing with a fingertip, she shuddered, as if she were absorbing the unknown. The feeling was unsettling, yet pleasantly sensual.

Would Jayse feel the same thing when she showed the paper to him?

"Oh," she exclaimed. "Look, at the top edge. The rest of the edges are a little ragged, like homemade paper. But the top edge is sharp. I'll bet this was cut with a finely honed blade." She angled the page against the light from the tall windows. "Probably not scissors, I'd guess a knife. And look at this." She pointed to a smudge of ink. "I'll bet this is the lower swirl to some letter. Someone cut whatever this is into at least two pieces."

"Ye dinna recognize the language?"

"No, but I'm not an expert in that area. Can we show this to Jayse when he gets back? Maybe it's written in some Faerie language."

"Aye, 'twould be a guid idea. Frcm the prominence this writin' held within Pagas' notes, I'm sure 'tis important. Though, I dinna believe he could read it either. Any other spells or charms he discovered, he copied an' translated fer his use. 'Twas nothin' wi' this."

"Then we have a mystery." She loved a mystery, however, with her life on the line, she wished she could close the book and ignore the possible endings.

A knock on the door drew her from musings growing increasingly morose. Jayse jumped through the opening and spread his arms. "Honey... I'm home."

The serious expression when she'd looked up fled her face and the brightness of her smile matched the elation in Jayse's heart. He waited impatiently for her to carefully place a narrow bit of parchment on the table. But once she had the paper safely tucked away, she leapt to her feet and met him halfway across the room.

The heat of her mouth on his, the warmth of her body as she melded to him, the soft sounds of welcome made deep in her throat...ah, if this was his homecoming, going away might— might—be tolerable.

Coralie chuckled as she passed them on her way from the room. "Ye must be hungry."

"Starved," he managed between kisses.

"I'll bring yer supper in here then."

"Yeah, food would be good, too."

He didn't notice when Coralie softly shut the door. All he cared about was the woman in his arms and the amazingly sensual things just holding her did to his body. Because of his vow, he'd never seriously considered the all-consuming plea-sures of sharing his body with the woman he loved. At this moment, he was consumed, and all it took was seeing her smile.

Moving his mouth to the arched column of her neck, he tasted her skin like the starving man he'd claimed to be. The man he was. She clenched her fingers tight on his shoulders when he yanked the hem of her shirt to the top swell of her breasts and suckled deeply on a lace-covered nipple.

"We can't... here," she gasped as he laved the other nipple and nipped the firm peak.

"Room's too far." He bent, dipped his tongue into her navel, then straightened and looked around the workroom. A door to one side of the exit to the deck looked promising so he backed her in that direction, his hands tight at her waist, his mouth locked upon hers. Angling them sideways, he opened the door to a neat closet with a variety of robes hanging from hooks lining the wall.

He tugged at several, dropping them to the floor to make a snug nest.

"A closet?" Lucidea gasped, then looked down at the pile of soft terrycloth and linked her fingers through his belt loops to pull him in into the cubicle. "Oh, Jayse."

With the door closed, the tiny space provided little maneuvering room, but, thankful she wore sweatpants, he easily shoved the fabric to her ankles. Her hands sped through unfastening his slacks and easing his boxers past his raging erection. There was no room to lay down, so he knelt, parted her folds with his thumbs, and tasted. No ambrosia could surpass the nectar he drew from her. Cupping her bottom, he held her writhing body against his tender assault until she moaned his name.

Moving to a cross-legged position, he encouraged her to straddle his lap and take him deep within her body. They rocked together, a slow urgency of sighs and moans, the sliding of his length, slick and hot, their tiny world filled with the expressions of love and desire. He knew nothing more. Cared for nothing more. Loved no one more.

Lucidea collapsed against him with a drawn out sigh. The clenching of her inner muscles arched his hips hard and high and he smiled at the silver and violet dancing in the darkness.

Pulled together and barely dressed, they escaped their tiny love nest only moments before Coralie carried a laden tray into the workroom. Silently, she gave them a smile, set the tray on the counter near the coffee carafe, and closed the door behind her.

"Do you think she suspects?" Lucidea asked as she rose to explore the delightful aroma rising from a covered plate.

Jayse chuckled. Maybe he could bring that cute blush to her cheeks. "No. I think she knows."

Lucidea glanced quickly at the closet, at the hall door, then at him, and he smiled. Bright pink infused her cheeks. She shook her finger at him. "You said that on purpose."

"Maybe, but she's not dumb. Bring that food over here, woman."

"Clear off the table, man. There's some papers there I don't want to get messy."

Jayse stacked the odd shaped pages and placed them at one corner. "Ready. What were you studying so intensely when I got here?" He had so much to tell her about his amazing discoveries that day, as well as his more mundane plans for the faire site. But, the expression on her face, the focus of her attention at that moment, was more important. There was plenty of time for his news.

"Looks good, huh?" Lucidea placed a large plate before him filled with roasted potatoes and vegetables and a thick filet of grilled fish.

The aroma of herbs tickled his nostrils and he inhaled deeply. "Sure does, but..." He gave her what he hoped was a lecherous grin. "It doesn't smell near as good as you do."

Lucidea covered her cheeks to hide her renewed blush so he wrapped his fingers around her wrists and pulled her hands away. "Please don't do that. I'm sorry. It's just that you're so cute when you blush."

She slapped at his shoulder. "I'll give you cute, buster."

"Promise? When?"

"Eat your dinner."

"Only if you answer my question. What were you thinking about when I got home?"

After sitting in her chair, she shuffled through the papers he'd so neatly stacked. She pulled out a narrow page and looked at it for a long time before handing it to him. "Can you read this?"

"What is it?"

A shrug lifted her shoulders. "We don't know. It was found in Pagas' notes. Coralie says he always translated any information or spells he found, but there's no translation for this. Look at the paper. It's ragged around the edges, except for at the top. I think this is part of something else and was cut apart with a knife. I wish we knew what it said. It might be important in figuring out where Pagas went."

Jayse chewed a bite of vegetables and swallowed as he remembered a message from Gowthaman. "Oh, by the way, I was supposed to tell you that Gowthaman talked to Derrik about a faerie shield over this place to match your Alfar protection. I'd say by now it's probably a done deal."

"Coralie mentioned that, too. Looks like we're dealing with two peas from the same pod with Pagas and Feidhlim. And we can't find either one."

The need to protect surged through him but his inadequacies made the paper rustle in his shaking hand. "We're all safe here. Promise."

"Thanks, but I know that's not a promise anyone can make when dealing with either one of these two... creeps. So, do you recognize the writing? Is it some Faerie language?"

He studied the flowing script. It wasn't Faerie but the odd form and strange combination of the letters looked familiar. "It's not Faerie, but it might be fairy."

"Huh? Care to clear that up for me?"

"It's not f-a-e-r-i-e Faerie, but I think it could be f-a-i-r-y fairy writing."

"Thanks. Clear as mud."

"Remember I told you that Korin is a fairy—slightly altered, but a fairy nonetheless."

"Then, maybe he can read it." She leaned forward eagerly and reached for the parchment.

"Maybe, but if this is an older form of their written language, I don't know." Disappointment flared in her eyes and he hated dulling her brightness. "However, my aunt Kaelea has studied the fairy language extensively and is the closest there is to an expert."

"Oh." The disappointment had taken root in her expression, but he knew a way to bring back her excitement.

"Eat your supper, then how about we take a walk. To the Otherworld."

· · ·

L ucidea raced through her meal, watching Jayse as he ate more leisurely. She knew he did it on purpose to draw out her misery. While fear of entering the Alfar-Sindhu world kept her on dry ground, the thought of visiting the Faerie Otherworld had her almost bouncing in her seat with impatience.

Finally, Jayse laid his napkin beside his plate, then handed her the parchment. "Keep that safe while we tell the others where we're going. Are you ready?"

Nodding, she dragged him laughing from the room. The others were lingering over their meal in the dining hall, and when Jayse announced their intensions, Nightshade asked to accompany them.

"I'll find my way home from there, sweet cheeks," he explained to Lucidea. "There's permanently open portals available for those who know how to see them."

Another delay gnawed at her belly, although Nightshade gathered his two packs quickly, spoke rapid farewells, and joined them in the courtyard. "When all this is over, this would be an excellent place for a permanent portal, Jayse," he said with a final wave to Breanna.

"Good idea. Ready, baby?"

Lucidea nodded and held her breath while Jayse created a portal. She angled forward, taking in the view of a lush green forest and bright evening sky surrounded by the soft shimmer. Would she feel anything when she stepped through? Maybe some magical jolt or something?

"Some people say they can feel the magic when they pass through a portal."

Her perceptive man guessed her concerns again.

He continued. "Korin had some difficulties at first because of prohibitions against his race entering our part of the Otherworld." A look of doubt crossed Jayse's face. "Since we didn't know about your race... if you feel anything uncomfortable tell me right away. Okay? Anything that feels... wrong."

"Yes, yes, I will. Can we go now?" She inched forward.

Jayse laughed and took her hand. Nightshade took her other hand and she smiled her thanks to each. As excited as she was for this experience, it was comforting to have someone with her. Maybe that's why she was so afraid to enter the Alfar world... she'd be alone.

"One, two, three," Nightshade counted and they moved forward together.

CHAPTER

TWENTY-TWO

L ucidea experienced no strange or unusual feelings as they passed into the shimmering oval, and slowly released her held breath. Stepping into the Faerie Otherworld was like stepping into a breath of fresh air. Colors as vivid as the auras she still saw when she lowered her mental guard burst onto her senses. It was as if she could pick out each leaf in clear definition. Would the human world appear this way without the haze of pollution? Her thoughts stalled. When did she start thinking in terms of the human world?

Shortly after they entered the small glade, Nightshade waved goodbye and jogged down a faint path. "How does he run in those sandals?" she asked Jayse as Nightshade disappeared into the trees.

Jayse shrugged. "I've given up trying to figure out anything with him. Every time I think I know him, something new pops up. Like this business in the Middle East. Come on, Kae should be glad to have some company. Except for coming to Chance's birth, she hasn't been allowed to use the portals lately."

Lucidea searched her memory. Jayse's aunt was one of the twins—the very pregnant twin. "So, there's a danger in using the portals while pregnant?"

The look he bestowed upon her made her wish she had a reason to know the answer, but it was too soon. There was so much uncertainty surrounding them; now wouldn't be a good time anyway. She fought a twinge of guilt, but couldn't determine if it was because she didn't want to be pregnant just then—or if she did.

"There doesn't appear to be any danger."

"Huh? Danger?" He grinned. Had he somehow followed her line of thought better than she had?

"In using portals while pregnant. Until this family came along, there really wasn't much reason to worry about it. There wasn't that much contact with the human world and the Faerie aren't a very, uh, prolific race."

"Couldn't prove it by your family." She nudged his ribs with her elbow.

"The healers believe it's because of our human blood. Makes us more... fertile." He waggled his eyebrows.

"If everyone's like you, it's not for lack of practice."

The kiss he teased her lips with needed no practice. But, the rustle of the parchment she'd wrapped in plain paper and tucked into her waistband stopped him from drawing her closer. The look in his eyes as he drew back begged forgiveness. "We'd better see what Kae has to say about this writing." He passed his hand over the curve of her bottom. "We can practice later."

She'd created a sensual monster. She liked it.

The door of a small cabin opened and Bard stepped onto the porch. He smiled and angled to call back inside. "More visitors, Kaelea."

Jayse led Lucidea across the clearing and into the tidy cabin. Kae sat next to Gowthaman at a round table. A large book of thick, handmade paper lay open before them.

Bard brought a fifth chair to the table. "What brings you here, Jayse?

Giving Bard a reproaching glare, the pregnant woman struggled to half rise and extend her hand toward Lucidea. "I'm Kaelea, Jayse's aunt. There were too many folks around when Chance was born so I never got to meet you properly." She turned her reproach on Jayse, then grinned. "Welcome to the family, Lucidea."

"Thanks." She didn't want to waste time in chit-chat, she had some practicing to do. Fighting the heat the thought brought to her face, she jumped right in with her concerns. "You've heard about my... heritage?"

"A little. Gowthaman's been pretty tight lipped about you."

Lucidea spread her hands. "I'm afraid I don't know very much myself. I didn't want to accept my heritage and now there hasn't been much time to explore futher. To get to the main issue, there's this guy who seems to be a lot like Feidhlim. Mostly because he wants to destroy me and my family and take over the Alfar-Sindhu."

Jayse shoved his chair back. "Dea Annie. This is...? There's really...?"

She leaned over to touch his shoulder. "Yes, I just figured it out this afternoon. Sorry I didn't say anything sooner. I already knew Pagas murdered my father and somehow magically called the fire elemental, hoping the creature would kill Morghan. Don't worry, though. Coralie says I've been protected. Now, especially, with your family. That's not the problem. That's not why we're here."

Slipping the papers from her waistband, she unwrapped the scrap of parchment. "This was found among Pagas' papers. Unlike his other... research, there was no translation. Jayse says it might be fairy. Oh, I mean Korin's language. He said maybe you could read this, Kaelea."

"Please, call me Kae." She took the offered parchment and studied it briefly before motioning to Gowthaman. He rose and leaned over her shoulder. After a moment, she glanced up at him. "What do you think?"

"The hand is similar. Perhaps it is the same."

"That's what I thought. Bard, would you get my brother and Korin? They need see this." Bard kissed her cheek and silently left the cabin.

"What? What do they need to see? What does that say?"

Lucidea scooted her chair sideways, stretching to see the parchment. With Kae's subdued reaction, this had to be something major. Maybe it was a clue to solving at least one of their problems.

Gowthaman turned to the large book and flipped through the pages. "After Jayse's discovery today—"

"A discovery of what?" Things were moving quickly and there was too much for Lucidea to learn and understand. She felt like she was taking two flailing steps back for every step forward.

"We spent time in another discovery." Jayse stared at the ceiling as he spoke, and his mouth twitched into a smile. He lowered his gaze to look at her. "We need to set aside some time... for talking. I think we both have a lot to say."

"No kidding. Tonight. As soon as we get home."

"Yes, dear." His deadpan expression brought laughter to the table.

"It's good to hear you laugh, Gowthaman."

"I have been somewhat somber of late. Facing the thing representing my fears appears to have given me some hope. I do not doubt that the fears remain, but for the time being, I am content."

Lucidea spread her hands and looked from one to the other around the table. If they kept talking in circles, she'd never understand anything. With a sigh, Gowthaman took pity on her. "Not long ago, Feidhlim held me captive and his seeker, a faerie with a talent to enter another's mind, learned my thoughts, my dreams, the darkness within me. It was... rape. Today, Jayse discovered the castle where I was held, hidden here in Faerie." He smiled, but the pain of his confession remained in his eyes. "We were discussing that castle when you arrived."

Kae rested her hand on Gowthaman's arm. "No wonder you haven't spoken of this before. I had no idea. I'm so sorry."

"I do not believe there is anything another can do. Breanna's healing can dull the pain, but can not take away the memory of what happened."

The ache she felt whenever she spoke to a victim curled deep in Lucidea's belly. Unable to imagine the rape of someone's mind, she could only draw upon her experience with other rape victims. Maybe... "Gowthaman, sometimes it really does help to talk about what happened. And with someone who understands."

He shook his head. "There is no one. I believe the power of the seeker's attack would destroy most minds. I do not know why mine was spared." He stared at the table. "There are moments... I wish it was not."

Lucidea wasn't about to give up on helping him. "Talk to Carrie. While her attack was different, I'm sure she's gone through many of the same kinds of feelings. She told me she's going to start volunteering at a crisis center, to be available to talk with others who've been assaulted. Try, Gowthaman. You might be pleasantly surprised."

A glimmer of hope swirled through his dark eyes. "Mayhaps. But now is not the time to speak of my concerns. The others have arrived."

Jayse leaned close to whisper. "Thanks."

She nodded. "I'm not going to let up on him. Once a victim starts talking about their abuse, it's often the key to healing."

With more chairs crowded around the table, the group settled back expectantly. Lucidea knew Jayse's father, so studied Korin. This man, with odd silver-gold hair, was once tiny and had wings? He caught her staring and smiled.

"My wings were destroyed in battle. In my choice to remain this size to be with Nanceen, it is a small sacrifice."

"Are all my thoughts just written across my face?" Or could this family really read minds?

"No," Korin stated. "I don't read minds. Your face is expressive, revealing your questions. You wonder what my wings looked like, don't you?"

"Uh, yeah. I can't imagine."

With a cocky grin, he rose. "Then watch and see."

Moments later Korin stood before her with huge blue and silver wings folded against his back. Then, the wings opened fully and she gasped. His butterfly wings looked so soft and she wished she could touch the fine texture. She sighed when the marvelous vision faded and Korin returned to his chair.

"Do you miss them?" Immediately regretting her spontaneous question, Lucidea tugged her lower lip between her teeth.

He arched one pale eyebrow. "At times. Now, why have you called us here?"

Kae cleared her throat, then began. "When Jayse accidentally found the castle today, Gowthaman noticed a crest above the doors and windows. He recognized that crest from this." She touched her fingertips to the large book. "Lucidea, you've been told that our family's connection to Oberon and Titania has only recently been discovered, right?"

She nodded and folded her hands to keep them from shaking with nervous excitement.

"This book is a journal, written by Oberon. It's really different because it's written backwards—I mean time wise, with the newest entries at the beginning. It was in the final entry, or the first entry, it's difficult to explain. Anyway, that's where we discovered our connection to those fey rulers. And the fact that Feidhlim has human blood as well."

"You're kidding. But, wasn't he trying to scour all traces of humans from Faerie?"

"Ironic, isn't it?" Kae lifted the Alfar-Sindhu parchment and held out her other hand. Gowthaman placed a similar slip of parchment on her palm. "Lucidea brought us a bit of writing found in her world. The script and handwriting matches that in the journal." She lifted one hand. "This was written by Oberon."

"How would it have gotten into my world?"

Jayse squeezed her hand and she realized how easily she'd claimed the Alfar-Sindhu world as hers. Some magic must be at work in her mind.

Gowthaman answered, "That is a question for which we need to seek an answer. Mayhaps as he studied, Pagas came across this and returned to your world with it. Another possibility—this was placed within your world for a reason. Mayhaps to await discovery at this time. None know the reasoning in Oberon's mind."

"What happened to Oberon? And Titania? So much history is related in Shakespeare's play, but not that."

Korin took up the tale. "My lands were long ruled by the Fir Dhaerrig, an unpleasant race of fairies. Their last king held in his possession a document that his family altered long ago to fortify their claim of kingship. This document had been written by Oberon and within it he named his successors. Both to my fairy realm and to the entire world we call the Otherworld. He and his love, Titania, had tired of their lives within these worlds and after his proclamation, they passed into still another world. No one knows where that world may be."

"Coralie will be thrilled to hear that," Lucidea mumbled. Then at the odd expressions of her tablemates, she explained, "She believes that there are hundreds of parallel worlds. In fact, she's sure that Pagas is hiding in one of them."

"A good possibility," Jaye said. "Now, what about the document Lucidea provided?"

Gowthaman turned to the front of the journal and pointed to a line drawing of a design. "The crest decorating the castle is this, Oberon's crest. I brought the journal here, for I have not yet become proficient in fairy languages, and asked Kae if she remembered any entries that may have mentioned the castle. As we searched the pages, we found a slip of ancient parchment, also written in Oberon's hand."

Kae held up the two pages. "It's obvious that these are part of the same document. The coloration and shape of the parchment is the same. Look how three edges of each are ragged, while the fourth is a straight cut."

"I think the cut was made by a knife." All eyes turned to Lucidea and she stammered to complete her thought. "There's no extra bend to the paper as if it were cut by scissors. And I'd say that's all there is to that page since there's no other cuts. Can you read it?"

With a glance that slid from Gowthaman to Korin, Kae nodded. "I can, but I have a feeling... Korin?"

"Place the cut edges together and we shall see."

While Gowthaman cleared the journal from the table and Kae carefully laid the two halves close together, Lucidea turned to Jayse. "What are they talking about? Why not just read it and let's find out what it says."

"Patience, Dea Annie."

Kae fit the two pieces together and stepped back.

Staring at the ceiling, Lucidea said, "Well, that's exciting."

Korin peered closely at the alignment, made a minute adjustment, then straightened. He spoke a single word that rolled like thunder through the small cabin. Before the echo faded, a faint glow of silver, gold, and emerald green lifted from each written word and swirled in a dance above the table. A low hum vibrated from the whirlwind of colors.

Lucidea gasped when she realized the hum had become words. Words she couldn't understand, but spoken in a voice so beautiful she couldn't keep tears from springing to her eyes. Caught in the spell of the voice, she cried out when the words ceased. The glowing swirl sank back to the parchment and with a brief blaze, rejoined the two halves to a single page.

When she could rip her gaze from the parchment, the faces around her glistened with tear-stained dampness. She hadn't been the only one affected.

"That was the voice of Oberon," Korin whispered, his melodious voice harsh after the beauty of the dancing words.

"Oh, my..." No statement, no praise was enough to express the joy, the sorrow, the pain and healing that filled her. How could anything be so beautiful? And yet, so terrifying in that beauty. She fought past her speechlessness. "But what... what did it... he say?"

Kae closed her eyes. "The last part... 'Thus say I the prophecy of Oberon'."

"What about the rest of it?" Impatient to know, Lucidea stared at each of the others. Yes, she'd been affected, but not as much as they had been. Was it because they had drops of Oberon's blood in their veins, and she didn't? An odd pain tightened around her heart. She'd give anything to be a part... no, she shook her head. She wouldn't fall into a trap created by the mesmerizing voice. She needed to know what this prophecy said and why it came to light now.

"Guys?" she whispered. What if they were in a trance she couldn't break through?

Bard caught her eye and winked. "Give them a few moments. This is always the way it is when Oberon's voice is heard." He shrugged. "It seems you and I have returned sooner than the rest."

"Any idea why? Could it be because we're not descended from him?"

"I hadn't considered that, but it's a good possibility. But see, the others have returned. Kaelea, can you translate the prophecy now?"

She blinked a few times, then rubbed her temple. "Prophecy?"

Lucidea hesitated, then touched the parchment. "That's what you said when the voice stopped. 'Thus say I the prophecy of Oberon'."

"Oh, I don't remember. Uh, sure, let me take a look at the parchments."

"There's only one now—it fused back together." Lucidea slid the prophecy across the table.

Kae carefully picked up the paper and studied both sides. She ran her finger gingerly along the repaired line of separation. "Interesting. I would guess that means it was really meant to be found now. Okay, give me a couple of seconds to look at it here."

The silence grew unbearable and Lucidea shifted in her chair. Jayse rested his hand on her thigh and gave a reassuring pat.

Finally, Kae looked up and smiled. "I'll read this now, since I know everyone's impatient. Then I'll copy down the translation so we can study it further."

She paused then began reading. "This first half is what was found in the journal.

'Alfar king away doth hide
Unbidden in ancient fire's mist
Blood of human rises high,
Deeply forgotten blade doth twist.
And so the prophets sing.
Daughter of Alfar! Son of Fey!
Worlds together bring!
Child of Darkness, brother of light,
Once found is sword, now born.
Child of light, sister of darkness
Charms to choose evil or the fair,'"

Kae looked around the table. "And this last part is what Lucidea brought to us.

'Of life or death until once more
Loud the prophets sing.
Daughter of Alfar! Son of Fey!
Worlds together bring!
Once lost, the newly known
The hidden King doth find.
The prison mist destroy,
The anguished mind restore.
Only then the prophets sing.
Daughter of Alfar! Son of Fey!
Worlds together bring!'"

TWENTY-THREE

P ropped against the headboard with a yellow legal pad resting on her thigh, Lucidea studied her copy of Oberon's prophecy. She tapped her pen against her lower lip. After a lengthy discussion of possible meanings for the prophecy, she wasn't sure they were any closer to discerning the truth than when they started. When she and Jayse returned to the manor, she'd copied sections of the words onto the pad, divided as the parchments had been before magic rejoined the two halves.

Jayse gave a soft, snorting snore and snuggled deeper into his pillow. With an indulgent smile, she tugged the blankets up over his shoulder then smoothed a strand of hair behind his ear. During the discussion at Kaelea's cabin, he'd explained how he'd literally found the castle of his dreams. She'd given deeper explanations of Pagas' actions, her uncle's disappearance and what little she knew of Alfar history. She paused now, wondering again at Gowthaman's startled reaction when she mentioned the Alfar ancestor, Dea Anu. There would be more long discussions in the future.

Returning to the prophecy, she examined the lines that they believed they'd deciphered. The Alfar king was Morghan, the references to fire and mist obviously pointing to that conclusion.

Although she hated to admit it, she was probably the daughter of Alfar, with Jayse the son of Fey. They'd already brought worlds together. Those conclusions were the easy part.

Blood of human rises high. That could refer to the blending of human and fey blood. She made a note next to that line. The sword? Jayse had dreamed of a sword. And a sword held a prominent place on Oberon's crest. But what did the sword twisting mean? Twisting into what?

The final lines of the prophecy gave her hope. To her, the lines meant Morghan would be released from his mist-laden incarceration. However, if she represented the child of Alfar, she wouldn't be the once lost, too. That would be too much for which to hope. So, who would release Morghan?

The remaining lines spoke of children. So many contrasts: light and dark, evil or fair, life or death. Try as she might, she found no answers.

What? Why? Who? The questions made her head pound, but she couldn't set them aside. The lines were confusing enough, but somehow she knew there was also a reason for the prophecy to have been divided. The Faerie-found portion spoke more of the Alfar, while the portion Coralie provided sang more to her of Faerie.

The gentle sounds of Jayse's sleep lulled her and although the whats and whys continued to pulse through her mind, she set her pad and pen aside, turned off the light and slipped down in bed.

"'Bout time. G'night, baby." Jayse spooned against her back and wrapped an arm over her waist. In the comfort of his sleepy embrace, the questions faded to darkness.

Feidhlim rolled from the bed, stretched, then covered himself with a silk robe. Crossing to a large desk under the room's single window, he contemplated his next moves. The large sheets scattered over the desk contained vast information, and painful realizations.

For nearly a week he had been able to shove aside the pain of bearing human blood in his veins, keeping his agony private. He'd studied the genealogies in minute detail and other than that single union, only pure faerie blood had entered his line. Only once, and that so long ago that even faerie memories grew dim and his ancestor had become legend. Yet, that taint remained always a part of him.

Was that tiny droplet of blood the reason for a human frailty, his inability to tolerate drink? Or perhaps why the taking of a human female was ultimately more satisfying than a tryst with a faerie maid? Why he hated Zeroun with an all-consuming passion?

Using slow, deliberate movements, he rolled two of the genealogies together and slipped them into a thick leather tube. The rest of the parchments he wadded into a tight ball and shoved to the floor. Kicking the paper ball, he moved toward the corner where a cushioned platform had been created for his meditations. Settling into a comfortable position, he took several long breaths, letting each out slowly.

He'd improved his technique and quickly found a place of silence within his mind. There, he called to his son.

After repeating the call, he waited, listening to the silence. It had been a disappointing week of attempts with no response, no contact, not even a hint of the connection that had unreasonably thrilled him.

Neither was there any taint of the force that had refused his single contact.

Unable to contact his child, unable to impose his will upon an infant, unable to control... Feidhlim slammed his fist against the wall. A low moan rose from the bed and he slowly turned his face toward the sound. Finding focus for his frustration, he dropped his robe as he crossed the room and crawled across the wide bed to the woman cowering against the wall.

Later, when the woman no longer cried out and her struggles weakened to a pathetic shaking of the chains binding her to the bed, he dressed and found Osric in a common room, lounging before the fireplace. Feidhlim took a nearby chair and stared into the fire. "What news?"

Osric straightened. "My lord, they have already begun preparing the land for building."

"So soon? Interesting."

"Yes, my lord. Your spies state that once the humans have completed providing power and other human requirements to the area, faerie builders will complete the project."

Feidhlim let his surprise show through his arched eyebrows. "What do you know of the plans, of what they mean to build?"

"Among smaller buildings, there are plans for a castle."

"Small wonder, then, that faerie builders are involved. Humans long ago lost interest in ancient constructions. This should be... entertaining."

"What devilment do you plan? How shall we disrupt their progress?" Eager, Osric sat on the edge of his chair and leaned his elbows on his knees.

"Devilment? Slow their progress?" Feidhlim shook his head. "No, I don't believe so."

"But, my lord?"

"Doubt my judgment, Osric?" Confusing this upstart pleased Feidhlim. After Osric's negative response, he explained. "We'll let them build to their heart's content with no interference. Let them become complacent once again. Let them believe we are no longer a threat. Then, and only then, will we make our move."

"My lord, they plan an event for the spring."

"Ah, and...?"

"At this time they will show the faire to other humans. I have not been able to discover further information, but given time I shall know what they know."

"Then we shall also plan for spring."

"For the first of May, my lord."

The first of May. Feidhlim rested his head against the chair back and stared at the plaster ceiling. Long ago, on another Bealtaine, he had been in true glory. Crowned as the horned forest

king, worshiped and adored, he had nearly taken then destroyed
Zeroun's daughter. He smiled. A fitting time for the final meeting.

"Excellent." Standing, he waved a hand toward the hall to his
room. "Remove the woman. I have finished with her."

"How shall I dispose of her, my lord?"

He pierced Osric with a disdaining look. "Simply put her back
where you found her."

In the three weeks since he first discovered Oberon's ruling
seat, Jayse had measured and mapped the entire structure.
Amazed at the striking similarities with his model and the
plans he'd created from his dreams, he stood in a tower room and
peered out a narrow window at the sea. The room was small and
a tiny rodent hole led into the neighboring room.

Once Gowthaman had begun speaking about his experiences,
his hesitant words described the evil Feidhlim created in these
rooms and when he followed Gowthaman and Bard into the
world between worlds. Shuddering, Jayse turned toward the
doorway, trying not to imagine the agonies that had torn the
gentle librarian's mind.

Thankfully, Gowthaman had taken Lucidea's advice and
spoke at length with Carrie, who was thrilled to have a way to
give something back to the family. As if loving Bryce wasn't
enough.

Jayse gave the room a final glance. The tower was an intrinsic
part of the castle, and a traditional feature faire-goers would
expect in his smaller version. He needed to find a way for the
space to function at the faire that wouldn't remind Gowthaman
or Bard of their time as Feidhlim's prisoners. Deep in thought, he
passed through a huge hall and a sparkle of light danced across
the floor before him. He peered up to a stained glass representation of Oberon's crest. The ruler was certainly fond of his symbol;
probably had it embroidered on his underwear.

His laugh ended mid-chuckle. An idea, bright and colorful, a joy-filled use for the tower area exploded fully developed into his mind.

Stumbling, he gasped and pressed his temples with his palms. Just as quickly the pressure was gone. But the idea remained.

A marvelous idea, one Lucidea would love.

A second idea formed, slower, much less startling. She might like this additional idea even more. Whistling, he stuffed his hands in his pockets and strolled from the castle. A quick portal transfer took him to the Zeroun's office.

He was working on his revised plans, searching the Internet for artisans and supplies, when Nightshade knocked on the open office door.

"Hey, Nightshade, come on in. We haven't see you lately." He shoved a chair toward Nightshade then frowned at the man's somber expression. "Sit. What's wrong?"

"Have there been any... communication attempts by Feidhlim?"

"Not one. Bryce has to return to work soon and he and Carrie are talking about moving back home."

"No." Nightshade lunged back to his feet and paced the small office. "They must not be allowed to return. Bryce can come with you through the portals every day, but Carrie and the kids must remain hidden."

"What's happened? What do you know?"

Nightshade perched on the edge of the desk. "I need to talk to Lucidea. Do you have any idea if she still has the renderings she did of Feidhlim?"

"I would imagine so. Probably on her laptop. Has he been seen?" His heart lurched before plunging heavily to the pit of his stomach. Had they really become so complacent in only a few weeks?

Leaning forward, Nightshade clasped his hands between his knees and turned his face to Jayse. "A couple weeks ago a dancer disappeared after a bachelor party. She'd gone off with customers before and stayed away from home for lengthy periods, so her roommate wasn't concerned until the hospital called a few days ago."

"You think Feidhlim had her?"

The flamboyant man's normally merry eyes turned stone cold. "She'd been chained, beaten, raped. Held for a week then dumped in a ditch outside the hotel she'd disappeared from."

Bile burned Jayse's stomach. "What do the police think?"

"She won't talk to them. Detective Corley called me in, but she's not one of my girls and only gave me the barest details. Things I could see for myself. Jayse, it's more than a fear of reprisal keeping her silent. It's as if she can't talk about what happened."

"And you think it's some sort of magical compulsion."

"Honey, wish I could say, but it sure looks that way. I'm hoping she'll respond to a picture. I didn't ask the detective for the drawing, didn't want to explain my reasons."

"Why didn't Detective Corley show her pictures? Unfortunately, they must have a file of rapists that haven't been caught."

Nightshade shrugged. "The detective had some photos and drawings, but nothing brought the girl out of her stupor. I'm thinking the only picture of Feidhlim they have is with the disguise he used when he attacked Carrie. I'm sure he no longer looks like that man. It doesn't appear Mr. Avery is a suspect... at this time. I plan to change that status."

Trusting Nightshade's instincts, Jayse dumped his papers into a folder and grabbed his jacket. "Let's go."

B reanna, dressed in a pale pink coat, looked up from the sandbox now occupying one corner of the courtyard and squealed a welcome. Nightshade knelt and embraced her. "How's my favorite girl?"

"Fine. Mommy's gonna be happy to see you."

"I'll go see her in a minute, sweetheart, but I need to talk to Lucidea first. Do you know where she is?"

Bree nodded happily, her curly pigtails bouncing around her

head. "She's with Gowthaman in the workroom. He's gonna sit by me at supper."

Winking at Jayse over her head, Nightshade rubbed his stomach and said, "Think I could finagle a place beside you, too? Nightshade's kinda hungry."

"Yea! I'll tell Coralie and Tori. They're cooking tonight." After a tight hug around his neck, she ran toward the dining hall doors. "Hi, Unca Jayse," she called as she passed.

"So, honey," Nightshade began as they followed the little girl into the manor. "The two Cs are getting along?"

"The two Cs?"

"Mmm, Coralie and Catori. Have you noticed, by chance, how similar they are? More than just subtleties in action and appearance, there's something else. Haven't been able to put my finger on it yet. But, never fear, Nightshade will solve this mystery, too."

"Yeah, I've noticed. It's eerie sometimes. Lucidea and I have talked about it, but haven't approached either of them yet."

"Start by finding out their family backgrounds."

Jayse grinned. "Advice from a pro?"

"Nope, honey, just common sense."

Lucidea looked up when Nightshade followed Jayse into the room and her expression blossomed into a smile of delight. "You're home early."

He circled the table and leaned close for a kiss. The touch of her tongue to the seam of his lips invited him to come home early every day. If only he had the talent for forming time portals like his sister. At a gentle cough, he drew back.

"Oh, honey, don't let us stop you. Right, Gowthaman?"

The faerie merely smiled beneath one arched eyebrow.

Lucidea conquered her urge to blush and joined in the laughter. "Okay, you guys. Enough. Obviously, I'm glad you're here, too, Nightshade."

"You might not be when we tell you why, sweet cheeks."

The excitement of the discovery Gowthaman brought her fled. The serious expressions stole her smile. "What's happened now?"

Pain and anger filled her heart as she listened in silence to

Nightshade's soft explanation. Even with the many cases of abuse and disappearance her skills had helped solve, she still couldn't believe how inhumanely one person could treat another. But then, Feidhlim wasn't truly human, was he?

When Nightshade's quiet voice faded, Gowthaman rose and stood looking out the tall windows, his forehead pressed against the glass.

She watched him for a long, sympathetic moment before speaking. "How can anyone be so cruel? Oh, I know it's a power thing, but still. He must have studied under the Marquise de Sade."

"Lucidea, he probably *was* de Sade. So, let's do what we can to stop this... animal. Now." The hard glint in Nightshade's eyes made her shiver. Good thing he was on their side, he would be a formidable opponent in whatever business he chose. Then his expression softened. "Let's not tell Carrie about this. Bryce, poor boy, will have to know so he can convince her she and the kids need to stay here. But, I don't want her to shoulder the extra burden. You know her. She'll assume all kinds of unreasonable guilt."

"Agreed," Jayse said. "I'll talk to Bryce this evening."

"I'll have to search through some disks to find that work. I was... I forgot to label it." Distracted at the time by Jayse and the hopes of getting to know him, she'd lapsed on many of her normal routines and practices. She ducked her head to hide a small grin. She rather liked the new routines, though. "I should be able to have them for you after supper."

Gowthaman silently returned to the table. Lucidea expected the dull, haunted expression to fill his eyes, but except for a lingering sadness that mirrored the expressions around the table, his face was calm. "It is a pleasant surprise to have you join us for the evening meal, Nightshade. I, for one, am pleased Jayse invited you when you met this afternoon."

"Good cover, Gowthaman." Nightshade saluted him. "Even if I did have to invite myself." He scooted his chair back, crossed one leg delicately over the other and waved his hand. "So, honeys, what was making the two of you smile so delightfully when we came in?"

The abrupt return of the flamboyant Nightshade startled Lucidea and she stared at him. He gave her a slow wink, a wicked contradiction to his behavior. Contradiction? He was a walking contradiction, and seemingly without thought or effort. Now that she knew more about him—she still knew nothing.

Setting aside her questions—again—she reached for a small volume resting at the center of the table. "Gowthaman brought this to show me."

Jayse turned the book to face him. "*Crystal Tarot?*"

"You can read this?" She traced the ornate lettering with her finger. The angles and swirls reminded her of an odd combination of flowing Arabic and more stark, ancient Celtic runes. "Oh, of course you can, it's your language, isn't it?"

"One of them."

"One of them? How many languages can you read?" Another surprise about the man she loved. She stored the warmth away for later.

Jayse made a show of counting the fingers on his left hand, pausing, then continuing his count as he wiggled the fingers of his right hand. His brow wrinkled and his lips settled into a straight, thin line. "Uh, two."

Trying to assimilate his words, she stared. Laughter burst from her lips. "Oh, you... joker."

"No, I really can read two languages. English and Faerie." He carefully opened the book toward the middle and studied the pages before him. "Although, this looks... well, it would be like you reading English written a few hundred years ago. Different spellings, different words, different meanings. I'm sure I could muddle through this, but it might take some time."

Lucidea leaned closer to look at the carefully inscribed pages. "I'd love it if you would try. With watching over all of us, Gowthaman doesn't have much time. He says..." Unsure she would make sense of what he'd told her earlier, she glanced at Gowthaman. "Would you explain this, please?"

"Jayse, when you first called Lucidea, Dea Annie, it struck an odd chord with me. Like a memory I could almost grasp and hold. I discounted the feeling, for I did not trust my memories at that time. But, when Lucidea supplied what little information she knew about her race history, I realized I recognized the name Dea Anu."

Jayse leaned on the table and tapped the book. "What does this have to do with all that?"

"He's getting to that. Please listen." With a start, she realized Jayse was more impatient to learn her heritage than she was. Failure toppled through her. Why was she so reluctant to learn about her people? Or herself? Coralie had answered her infrequent questions but offered little more, as if hoping she would continue the conversations.

She hadn't. Her friend had even stopped suggesting she enter the loch to discover if she did have the ability to breathe during the watery passage to the world of the Alfar-Sindhu.

Holding back a sigh, she admitted to herself she knew the reason.

Fear. Not fear of the water. Or fear of being of a different race. It was a fear of discovering who she was in light of the changes life recently brought to her. Was she still the Lucidea Ann Galvagin she'd taught herself to be—or had recognizing her strange talents changed her?

Would Jayse love only the Lucidea he first met, or did love grow along with the lovers? When he recognized changes in her, would he leave?

Contemplating her fears only gave them a stronger grip on her heart and soul. She struggled to keep her insecurity hidden— even from herself. It wasn't working. A small part of her wanted to return to the way her life had been, but the vibrant presence of Jayse in her life made that unthinkable.

In being honest with herself, she knew the changes in her were amazingly grand and glorious. Changes that made her more truly her.

That simple fact scared her spitless.

Warmth touched her side. In a crowded world—in any world
—she'd recognize the touch of Jayse's odd aura. Radiating
concern, he wrapped his arm around her shoulder and she leaned
into the offered comfort.

"Dea Annie?"

"I'm sorry. Just thinking."

Jayse stroked a few stray hairs behind her ear. "About what?"

The call to supper came before her answer and Catori's quiet
interruption brought a look to Lucidea's eyes that Jayse could
only interpret as relief. What kind of thoughts did she have that
she was so reluctant to share with him? Did those thoughts have
anything to do with the book?

Over the past days he'd caught her staring out over the loch,
her wistful expression hinting at fear. If only she would talk to
him and tell him what frightened her. Or at least explain why she
changed the subject whenever he tried to discuss her fey world.

Nightshade greeted Catori and rose, motioning for them to
follow. Giving Lucidea the opportunity to lag behind and talk a
few moments, he waved the others on and waited.

Lucidea stood and moved toward the door. "Aren't you
hungry? They planned a surprise menu for tonight and wouldn't
let anyone else near the kitchen. We'd better not keep them waiting. I don't want to be responsible for spoiling dinner."

Covering his sigh with the noisy movement of his chair across
the slate floor, he followed. Eventually she would have to talk to
him; this non-communication couldn't stand between them
much longer. As curious as he was about her world, if she chose
not to embrace that part of her life he would accept her reluctance. At this point, he honestly didn't believe she knew enough
about the Alfar-Sindhu to make such an important decision. And
certainly not alone, not now, not when he loved her. He remained
silent as they strolled hand in hand to the dining hall. Difficult as
it would be, he would bide his time and let her come to him when
she was ready.

They took their places at the table. Puzzled, Jayse gazed at the
empty chair between Gowthaman and Nightshade. Bree had been

so excited for supper, he'd thought she would be the first one at the table. He glanced at Carrie, but she was busy with the baby and hadn't noticed the empty seat.

Bryce rushed into the dining hall and cupped his hands to peer through the window into the shadowed courtyard. He jerked the door open and stepped outside, returning immediately. "Where's Bree? She's not in her room."

CHAPTER
TWENTY-FOUR

A rms laden with a heavy platter, Coralie entered the dining hall. "Bree? She was helpin' in the kitchen a bit ago. But, I sent her off to play while we finished. I dinna think... I believed she would... she dinna go to Gowthaman?"

Joining the others, Jayse looked at Gowthaman. His brown face tightened with agony and he closed his eyes. "She did not join us in the workroom."

Chance held tightly to her breast, Carrie struggled to rise. "Bryce, you looked—"

"Everywhere in the suite," he answered. "And she's not in the courtyard, the kitchen or the workroom."

"We know that, honey." Nightshade shoved his plate away and folded his hands on the table. "Get hold of yourself, man. She's probably playing a hiding game."

Carrie shook her head. "No, she wouldn't. I mean, she knows how dangerous that might be. She always tells someone where she's going. Oh, God. You don't suppose..."

Jayse had been fighting that same thought. Feidhlim. Had the bastard somehow found a way to circumvent the Alfar magic to take Breanna? But, if that was the case, wouldn't he have taken Chance instead? Jayse rose and braced himself, straight-armed, on the table. "Carrie, calm down. I'm sure she's here somewhere. We'll start a methodical search of the manor then... What?"

Lucidea had been pulling on his sleeve, and when she finally had his attention she wrapped her fingers around the chain at her neck and pulled the small charm from under her shirt. "What about Gowthaman's stones? Isn't that what they're for?"

The mingled sighs of relief sounding around the table dropped him back to his chair. "Thank you for your calm head, Dea Annie. Gowthaman?"

The tight set of Gowthaman's jaw remained but his eyes were clear as he tangled his fingers in the chain he wore about his neck and retrieved a stone swirling with clouds of red. "Forgive me. I should have remembered the locator. I shall..." He rose and moved a few steps from the table. In the clear space, he grasped the stone tightly in his hand and pressed the side of his fist to his forehead.

Lucidea gasped as deep crimson flared around him. At a questioning glance from Jayse, she whispered, "His aura." Nodding his understanding, he studied Gowthaman, tense and waiting—like every person at the table. Maybe Bree had just run off to play somewhere and lost track of time. As a child, she had done that herself, and been reprimanded for the behavior many times. Even as an adult, she easily lost track of time when something interested her.

Holding that possibility tightly, the sudden realization of the fearful focus of those around her brought another sharp intake of breath. Had Feidhlim taken Bree?

Jayse relaxed his stance and stepped closer to rest his hand on her shoulder. The soothing touch of his thumb stroking her neck didn't ease the anxiety, but she appreciated the effort.

A pink glow formed around Gowthaman's closed fist and his expression grew confused. "Is there... nearby... a cave?" He opened his eyes and stared at Lucidea.

The intensity of his gaze made her feel as though he looked into her soul. Lucidea shook her head. "Not that I know of."

"She is close, in a cave."

"Is she okay? What have they done to her?" Carrie's voice rose until Chance whimpered and pushed at her breast with his tiny fists.

Bryce held them close. "Shh, sweetheart. Gowthaman—"

"'Tis a cave." Coralie frowned when the focus moved from Gowthaman to her. "But I dinna ken how she could find the way. 'Tis at the edge of the loch. At the base of the tall outcropping."

"Where Morghan..." Lucidea felt her eyes go wide. Bree couldn't be there. No one went there. Not since her uncle had been sucked into the vortex. "Coralie, no, not there."

"Aye, milady. I fear 'tis so. There is a passage from the manor, but 'twas supposed to be shielded."

"We're going there now," Carrie demanded. "Gowthaman, you're sure she's safe?"

The lines of worry at Gowthaman's eyes eased and he tucked the stone under his tunic. "She is... playing. Coralie, will you take us to this place? I fear your beautiful meal is to be delayed."

Coralie led the anxious adults through a disguised panel in the kitchen pantry. As she trailed the others, Lucidea turned and walked backwards, staring at the opening. She had no idea there was a passageway from the manor to the outcropping. If she had known, maybe she could have used it to sneak up behind the fire elemental while Morghan fought him and... and what? Distracted her uncle so that he was killed instead of taken prisoner? There was so much she didn't know, so much she had to learn. How would she ever grasp even a tenth of what she needed to understand?

She ran into a solid body and froze. Nightshade's dry chuckle sounded close to her ear. "Not used to so many secrets, are you, sweet cheeks?"

Planting her hands firmly on her hips she whirled to face him. "Not like you are obviously." Shame at her snide outburst burned through her, but Nightshade only smiled with a knowing, benign stretch of his lips.

"So it would seem, honey. So it would seem. Let's go, Lucidea. I think you need to be there when we find Breanna."

She did. This was her home and the mystery of Morghan's disappearance hers to solve. In finding the cave, perhaps Bree had also led her to some clue, maybe even an answer. Her footsteps quickened. Nightshade continued chuckling and wrapped an arm about her shoulder as they followed the wide corridor.

The floor, though smooth and finished like an interior hall-way, rose and fell as if they strolled over ocean waves following the descent ever downward. Lucidea found no source for the light filling the long hall and thankfully the air remained fresh. Although she never feared being underground, something close to fright pushed her forward and simultaneously pulled her back.

"Breanna Joy MacAlister." Bryce's father voice echoed into the passageway.

"Uh-oh."

Lucidea bit back a grin at the tiny, contrite voice. Relief at finding the girl safe and unharmed chased away her personal concerns as she stepped into a large, round chamber.

Her first sight of the cave froze the breath in her lungs. Except for Bryce, Carrie, and Coralie, the others joined her in open-mouthed awe, turning slowly in place to take in the wonders of sparkling crystals against stark black stone. Close to where Bryce and Carrie spoke urgently with their daughter, the wall, covered with a thin film of water, shimmered in the pale light.

Drawn to the wall, she reached out and tentatively touched the water. Cool and damp, it flowed over her hand, but didn't run down her arm. The black stone was hard and smooth beneath her palm, but she saw an open space... the open sea. She jerked her hand back and cradled it against her chest. Only the stone glis-tened behind the ever-moving water.

Taking a deep breath, she touched one finger to the wall, and as the water flowed she again witnessed the vast expanse of the clear sea. Fish and odd nameless creatures swam before her, encouraging her, pulling her closer. She flattened her palm to the stone and an underwater palace appeared, vast as the sea but crumbled to ruin.

Jayse's presence at her side brought with it a strange flush of courage and she knew what she needed to do. Drawing her lower lip in between her teeth, she lifted her other hand, hesitated, then slowly pressed through the water to touch the stone. Warmth curled through the cool water and she entered the palace to stand at the entrance to a rubble-filled chamber. A pile of stones centered in the room steamed as if containing the remnants of eternal fire. The odd thought struck her deeply and she gnawed on her lip.

Centered above the destruction and surrounded by swirls of mist forming from the cool sea, a sword hung suspended in mid—sea?

Deep blue stones sparkled from the haft. She had to touch the gleaming weapon. She pushed upon the stone and the vision drew near. Moving just above her extended arm, Jayse's hand neared hers.

"I've seen this sword." He inched his hand back and she turned her face to look at him. "Many times."

"What is this place?" she whispered. "What kind of magic is this?"

"Mommy." Bree's voice rose with a child's exasperation. "I know. But it's the mermaid's sword."

Lucidea snatched her hands from the water and stared at her dry skin. Her hands were warm, not cool as the water had been. How was it possible to be dry when the water covered her hands? It should have run down her outstretched arms, dampened the sleeves of her shirt. She brushed her fingers along her arm, surprised to find no wetness there either.

"Sword?" Coralie hurried to Lucidea's side. "Milady? Do ye ken of what the child speaks?"

"There. Where the water flows down the wall." She indicated to the side with a sharp movement of her head.

"Aye?" Coralie prompted. "Only a few of these walls are found in our world. This one is the only such magic in this world."

"But, what is it for?"

"To view the Alfar world. I have no' been able to open the sight, 'tis naught but water to my touch. None understands the

276 · *LIZZIE STARR

magic an' none has been able to control any wall. No' even
Morghan. The magic is ancient—beyond memory perhaps. Ye
saw somethin'? Ye saw a sword?"

Lucidea nodded wearily. The excitement of discovering a new
magical talent was wearing thin—and she'd only experienced it a
few times. Now the entire group gathered around her and the
speculative curiosity in their eyes made her cringe. Jayse moved
behind her, his body a solid, warm security in the cold cavern.
Gentle and comforting, he rested his hands on her shoulders.

"I saw it, too."

"Ye did? Did ye touch the waters?"

"No. I wanted to, but something made me pull my hand back.
But I saw a round room, quite a bit like this one, only with a pile
of rocks in the center. Like some circular structure had imploded.
And hanging above it was a sword." His fingers tightened convul-
sively. "The sword... looks like the sword depicted on Oberon's
crest. Right down to the pattern of the blue stones. And, I think
it's the same sword I've been seeing in dreams almost every night.
I'd like to make sure. I need to see it again. Coralie, do you think
the wall will show us what we want to see?"

"I dinna believe so. Dinna I just say none has been able to
control the wall?" She softened her sharp reply with a sad smile.

Jayse turned Lucidea around to face him. "Will you try, baby? I
have the strongest feeling this is important."

"It is, Unca Jayse." Breanna smiled when he looked at her.
"'Cause it's the mermaid's sword, too. An' Auntie Dea is the
mermaid. It's hers."

"Mine?" Her voice squeaked. She didn't own a sword, never
wanted that kind of a weapon. She'd cut her own hand off just
moving it from one place to another. She chuckled nervously.
"What an imagination."

"Mayhaps..." Coralie drew out the word and Lucidea's
stomach discovered the ability to tie itself in knots.

"You can't mean that... it's mine?" She shook her head. "Nope.
No way. Nuh-uh."

"Legend says, milady, that two brothers created a sword

between them. The brothers were separated, and the sword placed into hidin'. Until such time as 'twas needed. To bring together the brothers. 'Tis also said none but a child of one of the brothers may touch the sword, an' release the blade from hidin'."

The knots that were once her stomach clenched tighter. This was even more unreal than being born half-fey. "If you say anything about only the rightwise born king being able to pull the sword from the stone, I think I'll scream."

"Lucidea? I dinna ken..."

She waved away Coralie's confusion. "It's from a human legend. About how only the rightful king is able to pull a sword from a stone, thereby proving he's the ruler."

Coralie nodded thoughtfully. "Aye, 'tis possible."

"Look." The dreamy voice stopped Lucidea's sarcastic response and she turned toward Catori. The young shaman had been silent during their search for Breanna, but now stood at the wall, her hand extended so her palm lay flat against the stone. The water parted around her hand and a vision overlay the black rock. "Do you hear it? The rattles."

Lucidea glanced at the others, but all shook their heads. She took a step toward Catori but refrained from touching her. Without knowing the effects the viewing wall had on any one of them, she didn't want to risk possible harm. "I don't hear anything, Tori," she said quietly.

"And see, there in the gray mist. A figure. He's using the rattle. He's... calling... no, begging for my help."

Feeling the others gathered close behind her, Lucidea peered into the vision. There was gray, and a darker shape that, if she squinted and used her imagination, could be a man. A spiral of mist spun out from the darker spot, whirling until it encompassed the figure in a spinning vortex and snapped it away.

A vortex? "Morghan," she cried and sank to her knees. "Come back. How do we help you? Morghan."

Catori stepped back, blinked, then knelt beside her. Lucidea clutched the woman's hands. "Was that my uncle?"

"I... I think so. He's trying to speak with us, but the vortex won't allow him words. All he has is the rattle. I've heard him... many times. I... oh." Catori slumped to the floor.

Nightshade crouched next to her and carefully touched her pulse points. "Catori?"

"I'm okay," she said without opening her eyes. She held her hand to her forehead. "Ow, this feels worse than any vision I've had before. I... need to sleep. But I don't think I'll make it back to my room without help."

"But..." Lucidea wanted answers, needed to know how to help Morghan.

"I don't know how to get him back, Lucidea." Catori sighed. "Yet. I'll concentrate... I'm... sorry."

Nightshade gathered her into his arms and rose. He glanced down at Lucidea. "She'll do what she says, sweet cheeks. After she's rested. I think it's time to get us all back to the manor. Maybe that book Gowthaman gave you will have some clues about this... water wall."

Adjusting the slim woman in his arms, he tossed back his hair, then smiled. "I'm still hungry. Think your supper is salvageable?"

After her weary nod, Nightshade called to the others. "Come on then, dearhearts. We'll talk about this place in the comfort of the dining hall. With full stomachs."

"Daddy?" Breanna tugged Bryce's pocket. "I know I did bad. But... can I walk back with Gowthaman?"

Bryce glanced at the dark-skinned faerie and nodded. "We'll talk about your punishment after supper."

"I know. Thank you, Daddy."

"For punishing you?" Bryce fought to keep his expression stern.

"No. I deserve that for scaring you and Mommy. Thank you for letting me go with Gowthaman."

Jayse offered Lucidea his hand and she gladly let him tug her to her feet. She ended in his arms. "Are you okay, baby?"

"Everything's happening so fast, but in some cases not fast enough."

"I know what you mean." He kissed the tip of her nose. "It'll all work out, you'll see."

He could make her believe just about anything, simply by saying it was so. She loved that about him, but hated knowing saying something was so didn't really make anything happen. Not the important stuff, anyway. She nodded that she was ready to go, but they waited as Gowthaman knelt beside Bree before following the others.

"You frightened your parents badly."

"I know. But..."

"There are no buts, little missy. You must be more careful, especially now when you have a brother to watch out for."

Bree touched Gowthaman's cheek. "I'm sorry I scared you. I didn't mean to."

He gathered her into a hug. "Ah, my soul. You must stay safe."

Gowthaman's aura flared and a swirl of pink entwined with the spiking crimson. Jayse whispered, "Soulfire. Bree says she's going to marry him when she grows up. From the looks of things, I'd say it's possible."

"But, she's so young."

"She won't always be. And Gowthaman... ages in the faerie way. It'll be a long time before he grows older. For now, he treats her as a loved child. When she's an adult..." He shrugged.

Lucidea held him back as Gowthaman carried Bree from the cavern. "How do faeries age, anyway? Will you stay the same, and I'll get older without you? Coralie's said that according to human timekeeping, she's very old, but still young as an Alfar-Sindhu. Does that mean I'll age differently? But I don't look any different than anyone else my age."

"Whoa. You're letting your thoughts run away with you, darlin'. In my race, children age the same rate as fully human children do. When we become adults, it's like the aging slows down. Even though Dad doesn't look it, he's in his sixties. Mom's in her seventies."

"You're kidding."

"Never kid about a woman's age. Didn't you know that? She's

thirteen years older than Dad and Tommy's just a little younger. Spending time in the Otherworld slows aging in humans, too."

"So, your race holds the secret to the fountain of youth." Lucidea laughed, letting the tension of the past hour escape with the happy sound. "Come on, knowing this crew, they won't leave anything for us to eat if we don't get there soon."

"One thing first." Jayse held her tightly and stared into her eyes. "I love you, you know."

"I know. But I'm hungry, so how about that kiss you've got on your mind and let's go eat."

"Think a kiss is all I'm considering?"

"I didn't notice a closet in here." The bronze flush burst over his cheeks and his honey brown eyes heated. He shook his head. "Actually, I was thinking about that book Gowthaman brought you."

"You were not. Kiss me."

"I was. I will." He did.

CHAPTER
TWENTY-FIVE

A blizzard blanketed the farmlands in deep waves of white. Feidhlim shivered as a blast of wind shuddered the house, easing through tiny cracks around the windows. Staring out over the frigid expanse of white, he searched for the row of ice-covered trees that marked the boundary between his property and that of the usurper's son. Already the high, rounded peaks of castle towers rose above the trees and the odd unease that had tickled at his senses from the beginning of construction returned with a cold to rival the wind.

Only a day previously Osric had managed to view the construction plans. Now he had sequestered himself away to place his memory on paper. Feidhlim was anxious to see the drawings, though he knew the plans intimately—each grand hall, each passage. This small structure would pale next to his castle in the Otherworld. How Zeroun discovered the seat he had chosen for his power remained a mystery.

Once Zeroun was destroyed, this pretender castle would fall, stone by stone, and he would return to the Otherworld. Magic be damned, it was his destiny to rule. And rule he would. By whatever means available to him.

He stepped back from the window and briefly admired the

fine lines and patterns etched in the frost. Once he stood in his rightful place, there would be time for beauty... and a woman. Zeroun's woman. Never far from his thoughts, the ache he felt for the human who'd bewitched him so long ago blossomed. She would suffer and he would find the pleasure denied him. Perhaps... he smiled as he left his room and paced the quiet hall to the basement stairs... perhaps he would take each of the Zeroun women. Let Allyn witness what she had denied to him. Then, she would come to him. His revenge would be complete.

Despite the winter's hold on the land, Bealtaine quickly approached. He'd not spoken of his personal plans to any, nor committed those plans to any means but his memory. Osric was a sly one, and would eventually discover his plans. But not until Feidhlim decided to let the fool know. They spoke now only of generalities while Osric continued to watch the construction progress. He would smile at Osric's suppositions, and occasionally gave veiled hints to his plans.

Toying with the fool was one pleasure he allowed himself.

He unlocked a heavy door and took a long sword from its resting place. Moving into the area designated for his training, he lifted the weapon and traced a line of fine scrollwork decorating the blade. After thinking long and hard about the method for Zeroun's destruction, he had chosen this. No modern human means, no rapid death. Too many years had been spent in only dreaming; the reality would be savored.

Silent, he moved through a series of exercises combining a world of methodologies. Chuckling, Feidhlim corrected a minute discrepancy in his stance. Not one world's skills, he would fight with skills of both worlds and of many times.

He slashed at the remains of some farm animal, hanging at man-height. Osric assured him that the blade pierced this animal with the same feeling, the same resistance as it would a human's flesh. Each thrust, each time he fought past the resistance of skin and bone, Feidhlim knew the increase of skill. In this skill lay his power. With this power he would destroy, regain, create and rule.

He fought the carcass until it lay in shreds on the cement

floor. So would the clan of Zeroun lie before him. He wiped the blade carefully with a soft cloth, polishing away the blood and gore, caressing the steel as he would a woman. Zeroun would not be the first to die.

First, Zeroun would see his children dead at Feidhlim's feet.

Zeroun had taken his son from him, hidden the child away, and denied him the chance to use the child, mold him, increase his power and control. Feidhlim returned the sword to the closet and securely locked the door.

A son for a son.

Zeroun's son would be the first to taste his power. The first to die.

"Are you ready for tomorrow?" Jayse lay on his side watching Lucidea prepare for bed. "A Yule celebration with my family's quite an undertaking. Thank you for allowing us to come here."

"It'll be fun. I always wanted to be part of a large family, especially at Christmas time. I know we could have all gone to the Otherworld, but there's no snow there. Besides, there's plenty of room. Bryce did a remarkable job decorating the courtyard. And that tree you guys found... how tall is it anyway? The ceilings in the dining hall have to be twenty feet high."

"Try about fifteen. We still had to cut off about two feet from the bottom of the tree to get it to fit. Glad you like it."

She bounced onto the bed. "Like it? I love it. I can't wait to see what it looks like all decorated. Tomorrow will be so much fun."

He gathered her to him. "Nice to be able to forget problems for a while, huh?"

Her hair tickled his bare chest when she nodded. "I'm glad we haven't heard anything about... him since that poor girl was found. Too bad I don't think he's given up. I have to keep reminding myself to be careful. Especially now that Carrie's going to the Rape Crisis Center every week."

"Do you think that counseling his last victim is helping her, too? I tried to get Bryce to talk Carrie out of working with her. Did you know the center did too? Guess they've never had a volunteer who wanted to work with someone who was the victim of the same attacker." He tried to control a shudder, but when it passed, Lucidea lifted her head to look into his eyes.

"It can't be easy. I do notice a difference in her though. So, it must be helping. She says the girl's doing well, too." She yawned. "Sorry. I know we should get to sleep, but we're almost done with the book. Are you awake enough to finish reading it to me tonight?"

"Get yourself comfortable, Dea Annie, and prepare for my amazing skills."

She moved away just far enough to prop the fluffy pillows behind her back. "Mmm. I'd like to finish the book first, though."

He swooped over her and kissed her forehead as he reached for the book on her nightstand. "Temptress."

"Think so?" She stretched her arms over her shoulders and arched, pressing her breasts against his chest. Even through the thick flannel nightshirt she wore against the winter chill, her firm nipples brushed his skin and sent his blood streaming low in his body. "I know so, baby." He nuzzled her neck, leaving a trail of damp, open-mouthed kisses. "Good thing there's not much left to translate. Don't know how well my brain'll work."

"As long as the other one does... later. Read for me, please?"

"Your wish, milady." He propped his back against the cold headboard hoping for temporary relief from the heat. Bending his knees, he opened the book to the page where they'd stopped the previous night and rested the ancient volume against his thighs.

Lucidea covered the page with her hand. "At times I'm so amazed at this. To think that it was relegated to a place with fictional tales in Gowthaman's library."

"The book did start out telling us it was a translation of an older document that the author found. That's a technique a number of human fiction writers have used. Why not a Faerie bard? The fact that Coralie confirms everything we tell her—"

"Did she show you the document she brought home yesterday?"

He shook his head.

"It's Alfar history. And the historian documented exactly the same things as we've been reading in this book."

"What's the ending?" If they didn't need to finish the book, they could move on to... other things.

"She wouldn't say. Of course, I can't read that writing either. She said it's up to us to experience the ending for ourselves. So, how about it? The sooner you read the end..."

Pink infused her face and Jayse studied the book to allow her the moment. She blushed easily and hated the visual reaction to her thoughts. Tonight wasn't the night to tease her. Not about that anyway. "Okay, baby. Last night you fell asleep during the battle between Wodhan and Brandr Ur."

"I can't believe I fell asleep during that. Will you read with your finger tonight?"

When she asked, he would point out the words as he read and sometimes she would speak a word or phrase before he did. She was learning the Faerie language, and had spent long hours in the Otherworld with him. Her willingness to be a part of his world thrilled him.

But she did so at the expense of her own heritage. He and Coralie had taken private moments to talk about Lucidea... and he knew when she found out he'd be in big trouble. Coralie was concerned at Lucidea's apparent lack of interest in her own world. Yes, she made decisions when called upon, but took little to no initiative to learn more about the Alfar-Sindhu.

Except for reading the book, *Crystal Tarot*, a history of ancient gods, of battles, and the parents of the child Dea Anu. Dea Anu, the ancestor of all Alfar. Her interest lay in the fire elemental Brandr Ur, who claimed Dea Anu as his mate when she was born. Much to the dismay of the god Wodhan, who also claimed the baby as his future wife. If this Brandr Ur was the same elemental that caused her uncle to be captured by the vortex, her interest made sense. Maybe she was searching for a way to reach Morghan.

"Well, what are you waiting for, Jayse? Read to me."

The pleasing sound of Jayse's voice rumbled softly in the night. His finger slid along the page and Lucidea translated along with him. She'd never thought to be able to learn another language, especially one written in symbols so different than the letters of the English alphabet. Through the process of reading with him, she thought she might actually be able to read by herself now. But she didn't want to confess that fact. She loved lying at his side, listening. When she closed her eyes, she could almost see the world of Haven and Zale, the world where the Alfar races originated.

The Alfar world... someday she'd have to find the courage and take the plunge. Literally. The only way she, as an Alfar-Sindhu, could enter that parallel world was through water. The deeper waters of a lake or an ocean would open to her, allowing her to pass into the Alfar world. In theory the transfer wasn't much different than using a faerie portal.

Except she would have to find her way alone. At least the first time. It was a rite of passage among her people. Once accomplished, Coralie told her there were ways for her to bring another through the transfer, even if they were not Alfar-Sindhu. So, she could show Jayse her world. In theory.

Only half listening to Jayse read, she fought a common rise of guilt. He'd been so generous with his world, and she'd returned nothing in kind. She hadn't even told him how much she'd been learning. Not even Coralie knew that. The guilt flared higher. Coralie despaired of her ever being interested in governing her people, or of even learning more about the Sindhu. How could she explain that when she began her self-education, she'd thought she was crazy?

Every day, when the others were busy with their concerns and the children safe under Coralie and Catori's watch, she'd been slipping away to the cavern and the watery vision wall. She'd never been able to raise a different vision. No matter what pleas she held in her mind or how much she wanted to see Morghan, she always returned to the underwater palace and the sword room.

There, she'd met her teacher.

The invisible presence wrapped her in comfort while his deep voice provided a rhythmic discourse on the Alfar-Sindhu. The words, lingering like a dream, nonetheless remained fixed in her memory.

She knew so much more than she let on, discovering the truth of the knowledge given to her in casual discussions with Coralie. How could she explain, without sounding crazy, that a disembodied voice spoke to her? Unbelievable as it was, a voice she suspected belonged to Wodhan.

"Baby, I'm going to stop here."

"Huh? Why? I thought we were going to finish tonight."

Jayse closed the book and set it aside. "You're not paying attention."

"I was, too."

"Uh-huh. What was the last part I read?"

A rapid search of her memory provided nothing, not even a clue she could use to bluff her way out of Jayse's accurate observation. She took a deep breath. "And they lived happily ever after?"

"Not even close. What were you thinking about?"

This she could bluff her way through easily. "Tomorrow."

Jayse's skeptical expression softened but retained his disbelief. "If you say so. Shall we get to sleep then?" He snuggled down in the bed, faced her and tugged the blanket over his shoulder. Exhaling a gentle sigh, he closed his eyes.

She turned off the light and pressed herself along his body. "Love me?"

A twitch in his lips created a dimple highlighted by moonlight from the window. "You know I do. Sleep well, baby."

Letting a soft growl rumble at the base of her throat, Lucidea slid one leg over his and angled her hips even closer. She traced her fingers over his chest and stroked his nipples. "That's not what I meant, and you know it."

His eyes opened lazily and he slipped his hand under her nightshirt to cup her bottom. "Your wish, milady."

T he noise in the dining hall was a low, constant roar, but Jayse wouldn't trade a decibel of the sound for anything. He stood in the corner opposite the tree, a cup of hot cider in his hands, admiring the decorations. Of course, the ornaments were thick close to the bottom of the immense tree where the kids helped and sparse higher where only a ladder could reach, but it looked great. With the number of children in the family, it hadn't taken long to create the holiday vision.

He scanned the room for Lucidea and grinned when he spotted her, tucked away in a corner with most of the kids. She held a book toward the children to show the pictures, then twisted her neck at what looked like an uncomfortable angle to read the text. All of the kids had taken to her, and she to them. She'd make a great mother.

He wondered briefly why they hadn't gotten pregnant yet, then set his concern aside. This was a day to celebrate the family they had, not to worry about what might happen later. Still, he couldn't wait to see her children... their children.

David moved easily around the room, one hand outstretched to warn him of obstacles. When the boy reached him, Jayse spoke a soft greeting. "Hey, David."

"Hi, Jayse. Can I talk to you for a minute?"

Curious at the boy's serious expression amidst the gaiety, Jayse nodded, then answered out loud for the sightless boy. "Sure. There's a couple chairs right here. Is that okay?"

After they sat, David leaned forward like he was looking out over the room. "I need to tell somebody something, but I don't want to tell my dads right now. Or Bryce, because I'm afraid it might not be true. If I tell you, you won't say anything, will you?" He turned his face to Jayse.

Startled at a subtle difference in the boy's eyes, Jayse leaned closer. "Is anything wrong?"

David shook his head. "No, I don't think so. You know the doctors can't find any reason for my blindness."

Jayse nodded. He'd been included in numerous discussions of how it was suspected David had suffered from traumatic abuse, and his blindness was a psychological defense. "Yeah, that's what I hear."

David turned back to the room. "The Christmas tree's really beautiful."

"That it is."

"I especially like the angel at the top. I think she looks like Searlait, don't you?"

Jayse chuckled. "Now that you mention it... David?" What was the boy telling him?

Facing him again, David nodded. "She has long blonde hair, like Searlait. I thought angels wore white, but the tree angel has on purple. Doesn't she?"

"Uh... yes, it's purple. How long have you been able to see?"

"Not long. A couple weeks. I'm afraid to say much, in case it doesn't last. But, I had to tell someone. Promise you won't tell?"

"David, you need to tell Tommy and Derrik. They'll be so happy. The whole family will. This is a great holiday present." Ready to leap to his feet and make the announcement, Jayse took David's hand, but the boy's expression halted him half from his seat.

"Please, Jayse. I trusted you with this secret. I'll tell, when I'm sure."

Jayse crouched in front of David and studied the boy's serious expression. "I'll keep quiet. I know how important keeping secrets can be. But, everybody'll be so happy, so don't wait too long. Is the world like you remembered it from before?"

A joy-filled smile burst across David's face. "It's even better than I remember."

"Any time you want to talk, I'm here. Now... how about we go raid the cookie tray?"

Having finished the story about a Christmas mouse, Lucidea sent the children off to find another storyteller. Stretching, she leaned back against the wall and watched the activity around the room. Jayse and David were heading for the table and she grinned. They'd each find plenty to satisfy their sweet tooths, including a chocolate cherry cookie she remembered her mom making. Holiday memories. After her father disappeared there hadn't been many. Her mother had sunk further and further into depression and with no other family to help, had pulled her daughter down with her.

Lucidea squared her shoulders and climbed to her feet. This was no place for the morose past. Pasting a smile on her face she moved from the corner. Nightshade stopped her with a hand on her arm.

"Great fake smile, sweet cheeks. Ain't going to fool anybody. Tell Nightshade what's wrong."

"Just old baggage. Nothing to be concerned with now, or ever." A commotion near the tree drew them closer, along with the entire family.

Catori stood next to an elderly Native American she'd introduced as her grandmother. While the old woman grinned, Catori's expression was confused. When she realized the attention of the entire room fell on them, her eyes cleared. "Grandmother told me something interesting last night." She looked around until she found Coralie then grinned. "Even though nobody's said anything, I know all of you have wondered why Coralie and I seem so much alike. We've both noticed you watching us with questions in your eyes. I might just know the reason why."

TWENTY-SIX

L ucidea welcomed Jayse at her side with a quick kiss and kept her attention on Catori. He took her hand and stood shoulder to shoulder with her. "Any idea what this is about?"

"None. I thought we'd been more circumspect in observing those two."

Jayse shrugged, rubbing their shoulders together. "Maybe we were, but if everyone in the family was looking, too... Maybe we should have said something sooner."

Amazingly, the crowded room fell silent. Even Chance's happy gurgles quieted. Catori bent her head close to her grandmother and nodded as the old woman whispered to her. Then she straightened and tugged on the end of her braid. The nervous gesture seemed to calm her and after a deep breath, she spoke. "This is difficult, but I'm not sure why. I guess when you find out what you thought was your personal history isn't, you get thrown for a major loop." She paused and her grandmother lifted a hand to take hers.

Jayse's fingers tightened around Lucidea's and she glanced at him. "Thanks."

Catori caught her eye. "Lucidea knows what I'm talking

about. It's like you're just going along great with the way things are and, bam, there's a major change."

She did know and, after the initial shock, realized time didn't make things easier. Instead one new loop after another had been thrown at her. Lucidea guessed she was doing okay with everything, but most of the time she wasn't so sure. Hopefully whatever Catori's situation was, she'd handle it better.

"I always thought my parents had been killed when I was a baby. That's what the tribal elders told me. Now, Grandmother tells me that's not the truth. The elders had no idea who my parents were or even where I came from. I was a foundling in the true sense of the word.

"Before I was found Grandmother had a dream, and because of the messages in that dream, I was given to her to raise. The elders didn't know what to do when I was called to be a shaman when I was only four. This wonderful woman did the best she could with a precocious child." She kissed her grandmother's cheek.

"But what about you and Coralie, honey? You've got us on pins and needles here, girlfriend." Nightshade crossed his arms and pretended to glare at her, receiving a wry smile in return.

"I don't understand all of it. There seems to be this really weird time warp thing going on. In human terms, Coralie's very old. Sorry, but it's true."

"Aye, I ken. 'Tis of no matter. Go on."

"Did you know her parents were killed, so she was raised in the household of the ruling family of the Alfar-Sindhu?"

Lucidea had known, but from the exclamations rising around her, few others did. Perhaps that was her fault. She'd focused on learning about the Faerie Otherworld and hadn't given information on her world in return. Before long, she'd try and rectify that purposeful oversight. She owed that much to Jayse.

"'Tis no' my tale yer telling, Tori." Coralie made a dismissive motion with her hand. "Tell yer tale."

"But, this is your tale, too. If what Grandmother says is true. If what I heard when I visited the cavern with the water wall really confirms her dreams."

Lucidea leaned forward. Catori had heard something in that room, too? Maybe her experience wasn't so unusual then. "What did you hear?"

"A voice. A woman's voice. She spoke to me of my family."

Disappointment tightened Lucidea's chest, then faded. Like the differing visions shown by the water wall, maybe each person who experienced a voice in the cavern heard something different. Since each person was probably searching for personal knowledge, the form the knowledge giver took would suit the individual. Well, that was a logical thought. Lucidea rolled her eyes to look at the ceiling. As much as everyone tried to make it appear so, logic really didn't have much going for it in this family. Even when she tried to solve a family problem logically... She sighed; thinking about logic made her head hurt.

"This voice told me that before the Elders discovered me hidden in a tiny cave, I had parents who had a forbidden affair. My father already had a wife. Nothing new in that scenario. But he and his wife also had a child. I have a half-sister. I know, this sounds like some old movie plot, and I didn't believe it. I wanted to, kind of like I really did know it was true, but I didn't want to believe. What would that do to Grandmother?"

The old woman smiled. "You've grown well, Granddaughter. No one could ask for more than that. I did my part. I've always known you had a difficult path to follow. Why else would you have been called by the spirits at so young an age? Why else would fate have brought you to this place? Just because you discover a new heritage doesn't mean you'll forget me, does it now?"

Catori hugged her. "Never, Grandmother. You're always in my heart."

Tears burned behind Lucidea's eyes. Jayse touched his fingertip to the corner of her eye, then replaced his finger with a kiss. "Anything I can do, baby?"

Damn perceptive man. She shook her head. Soon, she'd tell

him everything she knew about the Alfar-Sindhu. If only she could find the courage to enter her world so she could take him there as well. Maybe—in time.

Catori cleared her throat and dashed the dampness from her face. "So, to make a long story short, mostly because I can't explain the how and why, Coralie is my sister. Her mother was killed in an accident. Then after my parents were finally together, they both died, and somehow, something tossed me from some other world into this one. That part I really don't understand." She shook her head and chuckled. "That really does sound like a bad movie, doesn't it?"

The crowd of family parted as Coralie rushed forward. "I was so young then, an' was told both of my parents had died. Then no one spoke of them. I dinna ken ye were possible, yet here ye are. Blessed is A'maithair, Tori, we've found each other." She embraced Catori then turned to the gathered family. "I dinna ken how this happened either. An' I dinna care. I have a sister."

Grandmother gathered both women in her embrace before leading them from the dining hall. Kisses and congratulations slowed their exit. But as soon as they cleared the arched entry, speculation exploded.

Lucidea didn't know which way to turn, who to listen to... she suddenly wanted nothing more but to escape.

"Come on, Dea Annie." Jayse tugged on her hand. "Let's get some quiet."

He wrapped an arm about her shoulder and they left the hall in the opposite direction of the newly united sisters. When family members turned to them with questions, he subtly shook his head and they made their escape unmolested.

In the quiet of the front parlor, he sat and patted his lap. Lucidea curled against him and rested her head on his shoulder. He rubbed her back. "That's pretty amazing. Even living with the different flow of time in the Otherworld, I'm not sure how this thing with Tori worked. Usually the time passes slower somewhere other than the human world. Although, there was a distortion of time while Gowthaman and Bard were held..."

"Let's not talk about... that... or him today. This is a celebration. I'm just not used to such a large gathering. Your family's always been overwhelming."

He palmed her cheek. "I warned you, didn't I?"

"You did. Luckily there haven't been that many times when they're all together."

She drew in a sharp breath when he caressed her lower lip with his thumb then caught it between her teeth.

"Oh, baby, not now. We can't disappear for that long." He tilted her face, waited for her to release his thumb then crushed his mouth over hers. After a moment, he softened the pressure and slanted his lips at a new angle, smiling into the kiss. If they were gone from the dining hall too long—he knew his family. No one would say anything, but he wouldn't expose Lucidea to the knowing looks and suggestive jokes. Not today.

Though she maintained a strong outward appearance he could tell the stress of the day affected her more than she would admit. She melted against him and his body responded. Adjusting their positions slightly, he allowed her to feel his arousal, then captured her sigh with his kiss. Regret tinged his words when he twisted from her lips. "It'll be present time soon, we'd better go back."

"Presents?" It took a moment for the sensual haze to fade from her eyes. Male pride surged through him, burning with the blood throbbing in his groin. He'd put that lingering look on her face. Him, and no one else. She blinked twice. "I don't need any present but you."

"Mmm, baby. I couldn't agree more."

She leaned back and laughed. "You want you for Christmas? Pretty narcissistic, don't you think?"

"Cute." With his hands at her waist, he moved her until she perched on his knees. "Just for that remark I might not give you a present tonight."

Looking down, she traced her finger along his zipper. "Really? Think you can hold out on me?" The press of her palm along the hard ridge beneath the denim stole his breath. A firm stroke gasped the air back into his lungs.

"God, woman, the things you do," he managed to say.

Her second caress continued on to curve over his thigh. "Gonna take back that threat to withhold my present?"

TWENTY-SEVEN

Tiny purple flowers peeked through the remaining snow covering the courtyard. Lucidea smiled at the first signs of spring. Bryce had told her the names of the flowers when he planted the bulbs last fall, but she couldn't remember. Not that knowing the names mattered at all, she'd enjoy the color after the drab, gray winter. And it was a rare day with no one else in the manor.

Wrapping her arms about herself, she stared into the courtyard until her worries and concerns blurred the view. Three months after Tori announced that she and Coralie were sisters, Lucidea still found the revelation amazing. She was so happy for both of them. But jealous as well.

Catori had taken to being half Alfar-Sindhu like a fish to water.

Lucidea snorted at her analogy. After Coralie explained the process of opening gill slits, Catori had run to the workroom deck. Pausing only a moment to toss off her clothing, she dove directly into the frigid January waters of the loch. Coralie stood on the deck smiling, but Lucidea had clutched the railing, frantically searching the dark water for any sign of her friend. Minutes later Catori emerged from the water, dripping, shivering, and exultant.

That evening she had proudly shown off her newly opened gill slits to the family and chattered happily about the world she'd observed beneath the loch's surface.

Lucidea rested her forehead against the cold glass. She could still feel the touch of Jayse's questioning gaze. Had he been disappointed in her because she'd never taken that literal plunge? He'd said nothing, but that night when he held her, he had paid loving attention to the area behind her ears. Where she would have the slits if she could work up the courage to enter the water. She shivered at the erotic memory.

Why couldn't she take that step? At the holiday gathering she'd vowed to herself to tell him what she knew about her world, but conveniently had never found the time. What he now knew of the Alfar-Sindhu came from the sisters. Tori's excitement was contagious, but she couldn't hold on to the feeling for herself. Why was she such a failure?

She stared down at her hands. She hadn't even touched clay since coming to the manor in October. Maybe if she tried sculpting the familiarity of her actions would calm her distress and she'd be able to face the unknown. Sculpting a face over a skull was creating the known from the known, even if the identity of the sculpture was never discovered. But, if she started with a lump of clay there would be no expectations, no assumptions. Her fingers twitched and, recognizing the dizzying onset of a creative vision, she closed her eyes.

There, hovering before her, the face she would sculpt. A masculine face, beautiful and ethereal. She studied the face, knowing when she opened her eyes she'd be unable to describe the features with words. Only under the press of her fingers and the gentle touch of sculpting tools would the face appear again. Confidence and understanding flowed through her. By ignoring her creative side, she'd inhibited herself in other aspects of her life. She'd ask Jayse to bring her fresh clay tomorrow. Today she'd dig out her tools and set up the workroom.

Finding a purpose, she inhaled deeply and opened her eyes. In that new purpose, she also found the courage to express her fears about her heritage. She glanced over her shoulder at the clock. Five hours until Jayse would be home. Gnawing at her lower lip, she hoped she'd be able to maintain her minimal hold on that courage. She had a lot to tell him tonight.

As she was about to turn from the window, a shimmer reflected on the warming snow. A portal? Unable to control the leaping of her heart at the thought Jayse may have chosen that day to come home early, she rushed to the doors and out into the chilly courtyard.

Instead of forming at ground level, the portal hovered six feet above the ground. The light issuing from the oval shone with an odd greenish tint. A shadow floated to the center of the portal, then dropped to the ground. Laughter rang around the courtyard as she stared at the crumpled body.

A tight group of armed men ran through the doorway from the manor and surrounded the fallen man. Recognizing Alfar-Sindhu guards, Lucidea relaxed and waited until the closest knelt with his sword resting across his knee. "Milady. Our defenses failed, allowing this... I beg forgiveness."

"Oh, get up. Just tell me what's going on. I don't recognize that man. What the hell is he doing in my courtyard?"

One of the warriors turned the body and leapt back, sword pointed at the still chest. "Pagas, milady."

"Is he...?" The body exhibited no recognizable signs of life, but if it was Pagas, he wasn't human. There might be life in him yet.

The warrior poked Pagas with his sword, then knelt and checked the usual pulse points. Lucidea choked back laughter at the absurdity of the actions, so like a cop show on television. The guard shook his head. "He no longer lives, milady."

The guards milled about under the still open portal, watching. When a second portal flashed into existence behind her, they leapt to surround her then lowered their weapons when Searlait charged into the courtyard, sword high. Macaire followed on her heels.

Lucidea frowned. Now she was in the middle of a fantasy

movie. What was real life? There were times she couldn't tell anymore.

Searlait gave the body a cursory glance then peered into the hovering portal. Macaire moved closer to Lucidea. "We felt the opening portal slice through the Alfar shield." He gave her a terse smile. "Your guards reinforced the shielding, keeping us out as well. The balance of magics have now been restored—except for that portal."

Laughter rang from the portal. "Little warrior?"

Searlait growled and set her stance. She lifted her sword toward the portal. "Bocan. I destroyed ye."

"In one world. Nightmares of another give back life. Better life. More to eat. Bring present to thank you. This one not belong in new world." Like rock grinding against rock, the harsh voice sounded like a bad dream.

"Ye killed him."

"Oh? Not what Bocan supposed to do?" The laughter sent chills skittering over Lucidea's shoulders.

Searlait leapt trying to reach the portal. The oval lifted higher. "No, little warrior. I not fight again. I go back to nightmare world."

"Fight me," Searlait screamed.

"No, you bested Bocan once. Not again. I not come back to this world. Like new home. Good food."

Macaire jerked and turned, lifting his sword. Lucidea tore her gaze from the dead man in time to witness the formation of another portal.

She cried out as Jayse strode through, gave a frantic glance around, then ran to gather her in his arms. "What's going on?"

The courage and strength left her body in a rush and she clung to him. What was going on? The Alfar-Sindhu who killed her father was dead. Lying in a heap in her courtyard. Killed by a creature Searlait had once destroyed. There were guards and Alastriona all over. How had she thought she could deal with all this? She burst into tears.

With a nod, Macaire assured him the situation was under

control, so he led Lucidea into the dining hall and brought her back into a tight embrace. "Baby?"

"Oh, Jayse," she sobbed.

Stroking her hair and shoulders, he let her cry. He hadn't known how she had remained so calm, so strong all this time. Maybe this strange occurrence would be a catharsis for her, and she would talk to him of her fears, her concerns, her world. Keeping everything to herself wasn't healthy, not when he was there to support and help her in any way he could. He kissed her temple. "Talk to me, Dea Annie. Please, talk to me now."

She shook her head and he sighed. When would she open up that part of her life to him? How long could he afford to be patient when he could see how much it cost her emotionally and spiritually? How long could he wait until the woman he loved trusted him?

He blew out a second long breath. Forever. He'd wait forever.

Closing his eyes, he formed a wish. A wish that he wouldn't have to wait forever, and she'd talk to him soon. Wishes came true; he knew that for a fact. He held his dearest wish in his arms. He reinforced his new wish and loosened his embrace so he could lean back and peer into her tear-stained face.

She nodded. His heart turned over. Did this mean she was ready?

"I... I have a lot to tell you." She hiccupped and covered her mouth. "But... but..."

Another flip of his heart. Conditions. She was setting limits before she even spoke. He fought a rise of anger, but whether he was angry at her for her lack of communication or at himself for being impatient, he wasn't sure. Closing his eyes, he took a deep breath. A cleansing breath. A breath that did nothing but offer him air.

"I need to take care of that... mess in the courtyard first. Then... can we talk? In the cavern maybe... where no one will bother us?"

Not trusting the hope that would ring in his voice, he nodded. She'd never invited him to the cavern after the initial discovery. His curiosity about the strange watery wall had almost led him to sneak down there without her, but he'd held back. He promised himself he wouldn't invade her privacy—until she invited him.

"That body... that's Pagas. He's dead. Will you talk to Macaire and Searlait about what happened? They were here almost imme-diately." She gave him a watery smile. "The Alastriona response time gets high marks in my book. I'll get one of the guards to find Coralie so we can decide what to do about Pagas' body."

If Pagas was dead, she had nothing to fear from her people. At least, he didn't think she did. Maybe without the threat hanging over her, she'd be more willing to embrace her Alfar half. He added that to his wish. "I want to go take a look at the creep. Make sure he's really dead."

"Thank you. I want to get a good look at him, too. My father's murderer."

Jayse took her hands and they stood a few moments in silence with their foreheads pressed together. She stepped back. "I'm ready."

She walked calmly into the courtyard. The Alfar guards parted to let them pass and she glared at the first one who attempted to bow to her. Jayse's lips twitched. Lucidea, controlled and in charge, was back.

They stood over the torn and mutilated body. Jayse gulped back bile but Lucidea stared cold-eyed into the man's face. There was comparatively little damage to the face but the expression was frozen in stark terror. Glassy eyes stared sightless into the sky.

"Jayse, I need to do something. I can't believe this, but I need to. I have to."

"What? Can I help?"

She shook her head then turned to the nearest Alfar guard and held out her hand. "Your weapon... is it sharp?"

The guard frowned a moment as if affronted by the question. "Aye, of course, milady."

"Give it to me."

"Aye, milady."

Lucidea took the sword. She handled the long blade awkwardly but with a purpose Jayse began to guess. "Lucidea, I don't think you should do this."

She lifted her gaze to his. "I have to. I can't explain it, but if I don't..."

Understanding, he lowered his gaze and stepped back. "I wish I could do this for you."

"Me, too."

Using both hands, Lucidea lifted the slender sword over her head. "Pagas, murderer of my father... Pagas, conspirator against my people, the Alfar-Sindhu..." Tears streamed down her face. "Pagas... who caused my uncle... I, Lucidea, daughter of Cù Anu, take your power as you took my father's. I, Lucidea, daughter of Cù Anu..."

Her scream echoed long after the sword fell and parted Pagas' head from his body.

TWENTY-EIGHT

Pacing the cavern didn't help her nerves so Lucidea touched the water wall and stood back to study the sword the vision showed her. The tingling in her hands reminded her of holding a sword, lifting it, bringing down the blade. She shook her head violently. She'd never be able to rid herself of that memory, and she wasn't even sure why she felt so compelled to slice the head from her enemy. His head for her father's head. Revenge and retribution had never been a part of her emotional make up—was this an unwelcome legacy from her Alfar blood?

After Coralie arrived and confirmed Pagas' identity, the guards cleaned up the mess in the courtyard and took the body—and head—away. According to the guards, he had no family so she didn't care what they did with him.

She'd asked for a little time alone before facing Jayse, but not this much. She needed to talk to him before she lost her nerve again. He'd have even more questions now, questions she would try to answer.

Finally, she plopped down on the sofa and stared at the floor. "Hey." Jayse walked softly into the cavern. "When did you bring furniture down here?"

"Tori asked for it. She spends a lot of time just watching the wall. Says she sees all kinds of things. For me, it's like watching a television with only one channel. All I get to see is that stupid sword."

Jayse lifted his eyebrows at her tone but said nothing. He sat at the other end of the sofa and rested his arm along the back as he faced her. "So..."

"So... how're things going with the faire site? Any problems?"

His brows drew together. "I didn't think we were going to talk about my concerns right now."

"Please, a little everyday chit-chat. Just for a while. After what happened I need to feel a little normalcy."

"For a while then." Jayse shrugged one shoulder. "The building process is going great. Since I'm using mostly faerie labor, they've been able to do more than human workers over the winter. We should be set and ready to go for the planned opening."

"Still May first?"

"I was thinking about a family party on April thirtieth. That'll give us an opportunity to do some final checks. Since this is Zeroun's last event, Dad and Tommy will want the extra time to make sure everything's perfect."

"How do you feel about the family business closing?" She bit her lip. She hadn't meant to ask about feelings. That would open the door for his questions. She stared over his shoulder. Maybe it would be simpler if she let him ask questions, then all she would have to do was answer.

His bland expression hadn't changed. "Honestly, it's kind of sad. I mean, I've been a part of the business my entire life. But, I don't want to run it. I need to spend the time to make the faire site run smoothly. That's my dream. Luckily many of our employees are staying with me. We already have a full schedule for summer and fall, and even some events scheduled into next winter. It would appear folks in the area are interested in having their special events in a castle."

After a long pause, he asked. "Enough chit-chat for you?"

Her hackles rose at his snide tone. "What does that mean? All I asked for was a little consideration after a day I'd really rather forget. It's not often I've chopped somebody's head off, you know. Not that he didn't deserve it. All I wanted was a little quiet time before I had to face another unpleasant task."

"Talking to me is unpleasant? So, maybe we shouldn't talk."

She slammed her hand against the sofa back and coughed when the rising dust tickled her nose. "Damn it, that's the problem. I haven't been talking to you. Not really. Not about anything important."

He crossed his arms and turned his face away but not before she imagined the barest hint of a smile.

"Jayse, look at me."

He remained steadfastly glaring at the water wall.

"I'm so sorry." Those words were easy and she meant them will all her heart.

"Sorry for what?" He turned back to face her, his soft voice betraying no emotion. He wasn't going to make this easy for her. Why should he?

"You've shared so much of your family, of your world. You've taken me to the Faerie Otherworld, taught me to read your language..."

His eyebrows shot up at that, so she'd surprised him. Unfortunately, he might not take the other surprises so easily.

"You've made me welcome, happy, a part of your whole life. And I... I've hidden myself from you."

She paused, hoping he'd say something, but he remained silent, his expression neutral and waiting.

"I've hidden myself from me as well. I've been... afraid. I didn't, I don't know how to face being of a fey race. I don't know how to lead more than a handful of people. I don't... I'm afraid, Jayse. What if I can't do this?"

"Lucidea, I've talked with Dad about this."

"What is it with your family? Doesn't anyone mind their own business?"

"We all have very private lives. But I needed some insight on your situation."

"What would Jaye know about my situation?"

"Dad was placed in the human world as a baby, like Catori. But unlike her, he was never truly cared for—he existed in foster homes. That's why he's got such a strong work ethic. He knew he had to everything for himself. He was thirty before he found out about his fey blood. He accepted the news... much less easily than you. Dad's world was based in reality, a reality of his interpretation. There was no room for fantasy of any kind—except maybe when he fell in love with Mom. It was only when Mom was kidnapped by Feidhlim and taken to the Otherworld that Dad accepted who he was. He had to, otherwise none of us would be here. Then, he found out he was the chosen heir to rule our clan. That didn't sit well with him either."

"He does understand. I had no idea." What else had she missed or ignored by not being honest?

"Maybe, if we would have had this conversation sooner—"

"But it's more than that. I haven't shared my fears with you. I thought you knowing me as I was... before I found out about the Alfar-Sindhu... I thought that would be enough. Enough for you. Enough to hold on to you. I see now I was so wrong. How could you have been so patient with me? You've seldom questioned me. Never pressed for answers. Always supported me. How—"

"I love you."

His simple statement slammed into her heart with the force of an explosion. He'd said the words many times before, but this time she understood. He'd given her everything of himself and she'd ignored the precious gift. "I'm so sorry."

"That I love you?"

"No. Never that. I'm sorry I didn't understand. Maybe if we hadn't met when so many forces fought against us, I would have known sooner. Oh, no... one of those forces is what I kept from you, so that doesn't make sense. Maybe if we would have had more time..."

He smiled. "Dea Annie, you're blathering. I'll accept your

apology if you talk to me. Tell me what you feel. Tell me what you know about your world. What do we do now that Pagas is dead?"

"What do we do? I've got to learn about my people, really learn what I need to know. I need to find a way to release Morghan from his prison. I've got to find the courage to see if I can really enter the Alfar world. I've got to—"

"Baby, I said 'we'. Let me know what's going on and I'll do whatever I can to help."

"But, why?'

He shook his head as if in disbelief. "Because. I love you, Lucidea. Or is that one of the things you hide from yourself? Baby, I want you with me forever. Always. Even when you don't feel you can share with me, I'm here."

"Oh."

"Oh? Is that all, just 'oh'?" Jayse chuckled, slid close and took her hand. He stared at her fingers while he stroked her palm. "Something's missing."

The touch of his caress melted her bones, as it always did. "What?" she whispered.

He concentrated his attentions on one finger. "You need a ring here."

"Ring?"

"Baby, look at me. Lucidea Anne Galvagin, will you marry me?"

"Marry?"

"Yes, marry me. I love you. I need you for that forever and always. Together we can have our own fairy tale ending." He touched his lips to hers, giving her a kiss between each word. "Happily... ever... after."

She'd be happy with him forever. Her heart shouted yes with every rapid beat. But her head... damn her head. "Jayse, I... I don't know how to be married."

"Who does? We'll learn as we go along."

"I don't know if we can have children. What if Alfar and Faerie aren't compatible?"

"We're not compatible?" He kissed her again, lingering over

parting the seam of her lips with his tongue and exploring her mouth.

"Oh, that works," she muttered when he leaned back. "No, I mean... we've been having... we've done..."

"We've made love?"

Her face burned and she nodded. "But, I've never gotten pregnant. Maybe we can't have children."

Jayse cupped her cheek with his hand. "And maybe we just didn't hit the right time. Or maybe my virginal sperm isn't so active. Baby, there's lots of reasons couples don't get pregnant. Even if we never do, take a look at the family. Adoption's not a big issue, you know. There are lots of kids we could love." He smiled gently. "Next objection?"

"I need to know more about me first." There. She'd said it. As the words left her mouth, she knew them for the truth. How could she give her life to the man she loved when she didn't understand that life? "But if I'm a good study..."

Jayse laughed. "I'll help you study anytime. You'll let me know when I can ask you again?"

"You're not upset?"

He shook his head. "A little disappointed. I'm not gonna rush you into something else you're not ready for. Besides, it's not like we don't act married." He wrapped his arms around her and leaned back, holding her on top of him. Each kiss demanded more of her; more she gave willingly. Each caress grew in urgency, each piece of clothing an easily disposed of obstacle. Each thrust when he entered her became a promise. Each soft cry an answer and a promise of her own. Each shudder of completion a moment of eternity.

"My lord."

Osric stumbled down the basement steps and rushed forward, nearly impaling himself on Feidhlim's extended sword. A momentary disappointment wrinkled Feidhlim's brow. He ached to feel the sleek glide of his

sword into living flesh, and the fool would be as good a test
as any.

"You take great chances, disrupting my practice."

Osric looked from Feidhlim's face to the tip of the sword at his
chest. He took a deep breath and winced when point sliced
inward. Feidhlim waited then smiled and lowered the weapon
when a red stain dampened his underling's shirt.

"Your pardon, my lord. This could not wait."

"All we've been doing for months is wait. Why is this... whatever you have to tell me, so important?"

Osric leaned closer to whisper. "I know how to circumvent the
strange magic surrounding the place where your son is held."

"Indeed." His calm response obviously disappointed Osric,
while inside the excitement turned Feidhlim's stomach to a knot
of anticipation. "Come, I shall take a rest period and you will tell
me more."

He locked the sword away and led Osric to living room. They
sat before the cold fireplace. "Now. What did you do?"

"We witnessed a disturbance, and a portal created a narrow
fissure where it entered the manor grounds."

"Who created this portal?"

"That I haven't been able to discover." Osric stared at his
folded hands. "It was an unusual portal and slipped through the
fissure so quickly, I could not trace its origin."

"Surely they have repaired the fissure."

"Yes, my lord, almost instantly." He lifted his head and smiled
broadly. Feidhlim curled his lip at the proud expression but Osric
continued smiling. "But not the one I created."

"So, you are able... hmm, that offers us a multitude of possibilities."

"And, Feidhlim, I sense your son."

Feidhlim internally marked the familiarity, but let none of his
disapproval show. "Ah, my son. The child fares well?"

"From what we are able to determine. Shall I retrieve him for
you, Feid—my lord?"

Reclining in his chair, Feidhlim waved one hand. "Not just yet,

Osric. But, now that we are able to take the child at any time, I believe my plans need adjustment. Leave me."

Osric was unable to disguise the flash of anger before he bowed and left the room. Feidhlim snarled at his back, then smiled and stacked his hands behind his head. Ah, the fates were kind to him. As well they should be toward the future ruler of all Faerie. First he would try to reach the child. Perhaps the fissure would allow his thoughts to touch the boy. Then he would decide how best to use this new knowledge for his ultimate pleasure.

"You've never seen anything but the sword?" Jayse lay on the couch watching Lucidea as she paced before the water wall. She looked great in nothing but his shirt, her long legs exposed to the fullness of her bottom. Dragging his thoughts from her body he sat and struggled into his boxers and jeans. She was opening up to him, discussing her fears, her needs, her life with him. He had to keep his mind out of the bedroom now. She turned and the movement lifted the hem of his shirt exposing the curve of her hip.

"Uh, baby... could you get dressed?"

She cast him a sultry look over her shoulder. "I've got clothes on."

"Not enough. Not if you want to talk. You're not dressed for talking. You're not dressed for me to talk anyway."

"I love you, Jayse. Where'd you throw my jeans?"

He kneeled on the sofa and reached over the high back. "Here they are. But I think your shirt's..." He handed her the jeans as he glanced around the cavern. "Ah, over there." By the time he returned with her shirt, she'd quickly tugged on her jeans and was fastening her bra.

"Let me."

"I don't know. You're pretty good at unfastening this, think you can do it the other way?"

"I'm multi-talented." He made quick work of the simple hooks but before moving away slipped his hands around her to cup her lace covered breasts. He nipped at the spot where her neck joined her shoulder. "Mmm."

"Stop that. I want to try something."

He turned her and rubbed his nose against hers. "I'll try just about anything you want, baby."

"I'm going to have to get a copy of the Kama Sutra just to keep ahead of you. Here's your shirt." She shoved the material into his hand and stepped away to slip her shirt over her head. Unfortunately, even covered her body excited him. He hoped it would always be this way.

"I was thinking about what the prophecy said about daughter of Alfar, son of Fey. And wondering if you'd be willing to try an experiment with me."

"Sure. What do you want me to do?"

"I need to tell you something first." Her expression showed a tinge of fear, but she was willing to talk. He felt like singing, they'd made huge strides for their relationship that day.

"Okay, shoot."

She paced before him. "I'll admit I haven't come down here many times since we found Bree here. When I do, I touch the wall and get that." She swung her hand to the water wall and the vision of the sword suspended above a pile of rubble. "I've tried thinking of all kinds of things before I touch the wall, but nothing changes. Then, one day... I heard a voice. Not the same voice Tori hears. Mine's male. I... I don't know why I think this, but it's Wodhan."

"Wodhan? Like the god in the book?"

"Uh-huh. Wodhan, like the mate of Dea Anu. I don't always remember what the voice says, but I feel comforted after hearing him." She gave a wry chuckle. "You'd think I'd want to hear him more often then, wouldn't you?"

"And..."

"That's it. I wanted to tell you that I hear voices."

"Oh, baby, come here." Jayse opened his arms and she came to him. "What did you want to do today?"

"Well, if the daughter and son are supposed to bring together worlds, I wonder what will happen if we both touch the wall."

"Let's give it a try."

Glad that Jayse was willing to go along with her plan even after she told him about hearing Wodhan's voice, Lucidea took his hand as they faced the water wall. She nodded and they held their hands side by side and eased them through the water. Pinpricks of heat filled her palm when she touched the stone and she gasped in startled pain.

"Don't move," Jayse whispered.

"It hurts."

"I know. Just wait a couple seconds. I... feel more than magic."

Confusion colored his tone and, not knowing if it would help, she inched closer to his side.

Damp, water-rich air swirled around them and pressed at her back. Unable to resist the force she stumbled forward, crying out as she hit the rock wall and passed through the solid stone.

TWENTY-NINE

J ayse grabbed her around the waist before she tumbled forward into the steaming pile of rubble. Frantic, she looked around and her panic grew as she realized they'd somehow entered the room of the water wall vision.

"Do not be frightened, my children."

Jayse pulled her against his body and spun them to face the clear voice. A young man leaned against the remains of a thick pillar, one arm swung wide to the side in welcome. "I knew you would find the way."

Jayse angled her behind him and straightened his spine. "Who are you? How did you bring us here?"

The young man pointed to Lucidea as she peeked around Jayse's side. "She knows."

"You're Wodhan," Lucidea guessed.

"At your service." He bowed and his robes swirled around his feet. "You arrived here though a device as ancient as this well, even older than my father's recollection."

"Your father?" Lucidea thought back to the book Jayse read to her. "Your father is Rawdan?"

"You have learned your history well, child."

Lucidea giggled, then covered her mouth. She didn't need to start exhibiting hysterical behaviors now. However, Wodhan looked so young that calling her child seemed incongruous. He smiled as if he understood her thoughts. She took a deep breath. "Why did you bring us here?"

"I did not. The visions of the viewing waters show what you need. What you desire. What you must know. The waters simply allowed you passage."

"But, aren't you the god of waters in this world?" Jayse asked the question a moment before she could form the thought.

"Am I? Perhaps at one time. But as my father learned, times of the differing gods pass and so the gods pass from one world to the next. My time here is long done, but I have not been allowed to join my family in the next world. Only with the fulfillment of prophecy will I be allowed a passage of my own." He grew sad. "Long has it been since Dea Anu was taken from me. I ache with longing for her." He studied Jayse. "Son of Fey, you understand."

"Yes."

Lucidea moved to stand at Jayse's side. "Then we are the son and daughter of the prophecy."

Wodhan's smile returned. "Yes."

"What of the children of light and darkness?"

"Do you not know them? They reside in your household."

Jayse released a long breath. "Breanna and Chance."

"Very good, Son of Fey."

"Will evil take Chance? Will he follow his father's footsteps?"

Jayse balanced forward on the balls of his feet. She was anxious for the answer as well. The question had been an underlying concern since the boy's birth.

Wodhan shrugged. "That I am not allowed to disclose. If you already knew the answers, then prophecy would be worthless. Before you ask it of me, Daughter of Alfar, you are not the one destined to rescue the hidden king. That task is for another."

Lucidea sagged against Jayse, accepting the comfort of his arm about her. She had hoped to save her uncle. But now...

"Prophecy isn't always correct, is it? The actions of the participants can change the outcome."

"There is false prophecy, yes. Your actions, the choices you
make can determine the outcome—but only of the prophecy
naming you. The task that haunts your heart is determined for
another. Do not fear, my child. Now that Oberon's prophecy has
been found and the worlds joined, complete fulfillment will be
swift. This I tell you, this I promise as one time god of the Alfar."

Jayse released her and took a step toward the center of the
chamber. "Is this, then, this destruction... you called it a well. Was
this where the elemental was held?"

"Yes. By the same ancient magic that created what you call the
water wall. It was this magic that grew me from conception to
birth in minutes, to adult in days. It is magic that somehow my
brother harnessed, enabling us to create the sword and the magic
holding it there."

"Your brother?" Jayse scrubbed his hand over his face. "I don't
remember reading anything about your brother."

"Ah, perhaps that is because he is my half-brother. Born to
Rawdan and Gerde after the birth of Dea Anu."

Overwhelmed, Lucidea looked around and found a chunk of
broken stone to sit on before her legs collapsed. From his intense,
thoughtful expression, Jayse was on a fact-finding mission, one
she was happy to let him control. It was difficult to think, let
alone form coherent questions for Wodhan.

Wodhan. She closed her eyes in disbelief. She was talking to a
being her race had once considered a god. No wonder she was
having a hard time relating. Focusing on Jayse, she tried to
concentrate. If he asked the questions, she would help remember
the responses.

Jayse pointed at the sword. "I've seen this sword before."

"I know." Wodhan's half-grin brought Jayse a step closer.

"In dreams. In a family crest. The crest of one of my oldest
ancestors."

"A crest such as this?" Wodhan waved his hand and the sword
turned so the blade pointed upwards. An oddly distorted hour-

glass shape appeared surrounding the blade. A purple flower blossomed above the sword while below water swirled with sparkling jewels. A golden disc, spiked with radiating clear crystals settled into place behind the hourglass.

"Yes." Jayse reached dreamily toward the crest. "Like this."

"Jayse, don't touch it." Unreasonable fear burst through Lucidea and she rushed to his side and clung to his arm.

With the sharp closing of one of Wodhan's hands, the crest disappeared. Jayse stared at his palm and slowly drew it back to his side. Lucidea wrapped her fingers around his and held on tightly.

Wodhan closed his eyes and sighed. "It is my brother's crest. A symbol he took when he assumed rule of fey peoples in a different world than this." His eyes opened and he stared at Jayse. "My brother, Oberon."

"I don't believe this." Jayse shook his head, clearing the last foggy magic from his brain. "That can't be. How could Oberon be your brother?"

Wodhan's lips twitched. "I told you, we share the same father."

"No, I mean..." Jayse took a step back. "This is amazing. It'll take awhile for all this to settle in so I understand. Then is this..." He pointed to the sword that had returned to its original position. "... the sword of the prophecy?"

"If Oberon spoke the words, caused the prophecy to be hidden in your two worlds, would it not make sense for his sword to be included? He was extremely proud of his handiwork. None before and none after have been able to harness the power remaining in the well."

Lucidea rubbed her head. "Is that why I feel so funny?"

Moving to her side, Wodhan touched her shoulder and frowned. "Yes. You must go. The well will steal your power if you do not guard yourself. It is best not to remain long beside this magic."

Then he rested his hand on Jayse's shoulder. "Go now. Be

assured, you have chosen your paths with wisdom. Your love... ah, your love reminds me so of my Dea Anu and our love for one another." He kissed Lucidea's forehead. When he moved toward Jayse, Lucidea stifled an inappropriate giggle. But Jayse bowed his head and accepted the god's blessing. "Go now. Though I no longer am god in this world, I shall be with you should you have need of me."

Lucidea hit the cavern's smooth stone floor hard, her yelp of pain mixing with Jayse's startled grunt. "Ow, thanks Wodhan. Couldn't you have aimed for the sofa?"

Soft laughter caressed her and she sighed. She'd wanted to experience more than just the single scene the water wall showed her. Sure, it was the same vision, but she'd been there. "We were there. Oh my... we were, weren't we?"

Shaking his head, Jayse rolled to his hands and knees. "I can't get his voice out of my head." He rose up then sat back on his calves and held his head between his hands. "It won't stop."

"Wodhan?"

"No." He groaned and bent forward. "Oberon." With another groan he rolled into a ball, clutching his head. "I can't ... not... no..."

She stood and pounded her fist against the water wall. "Help him. Wodhan, help him."

A slender stream of water flowed from the wall, reaching out like a finger toward Jayse. Lucidea fell to her knees at his side and tried to still his agonized writhing while the water advanced. "Help him," she whispered.

The stream touched his forehead then wrapped fully around his head. His movements quieted, but he still mumbled as if answering questions she couldn't hear. Had they stayed near the magical well too long? A slender stream of water separated and rose to touch her cheek.

::No child, he will be well. My brother is... insistent in the demands he makes of his descendents. Be at peace.:: The finger of water retreated back to the wall.

"Yessss," Jayse whispered on a sigh. He grew still and turned his face to look at her. "You and me, Dea Annie." His eyelids drifted closed and he slept.

F eidhlim sent his followers from the farmhouse, demanding none remain even within sight of the building. Osric argued, citing the need to protect their lord, but Feidhlim laughed at him. He needed no protection, and he would tolerate none of the interruptions that had become much too common. Osric continued to watch him closely, or had others do so for him. Torquil's spawn had nearly outlived his usefulness. Feidhlim stood at the window and watched his followers enter a portal to the Otherworld.

Assured he was alone, he retreated to his room and the meditation corner. The excitement and anticipation of what would happen trembled through his muscles so he performed a few calming exercises. When he was sufficiently relaxed, he seated himself on the padded dais. Cleansing breaths, he reminded himself. Slow. Calm.

In the silence of his mind, he visualized the indigo aura he'd felt the first time he touched his son. He had no idea what his son looked like now, and really didn't care. A child was a child. The aura would lead him.

He soared high over the land ever reaching out with his thoughts. Ah. Hidden by a veil of the unknown magic he sensed his son. He searched the veil until he found the minute tear and Osric's mark. His thoughts slipped easily past the opening.

The aura was strong. His son, of course. Powerful magic called to him. The orange of his thoughts advanced. Touched. Ah. "My son," he whispered.

A fter Coralie found Lucidea and Jayse in the cavern and had the guards carry him to their room, he slept for nearly two days. Lucidea hovered over him, and while both Faerie and Alfar healers pronounced nothing amiss, she didn't trust their diagnosis. While his mother, Allyn, sat at his side, Lucidea tried her best to explain what had happened to the rest of the family.

While Jaye and Derrik discussed the situation with Coralie, she sat back and remained silent. Catori sat next to her and touched the back of her hand. "I was just in the cavern. Gerde spoke to me. He'll be okay. From what I understand, Oberon demanded something of him. Either Gerde didn't know what, or wouldn't say."

Lucidea gave a soft snort. "It's been my limited experience that those gods know a whole lot more than they let on. We've just got to figure all this out ourselves."

Smiling, Allyn appeared at her other side. "He wants to talk to you, darlin'."

"He's awake?"

The older woman laughed. "He doesn't talk in his sleep, does he?"

"No." She walked from the dining hall but the second she hit the hallway she broke into a run. Skidding into the bedroom, she stopped partway across the floor and simply looked at him. Propped against the headboard, he had his hands folded on his stomach and his eyes were closed. He hadn't fallen back to sleep, had he?

"Don't hover. You're worse than Mom. Come here, baby. I've missed holding you."

"I've been here."

"I know. I felt you. I just couldn't wake up. I hope I never experience anything like that again."

"Can you tell me what happened?"

"Crawl up here next to me. I can think better." She joined him on the bed but instead of lying next to him, sat facing him. He sighed. "Oh well, this is better than nothing."

"Jayse? It's been two days."

"Yeah, that's what Mom said. Baby, I need to ask a favor of you."

When she nodded, he continued. "This thing that happened...

I'm not sure about a lot of it. I need to think, to process what happened. I won't be able to tell you everything right away. Can you wait awhile? I'm not sure how long. I want to tell you—"

She rested her fingers over his mouth. "You've been patient with me for so long, how can I not return the favor? I'm here whenever you're ready."

"Thanks. It's weird, you know. Usually I can talk about anything."

"Can you tell me anything now? Your family's busy discussing all kinds of theories. I'd like to be able to give them a little focus if we can."

He chuckled, then pressed his hand to his forehead. "Ow, it still hurts. Do you remember the family's reactions when we heard Oberon's voice speak his prophecy? I know you weren't affected like the rest of us, but imagine that intensity concentrated... so beautiful that you never want the voice to stop even though the sweet sound is ripping your brain to shreds. That's what was in my head. Demanding."

"Demanding what?"

He carefully shook his head. "That's what I'm not sure of. What I need to think about awhile. Okay?"

"As long as you're fine." She ran her fingers over his face then leaned close to kiss him softly.

"I'm fine, baby. Sleepy."

"Then go back to sleep. We'll all be here when you wake up."

J ayse slept intermittently for the next full week, then rose one morning as if he'd never been ill. The women of the household coddled him and Bryce complained until he received similar pampering. Then he laughed and slapped Jayse on the shoulder in a show of male camaraderie.

Once the women left the room, Bryce grew serious. "About this prophecy thing."

Knowing that the questions would come didn't make hearing them any easier. Jayse nodded. "Yes, Bryce. Wodhan confirmed that the children of light and darkness are Chance and Bree, but he wouldn't say anything concerning the evil or the fair. Person- ally, I don't think there's any reason to believe Chance will be like his biological father. You're his father now."

"Nobody's ever solved the nature versus nurture issue."

"Nurture wins in this family. You'll see."

Bryce folded his hands and let them hang between his knees. Jayse felt his chosen brother's pain but didn't know what words might be comforting. So he let the silence stand between them until Bryce lifted his head.

"Something's been happening with Chance... every day for the past week. I don't know how to explain it. As far as I know, only Bree and I have witnessed the oddity. She... thank God for her, Jayse... she somehow protects him."

"Tell me what's happening."

Bryce tugged a watch from his pocket and stared at the face a moment. "It's almost always at the same time. In just a few minutes. Will you come? And bring Lucidea. She's seen his aura before, maybe she'll see something now."

The lines of strain around his friend's eyes deepened and he rose and paced slowly toward his suite of rooms. Shoulders rounded, he stuffed his hands in his pockets as he moved down the hall. Jayse watched until he was out of sight then went in search of Lucidea.

Taking her away from the others without letting them know the serious situation took levity and charm he had to strain to accomplish, but soon Lucidea joined him in the small side room designated as a nursery. Bryce sat on the wide window ledge and Bree lay on her belly on the floor reading a picture book. She looked up and grinned.

"You here to watch my brother today?"

"Sure are, darlin'." Jayse crouched beside her. "Can you tell me anything about what happens?"

"The bad man comes and I chase him away."

The bad man. Feidhlim.

"Jayse," Lucidea said as she softly shut the nursery door. "Look."

Chance lay on his back in the crib, arms and legs waving in the air. An assortment of soft, fuzzy blocks danced in the air above him. Gurgling happily, he chased the blocks with his tiny hands, caught one, and popped the corner into his mouth. Once the corner was chewed and slobbery, the block danced away and he grabbed for another.

"Bree, are you doing that?" Bryce asked.

The little girl looked up from her book. "No, Daddy. Chance does that. He likes blocks best. Sometimes, he dances his animals, too. 'Specially Unca Nightshade's bear."

Uninterested in the floating display, she turned the page and ran her fingers along the large print, mouthing words as she touched them.

Jayse looked from Bryce to the boy and back. "Is this what you wanted me to see?"

He shook his head. "I've never seen this before. Bree, honey. Are you sure your brother's making the blocks fly like that?"

"Uh-huh, Daddy, he does it all the time. He likes to laugh. Me, too. Sometimes he makes my dolls dance and we both laugh."

Jayse took a step back. Bree had shown magical talent at an extremely young age. But Chance was only six months old. This was... unprecedented. How were they going to deal with a child who could make his toys dance at just six months? What would he be able to do at a year? At five? "We've got to tell Dad about this."

Bryce sighed. "I agree. Carrie and I are gonna need a lot of help with these two. Especially if..."

"That won't happen. Chance will choose good."

Lucidea rested her hands on the crib rail and made a face at the baby. He laughed and cooed and danced a block into her hand. "Thank you, Chance," she said seriously. With her palm flat, she held the block until it lifted into the air and rejoined the dance. She spoke without turning to Jayse. "His aura's an even deeper indigo, so blue it's almost black. But the sparkles, his magic, they're silver, like yours."

Suddenly the blocks fell to the mattress and Chance's eyes widened briefly. Tossing his head, he squeezed his eyes shut. His soft mouth opened with an angry cry.

"I see it," Lucidea cried. "Orange, like misty streaks touching his aura. See how he's fighting."

Bryce and Jayse joined her in leaning over the crib. Bree gave an exasperated sigh and closed her book. "That's the bad man's color."

She climbed onto the bottom of the crib rail and stuck her arm through the slats to touch Chance's hand. His tiny fingers wrapped around hers. "It's okay, Chance. I'm here."

Lucidea gasped. "Her aura's surrounding his, almost merging where they meet. I see bits of purple. The orange can't touch him."

The baby had quieted but watched his sister with a serious expression. The ageless wisdom Jayse saw in Chance's eyes astonished him. Who was this child?

Bree stretched her free hand through the railing slats and waved it over her brother. "You can help me, you know. Then you'll know how to do it yourself." When Chance waved his free arm, she nodded. "Very good. No, don't wiggle your fingers. Keep your hand flat like mine to push the bad man away."

"They're doing it, they've pushed away the orange."

"'Course we are. Chance doesn't want the bad man. Wants the good daddy. Our daddy. Come on, let's play blocks again."

Milky bubbles dribbled from the side of the small boy's mouth when he chortled. Bree wrinkled her nose. "Ew, gross." She wiped his mouth with the edge of a towel hanging over the rail and stepped back to the floor. "I'm gonna read some more now."

Bryce ushered Lucidea and Jayse from the room. "That's pretty much it. What do you think?"

Lucidea glanced back at the room. "You're thinking about the prophecy, aren't you?" She took Bryce's hand between hers. "There's no way that boy will be anything but good. There's none of his sperm donor in him. Not with the way that he pushed that invasion away, even as young as he is."

Jayse tugged her to his side. "Yeah, what she said. However, I do think we need to get the Alfar guards and the Alastriona to upgrade their shieldings. And, we need to tell Carrie."

Bryce held back as they turned toward the manor's main living area. "Uh, I'll talk to the guards, you can tell my wife."

THIRTY

J ayse hadn't allowed the family to see the faire site during the last month of construction and now he stood at the gated entrance guarding the top of a hill and looked out over his land. Sunlight eased from behind a cloud and sparkled on the stones of his castle. Banners bearing Oberon's crest fluttered with the light breeze. His employees, already in costume, scurried about with their final duties. His vision, his dream, was now reality.

In less than an hour everyone would arrive for the special family gathering. Then tomorrow... opening day. He glanced to the side to an empty signpost. He'd yet to decide on a name for the faire but as he scanned the entire site, supposed it would be come to be known as simply The Castle. He had to admit, the building was a far more impressive sight than he'd imagined.

For a moment he wished Lucidea would arrive before everyone else. He needed time alone with her, time to share the excitement of his vision. But, that was time he didn't have. He nodded once in satisfaction and trotted down the hill. Like his father had at every Zeroun's event, he had to make sure of those last minute details. And he wasn't in costume yet.

He hadn't told anyone what he chose to wear that evening.

His normal faire-going attire was light mail when he was fighting, or simple peasant clothing when no exhibitions were scheduled. But tonight he would dress befitting a descendant of Oberon and heir to his father's Faerie rule. He donned a white silk tunic decorated with sapphire blue embroidery. After giving the white leather trousers the once over, he shook his head and slipped on the unusual clothing. Soft as chamois cloth and caressing his legs and lower body, the leather molded to him. He glanced down. Good thing he'd chosen a long tunic. A sapphire studded belt tied around his waist and a simple white scabbard hung at his side. For this occasion his sword was more ornamental than functional. He thought briefly of the sword suspended in Wodhan's world. That blade would be a perfect match to his outfit.

His folks must have had some idea how he would choose to dress. Earlier that day, they'd called him to the Otherworld and presented him with a circlet formed much like Korin's symbol of leadership. He took the circlet from the velvet-lined box. Interwoven strands of gold and silver intertwined with a thin ribbon of sapphire. It had to have been fairy made. Oberon's crest sparkled, centered at the front of the circlet. The way things were going, he'd have to adopt the crest as his own.

A sharp pain lanced through his head reminding him of promises, of a pledge he'd made to the voice of Oberon. A pledge he'd not spoken of to anyone. A pledge he would honor—he just wasn't sure how.

Standing before a long mirror, he set the circlet on his head. This would make a great wedding outfit. Maybe Lucidea would finally see him as a groom—her groom. He planned to ask her again, tonight, in the tower room. The room he'd created for her. The door to that room would remain locked and not be part of the tour until after he showed it to her privately. The anticipation brought a wide grin to his face.

When he stepped into the castle's great hall, all movement froze. The weight of every gaze fell on him. "Hey," he said as he shifted uncomfortably. "Is everything ready? Is there a problem? "

A low wolf-whistle sounded from the back of the room. Then

applause and cheers rose to fill the high rafters. Jayse chuckled and let the excitement build before he lifted his arms and the room quieted.

"You guys are great. As usual. Though tonight and tomorrow are the end of a legendary catering business..." He waited until the renewed cheers faded. "It's also the beginning of something grand and exciting. I'm glad you've chosen to stick around and be a part of all this."

"Three cheers for Jayse and The Castle."

He joined in the huzzahs and made a quick, final circle of the room. Everything was in place, as perfect as every Zeroun's event. He chuckled. The Castle. Already people were identifying his site that way. Maybe he shouldn't fight the tide.

"Oh, I can't wear that." Lucidea shook her head at the dress Coralie held before her. "It's much too... I'll get it all dir... It's too beautiful."

"An' ye would deny Jayse seein' ye in this?"

Lucidea touched the silken gauze fabric then rubbed a bit against her cheek. "Do you think he'd like it?"

"Aye, an' what's no' to like? Besides, milady. Ye must be seen as fittin' yer station."

"I agree. You'll be beautiful in that dress." Catori scooted from the bed where she'd been watching Lucidea's process of trying to decide what to wear. "But you'd better hurry. It's about time to go."

"I wish you were coming with us."

Catori shrugged. "Bryce and Carrie really need to get away and have some fun. But since... he's still at large it's better if they don't take Chance. I volunteered to stay here so everybody else can go to the faire. I'll go tomorrow with the rest of the public." She grinned. "Besides, Chance and I are gonna have a great time. I'm gonna teach him one of the games Grandmother kept me entertained with when I was a baby."

"Still..."

"Lucidea, ye must dress. An' I shall do yer hair."

"Okay, okay." Lucidea allowed Coralie to help her into the long, sapphire blue dress. The silky material fell in sensuous folds over her body, the train drifted behind her almost like a cloud. She wasn't sure she appreciated the really low neckline, but Jayse would. She felt like a princess and with a rueful roll of her eyes supposed she was.

Coralie sat her before the mirror and wove tiny crystals through her hair. The shape matched the locator stone she wore. Although simple, she supposed the charm would do for jewelry. Until Coralie draped a mesh of fine silver around her neck. Sparkling with crystals like her hair, the multitude of chains filled the expanse of skin then dipped seductively into her cleavage. "Oh. This is amazing. Where did you get this?"

She shrugged and turned to reach for something Catori held out to her. "'Tis part of yer heritage, Lucidea. As is this."

Lucidea sucked her bottom lip in between her teeth and stared wide-eyed into the mirror as Coralie positioned a silver band encrusted with clear crystals so that it sat at her hairline. "Uh, those are just crystals, aren't they?"

"As ye wish, milady." Coralie laughed. "'Tis happy I am to see ye wearin' this. Ye are our ruler, Lucidea Ann Galvagin Cù Anu. 'Tis this symbol provin' yer right. Fer if ye had no' the right, it would no' accept ye."

Lucidea blew out a long breath. "Looks like today I face who I am then." Rising, she gathered Coralie into a hug. "Thanks for being patient with me. I'm... thanks."

"Get along wi' ye then." Together the sisters shooed her from the room and into the courtyard.

"Where is everybody?"

Searlait and Macaire waited by an open portal. Macaire's eyes lit in appreciation while Searlait tilted her head to one side to study her. Then Searlait executed a deep curtsey.

"Oh, stop that. You guys look great. Searlait, I've never seen you in a dress before." Lucidea grinned as the young faerie blushed and Macaire took her hand.

"She is beauty, is she not?" Macaire grinned at Lucidea. "And you... I have not the words. Come. The others tired of waiting for you and have gone on ahead." Macaire nodded as Coralie joined them.

"Ah, the joy in my soul to escort three of the loveliest ladies in all the worlds."

F eidhlim turned to Osric. "You hold my wishes in your heart?"

"As always, my lord."

"When the sun sets?"

"It shall be as you decree." He tossed a small key and Osric caught it deftly. "Bring the sword while I prepare."

"My lord." Osric bowed and backed from the room.

T he family gathered before the closed gates. Except for Lucidea. Jayse tried to stand still, tried to appear calm, but his nerves kept him in motion. He moved from one small group to the next, chatting, his senses alert for the opening of the portal for his final guests. Finally, when he was ready to destroy the long-stemmed white rose in his hand with nervous frustration, she arrived.

Searlait and Coralie came through the portal first and moved to the side. With her hand resting on Macaire's outstretched arm, Lucidea stepped into the glow of the afternoon sun. The sight nearly drove him to his knees. Speechless, he stared.

"Honey," came Nightshade's awed whisper. "I'd give just about anything to wear that dress."

Laughter at Nightshade's reaction broke the stunned tension. Jayse handed Lucidea the rose then took her hands. Holding them out to her sides he looked, whistled softly, looked longer, then kissed the blush covering her cheeks. Still holding one of her hands, he turned to face his gathered loved ones. No one moved. The children remained silent.

Odd expressions filled adult faces. Oberon's laughter sounded in his head, a comfort this time rather than a pain.

Lucidea tugged on his hand. "Say something," she whispered.

"Uh, so, anybody wanna see The Castle?"

Amid acclamations of delight and surprise, he led the family over the site, explaining the uses of various small structures and open spaces. They stood for a long time at the children's play area watching tolerantly as the youngsters played with his granda's large black dog, Noid, and dirtying their faire clothing. David sat on a wooden railing, appearing as always, to look at everything. Jayse watched moments of delight fill his eyes, then be hidden away when the boy felt someone looking at him. Jayse took a deep breath. David needed to tell his folks he could see. The months since the Yule should have proven the return of his sight wasn't a fluke. He'd try and talk privately to David and convince him to spread the great news.

Lucidea had joined Kae on a bench where they cuddled Kae's new son. He was adorable, dressed in a tiny Henry the eighth outfit. Carrie watched from a nearby bench, obviously missing her own son. Noid approached and nudged her hand with his nose. Carrie rubbed his short ears then smiled and joined the others, dangling a tassel for the baby's enjoyment.

Jayse grinned. The animal played an important role in the family, both as a friend and a guardian for the children. It was fitting that Granda brought him to the grand celebration.

He glanced over his shoulder at the sun. "Hey, everybody. When the rays of the setting sun hit the crest over the castle doors, it's time for a tour of the castle itself. And then, our feast."

"About bloody time," Bryce called from where he pushed Bree on a dragon shaped swing. "'Tain't easy pushing a dragon around."

"Be glad I didn't ask you to do magic tonight," he called back.

Bryce stepped back from the swing, bowed, and pulled a live rose from the depths of his flowing sleeves. "Always prepared."

· · ·

"This is marvelous," Lucidea said after the castle tour. "I can't believe you built this. I love this space." She glanced around the flagstone patio behind the castle. Gathered there for pre-feast drinks, served in wooden goblets, the family conversations centered on the remarkable building. As the sun set on the other side of the castle, hidden lights came on, brightening the area and reflecting on the pond. She and Jayse stood at the edge of the patio listening to the sounds of spring twilight and the soft fall of water from the fountains positioned on the pond.

"There's one more place I want to show you. A little later, though."

"More? I'm on overload right now." Setting her goblet aside, she rested her hands on his shoulders. "You've done a wonderful job. This place is going to be so successful." She pressed against him and initiated the kiss she'd been longing to savor since she'd stepped from the portal into his fantasy world. She lingered over the taste of his lips and honey mead.

"Go." Derrik's sharp command jerked Jayse from her embrace.

A portal shimmered in the center of the patio. Searlait and Macaire disappeared into the oval. Moments later they reappeared with Macaire carrying Catori.

"Stay here," Jayse told her as he rushed toward Macaire.

"Oh, sure I will," she mumbled and followed.

Macaire whispered urgently to Derrik. Jaye knelt at Catori's side and examined the bruises and cuts covering her face and arms. Carrie cried out when she joined the tight cluster around Catori and clutched Jayse's sleeve. "She was with my baby. Where's Chance? Where is he?"

"Looking for this?"

The baby's cry announced Feidhlim and he stepped from the shadows into a pool of light, lifting his son before him. The shocked tableau frozen before him twisted his lips to a sarcastic grin. Osric had done well selecting the perfect time and place for him to renew his—acquaintance—with the usurper's clan.

"Give me my baby," a woman cried and he slowly slid his gaze to her. The dancer. A rush of heat flooded his loins. He shook his head.

"My son remains with me, bitch." The brat, responding to the woman's cries, squirmed and whimpered, pushing at him with tiny, ineffective fists.

The usurper crowded forward until the wave of Nechtan-Cattee surrounding the patio pointed their weapons toward him and advanced. He spread his hands. "What do you want, Feidhlim?"

"What I have always wanted, Zeroun. What was denied me by your birth. Your place in Faerie, your magic." He looked at the violet-eyed woman behind the usurper. "The witch, your woman."

Taking a deep breath, Feidhlim fixed his face with a bland expression and scanned the crowd. Denials formed on every lip, anger burned in every eye. His gaze paused on the usurper's son and, recognizing the symbol upon his forehead, frowned. They had even taken the crest from his hidden castle. After destroying his enemy, he would tear down the stones one by one. His seat of power had been sullied by Zeroun blood. He spat the vile taste from his mouth.

"You. Alastriona." His low command froze Derrik's stealthy movements. "Don't even try. A call to your warriors will not pass the shields I have caused to be set upon this place."

Jaye took a step forward. "This is between you and me. Let the others go. Give the baby back to Carrie."

"Is that what you believe, usurper? All I wish is you? No. One by one I shall destroy those you love. Each one shall die by my hand before you, begging for death, hating you for bringing them to this end. Be still, brat."

Feidhlim struggled to hold the squirming infant. The small hands waved and heat like fire burned his arm where the child lay. Each slap of the boy's open palm shot burning agony into his skin. "Osric," he called. "Take this abomination. I shall teach my son respect when I have finished here."

The dancer cried out and ran forward, reaching her arms toward the boy. Feidhlim met her advance and captured her chin with his fingers. Pressing hard, he forced her fear-filled eyes to focus on him. The contact delighted him and he slid his fingers to her throat and dug into her soft flesh. "Be still, woman, or the brat will know the taste of steel before his time has come."

Jayse swung his arm to the side to hold Bryce in place as Carrie slumped to the ground. Feidhlim glanced at him and smiled. "Very good. Each to their proper time and place, eh? You are mine. Now. Before the rest."

Jayse lunged forward but Feidhlim danced away lightly. Jayse circled slowly. If he could get Feidhlim away from the others...

"So, boy. You want to fight me? Believe you can save your family? Your devotion should sadden me, but it doesn't. Fool. Your father couldn't defeat me. The Alastriona couldn't control my magic. Even the world between worlds could not contain me. You think you can defeat me? Then try, boy. Try. It will be the last you do."

Noid's wild barking ended in a whine. A number of Feidhlim's followers held the animal captive. Feidhlim glanced once at the animal, scowled and arched one eyebrow.

"No, Jayse... please..." Lucidea's voice seemed so far away.

Jayse fought the echoes of Oberon's voice in his head to focus on Feidhlim. "Let everyone else leave. Including the baby. Then I'll fight."

"I don't believe that would be satisfactory. They must watch you fight. Watch you... die. That pretty little thing in blue, the one who cries for you, I've not seen her before. If you die well... I shall grant her special favors. Before she joins you in defeat."

Feidhlim was trying to get to him, to make him reckless by responding to his taunts. Jayse fought the urge for recklessness. Only calm fighting... the way he'd been trained his entire life. Only that would defeat Feidhlim.

::*You need my help as well, heir to my throne.*::

Shaking his head didn't rid him of Oberon. The voice needed to shut up so he could concentrate.

::*As you desire*.:: The sudden emptiness made him gasp.

"So," Feidhlim laughed. "You begin to understand that fate has dealt you a losing hand."

Jayse clenched his teeth. "I will not lose to you, Feidhlim."

Feidhlim unbuckled the scabbard from his side. His feral grin shone beneath the blue mask he'd painted on his face. A slender knotted design traveled from his temple down his neck to widen over his bare shoulder and circle his bicep. The design bulged when he drew his sword and tossed the scabbard to one side.

They continued circling as Feidhlim's followers herded their unwilling audience to the edges of the patio. Jayse reached for his own scabbard, drew the sword and dropped the protective hard leather to the ground. He kicked it off the edge of the patio into the darkness then glanced at his sword.

His stomach churned. This wasn't going to be good.

THIRTY-ONE

Lucidea stared at Jayse while he fingered the edge of his sword. Then she looked at Feidhlim's weapon. Long, slender, the blade was covered with a deeply etched design. The razor-sharp edge glinted when he moved the sword through the light. Her heart sank and she glanced back at her love's sword. Highly decorative, he'd explained earlier that the sword was more ornamental, lighter than what he would use for fighting. And, as a showpiece, not very sharp.

Determination set Jayse's jaw. He lifted the sword. Panic filled her. He couldn't fight with that sword. It wasn't a proper battle sword. He'd never be able to defeat... or even keep himself from... She covered her mouth with her hands and turned away. Any noise she made would distract Jayse, and that would be worse than fighting with a dull sword.

The first metallic clang made her cringe. The second weakened her knees. The third... she waited, but other than laughing taunts from Feidhlim, there was little sound. She had to do something.

Nightshade inched beside her. "Do something feminine."

Confused, she stared at him. "What?"

"You know, like faint, sweet cheeks. I need a distraction."

He started to move away and she clutched at his arm, whispering urgently, "No. I don't care who you really are, you can't do anything like that. Jayse can't be distracted."

"It's not him I want, honey."

"I know. But anything you do will take his attention from the fight. Nightshade, that's not a fighting sword Jayse is using. We can't do anything..."

"Honey? Are you sure?" Nightshade squinted to peer closely at Jayse. "Ah, I see. I'll... think of something else. Maybe I can find another sword around someplace." He slipped back into the shadows.

That was it. Another sword. But... where? It wasn't likely Jayse would keep a bunch of weapons lying around the castle. Maybe, though, if she could get inside, get some help from the staff...

The door to the great hall was closed and well guarded by four of Feidhlim's men. Where were her Alfar-Sindhu guards when she needed them? She sighed and watched the banter between the fighters. An occasional clash of swords shattered the quiet night, and Feidhlim seemed content at the lack of actual fighting. Lucidea chewed on her lip. He was wearing Jayse down. Making him tired. Trying to get him to do something reckless. She had to do something first.

Find a sword. No, she'd already decided that wasn't a viable option, so why did the thought keep popping into her head? Glaring at the guard behind her, she moved toward the edge of the patio and looked out over the pond.

::Find the sword. My brother's sword.::

::Wodhan?::

The clear voice was gone, but she had her answer. Oberon's sword. How would she get to the cavern if she couldn't get anyone to take her through the portal? As if sensing her distress, Coralie appeared at her side.

"There is a way, Lucidea."

Cautious, Lucidea asked, "Way for what?"

"Yer thinkin' milord Jayse needs a different sword."

"Yes. How...?"

Coralie winked. "Yer no' the only Alfar Wodhan has chosen to speak to."

"Oh. I need that sword, but I can't get back to the cavern."

"Nay, ye canna. However, here is water. Ye can accept yer heritage and I'm thinkin' once ye do, Wodhan will lead ye where ye need to go."

"Accept my heritage? I... I don't know if I can."

A shout of triumph sounded and the women whirled to face the combatants. Feidhlim danced a jig, waving his sword over his head. A thin red line trailed down one edge. Frantic, Lucidea searched for Jayse. Partially hidden by the crowd, he knelt, clutching his shoulder. Blood seeped through his fingers and spread quickly though the silk of his tunic.

"Son," Jaye called as he pulled off his shirt and tossed the wad of cloth to Jayse, who pressed it against his shoulder.

Feidhlim hummed a tune in time to his dance before stopping and pointing his sword at Jayse. "I shall wait as long as necessary for you to fight again, boy." He turned a glare on Jaye. "But you will not heal him."

Rotating his shoulder, Jayse rose slowly to his feet and tossed the shirt aside. "Only a scratch, Feidhlim. An irritation. Like you."

The slow advance and retreat began again. Lucidea grabbed Coralie's arm and drew her closer to the pond. "This water will work?"

"Aye."

"What do I have to do?"

Coralie leaned close to whisper rapid instructions. Lucidea nodded at each important point and hugged Coralie when she finished speaking. "You'll have to take care of this stuff for me," she whispered as she removed her circlet and the necklace. "Any-body watching?"

Coralie shook her head. "Blessings, milady."

With a final glance at Jayse, she whispered, "I love you," stripped out of her dress, and waded silently into the cold water. The soft waterfall of the fountains covered the splash of her awkward movements.

The pond wasn't large but the bottom dropped sharply not far from the edge. A sandpit, Lucidea reasoned as she swam quickly to deeper water. Lights from the patio reflected close to the shore, but not as far out as she floated. She heard the sounds, watched the distant fighters, and replayed what she needed to do. If it didn't work, they'd find her drowned body in the pond. If this didn't work, there wouldn't be anybody left to find her body.

All she had to do now was... she closed her eyes, blew out all the breath from her lungs and flipped to dive deep into the cold, dark, dark water.

A gentle thought entered Jayse's mind as he feinted with his sword in his off hand and lashed out with a kick. Distracted by Lucidea's love, he missed Feidhlim's midsection and had to swing his arm to regain balance. He tried to scan the anxious faces watching the fight without losing sight of his adversary but couldn't see her.

Feidhlim tsked at him. "Concentrate, boy. Don't steal my enjoyment too quickly, I beg of you."

"Beg? I'll make you beg." Lunging forward with renewed vigor, Jayse ignored the burning pain in his shoulder and attacked.

The burn in her lungs grew unbearable. She swam down. Her mind screamed for her to breathe. She swam down. Crying for oxygen, her heart pounded. She swam down. She opened her eyes in the darkness and Jayse's face wavered before her. She sent him her love. Maybe there was another world where lovers would meet again. She'd find him. She knew it as she knew death.

Giving in to the pressure in her chest, she opened her mouth and gulped water. Pain seared from her lungs to her neck as though lightning scorched her veins. The pain made her gasp and another lungful of water cooled the agony. The sound of ocean waves filled her mind. The babble of water over smooth stones in a mountain stream made her smile. The gentle splash of raindrops on the pond made her raise her head.

She took another breath and the sharp pain returned, this time behind her ears. In seconds the pain was gone and when she drew in what she truly believed was her final watery breath, oxygen surged through her veins. Startled, she recognized the liberating feeling and touched the skin behind her ears.

It happened. She'd done it. She. Had. Gills. She was breathing underwater. When she looked around, the pond waters were not dark, merely dim and she could see every creature inhabiting the sandy bottom. She looked up and blinked at the line marking the surface of the water. Lost in the delight of her new ability, she twirled and floated through the water, dancing with the startled fish, oblivious to the reasons she'd entered the pond.

::*Sword.*::

The single word plummeted her back to reality. Now what? How would she find the sword and return in time to save Jayse?

Without hearing Wodhan's voice, she knew what to do. Like opening a Faerie portal, all she had to do was create a clear picture in her mind of where she needed to be and... she was there.

Lucidea glanced around the chamber, but Wodhan didn't appear. She'd prevented Jayse from touching the sword, but she'd never been strongly affected by Oberon's voice, so she reached for the hanging weapon.

The sword hovered too high. She couldn't reach. Crying out with frustration, she tried climbing the stones, but the heat from under the rubble burned her exposed skin. She stamped her foot and winced at the pain. "Wodhan, help me."

"All you needed to do was ask of your own will, Lucidea." The sword lowered from its high perch and turned so she could grasp the haft. "Go now. Believe you will return but moments after you left, and it will be so."

"Time distortion," she whispered.

"Yes." Wodhan laughed. "Go now, Oberon's heir needs this weapon. And your love."

Lucidea closed her eyes and imagined herself back in the pond, only yards from the bank where the water first deepened.

Feidhlim opened a gash down Jayse's arm and chortled with glee. Jayse retrieved his father's shirt and pressed the dirty material to the deep cut. It hurt like hell. While Feidhlim postured and accepted accolades from his followers, Jayse took long, slow breaths bringing needed oxygen to his blood.

He was out of shape. How long had it been since he had done any serious training? He'd been so involved in getting the castle up and running, and loving Lucidea, he hadn't taken time to maintain his conditioning. He was a fool. And it wouldn't happen again. If he survived this encounter.

Out of the corner of his eye a movement drew his attention. He stretched as if testing his muscles and watched David leading Bree and Lara's two oldest around the edge of the patio. Following the children, Nightshade caught his eye and winked. They were headed toward the faerie holding Chance awkwardly. Jayse angled so no one would notice where he was looking and lifted his sword. The adults were heavily guarded, but evidently the Nechtan-Cattee didn't believe children, or Nightshade, to be a danger. Jayse smiled. They were wrong.

Feidhlim paused at his expression. "Are you enjoying this? I believe it's time to bring this to an end. I do have others to kill tonight, after all."

Jayse glanced down at his sword. Fat lot of good the nicked blade did him other than as a block for Feidhlim's attacks. He'd be better off just to whack his opponent on the head with the side of the blade.

He'd try, and buy Nightshade and the kids some time.

Saluting Feidhlim, he assumed one of the last defensive

postures he'd encountered, a tactical move he'd learned from
Bard. Then, he waited.

When she rose from the water, the chill air skittered goose
bumps over her body. She really didn't want to appear
naked before the family, but she didn't see Coralie waiting
near the pond. Holding the sword carefully, she wrapped her
arms over her breasts and waded the last few feet to the shore.

A muffled grunt of pain made her rush forward and she
stubbed her toes on the stone edging of the patio. She couldn't see
past the shoulders of the crowd but maniacal laughter told her
Jayse was the one in pain. She shoved against Feidhlim's guards'
backs then limped through the family. Biting back her cry, she
dropped the sword, fell to her knees, and gathered Jayse close. A
fresh, bright red stain spread over his side.

"What foolishness is this?" Feidhlim complained. "Take her
away."

Before his followers responded, Osric shouted and stumbled
backwards. As he fell over David, who was on his hands and knees
behind him, Nightshade snatched Chance from his arms. Then
the three smaller children sat on his chest. Bree shook her finger
in his face. "Don't you move."

The softness of a cape floated over Lucidea's shoulders and
she pulled it around to cover Jayse as well. He looked up at her
and smiled. "Baby."

"Don't... don't you dare die."

"I won't die. Flesh wound. Hurts though. Dad or Bree can fix it
after I take care of Feidhlim."

She pressed her hand over his side and gnawed on her lip. The
blood was so hot.

"He broke my sword."

She couldn't help smiling at his petulant tone. "I brought you
a new one."

Feidhlim stomped in a small circle. Children. Children and an effeminate. They had taken his son and defeated Osric. Impossible. He should have destroyed that fool himself, long ago. Protected now by a ring of adults, his son lay gurgling happily in the dancer's arms.

This would take longer than he anticipated.

He turned his attention back to the usurper's son. The last wound was deep, but by itself not life threatening. He'd made sure of that by pulling his thrust at the last minute. He wanted the usurper to see his son bloodied, his flesh shredded, his limbs useless, but still alive. Then the boy would beg for death. And if he felt merciful, perhaps he would grant that release. And move on to the usurper's fair daughter.

Feidhlim leaned back slightly in surprise. The woman coddling the wounded man wore nothing but a cape draped about her shoulders. Interest grew in his body. No. It was a ruse. Meant to distract him.

Lifting his sword, he stalked toward them.

Jayse knew the wound was worse than it looked, and would seriously affect his fighting, even with a better sword. Hopefully, he could make this quick. At first he'd wanted to capture Feidhlim so he could be brought to justice before the Faerie counsel. Now he saw the folly of that thinking. The only way to end this was to destroy Feidhlim. A wry thought passed through his pain. "Too bad we couldn't get rid of him as easily as Pagas."

As he hoped, Lucidea laughed. A watery, tear-filled sound, but her deep chuckle brought life to him. "Where'd you find a sword?"

She lifted the sword from her side and handed it to him. "It's Oberon's."

"No!" Feidhlim shouted. "That is mine by right. Give it to me."

He rushed the last few feet toward them. Lucidea screamed and grasped the haft behind Jayse's hand and lifted. The sword point wavered and dipped. With a grunt, Jayse lifted it higher.

Feidhlim froze and glared at the sword point a breath from his chest. He snarled, "The sword is mine."

Lucidea tightened her grip as Jayse laughed. He spoke, but it wasn't his voice that carried an imperious tone. "You claim the right? By my fair Titania, you have no right. Faerie hounds come for you, pretender."

"What trickery is this?" Feidhlim glared at Jayse, but Lucidea thought she saw doubt enter his eyes. He lifted his sword to knock Oberon's blade to the side.

Jayse adjusted his grip. "Help me, Dea Annie. Hold tight."

Frantic barking sounded from the far edge of the patio and a cry of pain echoed through the darkness. A black, furry blur burst across the flagstone and leapt at Feidhlim's back.

The force threw Feidhlim forward. His eyes widened. He gasped, looked down, dropped his sword and wrapped his hands about the blade imbedded in his chest. In the stunned silence, Noid sat on his haunches and smiled with canine satisfaction.

Feidhlim stumbled to the side. The sword jerked from Jayse's and Lucidea's hands. The blade twisted slowly, burying itself deeper in his convulsing body. His screams, a combination of anger, denial, and pain pierced the air.

"Deeply forgotten blade doth twist." Oberon's voice rang over the echoes of Feidhlim's agony. The blade twisted again but Feidhlim made no sound. A third twist and Feidhlim collapsed. "Of life or death..."

The sword ripped from Feidhlim's body and returned to Jayse's hand. "This is my chosen heir, my true heir, the Son of Fey. His mate, Daughter of Alfar. Your worlds are one as they were meant to become long ago. Now, my brother and I join our father to create, to build..."

A shout from the lake roused the stunned crowd, and a legion of Alfar guards surrounded the patio. Derrik shouted directions and within moments the leaderless Nechtan-Cattee were subdued.

Nightshade snatched a sword from a passing guard and advanced on Feidhlim. After a couple of pokes, he knelt and examined the fatal wound. Then he stood, handed the impatient guard his sword and wiped his hands delicately on the guard's tunic.

"He's dead."

"Not yet." Jayse struggled to stand and Lucidea angled herself to hold the sword and support him as they rose. As they approached Feidhlim's body, the family and Alfar guards backed away.

"Not yet," Jayse growled when he stood over his family's life-long enemy. Cold blue eyes stared sightlessly up at him. "He's mine," he whispered and Lucidea handed him the sword and stepped to the side.

Oberon's fading laughter resounded through his mind as he lifted the ornate sword high over his head. He thought no words were necessary, for the thing he was about to do was in the heart of every member of his family.

However, Lucidea spoke softly, for his ears only. "I, Lucidea Cù Anu, condemn you, as I condemned Pagas. Murderers both."

Jayse took a deep breath, stared at Feidhlim and, with a low grunt, forced the sword down on the outstretched neck.

The ringing of metal upon stone severed Feidhlim's head from his body. Jayse lifted the bloody sword and rested the blade against his palm. He turned to the stunned faces of his family.

"Now, he's dead."

THIRTY-TWO

"What do you think Oberon meant when he said you were his heir?" Lucidea fussed over Jayse although his father had easily healed the wounds.

"I... remember after we met Wodhan and I had all that pain?"

"How could I forget? This scared me a whole lot more. Are you sure you're okay?"

"Right as rain, darlin'. The pain was from Oberon's voice in my head. He made demands. But, now it's like a dream that you're convinced you'll remember all your life but that you forget even before breakfast is over. Ever since Dad inherited the rule from his aunt, I've been his heir. Since we're descended from Oberon, maybe that's all it means. I'm not gonna worry about it. And neither should you."

"He's really dead. It's really over. For both of us. Both Pagas and Feidhlim. I'm not sure I'm going to know how to act without their threats hanging over us."

"There's a lot more for us, baby. Will you let me show you something?"

Lucidea smiled. He could show her anything. But first... "You haven't asked how I got the sword."

He ducked his head and that adorable bronze flush tinted his cheeks. "Sorry."

"Don't be. I... conquered my fears and discovered my heritage."

"Let me see."

Lucidea pulled her hair to one side and exposed the skin behind her ear. His warm breath tickled her neck and she thought she felt a tiny flutter of the gill slits. "Thin, barely noticeable. But, they're there. Congratulations, Dea Annie." He kissed the spot tenderly and twin spirals of intense desire centered on her nipples.

"Oh."

He carefully tilted her head the other way and kissed the matching spot behind her other ear. The liquid spiral flowed lower. "Oh."

"Mmm, looks like another purpose for these rather... sensitive spots." He smoothed her hair behind her ears. "Now can I show you something?"

She wasn't sure she'd be able to walk with her wobbly knees, but nodded and they waved at the family as they passed through the great hall.

"They're going to be talking for hours about this," Jayse said. "And celebrating something really wonderful. David's regained his eyesight. He's been able to see since Christmas, but didn't tell anyone until tonight."

"Amazing. I'll have to congratulate him. And Tommy and Derrik of course. That's gonna be a much better memory for today."

"We'll have plenty of time to get in on the celebration later. This... I designed this... I hope you like it."

He took the key hanging near a wide double door and unlocked one side. He led her into the center of an open space, gave her a quick kiss then backed away. Closing the door cocooned them in darkness. "Welcome to the Kaleidoscope Tower, baby."

He turned on high overhead lights, which shone down on a

lowered ceiling made of stained glass. Colors surrounded her and she held out her arms as if to catch them. "This is... beautiful."

"Wait." Jayse touched a switch and the ceiling rotated slowly. A second layer of stained glass created an ever-changing pattern of colors on the floor, on the walls, everywhere.

"Oh, my God. How did you do this?"

"Engineers can build remarkable things, don't you think?" He joined her in the center of the round room and held her close.

"You know what this room would be great for, Jayse?"

"Hmm." He pressed his lips to her forehead.

"Weddings."

"There's already quite a few on the schedule. You romantics love stuff like this."

"Romantics, huh? Oh, it is beautiful. When's the first wedding scheduled?"

"Not until next month. I wanted to make sure all the kinks were worked out first."

She rested her head against his chest and listened to the beating of his heart. The beat of life; strong, loving. He was her life. "You know, a lot of things happened that day in the cavern."

"Yeah." Humming softly in her ear, he danced them in a smooth circle.

"And a lot has changed since that day, too."

"Uh-huh. Not how much I love you." He continued his soothing song.

"I love you, too. That day, I wasn't ready. Today. Oh, today I am."

He paused and leaned back. Confusion drew his brows together. "Ready for what, Dea Annie."

"Dance with me some more." When he complied, she said softly. "I think we need to try out a complete wedding in the castle, and in this room before next month."

Jayse froze. "Baby?"

She looked into his eyes and rested her palm against his heart. The beat was faster, as anxious as his expression. "Uh-huh. Yours and mine. I'm ready now. If you're not going to ask right this second, I will. Jaysson Allen Zeroun, will you marry me?"

He stared at her for a second and for a moment she feared he would speak the word she dreaded. Instead, a slow grin spread across his face and he spun her in a circle, lifting her feet from the floor.

"Yes!" he shouted to the colorful ceiling. "Yes," he whispered before claiming her lips.

A cheer rose from beyond the closed door. Lucidea pulled away just enough to ask, "Think that means they suspect?"

He glanced toward the door. "I'd say more like they know."

"Good." She lifted her hands to his ears and tugged gently to close the distance between their mouths. "Then we won't have to hurry."

DEAR READER

Thank you for reading this tale. Bringing stories to life is one of my greatest delights and I hope you enjoyed your time in one of my worlds. Readers like you spark the energy needed to tell these tales. Again, thank you.

With today's world of vast reading choices, word of mouth is the best advertising. So please let others know about this book. Tell your friends, relatives, acquaintances, the dog next door (hey, you never know...). And please consider leaving a review at your favorite retailer or a review site like Goodreads or Bookbub.

To keep up with new releases, sign up for *Starr Words*. Yes, it's a newsletter, but will appear in your email only occasionally. Your email is safe with me, will never be shared, and you can, of course, unsubscribe at any time. You can find the link on my website www.lizziestarr.com

Enjoy the love and discovery! Happy reading!

Lizzie Starr

NEXT FROM THE KELTIC MULTIVERSE

Blue Keltic Moon: Children of the Triad 1

Love and redemption? Only under the blue Keltic moon.

It's been twenty years since Morghan, leader of the Alfar-Sindhu, was trapped in the desolate World Between Worlds. Now blue moons are aligning in a multitude of worlds, signaling a magical opportunity.

Devoting his life to the Fey library hasn't saved Gowthaman from the agonies  of his past, and the long moments he spent in the World Between Worlds. Now, the woman he loves stands ready to lead others into that cursed place. Only he holds the knowledge enabling them to enter. And with luck, safely return with the prince. The risk to his mind doesn't matter, as long as he keeps Breanna from harm.

A competent warrior, Breanna sets aside her personal desires to lead the rescue mission, facing the unknown to bring Morghan home. While she's loved Gowthaman forever, he claims their age difference is too great. But she's seen their soulfire and knows he loves her as well.

Together they must face the World Between Worlds. Can a place filled with despair and loss also be a discovery of love and redemption? Perhaps... only under the blue Keltic moon.

THE KELTIC MULTIVERSE

By Keltic Design: *Double Keltic Triad 1*

It ain't easy to be fey when you don't believe in fairy tales.

In the fey Otherworld, a half-faerie child is born. To protect him from evil's crusade to ensure the purity of the faerie race, he is abandoned in the human world, never to know of his magical heritage.

Now Jaye Zeroun is a successful businessman, rooted in reality. Fantasy is only something from an undisciplined imagination. Until he meets Celtic artist and friend of Faerie, Allyn Keeley.

Allyn has found the man she can love but fears their age difference and the overwhelming task of helping him realize his destiny will tear them apart. But Allyn knots her way around Jaye's heart and fills his life with a fantasy he refuses to believe.

Until danger threatens their love, forcing him to either accept a deadly battle or lose the very things he never planned for in his life' a family and a love beyond his wildest imaginings.

Fires of a Keltic Moon: Double Keltic Triad 2

Can love find a way through time?

Lara Zeroun needs an adventure, so she opens a portal in time and travels to the ancient Scottish Highlands. She meets two mysterious men but dares not trust her heart with either.

Under a matriarchal line of succession, Iain is unable to claim his father's holdings--his home. With no lands or possessions, he fights the temptation of a golden-haired woman who came to the manor on the arm of a wandering storyteller.

The storyteller's deceptions bring danger in Iain's time and threaten the destruction of Lara's present. Will Lara and Iain defeat the power of this growing evil and find their ways through time to the love they both desire?

Keltic Flight: *Double Keltic Triad 3*

What does she need to believe in love?

Even as a mythical faerie, Nanceen doesn't believe in the legends of tiny winged fey. Until a soft voice compels her to search... for love. She doesn't know what she believes but what she discovers changes everything.

Korin Goodfellow has loved the gentry maid from afar. But showing himself to her is forbidden by the fairy king, until using deceptions hidden by dark plans, the king forces Korin into an agreement with seemingly impossible conditions. Fueled by his pure emotions, Korin appears to Nanceen as a wingless man. One she can see. Touch. Believe in.

The evil fairy king keeps Korin's heritage hidden, warping the conditions to force Korin into battle after battle until he discovers his true place in the fairy world. Will Nanceen stand at his side as he risks everything for love?

Wild Keltic Carouselle: *Double Keltic Triad 4*

Falling in love is easy, the possibilities endless.

After months of searching, Bryce accepts he'll never find the masked dancer who captured his heart. Time to get on with life. But when his darlin' daughter climbs onto the lap of a captivating woman in a coffee shop and calls her Mommy, he certainly wouldn't mind exploring the possibility.

After a lengthy vacation, Carrie dreads returning to the job she once loved. Especially when a blond-haired cherub insists on calling her Mommy. The tiny girl's father is intriguing, and Carrie believes she's ready for a real relationship. But memories of a horrific attack surface making her doubt and fear a happy future.

Although he's human, Bryce's family ties are to the Faerie Otherworld, so when one of his fathers is kidnapped, no one knows if the abduction was of human or fey origins.

Falling in love was easy. Telling Carrie about the Otherworld risks that love. But demons resurfacing from both their pasts and evil-doers intent of destroying the present are intent on tearing them from their newfound love. Will their love survive a world of deception, lies and revenge?

Keltic Dreams: *Double Keltic Triad 5*

Passion blazes hotter than the desert sun.

A spiritual quest throws Bard, naked and alone, from his world to the desert Sahara. In search of answers, each grueling step through the shifting sands only adds to his questions and confusion. What did the seven Guardians mean for him to learn in this strange place?

An ever-present evil continues to stalk her family, so Kaelea researches possible protections at the Fey Library of Alexandria. The appearance of a stranger at the oasis is an unwelcome interruption. Her instant fascination with the man, and the overly possessive actions of a fellow researcher are even more distracting.

Time alone might bring solutions to Bard's quest. But will unknown danger and the search for knowledge drive a wedge between him and Kaelea? Will they survive a passion that burns hotter than the desert sun?

(Author's note: The action of the book *Prince of Dark Ness* takes place between Triad books 5 and 6. While it's not necessary to read *Prince of Dark Ness* here, it does give background into Lucidea's life prior to meeting Jaysson.)

A Faire Keltic Renaissance: *Double Keltic Triad 6*

It ain't easy being fey... and the subject of prophecy

Lucidea had no idea her father wasn't human—until a chance assignment as a forensic artist leads her to Scotland and a family she never knew. With her uncle imprisoned in the World Between Worlds, she's forced to assume leadership of a parallel, underwater world as his half Alfar-Sindhu heir.

Then she meets Jaysson Zeroun who has Otherworldly issues of his own. Once again evil plagues his clan and protecting a newborn child takes priority over personal dreams. When Lucidea offers to hide the family at her uncle's manor, Jayse accompanies them to Scotland. He's falling for Lucidea, but he fears how she'll react to the fact he's part Faerie.

Three worlds are in peril. A pieced together ancient prophecy might defeat the separate evils, but will it also bring them love?

Prince of Dark Ness: Keltic Mulitverse

A romantic fantasy

(Author's note: This story takes place between books 5 and 6 of the *Double Keltic Triad* and introduces the heroine of book 6.)

An ill-prepared Alfar-Sindhu prince struggles to protect two worlds from an ancient fire elemental.

Torn between duty and love, Morghan stands alone to protect both his Alfar-Sindhu underwater world and humanity from an ancient fire elemental bent on escaping the World Between Worlds. While he's loved Coralie long upon long, he never acted on his desire.

Raised in the royal household, Coralie has remained steadfast at Morghan's side through long human years. She's hidden her true feeling for him, even from herself.

A forensic artist from America, Lucidea Galvagin travels to Scotland to determine the identity of a skull found on Morghan's land. What she discovers changes her life and possibly the fate of two worlds.

Will Morghan's two worlds be lost if he chooses family and Coralie over battle? Or will his actions doom a multiverse of worlds to fiery destruction?

Blue Keltic Moon: Children of the Triad 1

Love and redemption? Only under the blue Keltic moon.

It's been twenty years since Morghan, leader of the Alfar-Sindhu, was trapped in the desolate World Between Worlds. Now blue moons are aligning in a multitude of worlds, signaling a magical opportunity.

Devoting his life to the Fey library hasn't saved Gowthaman from the agonies of his past, and the long moments he

360 · THE KELTIC MULTIVERSE

spent in the World Between Worlds. Now, the woman he loves stands ready to lead others into that cursed place. Only he holds the knowledge enabling them to enter. And with luck, safely return with the prince. The risk to his mind doesn't matter, as long as he keeps Breanna from harm.

A competent warrior, Breanna sets aside her personal desires to lead the rescue mission, facing the unknown to bring Morghan home. While she's loved Gowthaman forever, he claims their age difference is too great. But she's seen their soulfire and knows he loves her as well.

Together they must face the World Between Worlds. Can a place filled with despair and loss also be a discovery of love and redemption? Perhaps... only under the blue Keltic moon.

Candy Guy and the Chocolate Brownie: *Keltic Mulitverse*

A short story

Who better to assist a struggling choco- latier than a Brownie?

Candy Guy is in trouble. Winning a design contest will prove his abilities as a chocolatier, but creativity eludes him. An enchanting intruder invades Trace's work- space. She may be real, or she might be a dream. It doesn't matter. Desire consumes him at her lingering touch and the deep chocolate flavor of her kiss.

Deleesi hopes to end the ancient fey curse haunting her family, but the handsome wisher defies her sleep-inducing magic. Something about this human calls to her soul, and, unbelievably, to her heart. The sensual distraction proves impossible to ignore, even while granting his unspoken wish.

By the end of the rainy afternoon, Trace has his inspiration. But will he ever again see the tiny woman who captivated his heart and became his muse?

THE ASPEN GOLD SERIES

The Aspen Gold Series is a multi-author series set in the small, but affluent tourist town of Spenser, Colorado. I'm delighted to join with these six fantastic authors to bring you these tales. Find out more about the entire series at www.aspengoldseries.com.

These are my contributions to the series... so far.

Ryder's Heart: *Aspen Gold Series Book 3*

Ryder discovers an intriguing woman in his bed...

Five celibate years in Hollywood didn't ease Ryder Barlow's guilt over his father's death, and now he's coming home to Spencer with a new purpose—to create a camp specializing in equine therapy. When he discovers a beautiful woman in his bed, his plans aren't exactly derailed, but definitely knocked off kilter.

Escaping her past hasn't been easy for Vianna Harrison, but she thinks she's found a welcoming home in Spencer—as long as she can keep her ability as a psychic medium hidden. Not an easy task when spirits need to speak of forgiveness and joy to so many loved ones. Or when the owner of the exquisite cabin she's been allowed to live in comes home unexpectedly.

Neither can start a new chapter in their lives until they stop rereading the old ones. Will acceptance overcome their secrets and show them their Rocky Mountain path to love?

For Keeps: *Aspen Gold Series Book 4*

Hiding the truth is like denying the sun.

Widow Kate Michaels kept a secret from the man she loves, and from the entire community of Spencer, Colorado. She's content running her bookstore and life is good. But in order to pay for his medical care, she must sell the ranch that was her father's dream, and in doing so disappoint her 8-year-old, horse loving daughter. Madison makes an unlikely friend in someone Kate would rather forget.

Veterinarian Jackson Samuels is intrigued by the charming girl, and occasionally lets her shadow him in his nearby clinic. He's enamored with the child's mother, but her defenses are so sturdy, not even his charm or their shared past can make a dent. When Jack uncovers a family secret, the truth makes him question who he thought he was.

Will two people who once shared a heartfelt love, allow their lonely secrets to consume and define them? Or will they help each other, forgive each other, and build a future together—For Keeps?

(Author's note: Barbara Gwen was one of the original authors who created the Aspen Gold Series. When I joined the group and planned my own story, we discovered our heroes were best friends. When Barb left this world much too soon, how could I not finish the book of her heart. **For Keeps** *is by her and for her.)*

Speechless: *Aspen Gold Series Book 8*

How many peonies does it take to get married?

It's a beautiful day in Spencer, Colorado, and the peonies are in bloom. A perfect day to gather for a wedding, filled with love, traditions, fun, and maybe even a prank or two.

Vianna Harrison and Ryder Barlow would love the honor of your presence as they celebrate their marriage.

Fortunate Cookie: *Aspen Gold Book 11*

This woman. Wearing Frosting. And nothing else...

Cookie Lamont owns a successful cupcake shop in Spencer's trendy tourist center. Life would be perfect if not for the escalating unwanted attention from a self-important town trustee. She has everything she needs—and a man is the last thing on her mind.

Until he walks into her shop.

Treehouse builder and TV personality Anthony Burnham returns to Spencer and finds focus building cabins for a new camp. His passion for treehouses is rekindled as a sweet, sexy new love blooms.

But the past haunts his steps and threatens his growing relationship with the alluring baker.

Some Days are Diamonds, is a short story included in:
Yesterday's Promise: *Aspen Gold Series Book 16*

A high-stakes poker game, first meets, a dog rescue, loves lost and rekindled, and life-altering choices fill the history of Spencer, Colorado. Discover the challenges faced in these heartwarming stories crafted by the multi-author group who brings you romantic fiction at its finest in The Aspen Gold Series.

This collection includes:

The Card Game~~ M.A.Jewell

Some Days Are Diamonds~~ *lizzie starr

Ah, Venice ~~ Debra Hines

First Chance ~~ Donna Kaye

Racing Hearts~~ Bernadette Jones

Rescue Me ~~ Cheryl St.John

FANTASY ROMANCE

Double Moon Destiny

Fantasy Romance

On the night of the Double Moon a child is born, and the destinies of an acolyte and a rebel are changed forever.

Jermanah, acolyte of the religious Compound, has never been given the opportunity to make her own choices. Although she accepts her way of life and yearns to rise higher in the order, she learns ancient, forbidden healing from the Seer. On the night of the Double Moons, a child is born and given into Jermanah's care until the boy is taken to the king.

Kierigh was born moments before the rising of the Double Moons, but his twin brother wasn't so lucky. Rumors flow from the Stronghold—following an ancient prophecy, the king sacrifices the baby boys to increase his power. But Kierigh senses that even after five cycles, his brother still lives.

When Kierigh's rebels attack the procession, he takes the babe, and Jermanah, to his hidden camp. The captivating acolyte disrupts Kierigh's ordered and simple life. He opposes her religion and all the

Compound claims to stand for. She's everything he doesn't need in his life. Yet she is everything he desires.

No longer considering herself one of the Compound, Jermanah discovers freedom, and truths she finds difficult to believe. But when the babe is taken from the forest, she will do anything to save the child, including face the leader of the Compound—and the king.

Can a rebel and an acolyte set aside pride and differences to find a lost brother, defeat evil, and discover their prophecy fulfilling destinies?

CONTEMPORARY ROMANCE

Birds Do It!
Contemporary Romance

A search for truth, switched babies, and a threat from the past
Macaws as lovebirds?
An avian expert, Birdie Simons is called to help control a cantan-
kerous hyacinth macaw during a young girl's birthday party.
Inexorably drawn to each other, she and single father Garr Logan

share an afternoon of joy and bittersweet memories, for Garr's wife died the same day as Birdie's newborn child.

Something about Rachelle makes Birdie wonder if the golden-haired girl is her daughter, switched at birth. Then her child's father returns, dogging her search for understanding and throwing her deeper into fear and confusion.

Ready to move on after his wife's death, Garr wants the intriguing woman, but Birdie keeps the search, threats, and hidden relationships to herself, driving a wedge between them.

Will discovering the truth from nine years ago bring them closer, or forever tear them apart?

SHORT STORIES

Written in Stone: *'Structs in the City 1*
Fantasy Romance

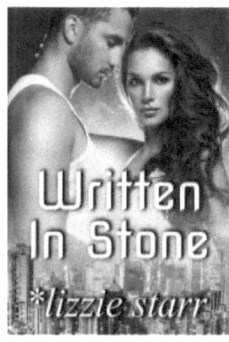

Undercover agent Stone Mason must find a data-link before a demonstration for underground bidders leads to mass destruction. His search of a posh hotel is risky, but time is up.

Monika Linberg returns to her hotel room after her boss dumps her and assumes the striking, robotic sex-struct is her consolation prize.

Stone is no construct, but a living, breathing man whose touch and need for information and assistance turn her world upside down. Will working with the sexy agent to keep the city safe be too dangerous for her heart?

Dead Lily Blooms: *At Death's Gates 1*

Fantasy Romance

For ages uncounted, Master Death has assisted souls in transition. But what happens when love gets in the way?

Someone wants vampyre Lily dead, and a bargain with Death has been struck. Death sends servant Agaar to bring Lily to him, but the task becomes more complicated than either Death or Agaar anticipated.

This short story originally appeared in the anthology **Tales From The Mist**. *This re-release has had minor corrections from the original edition.*

Death and the Dryad: *At Death's Gates 2*

Fantasy Romance

For ages uncounted, Master Death has assisted souls in transition. But what happens when love gets in the way?

What's Death to do when a dryad appears at his gate without her soul? She can't move on, nor go back. Will Death find a place for her--at his side?

This tale appeared originally in the **Martini Madness** *anthology and this re-release has had minor corrections and additions from the original.*

FUN STUFF

*lizzie also enjoys creating journals and guided workbooks for authors and other creatives. Look for them on her website.

About the Author

*lizzie always made up games and stories to keep her company. So, a cunning witch lived in Grampa's weather research station and was only held at bay by waving a certain weed. An ancient road grader morphed into a boat carrying wild adventurers to islands filled with fierce lions and dangerous cannibals, which really looked a lot like sheep.

Now filled with fantasy, love, and romance with a sparkling twist, the stories of her imagination swirl their way into the mundane world.

*lizzie recently retired from her more routine life of being *the Lunch Lady* at a private school. According to the kids, she was 'the best cooker!' Yes, she misses the students and teachers, but is delighted now to start her days by telling stories rather than opening cases of chicken nuggets and counting milk cartons.

Her tag line of *Author and lunch lady~~what a combination!* no longer holds true (which makes her sad because she really liked that one).

Now you'll know *lizzie by her tales of...
~~*Romance with a sparkling twist*~~

Want to keep up to date with all of *lizzie's worlds? Sign up for her newsletter:
https://landing.mailerlite.com/webforms/landing/o9q4q4

facebook.com/authorlizziestarr

twitter.com/lizziestarr

instagram.com/lizistarr

amazon.com/*lizzie-starr/e/B003F33Y0W

bookbub.com/profile/lizzie-starr

goodreads.com/lizziestarr

pinterest.com/lizziestarr

tiktok.com/@authorlizziestarr